D1342457

# FOURTH DOWN, DEATH

# Michael T. Hinkemeyer

# FOURTH DOWN, DEATH

A Critic's Choice paperback
from Lorevan Publishing, Inc.
New York, New York

Reprinted by arrangement with St. Martin's Press

ISBN: 1-55547-145-5

First Critic's Choice edition: 1987

From LOREVAN PUBLISHING, INC.

Critic's Choice Paperbacks
31 E. 28th St.
New York, New York 10016

Manufactured in the United States of America

I want to thank Jim Shevlin for a suggestion,
Joe at the Brasserie St. Germain for point spreads,
and Father Ray Runde on general principles.

# Author's Note

*Fourth Down, Death* marks Emil Whippletree's third appearance as a crime-solver in my fictional version of Stearns County, Minnesota, the North Star State. In *The Fields of Eden*, he was serving a second term as sheriff. In *A Time to Reap*, he was retired. Now he is back on the job, ten years younger than he was in his last adventure. Well, Emil told me that he didn't want to get old just yet and, anyway, time is relative. Sheriff Whippletree's jurisdiction is a county of the imagination.

—MTH

*Power is the ability to sustain illusion.*

—Dr. Rexford Anderson
President
North Star University
Minnesota

Emil contemplated point spreads that September afternoon, wishing he could get away to catch the Minnesota Vikings–Denver Broncos clash in Minneapolis on Sunday. The Vikings weren't favored—the spread was five points—so if he wanted to win a couple of bucks, home-state loyalty sure looked to be a candidate for sacrificial lamb.

Next, he considered the amount of wager. Five dollars seemed pathetically inadequate, betraying a lack of confidence. Twenty was too much, besides which he'd promised his wife, Sarah, to keep his bets down this fall. Ten was his usual shot, but, truth to tell, he'd lost a sawbuck almost every weekend last season and it had added up. Sheriff of Stearns County was a good enough title but the pay wasn't all that great, and Emil was saving up for a trip to the Rose Bowl come New Year's Day.

He stuck a plug of Copenhagen between cheek and gum, put his feet up on the battered, paper-cluttered desk, thought the whole thing over again, and decided to go with a five-buck bet. Too bad he wouldn't be able to get to the game: one of his four deputies was down with the flu (bourbon hangover), another had gone up to Leech Lake to visit a sick aunt (assuming said aunt wanted to share a fishing boat for the weekend), and the other two were out on assignment. That left only Emil to cover the office, which was no place to be. The weather was gorgeous: sunny, warm, clear. The gilded dome of the St. Cloud courthouse across the street glittered beneath a sky of cornflower blue. Trees were beginning to show reds and golds among the deep-green leaves of early autumn. Emil could almost feel the snap, see the runner feint and break free, hear the roar of the crowd.

The radio in the outer office crackled but Emil paid no attention until Alyce, his departmental secretary, stuck her tousled head around the doorjamb and announced, "Hey, Sheriff Whippletree, it's Axel. He's on the road near the North Star football stadium. There's some sort of trouble out there and he wants to talk to you."

North Star University, located among the forested hills of white pine five miles north of St. Cloud, perenially fielded powerful football teams. The "Noble Norsemen"—they excelled at the running game—had brought home a long string of championships and a handful of Heisman Trophy winners over the years. Today was the season opener against Northwestern, and Deputy Axel Vogel, who was investigating a theft at Norb Heffner's gas station in Avon, had planned to cut cross-country and catch a bit of the game.

Emil swung his boots off the desk, spat into the ancient brass cuspidor next to his swivel chair, got up, and walked out to the radio. He was a big, rangy man, nearly six-two, but he was also sixty-two and he felt his back creak as he bent over the microphone.

"Yeah, Axel? What's up?"

"Well, Sheriff, it's sort of a mess and I don't quite know what to make of it."

"Anybody in immediate danger?" Emil demanded, getting to the most important thing right away.

"Nope. Not that I know of. You see, there's this big traffic jam . . ."

North Star's legendary football crowds were huge, due to the team's national reputation.

"Some sort of protest?" Whippletree wondered. That didn't seem likely. North Star's undergraduates, male and female, were pretty much models of decorum. University President Rexford "Rector Rex" Anderson ran a tight ship. Emil's niece, Dee-Dee Tiernan, was a senior at NS.

"I don't know what the hell it is," Axel was saying over the radio. "All's I know is there's this bunch of people 'bout a quarter mile up the road. They're all excited about something, running around like crazy. It's makin' me feel funny. I feel sort of jittery, like there's something weird goin' on."

"Where's Butch Lodge?"

Butch, a retired United States Army master sergeant, was in charge

2

of university security, although it was no secret that he had his eye on bigger things in the field of law enforcement. Like sheriff.

"I can't see Butch. Want me to go on up there and check the deal out?"

"Might be a good idea," said Emil. "By the way, what was the story at Heffner's gas station?"

"Thief got away with four white-walled radials and a case of ten-W-forty oil. Sometime last night. I found an old hubcap lying at the curb. Could've come off the perpetrator's vehicle."

"I'm on my way out there to North Star," Emil told his deputy. "Do what you can to get traffic moving and see if you can scare up Butch Lodge. And make sure nobody gets hurt." Injury to life and limb, anywhere in Stearns County, came under his jurisdiction.

"Headin' for the university to help unclog some sort of a bottleneck," Emil told Alyce. Then he left the squat, brick building that was both sheriff's office and jail, climbed into the black-and-white Ford that his deputies called "Stearns County One," and gunned north past the hospital and out of town.

Traffic on the main highway started to back up two miles from the university. Sensing that something serious had really happened, Emil switched on the blue-and-red flasher, which he hated to do because the lights always evoked so many startled, guilty stares, and swung into the oncoming lane. Not much traffic there: Stearns was mainly a rural county of about eighty thousand people, half of them living in St. Cloud, a super-clean, buttoned-down little city on the banks of the Mississippi, seventy miles north of Minneapolis.

In a couple of minutes, doing sixty-five in the illegal lane, Emil reached the turn-off to the university, where a massive red-, white-, and-blue football-shaped billboard announced:

NORTH STAR UNIVERSITY
HOME OF THE
NOBLE NORSEMEN

Drivers and passengers were standing outside their cars here, angry about the back-up, furious that they might miss kickoff. People cheered as Emil swept into the curve leading to campus.

3

"Here comes the cavalry!" somebody yelled.

"Good luck," shouted another.

Emil needed it. When he turned onto the pine-fringed asphalt drive, he saw that both lanes were jam-packed. So he crawled out of his patrol car and, joints protesting at the effort, climbed onto the hood. The drive itself ran for a straight narrow mile to the looming bulk of Granitelli Stadium and the pine-shrouded cluster of university buildings. Bordered on one side by a heavily wooded ravine through which the Sauk River flowed and on the other by a stately row of white pine that fringed the golf course, the drive offered little room for maneuver.

In the distance, thrusting above the pine-covered hills, Emil saw the famous Sacred Steeple of the campus church. It was North Star's trademark symbol: thousands of miniature Nerf footballs emblazoned with an image of the Sacred Steeple were given away each year as a public relations ploy. President Anderson had made great strides in forging the university's academic reputation, but the continuing dominance of sports was symbolized by a gigantic statue of Jesus—arms upraised—that stood beside the stadium. Late on autumn Saturdays, with the sun just right, the shadows of Christ's upthrust arms seemed to embrace the playing field.

From atop his car, Sheriff Whippletree could hear the expectant rumble of the crowd already in the stadium, as well as the cries of people all around him, up and down the drive.

"Sheriff, do something!"

"We won't have time for our tailgate lunch," one woman complained. "My fried chicken is turning into ptomaine and salmonella right in the wicker basket!"

Then Emil spotted the source of the bottleneck. About half a mile ahead, the road was blocked by a swirling, tightly packed crowd, the kind of group that gravitates to the scene of a disaster. The mass was centered on something either in the drive or just alongside it. People spilled over onto the golf course too. And Emil noticed a strangeness as well: a pulsating current that flashed and flickered like raw energy through the taut, invisible air. But meaning was elusive, offering him only the half-formed image of an opening far out upon fields of time, where darkness met night.

4

Emil got back into his car, eased it between two pine trees and onto the golf course. He charitably skirted the eleventh green and braked to a stop at the edge of the roiling crowd. Deputy Axel Vogel, all six-feet-six and three hundred pounds of him, lumbered over to meet Emil as he got out of the patrol car.

"Thank God you're here, Sheriff. Nobody can figure out what to do." Axel led the way, moving through the throng like a bull in a cornfield, or like Gunnar Rutkow, North Star's star defensive lineman, cracking through for a sack. The people parted and made way for Axel and the sheriff.

Emil had only managed to finish eighth grade before his father died, leaving him to run the farm, but he'd always secretly thanked the Good Lord for quickness of perception and sureness of hunch (football wagers excepted), and he sensed among the people here a strange mood, almost of elation, yet with a tinge of bemusement to it, as if they could not quite bring themselves to believe in a suddenly observable truth to which they'd always sworn private fealty. They felt, as Emil had, that quivering imminence in the very air. Emil, who knew the various characteristics of sports crowds, political rallies, church picnics, tavern brawls, and plain old family hassles—Mom, Dad, and the kids in butcher-knife free-for-alls—had never seen a group of people behave like this.

Axel brought the sheriff to the center of that enigmatic human swarm, shrugged, and pointed. "She won't move, Emil. That's the cause of the problem."

"What the hell," Emil said.

A woman knelt at the side of the asphalt drive. She was hunched down on the pavement just next to a blue Datsun that was stopped with its doors ajar in the middle of the road. And she gazed, transfixed, at the tall white pine directly in front of her, as if all the world and everyone in it had disappeared and only that pine tree remained. Middle-aged, with features that still showed how pretty she'd once been, she wore brown slacks and a beige windbreaker. A faded yellow scarf partially covered her graying hair. Emil knew her: Bunny Hollman. She belonged to Holy Angels Parish in St. Cloud, as did the sheriff.

Behind Emil, horns continued to honk. Up the drive, in Granitelli Stadium, spectators shouted in anticipation of kickoff and the band blared the brassy fight song: "North Star, red, white and blue, North Star, always be true . . ." The gigantic statue of Jesus brooded over the campus and two men hovered protectively over Bunny: a thin, young guy who looked vaguely familiar to Emil, and a crisp, chubby little fellow, fifty years old maybe, Professor Charlie Hollman, Bunny's husband. He was chairman of the North Star history department.

"What's the matter with Bunny, Prof?" asked Emil.

"If it's what I think it is, God be praised." Charlie spoke ponderously, aware of the importance of every word, in a voice that was rich and disconcertingly deep.

"Amen," said the slender young man, bending over Bunny as if to shield her from Emil's gaze.

"Could you be a little more specific, Charlie?" Emil asked. "We've got to move this crowd and clear the road. Where is Butch Lodge? We've got to—"

"Don't you do a thing!" the young fellow snapped, facing Emil challengingly.

"That's right," agreed the professor, crossing his arms. He wore an old tweed jacket with leather patches at the elbows. It concealed a tubby girth and lent him a dignity that his stature did not. "You must not interfere."

Exasperated, Emil turned away from the two. "Folks, we'll have you rolling in just a minute . . ." He felt thin fingers gripping the sleeve of his dark-blue uniform shirt.

"We *told* you not to interfere," said the kid.

Bewildered, Emil swung around to face him. This was his fourth term in office—four years per term—and people generally refrained from bothering him when he was doing the job. He bent over backwards to be fair, and folks knew it.

"What'd you say?" Emil asked quietly, as if he might've heard wrong. Yes, he was sure he'd seen this young whippersnapper before, with his thin, sallow face and a very prominent nose that supported wire-rimmed glasses.

The kid was about to reply, but Bunny Hollman, still kneeling

6

there on the asphalt, groaned suddenly, huskily, deep in her throat. Her eyes were rapt and shining; on her face was a dazed expression combining overwhelming awe and excruciating pleasure. Her soft moaning, the flushed glow on her cheeks, slightly parted lips: these signified the unmistakable presence of ecstasy. Something was wrong. Bunny was definitely not the type to pull this kind of stuff in public.

Emil glanced around. More and more people were pushing toward Bunny. A deafening roar from the stadium signaled kickoff.

"You see," Charlie said in his somber baritone, "Bunny is a Charismatic." He turned toward the onlookers and addressed them too. "Lately, she's felt herself to be on the edge of a transcendent experience. . . ."

Emil's wife, Sarah, had mentioned to him that there was a new group of Charismatics in town. "They get very emotional," she'd said. "I think it's another form of prayer."

"Consider it in terms of a breakthrough," Charlie explained. "My wife has felt very close to heaven, to the spiritual reality that lies just beyond our usual field of perception. And today as we were driving to the stadium, it happened."

"*What* happened?" Emil asked doubtfully. He wasn't at all sure what "transcendent" meant either.

"We were coming up the drive," Charlie told the throng, "and suddenly my wife said, 'It's here, stop the car.' Naturally, I did. She got out and knelt down on the pavement, her eyes on that pine tree. She hasn't stirred since. We must let her luminous moment run its course."

A low hum of excitement and wonder arose from the crowd. A lot of these fans were from Stearns County, which had a strong religious tradition. Many of them had attended North Star, purveyor and celebrant of a staunch, conservative Christian heritage. The concept of a spiritual dimension, existing just beside or beyond the everyday world, was not at all alien here.

"Let's get her off the road at least," Emil suggested to Charlie, "and move your Datsun so the cars can get by."

He bent to lift Bunny, slipping his big, rough hands beneath her

7

armpits. A shudder passed through her rigid body. Emil felt it shoot into his hands and up his arms. Once, by mistake, he'd grabbed hold of an electric fence. The shock from Mrs. Hollman's body was something like the jolt he'd received from that charged fence-wire. He jerked his hands away from her. Emil could have sworn he felt the earth tremble beneath his boots. An image of a door came to him then, a faraway door opening with exquisite slowness, and beyond it rolled fields of purple fog, a gloom illuminated by crackling flashes of light. And Bunny Hollman cried out in a voice that might still have been her own:

*"Our Lady is about to speak!"*

"What'd she say?"

Emil looked down at Bunny, in her yellow scarf and simple beige windbreaker. He felt a quiver of dark alarm similar to the time he'd encountered a burglar in an alley behind the Hannorhed Bank in town. It had been night, he'd seen barely a shadow of the figure moving in darkness, but he'd known, with the sure sixth sense by which one knows disaster, that the shotgun-wielding stranger inhabited a world in which all laws were different, where ambiguity reigned supreme.

*"The soul of man is a knife upon the altar,"* cried Bunny. *"Of woman it is silken softness for the piercing."* Her voice was weird and shivery, her eyes still fixed upon the pine tree. *"Our Lady is speaking to me . . . She is telling me . . . she is telling me . . ."*

The rumble from Granitelli Stadium continued, but among the people here by the golf course and along the roadside there was scarcely a sound.

*"Our Lady is telling me . . . about John F. Kennedy,"* Bunny gasped, almost sobbing now, stricken to the depths of flesh, *". . . and she says . . . she says . . . that yesterday our beloved president left purgatory to dwell in heaven."*

Now Emil had no idea what in hell to think, much less to do. Axel stood there, head and shoulders above everybody, staring at Bunny. All eyes were on her, entranced by something so innocent, yet so compelling, that it could not be denied. Some people crossed themselves and fell to their knees.

8

Charlie was gazing at the pine tree. Emil looked at the tree himself. He didn't see the Blessed Virgin, just a white pine, but he recalled from long-ago Catechism classes that Mary had made appearances in trees or bushes before, and that pilgrims still flocked to various shrines all over the world.

He shook his head and looked around. Purgatory? Nobody talked much about purgatory anymore, the place where residual guilt of earthly sins was expunged from the souls of the dead.

"*The Blessed Mother wishes all those who love her to come here each day and pray!*" Bunny cried, her voice trembling now at a crescendo of fierce intensity. "*And if we pray each day she may give us a message from her Divine Son.*" Then she fell face down on the grass and lay still.

Everybody shouted at once, pressing forward. "Axel," ordered the sheriff, "get 'em back. Push 'em if you have to."

Charlie Hollman was stunned and unmoving, staring at his wife, so Emil reached Bunny first. He bent down, took a strong hold—no shock this time—and lifted her to her feet. The crowd was making a lot of noise, so Emil alone heard Bunny's final message. "Thirty-eight . . . thirty-eight to three . . ." she said.

Sounded to Emil like the score in a one-sided football game. "What'd you say?" he asked, half walking, half carrying her to the shade of the pine trees.

Bunny's blue eyes cleared. She looked around, puzzled. "What . . . ? Emil? Where . . . ? Why are you holding onto me?"

"It's all right, dear, it's all right," soothed Charlie, rushing over. "Sheriff, why don't you let her lie down on the grass?"

Emil eased her down gently until she was resting on the ground and looking up into the long-needled branches of the pine.

"Oh my God!" she cried out. Her eyes flew immediately upward, searching the dark, slender branches of the tree. "Oh, sweet Jesus, it *did* happen, didn't it?"

"Yes, dear, it did," replied the professor proudly, "and I have a feeling that this is just the beginning."

Emil took a moment to examine his perceptions. Whatever he'd felt earlier was gone now. A warm September day glowed all about, in blue and green and gold. The people were heading back toward their cars, except for perhaps fifty or so who stood watching in silence at a respectful distance.

Bunny sat up and saw the people, saw not only their eyes on her but also the hunger in those eyes, a craving, a need to believe in the authenticity of her experience. Emil sensed this need too, along with Bunny's yearning desire to fulfill it, even as his hardy, nuts-and-bolts Stearns County soul explained to him that what had happened was nothing more than a product of football, excitement, frustration, novelty, and fleeting hysteria.

A terrible roar, followed by blasting bugles and the fight song heralded the first North Star touchdown.

"Better get Bunny to a doctor, Prof," Emil said. "And you'll have to move your Datsun pronto."

Charlie didn't say anything, for once, but went helpfully to his car. Traffic began to move at a pretty fair clip. The bespectacled young guy came over and helped Mrs. Hollman to her feet.

"I saw the Mother of God," she told him dazedly.

"I know, I know."

"What'd she look like?" Emil asked, curious.

"Like a light. Just a . . . a face that was all light. But I know it was she. I felt her presence."

"Sure it wasn't just the sun? It can still be pretty bright this time of year."

She didn't reply. The kid walked her over toward the Datsun, in which Charlie waited. A half-dozen security men, led by Butch Lodge, came trotting across the golf course from the stadium. Jogging along with them was Roy Riley, reporter for the St. Cloud *Tribune*. The Datsun moved off in a cloud of blue smoke.

"Hey, Emil," said Butch when he reached the sheriff. "What brings you out to my territory?"

"Hell, I'm not even sure. Unplugged a jam for you though."

"We never had a traffic back-up before," said Lodge, with a touch of apology in his voice. "The drive never clogs up because my men in the lots park 'em as fast as they come in."

The security boss was a trim, big-shouldered man with quick

black eyes, close-cropped black hair, and a face that looked to be about one-half jaw. He'd returned to Stearns County after two decades in the Army. Emil had heard that Butch played a major role in getting civilians out of the U. S. embassy when Saigon fell to the communists, and he'd recently read in the *Trib* that Lodge's third wife, Trudilynn, had divorced him, no reason given by the paper.

"Axel radioed me about the jam," Emil said. "I don't think it could've been foreseen or prevented. Charlie Hollman's missus caught a glimpse of the Virgin Mary in that tree there"—he pointed—"a crowd gathered, and that's all she wrote."

Butch and his men and reporter Riley glanced first at the tree and then at the small group standing or kneeling in prayer on the golf course.

"Hollman?" wondered Butch Lodge. "He goes around acting like he runs this place. I wish Rector Rex would tell him where to get off."

"You did say his wife saw *the* Virgin Mary?" inquired reporter Riley. "That is, the woman who lived about two thousand years ago, had a very understanding husband called Joseph, and—"

"That's the one, all right," Emil said.

Riley, who was as round and hard as a cannonball, but more aggressive, indulged himself in a big smile of cynical delight. "Fantastic," he said, reaching for his notepad. "I'll give her a call. I can probably get this on the wire services. Look at all the people who believed *The Amityville Horror*. Did she say anything?"

"Well, yeah, I guess so. She said the Virgin told her Jack Kennedy is no longer in purgatory. They let him into heaven yesterday."

"You mean Jack Kennedy who ran the bait shop out on Grand Lake before he died of tequila?"

"No, the other one."

"Don't shit me, Emil," Riley said. "This story is weird enough. I don't need embellishments."

"This is the straight stuff, I swear it," said Emil, as Butch and the boys laughed. "Ask Axel."

11

"Emil's telling the truth," asserted the big deputy seriously.

"Bunny even gave what could have been a score for today's game," continued Emil. He was about to mention the 38–3 tally that Mrs. Hollman had predicted, but held back. Why give away an inside tip?

"Would you base a wager on Bunny's vision, Emil?" Riley asked. He and the rest knew of Emil's prudent adherence to penny-ante bets. It was sort of a joke that the old sheriff never bet "real" money.

"I'm a wait-and-see kind of guy," Emil said.

"Think anybody will show up here to pray in the coming days?" Riley wondered.

Emil knew his county and the awesome expanse of its grapevine. "Today's traffic jam is a fender-bender compared to what's gonna happen when news of this gets out. Roy, do us all a big favor and keep this story local, okay?"

"No comment." The reporter smirked. "Sheee-it, Charlie and Bunny Hollman. She's so sweet and harmless. He's an egomaniac. Ever read the letters he sends to the *Trib*? Slightly to the right of Attila the Hun."

"Who's he?" inquired Axel Vogel.

"First draft choice, Pittsburgh Steelers," said Butch.

"Right." Axel nodded cannily.

Riley walked away, pocketing his notepad. Emil watched the last of the cars go by, faster and faster, until the drive was clear.

"Well, Emil," said Butch, "I guess that takes care of it."

But the whippersnapper appeared again, slouching across the golf course. He stopped in front of Emil and glared.

"Yes?" said the sheriff. "Where's Bunny?"

"In the university infirmary. Sheriff Whippletree, I intend to lodge a formal complaint against you. Do you want to know why?"

"Not particularly."

"It's because of the way you manhandled Mrs. Hollman when she was experiencing that divine . . . experience. Something like that is given to perhaps one in a hundred thousand million souls, and you—"

12

"Look, son, don't make me embarrass you here. I've known Bunny Hollman for more years than you've been around."

"She *saw* our Holy Mother."

"Could also have been the sun behind the tree. Mind if I ask who you are?"

The kid drew himself up to his full height, which was about five-ten. "I am Brewster Titchell, Jr."

Oh God, thought Emil, I should have known from the big schnoz. The senior Brewster Titchell had one just like it. He was Stearns County's preeminent judge, with whom Emil occasionally differed as to the theory and practice of law enforcement. Emil was the more liberal.

Again, a great tide of sound from the stadium. Another Norse touchdown.

"Reckon you ought to move along now, son," Axel suggested.

"When I want garbage out of you, I'll squeeze your head, fatso," the kid shot back.

Uh-oh, thought Emil. Axel's beer belly did hang way out over his belt but even a strong man might sprain his hand taking a punch at it.

"You know," drawled the deputy, "I been listenin' to you chirp at Emil for the last half hour. He's a patient kind of man, puts up with almost every sort of asshole, of which you are damn sure one. But I am gettin' just a little sick of hearing your puny voice." He reached for the handcuffs attached to his big belt. "Put 'em behind you, Titch. You gone an' interfered with law officers in the performance of their duties. You're under arrest."

Brewster's eyes snapped wide in disbelief. Life as he had learned it simply did not go this way. "Sheriff?" he faltered.

"It's out of my hands," Emil said.

Titchell made his decision, turned, and ran, heading across the road toward the ravine. The men heard him scrambling down the embankment toward the Sauk River. Axel followed.

"You really *want* my job?" Emil asked Butch. "Well, 'scuse me, I'd better save young Brewster."

He knew Axel wouldn't really hurt the punk, but it was possible that Titchell, Jr., might trip on a root and break his neck or stumble over a rock, fall into the Sauk River, and drown.

He crossed the drive and ducked into the scrub brush. Sounds of the marching band drifted over from the stadium. Half-time. Score would be pretty one-sided now, favor of the Noble Norsemen. In order for the game to end as Bunny had predicted, North Star had to score several more touchdowns and a field goal, and Northwestern had to part the uprights too. Jesus, it could happen, quite easily, couldn't it? Too late to bet the game, Emil thought, smiling to himself. Half the people in the Upper Midwest had money riding on North Star and its Terrible Trio: Lem Duffy, Gunnar Rutkow, and quarterback Rusty Rollins.

"Axel?" Emil called, skidding down the embankment toward the river.

The Sauk, which bordered one side of the campus, was narrow and shallow, but sort of pretty too. A leaf- and vine-covered path ran alongside it. North Star students came to stroll and neck here, in spite of the fact that President Rexford had ordered Butch Lodge and his men to keep such carnal fraternizing to a minimum.

"Axel?" the sheriff called again. It was chilly down here in the river-cooled shadows. Emil suppressed a shiver. Way up the path, he thought he heard the muffled sound of someone running over trampled grass and leaves.

"Hey, Axel! Where are you?"

For a moment, there was no sound at all, then a blood-stilling shriek pierced the air and echoed along the Sauk, a cry something like *EEEESSSSHHH* or *LEEEESSSSSHH*, followed by a wail that ended in a dead gurgle.

Titchell, for sure. What had Axel done to him? Emil felt a flash of the same fear he'd experienced while staring at the maniac's shotgun in the alley behind the Hannorhed Bank. A second horrified yell came then, somewhere up the path. "*Emil?*"

"Right here."

"Oh God," the big deputy shouted. "Emil, you better come here right away and take a look."

## 2

Axel's discovery lay half-hidden at the side of the path, beneath tall, twisted grass and tangled vines. Judging on the bases of rigidity and coloration, Emil guessed it must have lain there for at least twelve hours. Branches and vine leaves formed a soft canopy that filtered the sunlight, dappling and partially camouflaging the corpse.

"A looker," Axel allowed.

"Was," corrected the sheriff.

"What now, Boss?" asked Axel. "We got junior to worry about too."

Brewster Titchell lay face-down on the pathway, a couple of yards from the girl's body.

"He just let out a yell and fainted dead away when he saw her," Axel said.

"Better revive him. Get some water from the river and splash it on his face."

Axel clumped down to the slow-moving river and Emil studied the body, forcing himself to observe, concentrate, and remember. Expensive sneakers, the kind millionaire tennis players extol on TV. White, knee-length woolen stockings. Long, slim, tanned legs, recently shaved to just above the knee, as if the girl had gotten ready to go somewhere quickly, hadn't bothered with an all-over job. Plaid, woolen skirt, with a big, gold, decorative safety pin, the skirt bunched unevenly at the waist. A pair of ripped red panties clung to the left thigh, which was as tan as the smooth, flat belly. Slightly convex navel. Neatly trimmed, russet-colored pubic hair. Unbuttoned white-silk blouse. Red bra askew, one breast exposed, one not. Breast smallish, well shaped. Long, thick reddish hair. Green, black-lashed eyes, wide open. The face was distorted, however, by something partially protruding from the mouth. Emil

15

bent to look, his old back protesting at the effort, and let out a groan of disbelief and disgust. Jammed between the young woman's teeth was one of those miniature Nerf footballs that the university publicity department gave away to visitors and fans and alumni and the children of alumni. This one showed, in addition to an image of the Sacred Steeple, the signature of football coach Sosthenes "Snopes" Avano in black magic-marker.

The dead girl looked to have been about twenty years old.

There were bruises around her neck.

Which was broken.

Both wrists were broken too.

Yet there was not a button missing from the open blouse, nor a tear in the fabric.

Emil knew that times had changed. A lot of women ran about with plenty open and even more hanging out. But few of them— he guessed—walked around at night, way out in the country, totally unbuttoned. Was this corpse the product of a Sauk River rendezvous gone suddenly, horribly wrong?

He had registered the particulars, so he stood up and thought about the person. The victim. Young and very lovely. All of life ahead, as they say. Emil felt his throat get hot and tight. Once, a long, long time ago, he and Sarah had lost their only child, a little girl, Susan, when she'd been only four years old. Now, every time he saw a young woman he always thought, Susan would have been exactly this age once, for an instant of time.

It was hard for Emil to gaze upon the red-haired girl. It was like losing his daughter all over again. I'll find out who did this to you, he promised. I'll give it everything I've got.

"Hey, Emil, I think the kid's coming around now," Axel Vogel called, bending over Brewster. The big deputy had flipped Titchell Junior over onto his back and was pouring a steady stream of algae-laden river water from his sodden trooper's hat. It splashed all over Brewster's face and neck. He had begun to sputter and writhe. Speech followed.

"Hellllppppp," Titchell gurgled.

The deputy ceased his ministrations. Titchell wiped his glasses

16

with a shirtsleeve and stared up at the lawmen. He remembered who he was, where he was, and what he'd seen.

"Let me up," he said, struggling, "I saw—"

"We know what you saw. Calm down."

The young man began to shiver with fright and tension.

"You hollered something just before you conked out," Emil reminded him. "Recall what it was?"

"Yes. Lish. Alicia Stanhope. She's . . ." He jerked his head in the direction of the corpse, his whole body shaking like somebody on the dance floor at The Bucket, a notorious singles bar in town. "She's a senior here at NS. We called her Lish, for short."

"You knew her?"

A nod. "She and I were in Professor Torbert's special seminar."

"So you're a student here. What's a special seminar?"

"It's Professor Hollman's idea, one of his best. Small groups of students meet with a teacher to study the values of our culture."

This was academic talk, which Emil didn't know a whole lot about.

"Professor Hollman wants to see North Star achieve real intellectual distinction," continued Titchell, hugging himself and shaking, "like the big schools back East."

"Who's in Torbert's seminar?" Whippletree asked.

"Well, there was Lish and me. Tony Wiggins. He's a real brain from Ely, up North. And Lish's roommate, Dee-Dee Tiernan . . ."

My niece? thought Emil. It jolted him to hear her name connected, however tangentially, to this tragedy, and a sensation of half-formed dread blossomed beneath his breastbone.

". . . and then we had the jocks," Titchell finished.

"The jocks?"

"Gunnar Rutkow, Lem Duffy, and Rusty Rollins."

Emil was impressed. The Terrible Trio, as they were known to Norse fans, and all of them together in Torbert's special class. Rutkow led the conference in sacks. Lem Duffy, tight end, caught just about everything thrown his way, thrown by Rusty Rollins, all-American quarterback. All three were sure to make the pros.

"President Rexford assigned some jocks to each of the seminars," Titchell said, "although not all of them can handle the work. Rector Rex's afraid that the National College Athletic Association might come around here and find most of the jocks taking courses in basketweaving."

Emil recalled reading something about the recent NCAA study. It seemed that up to seventy percent of college athletes never graduated *at all*. The association was cracking down on schools that put sports ahead of education. Many critics had contended over the years that North Star was one such school.

"When did that seminar meet?" Emil asked.

"Last night."

"Funny time for it. Friday night."

"It's scheduled for Wednesdays, but Professor Torbert couldn't make it this week. He had a meeting to attend."

"What kind of meeting?"

"Ask him about it."

"I will. So you were dismissed at . . . ?"

"Ten-thirty."

"Where'd you go after it was over?"

"To Professor Hollman's office. He'd promised to drive me into St. Cloud. I stay with my parents on weekends." Titchell was shaking as if he had the palsy now.

Emil angled for a few more quick facts. "Did you notice where the rest of the students went?"

"No, but I assume the jocks headed for Valhalla. Their curfew's eleven on the night before a game."

The athletes lived in a special dorm, Thomas Hall, in quarters somewhat larger and more luxurious than those occupied by regular students. An irreverent campus wag had dubbed it Valhalla.

"So you and Dr. Hollman drove into town?"

"Yes, and then I came back out here today with him and Mrs. Hollman. To see the game."

"Okay. You've been helpful. Tell you what. We'll forget about your interfering with law officers . . ."

Axel looked disappointed.

". . . and I wouldn't want to embarrass your dad by hauling you in . . ."

It occurred to Emil that Judge Titchell would be disposed to throw the book at any kid (except his own) for a lesser matter than this one.

". . . if you promise not to do it again."

Brewster ducked his head, a weak gesture of assent.

"But one more question. Do you know anyone who might have had reason to kill Miss Stanhope?"

Titchell hesitated. He didn't hesitate long, but he did. Bingo! thought the sheriff. He knows something, or he thinks he does.

"No," said the boy.

Emil pulled the kid to his hush-puppied feet. "Let's get you to the infirmary. They can give you a sedative, or something. Axel, wait here. Don't let anyone walk through this area. We'll have to rope it off and search all around."

"Right, Emil." Axel did not look too happy about being left alone with the body.

"I'll radio Doc Divot and have him come on out here." Percival Divot, former surgeon, was Emil's longtime fishing buddy and first-term county coroner.

Emil half dragged, half carried the whippersnapper back up the ravine's embankment, worrying about what he'd learned. Seven people had been at the seminar with Alicia, including Dee-Dee. All of them would have to be interviewed, no way of knowing if the effort would be productive, but the thought of his niece bothered Emil most. She was his wife's sister's girl, but to him she'd always been a secret substitute for his own lost daughter, Susan. Emil had watched her grow from a little babbling tyke to a gregarious tomboy to the whip-smart, honey-haired young beauty she was now.

*If something's happened to Dee-Dee, I couldn't take it, I just couldn't.*

Whippletree and the kid came up out of the trees and onto the asphalt drive. *Several hundred* people were kneeling on the golf course now, praying to the pine tree. Word of Bunny's vision must

19

have spread into the stadium crowd. Bored with the apparently one-sided gridiron contest—a swelling roar meant still another Norse score—they drifted over to the tree in twos and threes and fours, falling to their knees and joining the hushed, reverent mass.

Butch and a couple of his men were standing around, smoking cigarettes, waiting for the game to end, watching the people worship the pine tree. The security guys showed a mixture of amusement, disbelief, and awe. Butch just looked worried. He was thinking of larger crowds in days to come. "Emil," he said in greeting. "Hey, what'd you do to the kid? He don't look so hot."

Obligingly, Titchell retched, relieving himself of a mess that looked like popcorn and candied apple.

"Butch, I got bad news for the both of us. There's a dead girl down by the river. A North Star coed. I need your help. We've got to rope off the area and fine-tooth-comb it for evidence."

Emil watched the security chief's face carefully as he spoke. Butch reacted to the news as if somebody'd rammed a red-hot poker up his nether orifice. There was no question about it: his hard face sagged, becoming for an instant a pale mask of complete fear. He pulled himself together quickly.

"Sure she's one of ours?"

"Yep," said Emil. "Titchell comfirmed it. He knew her."

Butch gave some orders. Emil walked to his patrol car, still parked there on the golf course. He got behind the wheel, picked up the mike, and flipped a switch.

"Alyce? Alyce, it's me."

Crackle and a pause. Sound of chewing gum snapping. "Yeah, Sheriff?"

"Alyce, I've got a homicide out here at NSU. Raise Doc Divot and tell him to head on out here PDQ."

"Oh Jeeez, Emil! A murder? Who?"

"One of the students. It's pretty bad. Call Deputy Poll and tell him to get here too. He'll sober up fast when he sees what we're up against. And contact Jamie Gosch up at Leech Lake. Tell him to pack his fishing gear and start home."

Alyce complained about extra work on Saturday, but the sheriff promised to make it up to her. ". . . And call my wife," he said. "I'll be home a little later than usual."

When Emil got out of the car, Butch was standing there, tense but composed. He'd earned almost every ribbon or medal the Army could bestow, according to reports. But Emil didn't know him, didn't have a feel for the guy, and the ex-sergeant seemed just a little tentative for a man who'd been a hero in Saigon. Still, wasn't a hero just a person who kept his wits a minute longer than everybody else, then sat there in the dirt with everybody else, shaking and sweating and wondering what had happened?

"My men are bringing some rope, Emil."

"Thanks. We have to get it strung so people don't mess up the area."

"Emil, shouldn't higher authority be told of the . . . incident?"

"Thought I *was* higher authority."

"The university, I mean."

"Oh. Right. President Anderson. Go ahead and do it."

"I . . . ah . . ." Butch faltered. "I . . . don't think it's my job to tell him. This is a murder. It's out of my league."

Whippletree frowned. Technically, Butch was right. Homicides didn't come under the jurisdiction of university security. No sense arguing about it. Besides, Emil would have to deal with President Anderson soon enough. And, frankly, he'd always wondered what Rector Rex was really like. The man was probably Minnesota's most renowned citizen, his reputation as executive, educator, thinker, and public figure illustrious and unchallenged.

"All right, I'll do it," Emil decided.

"He's at the football game."

"Okay. Do me a favor. When that rope shows up, take it down to Axel and help him get started. It's getting dark early these days. Get yourself a little experience in the sheriff game, too," he couldn't help adding.

Almost everybody in Stearns County knew Emil. Fans, vendors, custodians, and ticket-takers greeted him as he entered one of the stadium's big gates and made his way through a concrete tunnel toward the playing field.

"Hey, Sheriff! Come to catch some of the game? You're late. Not much time to go."

"Got to see President Anderson about something." Emil grinned, with an easy wave, not letting on that the university head was not going to remember this visit with delight.

"He's in his box on the fifty-yard line with Senator Durenberger and the governor."

"I'll find him. What's the score?"

"Thirty-eight to nothing, favor of the Norsemen, of course. Northwestern hasn't won a game in years."

Emil felt the ghost of a shiver work its way up his spine. He'd pretty much discounted Bunny's prediction that the game would end at thirty-eight to three. If she's right, I'm gonna have to be real friendly to her, Emil told himself.

He came out of the concrete passageway and onto the field. It was always a thrill to enter Granitelli Stadium, site of so many momentous clashes that had roused the old sheriff's blood in the past. A vast, sweeping bowl of light, sound, color, it symbolized a yearning for excellence that the best human hearts would always celebrate and hold dear. Cheerleaders of innocent or not-so-innocent beauty, but breathtaking in their sheer youthfulness, whirled and cavorted; fans were on their feet, yelling and screaming, making strange, tribalistic, pushing gestures with their arms; multi-colored flags flew from the top tier of the bowl. And gigantic Jesus blessed it all, the stadium and everyone in it, His arms lengthening on the gridded grass as the afternoon wore on. The artifice had a huge crown of concrete thorns; it resembled the Statue of Liberty.

A huge electronic scoreboard told the tale:

| NORSEMEN 38 | | WILDCATS 0 |
|---|---|---|
| QUARTER 4 | DOWN 4 | YARDAGE 7 |
| | TIME 1:17 | |

Northwestern had the ball on North Star's forty-two-yard line. There was a time-out on the field.

Along the sidelines, in front of the Patriot bench, Coach Snopes

Avano paced back and forth, back and forth. He never relaxed, not even with a thirty-eight-point lead and less than two minutes to play. Avano was in his seventeenth year as North Star's head football coach. He'd achieved a record of one hundred and thirty-two wins, thirty-one losses, and three ties, invitational bowl games included. It was his oft-stated dream to surpass the two hundred and two victories racked up by the legendary Rocco Granitelli, but Snopes was already sixty-two—just like the sheriff—and he knew that time was not on his side. Still, in his crushed cap, with tinted aviator glasses and a lacquered corncob pipe jammed between his teeth, Snopes radiated defiance, determination, and will—inflexible will. No mentor had ever elicited more loyalty from his players, a dedication Snopes returned in full measure.

Trying to keep his bearing casual, Emil strolled toward the president's box. He recognized Minnesota's Senator Durenberger, Governor Bauch, and his lovely wife, Mary. Seated with them was Dr. Anderson, old now but lean and tall, with shining, thick, silvery-white hair. His strong, craggy face was tanned and deeply lined, and he wore a simple blue suit with a gold football pin on the left lapel. Next to him was a younger man, almost a copy of Anderson, except that his hair was only touched by gray and his face not as weathered by time. He was Fagin Dexter, North Star's newly appointed executive vice-president. Roy Riley had done a profile piece on Dexter for the *Trib*. The president would periodically aver that he had had enough, he'd soon be stepping down, and an heir apparent would be installed. But after a few months, Anderson would state that the trustees didn't want him to retire just yet, the putative successor moved on to another job, and everything settled down until Rector Rex started pondering retirement again.

"Dr. Anderson," Emil said, reaching the box. "I'm Emil Whippletree and—"

"Sheriff Whippletree. Yes, of course," exclaimed the president, half rising to shake hands.

In most ways, Emil was more than content with his life. Yet he'd always wondered how things might have gone if he'd been able to get a good education. What would it be like to have real "book learning," and be able to talk knowledgeably and well about all sorts of things, the way people talked on "MacNeil-Lehrer" and "Meet the Press"? Emil felt a little awed by President Anderson, who had been on those programs and others like it. Education had incalculable benefits, Emil knew. It made a man's mind keener. But did it make the man himself better? Emil's optimistic nature told him yes, but a small quirk way back there in his Minnesota populist soul said no, not necessarily. He was just about to deliver his bad tidings when the scoreboard clock started up again.

"Let's watch this, shall we?" suggested Rector Rex. "Northwestern's going to try for a field goal."

With Bunny Hollman's prediction on his mind, Emil waited. For a matter-of-fact guy, he felt a thrilling and pretty damn disquieting quiver of fate, or destiny, or whatever you wanted to call it. Spooky, he called it. Joey "Tank" Furillo, Northwestern's second-string quarterback, was set to take the snap from center and hold the ball for the kicking artist, LaVandar "Fistfoot" Zipp, whose field-goal percentage was around .956 or thereabouts, mainly because NW seldom got within field-goal range. In North Star's line, huge Gunnar Rutkow shifted into a more threatening position.

Then the snap. It was straight and sure to Furillo, who caught it and set it in place. Zipp was already moving forward, his bared kicking foot downswinging into the arc.

The crowd roared, savoring the existential moment. Gunnar Rutkow, as usual, had broken through the Wildcat line. He plunged toward Zipp, his thick arms raised and waving to block the kick.

Zipp's flashing foot made slapping contact with the ball.

The crowd was roaring.

Gunnar Rutkow was almost there.

But he didn't make it in time. Smart smack of flesh against leather, and the football soared into the sky, above the disarray of linemen, medieval knights in fray, toward the silver goalposts.

Emil's heart didn't stop, but his breathing did. He watched the ball go up, up, reach its apogee, and begin to descend. The fans were yelling and the referee scissored his arms energetically at knee level.

"Northwestern field goal attempt no good," said the announcer over the booming public address. "Norsemen's ball on their own forty-two-yard line."

The game was, in effect, over already, Snopes Avano's one hundred and thirty-third victory. Emil reflected, with no little wonder, how close Bunny had come to calling the contest. Whew! Had to be more than chance, didn't it? Yet, how on earth . . . ?

"What can I do for you, Sheriff?" Rector Rex was asking.

Emil nodded toward the others in the box. "It's sort of an official matter . . ."

Anderson understood immediately. Excusing himself adroitly, he left the box, and the two men walked to a grassy spot between the bleachers and the Norse bench. The players were bunched there, counting down the final seconds of the game. Emil was a little stunned at the size of them, wide and towering and anonymously threatening behind their face guards.

"Well, Sheriff, I guess Snopes and the boys skunked 'em," Dr. Anderson said with relish.

Emil nodded, steeling himself. No other way but to come right out with it. "Doctor, I hate to have to tell you this, but a body's been found here on campus. Down by the Sauk. 'Fraid it looks like homicide, and maybe rape too. Coroner's on his way out."

Dr. Anderson's face remained smooth for a moment as he registered the news, then showed veiled alarm. "Well, Sheriff, I'm sorry to hear that. And, of course, we'll cooperate in any way we can. But it doesn't really involve the university, does it?"

"The victim's one of your students," Emil told the elegant president. "Her name's Alicia Stanhope . . ."

"Alicia!" gasped Anderson. "Oh good Lord . . . how . . . ?"

North Star had over four thousand students, and Emil was impressed that the president was instantly familiar with a single name.

"When did it happen?" the president asked.

"Sometime last night or early this morning. We'll find out. How well did you know her?"

"Quite . . . well. She was active in our special seminars pro-

25

gram. Sheriff, the school, myself, all my people: we put ourselves behind you in every way."

"Thanks, I'll need all the help I can get." Emil decided to spare him the details of Alicia's state. The final gun had sounded and the stands were emptying.

"My niece studies here," Emil said proudly. "Dee-Dee Tiernan. She's a senior."

Anderson nodded distractedly. Emil was a little miffed. Why would he know Alicia Stanhope and not Dee-Dee, who had to be the best student at North Star?

"She's Miss Stanhope's roommate," he told the president.

"Oh? Oh, *yes*. Perhaps she knows something that will aid us. . . ."

"I hope so. I'll have to talk to her and some others." He mentioned Professor Torbert and the members of the seminar.

"The football players were in that seminar?" Anderson mused. "Yes, I guess I knew that. . . ."

"Sir?" prodded Vice-President Dexter, standing with the distinguished guests. "Will we be leaving?"

Anderson turned toward his subordinate. "Please come here, would you?"

Dexter obeyed, and Emil was introduced to a serious, capable-looking man of perhaps forty-five, who seemed attractively modest, competent, and attentive. The president conveyed news of the tragedy—to which Dexter reacted with muted shock—and gave the names of the seminar personnel.

"Fagin, I'd like you to arrange for Sheriff Whippletree to meet with all of them. What time is best for you, Sheriff?"

"I've got to search the area for evidence right now," Emil said. "For the time being, see if you can determine where they all are— we know about the players, naturally—and first thing tomorrow morning I'll drive out here and interview them."

"Very good, I'll take care of it," said Dexter.

"Guess that'll be it for now, thanks," said Emil. "Oh, by the way, have you heard about Bunny Hollman?"

They hadn't, so he told them.

26

"Charlie Hollman's *wife?*" said Millhouse. Then he smiled. "Sheriff, you don't have to worry about *that*. It's a college president's problem, I'm afraid."

"You can have it," Emil said.

"It'll be taken care of," Anderson replied. "It's nothing that can't be handled."

Emil felt pleased with the way things had gone. He'd just participated in a one-on-one with the most distinguished man he'd ever met and he'd held his own all right.

So he thought.

The drive was packed with cars moving slowly off campus as Emil headed across the golf course and back toward the ravine. There were at least five hundred people at prayer beneath the pine tree. Somebody had tacked a small cross to its trunk. Clusters of sunflowers and wild roses had been placed at its base.

Dr. Percival Divot, county coroner, had arrived. He was waiting for Emil at the side of the road, leaning against his red-and-white van. He and Emil had known each other for over thirty years, ever since Emil had gone to him for a checkup shortly after Doc had hung out his shingle in St. Cloud. "I like you," Divot had said in his blunt way. "You're an improvement over those assholes in med school." Emil didn't know how bad the med-school assholes had been, but he'd taken the remark as a compliment. He and Doc had been sharing six-packs in fishing boats ever since.

"Dammit, Emil," said Doc. "I was out at the country club when your secretary called. Two under par on the thirteenth hole and fifteen bucks ahead of T. R. Steinhaus. This better be good."

"Consider it a professional challenge, Doc."

Divot was a couple of years older than Emil, but still plenty agile. The two men parted low-hanging branches and slid down the embankment toward the Sauk River. Axel, along with Butch and his men, had roped off the area thoroughly and professionally. Emil thanked them. Deputy Pete Poll had arrived, still shaky and a little hung over—Friday nights were hard on him—and so had young Deputy Farley, who was always complaining about how boring Stearns County was.

"We finally scraped up a little excitement for you, Benny," said the sheriff.

Farley grinned sheepishly, looking sick. Butch Lodge didn't look too well either, noted Emil, for a guy who must've known his share of death.

Divot bent to untangle a pesky vine that had wrapped itself around his ankle and took a look at the body. "Broken neck. Probably C.O.D."

"C.O.D?" wondered Farley.

"Cause of death. And broken wrists. Snapped clean. No cuts, no abrasions, no other marks I can see right off. She came up against a powerful sumbitch, though. Ain't that easy to break a bone, let alone a neck. No buttons torn off, though. Interesting." He peered at the russety muff. "Have to check for evidence of sexual activity when I get her back to the lab. Couple you guys trot up to my meat wagon and bring down a stretcher."

Poll and young Farley complied without protest. Divot felt gingerly around the body and then beneath it, grunted, and pulled a small leather handbag into view.

"Inventory," he rasped, unsnapping the clasp and puttering around inside. "Comb. Hairbrush. Compact. Ten, twelve, eighteen . . . twenty-three bucks and coin." Then he removed a seashell-shaped plastic container. "And diaphragm," he said.

"Hey!" protested Axel, "I thought North Star girls wasn't supposed to do it. That's what I always heard."

"Everybody does it," grunted the Doc. "Don't let 'em tell you different."

"The question," said Butch, "is who'd she do it with? And if she did it here, I guess she forgot to use her comestopper."

Emil, who'd been idly probing the vine leaves with the toe of

28

his boot, caught a glimpse of something crinkly and shiny down in the grass.

"And what the hell is this? A football in her mouth?" Divot exclaimed with considerable interest. "Now that's a psycho touch for sure."

Emil eased himself down into a crouch and picked up the object that had caught his eye, holding it carefully between his fingernails. "This could be why she didn't bother with the diaphragm," he said, showing the others the empty foil container. It had, according to its markings, once held a lubricated Trojan-Enz prophylactic. "Seems like her partner might have been considerate enough to take the precautions."

Everybody looked at the foil, then at each other.

"Rape with a rubber?" Axel wondered in amazement.

"We don't know if it's rape," said Doc. "Can't even tell about penetration out here in the wilderness."

Poll and Farley stumbled back with the stretcher and laid it down next to Alicia Stanhope.

"I'll do it," offered Butch Lodge, and, with obvious gentleness, he smoothed the girl's clothing, eased her almost tenderly onto the stretcher. Then, as if noting that something seemed incomplete, he stripped off his quasi-military guard's jacket and laid it carefully over her face.

"Don't touch the football," Doc warned. "Got to check it for prints."

Butch nodded to Axel. He and the big deputy carried Alicia Stanhope up through the trees toward Divot's van. Doc said so long to Emil and followed them.

Emil stood there for a moment, thinking things over. There'd been a murder all right and sex had been involved. But what kind of sex? He had the feeling that the little Nerf football ought to be telling him something. "Okay," he said to his deputies and Butch's men, "let's start looking."

"What are we lookin' for?" asked bourbon-battered Poll in a husky voice.

"A used rubber, for starters. Semen can be typed, like blood."

29

After ten minutes, however, their search turned up over a dozen discarded prophylactics, as well as combs, earrings, barrettes, and a man's loafer. They found some hosiery too and even a few pairs of panties in various stages of mildewed deterioration.

"All right, forget about that," said Emil. "Let's sweep east to west inside the roped-off area and see what else we can find."

Dusk fell and Emil knew he'd have to call off the hunt pretty soon. Poll and Farley were shambling profitlessly through the underbrush. The sheriff paused and leaned against the trunk of an ancient birch. Its grotesquely twisted roots snaked up out of the earth. Emil thought of a dying creature, writhing in protest as it sensed the withdrawal of the life force. He bent to examine the roots.

On a piece of curled whitish bark, he saw a reddish-black smear. Dried blood?

And, clinging to a chokecherry twig, he spied a scrap of torn, filmy fabric.

Nylon.

With his heart beating just a little faster, Emil carefully twisted the fabric from the twig. He smelled something, fragrant and very strong. He sniffed the cloth. A powerful, sweetish, musky scent filled his sinuses. Whoever'd snagged her hose on the chokecherry didn't shrink from splashing on the stuff!

An image came to him, a kind of superanimated mental movie of a frightened woman ducking desperately behind this birch, wanting to get out of sight, wanting to get away from . . .

He crouched down behind the gnarled roots and peered over them in the direction of the murder site. He could see it easily.

It had been a clear, still night; there'd been a moon. He studied his position behind the tree. If he'd dived in here hurriedly, just so, he might have smashed knee or arm or even head on the root. It might have drawn blood. And the chokecherry bush could have caught his pants leg. But why would he want to jump back here in such haste?

Why would *she* have, assuming—as seemed logical—that a woman had worn this fragrant bit of cloth?

Because she herself had caught sight of something threatening and dangerous.

Emil felt a tingling at his temples and along his hairline (which hadn't receded at all over the years: Sarah always said that he and Ronald Reagan shared a lucky gene). This prickly sensation was always a sign of intuition for him.

Someone might have hidden here, witnessing Alicia Stanhope's last moments on earth. Emil felt encouraged for a moment, until he considered the parameters of time. About eighteen hours had passed since the killing and no such witness had come forward.

Perhaps that witness was dead too.

And then Emil's gentle old heart began pumping the fierce blood of panic. What if Alicia and Dee-Dee had decided to take an unauthorized absence from campus? He didn't want to think she would do that, but she was a spirited young woman. And, judging from the articles found here in the underbrush, student life at North Star was not exactly what university public relations proclaimed it to be.

No, not Dee-Dee, Emil prayed, getting slowly to his feet. She was the first child in the family even to go to college, she wanted to teach little kids, she was getting almost all As. Not Dee-Dee.

Night was falling, and a piece of night had fallen upon his heart. Emil slipped the piece of nylon into his wallet, peeled the blood-smeared bark from the birch—he'd take it into town for Divot's analysis—and put it into his breast pocket. "That's all for now, you guys," he called in an unsteady voice. "Too dark to do any more. Let's go home."

Nobody protested.

There were still a couple of dozen worshippers beneath the white pine when Emil climbed back up from the riverbank and told Poll and Farley to go on into town. Then he saw Butch Lodge and

President Anderson standing next to his car. Butch leaned uneasily against a fender, shifting his weight nervously. Rector Rex, tall and slightly stooped, looked lean and steely calm against the twilight.

"Did you and your men find anything?" he asked.

"I'm not sure yet," sighed Emil, thinking of the bloody birch bark and the scrap of nylon. "I'm heading into St. Cloud to huddle with Divot. Maybe he'll come up with something we can use."

"Sergeant Lodge may have had a bit of luck," observed the president. Emil was immensely impressed with the naturalness, the genuineness of the man's personality.

"I checked the reports filed by my men last night," Butch said. "Should have done it this morning, but with the football game and all"—he made a loose throwaway gesture—"I just didn't. Anyway, I found something that might give us a lead. There was an incident outside the cafeteria. At about nine o'clock. A townie had driven onto campus, must have slipped by the gate. He was asking for Alicia Stanhope."

A townie was anybody from St. Cloud who did not attend North Star. There was some town-gown conflict in the county, but not too much. Rector Rex believed that good fences made good neighbors.

"Get a description of the guy?" Emil asked.

"Sort of a greaser." Butch shrugged. "And he wasn't shy. He gave his name before he left. You ever heard of a John Pflüger, Emil?"

The sheriff laughed.

"You recognize the name," Anderson observed.

"Hell, yes . . . sorry, sir . . . yes, I do. Butch, you've been away from Stearns too long. Cowboy John is a public figure. I've arrested him at least a dozen times and every one of my deputies can probably make the same claim. But murder is out of his line. He's more a bad-check artist and a contested-paternity-suit kind of guy."

Women—a certain kind of woman—kept calling the various bars of Stearns County, seeking a few ecstatic hours of Johnny Pflüger's questionable charms.

"Still, I believe it ought to be looked into," said Anderson.

"Oh, it will be. I'll pick him up for questioning tonight. He's almost always drinking at The Bucket on Saturday nights. But a girl like Alicia Stanhope wouldn't have given a jerk like Johnny the time of day."

"He was here," said Butch. "He knew her name."

"It might be wise," suggested the president quietly, "to remember that each personality has many facets. What appears obvious can often be discounted."

In Emil's limited experience with homicide, that was and wasn't true. He'd solved one case in which a minister had killed his wife and children in order to be free to marry a shady lady. In another, a county oldtimer had dealt frontier justice to a promiscuous woman and her thieving son. "It's usually obvious in hindsight," Emil said. "I'll guarantee you that."

"I have a visceral feeling that this unpleasant Mr. Pflüger is the man we are looking for," Anderson asserted.

"Well, we'll know soon enough."

"As for tomorrow morning," said the president, "Vice-President Dexter has arranged for you to meet with the football players, Rutkow, Rollins, and Duffy. Professor Torbert has gone to Minneapolis for the weekend to do research at the University of Minnesota, but we are trying to reach him. Anthony Wiggins will be available. He's right here on campus. And Miss Tiernan, whom you know, signed out to spend the weekend at her home in St. Cloud."

Thank God! exulted the sheriff.

"However," continued Anderson, "she was not at home when Dexter phoned."

Emil's spirit, so briefly soaring, plummeted. Dee-Dee might be out shopping, or fooling around with her friends, but that dark premonition inside his rib cage was still very much present. Rector Rex did nothing to dislodge it when he said, "The girl's mother seemed unaware that Miss Tiernan intended to come home."

There was a note of reproach in his voice. Emil knew why. It was a violation of North Star's vaunted honor system to trifle with

33

the privileges and procedures of off-campus forays. A student could get into big trouble for so doing.

"She's probably out shopping," Emil said. "I'm sure there must have been a little misunderstanding."

"Dexter will continue trying to reach her," Anderson said. "I personally phoned the Stanhopes. I believe it was just about the hardest thing I've ever had to do. They will be in St. Cloud tomorrow afternoon to claim the body. Will that be convenient for you?"

"I'll check with the coroner, but I think so."

"Alicia Stanhope didn't sign out at all," offered Butch. Anderson nodded in corroboration.

"Maybe she didn't intend to leave campus," Emil said. If that were true, then one of his earliest impulses might have been correct: she'd planned to meet someone, a lover's lane rendezvous.

"Belief," said Anderson, in a tone Emil could not interpret. It was quite dark now and the president's face was only an outline against the sky, like the Sacred Steeple and the statue of Jesus. The president might have been amused or whimsical or even angry. Emil couldn't tell. But he remembered very clearly his peculiar sensations earlier in the day, when he'd arrived on campus to perceive, however obscurely, a door opening at the edges of the world.

"What do you think of this vision business?" Emil asked.

"It depends on who I am," answered Anderson, in that same unreadable voice.

"I . . . beg your pardon?" Emil felt a bit embarrassed. He was afraid he'd missed something that anybody with even half an education would have picked up right away.

Rector Rex laughed quietly. "Sorry," he said. "I didn't mean to sound mysterious. But, you see, belief defines person. Find a human being's basic belief and you can almost always predict what he—or she—will do if given a certain stimulus."

"What's your basic belief, Emil?" interrupted Butch, who (Emil was sure) didn't understand what Anderson was talking about any more clearly than he did himself.

"Well," Emil began, pretty sure of himself, "the most important thing I believe is . . ."

And through his mind there raced all kinds of things he believed in: love and his job and having people think well of him and sitting in a duck blind with Doc Divot and a pint of Old Crow on a brisk November morning . . .

"Cat gotcha tongue, Emil?" Butch guffawed.

Rector Rex was more understanding. "You see what I mean now," he said. "What do I think of Mrs. Hollman's vision? Well, the Virgin was sighted in bushes and trees before, at Fatima and Guadaloupe and Lourdes, or so thousands of people believed, and I feel that Mrs. Hollman *thinks* she had a vision. As a Christian, a part of me would like to believe that she did. It would constitute reassuring evidence, so to speak. As a scholar not unfamiliar with psychology, I would speculate that Bunny is in the grip of an hysteria powerful enough to affect many others. As a man trained in scientific method, I would conclude that there is no basis whatever to her claims, because I would deny any reality beyond that which can be observed on this earth. But, as president of North Star University, I can say for sure that Bunny Hollman's vision, real or not, is going to cause all of us a lot of trouble."

"You can sure count on some big crowds for a while," Emil said.

Butch groaned. "Next Saturday is no real problem. The team will be in Indiana, playing Notre Dame. But the following week it's homecoming against Illinois and, well, you saw the mess we had here just today."

"Ten years ago in New York," said Rector Rex, "some woman claimed she saw the Virgin in a maple tree right outside her parish church. She lived in a heavily populated residential neighborhood. The place turned into a zoo. Busloads of people showed up. Pilgrims from Quebec arrived. Ice-cream vendors rolled in with their white trucks . . ."

"Charlie Hollman works for you, doesn't he? Just ask him to tell Bunny to have her vision someplace else," Emil suggested.

There was a slight pause. Then Anderson said, "Sheriff, I think this matter falls under your jurisdiction. The crowds we can expect constitute a clear and present physical menace."

"Why don't you just talk to Charlie, like I said?"

"The university is somewhat complicated, Sheriff. Dr. Hollman is a powerful member of the faculty."

"You mean you can't tell him what to do?"

"In some things, no. And you must keep in mind that this is an institution sworn to uphold ideals. Like it or not, we are in the public eye."

Emil sensed Butch's tension; he was waiting for the old sheriff's response.

Then Emil understood. Rector Rex and Butch didn't want the university to bear the onus of having to deal with crowds of believers. How would it look if North Star, a Christian place, had to get tough with people who had come there to pray? No, they figured it would be a lot more comfortable for them if Emil shouldered the burden.

"If anything unlawful occurs," he said agreeably, "if there's any danger to the peace, you can count on me. But it is your land and you *do* have a security force to tend it."

The ensuing silence proved that each man fully realized the terms of the transaction that had been proposed here, and understood just as completely that Emil had said "No deal."

Rector Rex tried to pull a fast one on me, thought Emil, astonished. No, maybe I'm just tired. These intellectuals have a reputation for being indirect. Still . . .

"See you in the morning," he said, climbing into his patrol car. "You guys handle the religion. I'm gonna have my hands too full with homicide."

There was almost no traffic on the drive into St. Cloud. Emil radioed the office to tell Alyce it was all right to go home, learned that she already had, and that Jamie Gosch, fisherman, had returned from Up North. It was always called Up North, just as Minneapolis and St. Paul were known as The Cities.

"Glad you're back, Jamie. You missed one hell of a day. Catch anything?"

36

"Yeah, Sheriff, I got three big walleyes and—"

"Great. Glad to hear it. You're on duty tonight. I'm stopping at the coroner's, then at The Bucket, then—"

"You goin' out drinkin', hey, Sheriff?"

"No, I'm going fishing for Pflüger."

Divot had completed the autopsy. Alicia Stanhope's body lay on the operating table under a grayish-white surgical sheet. Doc didn't seem to mind, but the preternatural stillness, the pure motionlessness of that sheet gave Emil the jitters.

"Hey, Emil," said Divot in greeting.

The sheriff stuck a wad of Copenhagen inside his cheek. "Learn anything?" he asked.

Divot shrugged. "She was in damn good physical condition, I'll tell you that. Like new."

"She was new."

"As to evidence, several things. Could help you out, I think. Under the fingernails of her right hand, blood. Type A, positive. She got her claws on the guy, at least. Under the left-hand fingernails, I found bits of a rubberized synthetic fabric, blue in color. Maybe a jacket, windbreaker, something like that."

"Anything of a sexual nature?"

"Well, no semen. But I did find traces of the kind of lubricant they put on prophylactics." He gestured toward a table where the little football lay on a white cloth. "No fingerprints on the ball he'd shoved in her mouth, though. I'd judge that to be a probable sign of some off-the-wall perversion."

Emil nodded. "Think it was rape?"

"With a rubber? That'd be awful weird. Still, it could have been. We've got some pretty strange ones running around these days. Maybe sex first, murder afterwards. That unbuttoned, untorn blouse intrigues me."

Divot washed his hands, found a thin, brown cigarillo in the pocket of his surgical jacket and lit it. "Wonder where she was headed when it happened? Purse, money, diaphragm, and the rest?"

"Night on the town, maybe." Emil remembered the piece of birch bark. He laid it on the table next to the Nerf football, and explained the situation.

"I'll give it a look-see first thing in the morning," Divot said. "By the way, you betting on that Vikes—Broncs game?"

"I guess so."

"I'm afraid the Vikings are gonna get whupped again."

"Could be." It occurred to Emil that maybe he should ask Bunny Hollman. "Say, Doc, mind if I ask you something? How well do you know Rexford Anderson?"

"I don't. Met him at a couple of local fund-raisers, is all. We move in different circles. Why?"

"I'm not sure. But I think he tried to stick me with crowd control, in the event that Bunny Hollman starts attracting a lot of attention." Briefly, he explained the situation, expressing an apprehension that the pious as well as the curious would soon begin to show up at North Star in droves.

"If I were Anderson, I'd be a little wary too," Doc said. "Butch Lodge isn't equipped to deal with a mob in addition to the football crowd. He hasn't got the manpower or the statutory clout."

"I haven't got the manpower either."

"Oh, Emil, don't worry about it. Wait and see what happens. Say, you want to slip out and have a quick one? I'll be through here pretty soon."

"I better not. Got a stop to make on the way home as it is, and Sarah will be worrying."

Divot promised to run a test on the birch bark and call Emil with the results. The sheriff slid wearily into his patrol car and drove on over to The Bucket. At one point in its evolution from frontier town to the "hub" of central Minnesota, St. Cloud had boasted more churches than bars. The old-timers hadn't spent much time on trivial diversions. Their descendants, however, enjoyed supper clubs and discos and plenty of taverns. One of these was The Bucket, where Johnny Pflüger hung out quite a bit.

Emil pulled his car into the back lot, where it wouldn't be obvious, and walked around to the front. The Bucket was a low-slung clapboard building, painted off-white, that featured a long bar, a jukebox, a dance floor, flashing lights, and a rock band that played every Friday and Saturday night.

Pflüger, who worked at the paper mill in Sartell when he did anything, drove a dilapidated 1967 Caddy deVille, which crouched on tired shock absorbers in front of the bar. Its right front hubcap was missing. Hanging on a chain from the rearview mirror was a North Star Nerf football.

The rock band had not yet begun its evening gig, so when Emil entered The Bucket he heard the jukebox blaring an awful bit of rot called "Cowboy John." Pflüger identified with the lyrics and played the song every time he got the chance.

> *"Drove a pickup truck, packed a shotgun,*
> *Stood about six-foot-nahn . . ."*

The bar was fairly crowded. Emil saw Johnny and his drinking buddy, Byron Tillman, down at the end, sipping draft beer. Pflüger was five-eleven in his engineer boots and weighed maybe a hundred and forty-five soaking wet.

> *"John'd smack you a clip*
> *If you gave him lip,*
> *Right up-side yo' haid . . ."*

In Pflüger's case, he was the one who gave lip.

"'Lo, Emil," said Rafe Schwinghammer, from behind the bar. His expression revealed just the slightest bit of apprehension. Emil's visits in the past had been mainly to break up fistfights. The regulars turned from glasses or mugs to nod or say "Hi" or "Hey, Emil, what's up?" Emil strode across the floor and slipped onto a barstool next to Pflüger.

Johnny half turned, real slow, cool. Tillman, his buddy, aped him perfectly, right up to the curl of the lip. Emil saw that Pflüger was wearing an old blue windbreaker with a small tear on the left sleeve. Two jagged scratches ran down his right cheek, partially obscured by a couple day's growth of beard.

"Hi, Sheriff," he said. "Rafe, give the law a beer."

Emil nodded to Schwinghammer.

> *"Killed many a man with his shotgun,*
> *Ne'er drove nothin' but a Ford,*
> *It's true he liked*
> *Likker and wimmen,*
> *But he really loved*
> *The Lord . . ."*

Pflüger was always saying that he was a lover, not a fighter, and he had the reputation to back it up. The kind of women he attracted were partial to his sleepy, dissipated pretty-boy looks and to his devil-may-care cockiness.

"How they hangin', Emil?" Johnny asked with a snicker.

Byron Tillman practically fell off his stool laughing. Rafe brought over a glass of beer and Emil took a swallow.

> *"Cowboy John . . .*
> *Cowboy John . . ."*

"Aw *right*," said Pflüger, as the song ended. "Tillman, put in another quarter and play it again."

Byron raced over to the jukebox.

"John" said Emil, "we got to talk professionally."

"No skin off my ass. Rafe, give me a shot of Guggenheimer's."

"You need some courage?" Emil asked.

"Hell no."

Schwinghammer brought over the whiskey and Johnny downed it in a gulp. If he'd committed murder less than twenty-four hours ago, he looked awfully cool. But then he always looked that way. The sheriff was amazed. Johnny was as close to a total loser as Emil had ever met, yet he survived, exemplar par excellence of Stearns County's darker side. Farm boy from St. Alazara, two bewildered parents, and fifteen siblings. (The local bishop was still pushing the idea of big families in a time when very few could make a living off the land any more.) Johnny'd finished grade school, then hung around the farm until he was old enough for "The Service." His old man had thrown a big send-off party—hundreds of snaggle-toothed relatives attended—and everybody secretly hoped Johnny's "problem" would disappear under the discipline of military life.

He was back in Stearns County three weeks after he'd left.

Bed wetter.

Yet, however poorly his peter functioned in one department, he found that it worked very well in another.

"Cowboy John" started up again; Pflüger tapped rhythm on the bar.

"Where'd you get those scratches on your mug, John?" Emil asked.

Smirk. "Broad give 'em to me. I got tired after the eleventh time 'n' she was pissed."

"Got a rip in your jacket too, I see?"

A dull awareness appeared in Pflüger's pale eyes. He realized that Emil wasn't asking this stuff for his health. "Caught the fucker on a nail," he said.

> *"John was born with his boots on,*
> *Was a cold gray windy dawn,*
> *An' his po' momma sighed . . ."*

"You know a girl name of Alicia Stanhope?" Emil asked sharply.

"Give me that name again?"

"Stanhope. Alicia."

"Can't say as I do. Who is she?"

"Don't lie to me," Emil snarled, so effectively that Johnny jumped about an inch. "Butch Lodge told me you were out at North Star looking for her last night."

"So? What's it to ya? Any law against a guy goin' lookin' for a little?" Then he lapsed into a momentary silence, studying Emil with small peasant eyes, and decided to reverse his strategy. "Yeah," he admitted casually, "I know her."

41

"How?"

"Met her in here. Sometime last spring, I think it was."

So Miss Stanhope was no stranger to the high life of St. Cloud, Emil realized. "How well do you know her?" he asked.

Johnny leered. "She's got the strongest pussy I ever had, Sheriff, and I kid you not. Grip like a big man's handshake. I scrogged her up one side and down the other. . . ."

If this is true, Emil thought, there may be a lot about Alicia that I don't know.

"Why are you so interested?" Pflüger demanded. "Did the college complain about me being there last night, or something?"

"You might say that."

"Fuck them. The stuck-up bastards. They just don't want to believe a guy like me can get it on with one of the little princesses. But I can and I did. Yeah, I was supposed to pick up Lish for the weekend. We were gonna hole up at the Pine Tree Inn in Big Fall and ball our brains out."

"But you didn't?"

"Nope. Dammit. She never showed. The bitch. That's how she is. Does whatever she wants to. Probably ran off with some stud wears an alligator on his shirt."

Pflüger was being pretty convincing. Anderson's intuition notwithstanding, it was hard to accept Johnny as homicidal. Still . . .

"Do you know a girl named Dee-Dee Tiernan?" Emil asked with some hesitation.

"Yeah. Rooms with Lish. I met her. She's not my type . . ."

You can say that again, thought Emil, pleased.

". . . anyway," Johnny continued, "she's humping some other dude. I'd scrog her if I had the chance, though."

Emil was trying to keep his temper in check. "Who was it?" he asked. "That Miss Tiernan was seeing?" As far as he knew, Dee-Dee was still missing. If she had gotten serious with a man, she'd have mentioned it to her mother, Barbara, who would have told Sarah, who would have let Emil know.

"Hell, I don't know who it is," said Johnny, sipping his beer. "Why the hell should I care?"

Angered and worried, Emil decided on the shock treatment to take a little wind out of Pflüger's sails.

"Alicia Stanhope was killed last night," he said quietly, his eyes hard on Johnny, "right on campus."

Pflüger looked as if he'd been pole-axed.

"Whoever did it sustained some damage. She had traces of blood and fabric under her fingernails. I see your face and I note the rip in your jacket—"

"You can't . . . you ain't gonna pin this on me—"

"How about coming with me, Johnny? A little blood test could put you in the clear."

> ". . . Afore she died,
> 'Y'all name him
> Cowboy John . . .'"

Pflüger was halfway to the door before Emil could slide off his barstool. He was out the door before the sheriff's hand closed around the grip of his .38. The regulars at the bar had whirled around in surprise, watching Pflüger's flight, and Byron Tillman let out a yell of fear.

"Jesus," said Whippletree. He ran across the dance floor and shouldered the door open. Pflüger was already in his Caddy, revving the ancient engine. Clouds of oily exhaust rose from the sagging tailpipe and hung in the air. Then he slammed the car into reverse and shot backward across the parking lot, the Nerf football swinging wildly on its chain. In a minute, Johnny would be gone. Emil didn't want to deal with the hassle of finding him, or with the inevitable stories of how Cowboy John had made a dramatic escape from right under the sheriff's nose. He gripped his weapon with both hands, got into position, aimed at Pflüger's right front tire—the one without a hubcap—and blasted away.

Bull's-eye. The tire exploded.

Johnny, backing sharply at about thirty miles an hour, lost control. The Caddy lurched to one side and slammed into a utility pole at the edge of the parking lot, denting a fender, demolishing a tail fin, and popping the trunk open. The engine roared, then stalled, as Pflüger tried to shift into drive and limp away on three tires.

"Okay, John," said Emil, walking over, holding the .38, "get out of the car."

Pflüger obeyed. Tillman, Schwinghammer, and the regulars were watching from the door of the tavern.

Emil glanced into the open trunk. "Well, now. Seems you got yourself a nice new set of radials. And you sure won't be hurtin' for motor oil, will you?"

"I ain't never seen none of that stuff before!" cried Pflüger. "Somebody must've planted it there."

"Ever do business at Heffner's gas station in Avon, John?"

"Never heard of the place!"

"Better shut up. Anything you say may be used against you. And I think I heard Judge Titchell say that the next time you show up in his courtroom, he'll be inclined to treat you to a stint in the reformatory."

"We'll ___ about that," Pflüger managed, a show of defiance for the benefit of The Bucket crowd. "I wanna see a lawyer. I ain't sayin' one word until I do."

Sarah was peeking out of the corner of the living-room window when Emil pulled into the driveway. She didn't want him to see her worrying, and ducked back quickly out of sight. He smiled, switched off the ignition, waited a minute, listening to the ping of the cooling engine, and went inside the house.

"Oh, hi," Sarah called from the kitchen, as if she'd been there all the time. "Shall I put the steaks on right away? Or do you want a cold beer first?"

"Make it two cold beers to start with," Emil said. Until he'd

44

entered the house, he hadn't realized how tired he was, and the thought of Dee-Dee preyed on his mind.

Emil hung up his hat. Sarah came over and kissed him. She was a tallish woman, a little over five-seven, still size ten, with sensitive, softly molded features and expressive blue eyes. She was smiling, but they'd been through a lot together and he could tell that she was worried. He gave her a reassuring hug. His badge got caught on her blouse and she unsnagged it carefully.

"I know about the murder," she said. "I wormed it out of Alyce when she called to say you'd be a little late. Has Dee-Dee been found yet?"

Uh-oh, he thought. The premonition down there beneath his breastbone dropped into his gut and curled up to stay awhile.

"All's I know is that she signed out for home," he said. "What's the story?"

"My sister called earlier. She'd been contacted by Vice-President Dexter from the university. She'll be stopping over in a little while. She's very worried. Is there anything you can do?"

"Well, let's try to reassure her. Try not to panic. I'm sure she's safe . . ."

He wasn't sure at all.

". . . but we can be on the lookout, and we can broadcast on the radio if we have to."

"Barb said she and Dee-Dee had a little squabble last weekend."

"Oh? What about?"

"Dee-Dee's gotten secretive lately, and that's not like her at all."

"There you have it. Probably just a mother–daughter thing."

"Oh, Emil, I hope so. What happened out there at North Star anyway?"

"Whew! Soon's I pop a cold beer I'll tell you."

They went into the kitchen. Emil got a beer out of the refrigerator and sat down at the table. Sarah put two big sirloins on the broiler. He outlined the basic facts of the case, while the steak sizzled and Sarah made a tossed salad. The first beer went down very easily, so Emil started a second.

"Do you have *any* idea who might've done it?"

"No. I've got Johnny Pflüger in jail right now. There's a chance he might be able to provide a bit of useful information if he decides to talk, but I pretty much doubt it'll be of value. Tomorrow morning I'll be interviewing the people who saw Miss Stanhope last. Maybe I'll get a lead from one of them. I sure hope so."

Sarah served the steak and sat down with him. "Let's not talk about that any more right now." She smiled. "The whole town's abuzz about Bunny Hollman. That young Father Ryder, from Holy Angels Parish, is going to say Mass tomorrow morning under the pine tree. Bunny will be there. And Emil?"

"Yes?"

"I think I'll go too."

"Why not? Can't see what harm it'll do. You've always seemed pretty level-headed to me."

Sarah was quiet for a while. Emil began to notice the silence. "Thinkin' about something?"

"I guess so. I was just wondering. Do you think Bunny really did see something in that tree?"

"I know she thinks she did. And even Rector Rex feels that she believes she did." He remembered, with a sudden surge of intensity, that feeling of eerie unreality that had descended upon him on the golf course.

"I'd *like* to believe it," Sarah admitted. "Wouldn't it be wonderful to know that heaven is really there, that all the people we've known and loved are safe and happy?"

She's thinking about our daughter Susan, Emil realized.

"Can't argue with you there, honey," he said, concealing a flood of emotion in casual gruffness. Susan had died forty years ago, but whenever Emil thought about it, all the pain, the doubt, and self-accusation, came roaring back. The hurt would never heal; there seemed nothing on this earth to salve the wound. He thought of the Stanhopes too: the pain just beginning for them. Only this morning they had been happy, enjoying their lives, looking forward to a gorgeous fall day, proud to have their beautiful daughter away at a fine college . . .

"Oh," exclaimed Sarah, "I forgot to tell you. I received that genealogical material in the mail today." Sarah had become involved in tracing the family's roots in recent years.

The phone rang. They both tensed. A break in the case? Emil got up from the table—the phone was on the wall next to the refrigerator—and answered. It was Doc Divot.

"Blood on that birch bark was type O, Emil. You wanted to know."

"Thanks. And Miss Stanhope's?"

"Type B."

"Okay. Thanks." He hung up and sat down again.

"Good news?" Sarah asked.

"Can't tell yet." It was unlikely that Sarah would know Dee-Dee's blood type, and he didn't want to get started on the subject of Dee-Dee again.

"Anyway," Sarah said, "the packet came in the mail. Dr. Steubenkopf managed to trace my side of the family all the way back to 1542. Isn't that exciting?"

"Sure is," he said, taking a second helping of salad. Just this past June, he and Sarah had flown to Saxony in West Germany, and there they had engaged Dr. Steubenkopf, a researcher, to do the necessary tracing of records. Emil's own hunt for his past had been much less successful. A visit to Godalming, a little town in Surrey, southwest of London, had yielded not the church records he'd hoped to find, but only an incredibly weathered gravestone in an overgrown cemetery. *"Whiffletree,"* it had read, *p*'s like *f*'s, *"1694–1731."* One single ancestor, no trace of any others. Emil's father had emigrated to Minnesota, an orphan, in the late 1880s, and he himself had no children. Roots obscure, and fleeting reputation the only heritage he had to leave.

The phone rang again, and this time Sarah answered. She covered the receiver and whispered, "It's Ethan Pappendorf, dear. That investment counselor who's always pestering you."

Emil got up and slouched to the phone. Ethan "Wienie" Pappendorf was the town bookie, a fact Emil figured Sarah didn't really need to know in order to live a full and happy life. With the small amounts he wagered, Emil didn't really need a bookie. He could have chanced his fives and tens with Axel Vogel or anybody. But he liked the ritual and Wienie felt honored to number the sheriff among his many clients.

"Hello?"

"Emil, it's Wienie. Safe to talk business?"

"I s'pose."

"Want in on the Vikings–Broncos action?"

"I think I'd look favorably on that."

"Your usual ten bucks, like last year?"

"Well, the economy hasn't been too great, and I'm saving up to take my wife to the Rose Bowl."

"Ha ha," said Sarah.

Wienie delivered himself of certain arcana regarding spread, odds, and the opinions of Jimmy the Greek. "Do a ten at least, Emil. How about it?"

"Well, all right," agreed the sheriff. He hung up.

"What'd he want this time?" Sarah asked.

"Not much. Something about a prospectus. I think he'll be mailing it over. Said I'd take a look."

"That won't do any harm," said Sarah. "It's certainly more mature than throwing your money away on football games."


Emil called the office after dinner and learned from Deputy Jamie Gosch that Cowboy John had retained Ricky Stein, an attorney from Apple Valley. Tricky Ricky, as he was known in the Courthouse Bar and Grill, had advised his client to say nothing pending arraignment in Judge Brewster Titchell, Sr.'s courtroom Monday morning.

"He's not permitting any blood test either," Jamie said.

Damn, thought Emil. And meanwhile those scratches on Pflüger's face had more time to heal. He ordered Jamie to alert the St. Cloud police and all county constables to be on the lookout for Miss Diane Tiernan, age twenty, height five-six, weight approximately one hundred ten to fifteen, hair blond, eyes green, but he had the sick feeling that his action wasn't going to do any good.

Barbara showed up a little while later. Sarah commiserated with her and Emil told her that everything was going to be all right, just wait and see.

"She just hasn't been herself lately," Sarah's younger sister worried. She was a few inches larger than Sarah in everything except height, but a handsome woman and, just now, a very troubled one. "I know she's been keeping something from me."

"Has she been ill?" Sarah asked. "Have her grades at school been suffering?"

"No, no. Nothing like that. But she might get into trouble now with this sign-out business, and after all the work and effort she's put into getting her degree. . . . Vice-President Dexter was too nice to mention it, but he seemed awful surprised when I told him that Dee-Dee wasn't home, like she was supposed to be. And you know the strict rules they have there at North Star."

"Well," drawled Emil, with a confidence he did not feel, "maybe she just went off on her own to think a few things over. She'll be graduating next spring and she probably has quite a few de...ons to make."

"But we always talked things over together," Barbara mourned.

"Kids have to do that kind of thing," Emil went on. "They have to break away and make plans on their own. But if you let them do it, they always come back."

Then he remembered the shred of perfumed nylon in his billfold. He pulled it out now—the whole billfold smelled like a house best entered in darkness through the back door—and handed it to Barbara.

"What's that?" Sarah wanted to know.

"Piece of cloth found at the scene. Dee-Dee ever wear a fragrance like that?"

"Fragrance!" exclaimed Barbara, wrinkling her nose in distaste. "I'd call that a stink."

Emil felt a little better for the first time since he'd heard Titchell, Jr., mention Dee-Dee's name. Perhaps she wasn't connected with the situation at all.

After Barbara had gone home and Sarah was upstairs taking her bath, Emil dialled Sister Yvette over at the St. Cloud hospital.

He'd nabbed some teenage vandals there once and she thought he was the best lawman since Bat Masterson.

"Sister, Emil Whippletree here. I wonder if I could trouble you to look up the blood type on a baby born September 7, 1965. Tiernan, Diane Lee."

The wait was short—hospital had just about everything on computers now—but Emil wished it'd been a lot, lot longer.

"Sheriff," said the nun, "that baby had type O blood. Can I help with anything else?"

A buckshot pellet worked its way out of Emil's shoulder and fell to the floor as he put on his pajamas. It had been dark in the alley behind the Hannorhed bank, and Emil had sensed rather than seen the maniac's fingers tightening on the trigger. He'd spun around and flung himself sideways against the granite wall of the bank. Even so, part of one barrel's blast had hit him, knocked him unconscious. Doc Divot operated for six hours, removing eighty-three pellets from Emil's skull and back. That had been ten years ago, yet every now and then Emil would be combing his hair or sitting in a chair reading the *Trib* and a refugee piece of buckshot would pop out of his scalp or flesh, expelled after all this time by the mysterious forces of the body. He picked up the pellet, examined it, then dropped it into a little jar with its companions, wondering what fate the maniac had found. Sometimes the sheriff almost believed that the gunman hadn't existed at all, so sudden was his appearance, so completely had he vanished. But Emil had that jar of buckshot to remind him of reality, and it was no mere vision.

Drifting into sleep beside Sarah, Emil had the radio at low volume, tuned to a Minneapolis station. He and Sarah had played the courting game way back there in the late 1930s, and the station was having a Bing Crosby hour, so Emil was pleasantly nostalgic until the news came on. Several foreign crises were noted first, and then the brutal murder of a North Star coed. Emil heard his name. He could have lived without the experience. Finally, the announcer said, "A St. Cloud woman claimed today to have

50

seen the Blessed Virgin Mary in a pine tree on the campus of North Star University. A spokesperson for the Archdiocese of St. Paul has declined comment, but it has been learned that several busloads of believers will leave The Cities early tomorrow on a prayer pilgrimage to the campus. . . ."

Thank you, Roy Riley, Emil thought. He did not know that, in a week, shoppers at checkout stands all over the country would be staring at tabloid headlines telling them:

MIDWEST FEM SPOTS HOLY MOTHER
VIRGIN SEEN IN MINNESOTA TREE

Emil lay there, thinking of his ancestor, *Whiffletree,* asleep for centuries beneath green English sod, no trials, no doubts, no pain for all that time, and of the time he'd taken little Susan, who was then about three, on a joy ride on the milk train to Melrose. They were the only passengers on the train, except for a conductor, of whose presence Emil was but vaguely aware. The fields across which the train rolled were green and golden, the air heavy with pollen of wheat and corn. Susan laughed and jabbered; Whippletree's heart was all but undone by love. Then, in an instant, the vista changed. Where there had been blooming fields, now there were houses, strange, beautiful houses, perfect and white and silent upon great sweeping stretches of immaculate grass. Mystified, Emil stared out the train window at these dead palaces. There was not a living human being in sight. Susan stopped laughing. Emil was aware of the conductor in the vestibule at the end of the car.

Then the train entered an area in which the houses were unpainted, dilapidated, shuttered. There was something monstrous about them, but he did not know exactly what. When the train stopped suddenly, curiosity impelled him to step out—oddly, the door was open—and have a look around.

Obviously, they'd reached the end of the line. Emil heard a door open at the end of the car, heard some sort of switch being thrown. The conductor is reversing a mechanism so that we can go back the way we came, Emil thought. He walked around to the

51

back of the car, planning to ask the trainman why they'd entered such a remote and alien place. But before he got around the corner—he never even had a glimpse of the man—the train doors slid shut with a deadly hiss. Turning, Whippletree saw not a train but only a single car, a smooth, glistening box of polished wood on silver tracks.

And it began to move.

"Wait!" he shouted. "Wait! I'm still out here!"

Surely there was some mistake. The conductor hadn't seen him get off. He ran alongside the fearful wooden car—which reminded him of something, what was it?—shouting and hollering and looking for a window. Finally he found one. Little Susan's face was pressed against the glass.

"Daddy!" she cried.

Whippletree was amazed, but relieved. She did not appear to be afraid.

"Honey," he shouted, running faster as the car picked up speed, "tell the man to stop! Tell him I'm still out here!"

"I told him the story already, Daddy," she said, in a voice that came from far away. "And he said he's just pretending."

The conductor is lying to her, Emil knew. He's taking her away! He sought a foothold, a handhold on the smooth, shiny car—he could barely keep pace with it—but it was too slick. Besides, trees pressed close to the track now; he could no longer run next to the train. So he dropped back, hoping to hop onto the rear of the car. But it was as smooth as glass.

Then he stumbled, and by the time he picked himself up, the coffin was far away, sliding into the wooded distance on those ominous silver tracks. I'll follow the tracks, he thought in panic. I'll follow the tracks. They have to end somewhere.

So he set out, running, jogging, walking. Until he reached the place where the tracks ended in a forested wilderness. A living wall, the border of infinity.

He awoke, sweaty and despondent, with tears just behind his eyes. The dream of loss again. He clung desperately to the memory of Susan's sweet little face, and to the knowledge that she had not been afraid.

Now he knew that those perfect, heart-stopping houses had been tombstones, and the strange land a cemetery. But, in the dream, he'd been the one who was left there. She had gone on.

Yet he was the one who still lived.

Or did he?

After that, Emil did not sleep well, imagining beneath those fields of fog at the edges of the world a pair of silver tracks
that he would one day find and follow
to Susan
to the source of
eternal life and joy.

They met at the office early Sunday morning, the sheriff and his four deputies. Emil felt a little tired, but calm. There'd been no word on Dee-Dee and no news—being the only news—had to count as good. Pete Poll looked sober and ready to go. Ben Farley was a little jittery. Axel wolfed sausage rolls happily and guzzled hot chocolate from a quart-sized container. Jamie Gosch was dead on his feet from a night at the radio, although there hadn't been much action. Fistfight at a St. Augusta dance hall over the relative merits of two competing makes of snowmobiles. Breaking and entering at the Bryant Library in Sauk Centre, which housed Sinclair Lewis memorabilia. A John Deere combine stolen from a field near Holdingford.

Cowboy John had adjusted well to cell life, which was not unusual since he'd known it before. He declined to talk about anything, or to take a blood test, and called for breakfast, the Sunday comics, and a television set. Emil approved the first two demands.

"Mr. and Mrs. Stanhope are due here this afternoon," yawned Gosch. "Can I go home now?"

"Yep," said Emil. "Farley, you take the radio today. Poll, stay here on call, in case something comes up."

Then Axel and the sheriff headed for North Star in Stearns County One. Emil was prepared to see a small crowd around the pine tree, but not the huge throng that spread out all over the golf course. Cars were parked on both sides of the asphalt drive—Butch Lodge and his boys had managed to retain a narrow aisle for traffic—and five big scenicruisers from The Cities stood close to the tree. A hand-lettered placard in the window of one bus read NORTH STAR PRAYER PILGRIMAGE.

"Got to be five hundred people at least," said Axel, slowing the patrol car.

"Weather's contributing," allowed Emil. Another perfect September day, temperature in the low sixties. Sunlight glinting off the Sacred Steeple hurt his eyes; copper-toned Jesus glowed. A team of teenagers in cassocks was erecting a portable altar beneath the pine tree. Emil caught sight of Butch Lodge talking with Professor and Mrs. Hollman.

"Axel, stop and let me out. I'll join you up at the Administration Building in a couple minutes."

"Sure thing, Boss."

Emil got out of the car, put on his wide-brimmed hat, shifted his holstered .38 to a more comfortable position on his hip, and strolled across the grass. He said "hi" to the three and tipped his hat to Bunny. She was nicely dressed in a neat blue-cotton shift and matching pillbox hat.

"Mornin', Emil," said Butch. "Any news on the case? Did you pick up that Pflüger character?"

"We've got him, and he did know the dead girl, but I doubt he had anything to do with it."

"Dead girl?" asked Bunny Hollman, alarmed.

Charlie shot Emil a warning glance. "I didn't wish to upset you, dear," he told his wife in his Henry Kissinger tones, "but one of our girls was murdered here Friday night."

"Oh, how horrible," Mrs. Hollman exclaimed, putting a hand to her breast. "Oh, my . . ."

"You know a professor named Dale Torbert, Charlie?" Emil asked.

"Of course. I hired him. He teaches the seminar in which Miss Stanhope was a student."

"What's your opinion of the guy?"

Charlie shook his head in apparent discouragement. "Torbert was one of my personnel errors," he said.

"In what way?"

"It's a professional matter."

"The guy's a bad actor, or something?"

"He just isn't right for North Star."

"Bad habits? Unsavory friends?"

"He's simply too liberal for us."

That didn't sound terribly sinister to Emil, who'd been an ardent Humphrey Democrat. "Think you and I could have a little talk later on?" Emil asked, turning to Bunny.

"Please, Sheriff," complained the professor. "There's a Mass coming up, and we pray that the Virgin will again make her presence known. My wife is under quite a strain."

"No, I feel fine," protested Bunny. "Of course I'll talk to you, Emil."

"Who would you pick between the Vikings and the Broncos this afternoon?" Emil asked the woman.

"Why, I don't know," she replied, mystified. "I'm afraid I don't know anything about football."

Emil and Butch Lodge exchanged a glance. "Well, so long," said the sheriff, tipping his hat again.

Butch caught up with him as he was walking away. "Wait up, Emil."

Whippletree halted and turned around. "Yep?"

The security boss grinned slyly. "Just how close *did* Bunny come to predicting the score of yesterday's game?"

"Not close enough to do any good for me," said Emil evasively. "Funny, she doesn't seem to remember anything about it."

But Butch had something else on his mind besides football. "Emil, you know yesterday when President Anderson asked you to give me some help if we start getting big crowds here? Well, you don't have to. I can take care of things all right."

Beneath the ex-master sergeant's tough, in-charge exterior, Emil was beginning to sense a complex and sensitive man. "How you doin' in general?" asked the sheriff.

"Oh, all right, I guess. The divorce from my third wife was a downer though. I thought I was gonna go all the way with this one. And Trudilynn went and got remarried last week to some guy in town, T. R. Steinhaus."

"Right." Emil nodded. He knew T. R., who sometimes played golf with Doc Divot and had a well-earned reputation as a playboy.

"They're calling themselves the fun couple," Lodge mourned. "Ain't that something?"

"It hurts but you live," said Emil. Wasn't much else you could say.

"So you really don't think Pflüger did it?" Butch was saying. "Rector Rex does."

"I'm sure he wants to get things solved and settled, and I don't blame him. So do I."

"Could put a damper on the election next year, couldn't it?" hoped Butch disingenuously. "If the case isn't solved?"

Emil allowed himself a smile. "Well, we all have to be thinking ahead, don't we?"


Axel was waiting at the entrance to the administration building, known formally as Cuthbert Center.

"Axel, I'd like you to go on down to the riverbank and take another look around. We might've missed something yesterday. Then check out the prayer meeting. I'll meet you there."

"Gotcha, Boss."

Emil took the elevator up to President Anderson's office on the seventh (and top) floor. Cuthbert Center was located on a substantial hill, and the vast floor-to-ceiling windows of the executive wing offered a breathtaking view. Emil had the sensation that he was floating above campus. The statue of Jesus seemed close enough to touch, bronze eyeballs five yards wide, implacable and disquieting. Granitelli Stadium was a modern Colosseum—tiny figures darted about the playing field—and beyond the Sacred Steeple rolled the fields of Minnesota that Emil loved so well, and the deep blue lakes, and the pine forests that ran on for a thousand miles. From the seventh floor, Emil could also see Bunny Hollman's crowd growing by the minute. Cars and buses were arriving even as he watched, their occupants joining the small army already on the golf course. Emil was a bit puzzled. Upon meeting Rector Rex yesterday, the president had implied that the vision was "university business" that could be dealt with. But later, talking with Emil and Butch on the golf course, he'd been less certain, he'd spoken of Charlie Hollman's power.

Couldn't a man who went horseback riding with Ronald Reagan, who joked about his tennis game with "The Tonight Show's" Johnny Carson, who'd figuratively mopped the floor with William F. Buckley, Jr., also find a way to deal with Professor Hollman and his dutiful wife, Bunny?

President Anderson was waiting in his office doorway, from which he too could see the golf course. "Belief is a powerful thing, isn't it?" he asked. "That's why a proper education is so terribly important. Else who knows what will take root in the human soul."

"You're talking about pretty fertile soil," said Emil, shaking the president's hand. "Something wants to grow there, it generally does. Are you suggesting that Bunny Hollman ought to get herself a hoe?"

Anderson laughed, and Emil was pleased. Here, in spite of his accomplishments and renown, was a regular guy. Anderson led Emil through a dark-grained wooden door, on which a simple gold plaque said *President* in delicate letters. Vice-President Fagin Dexter was waiting inside the office.

"Any word on your niece, Sheriff?" Anderson asked solicitously.

"No, but I'm sure she's fine. She's a level-headed young woman."

"Naturally, we're concerned. Because of Miss Stanhope."

You and me both, Emil thought, as President Anderson motioned him toward a leather-upholstered chair beside the presidential desk. The office seemed to have about an acre of floor, partially covered by a stunning Asiatic rug of browns and beiges, golds and muted reds. Thousands of books filled shelves along two walls, along with signed photographs of Anderson and famous Americans from all walks of life. The other two walls were windows, looking out across campus.

Anderson took a seat behind his desk. Dexter remained standing. His deference to the president, Emil gauged, was not entirely natural; his mind's eye was already on the big chair in which Rector Rex sat.

"You've apprehended Mr. Pflüger?" Anderson asked.

"That's right."

"I'll be surprised if he's not the killer."

"Sorry, but I'll be surprised if he is."

Anderson looked pained. "When you see the Stanhopes," he said, "please convey my deepest grief. They are both very· bitter toward the university, and refuse to speak to us."

"I will," said Emil. "I don't know how it could be your fault, though."

"It is part of the dynamics of grief. They must blame someone. We offered to have the funeral held here, but we were rejected."

Emil nodded.

Anderson turned, somewhat morosely, and stared out the big windows and down onto the golf course. "This is tragic for the university," he said. "The killing symbolizes a failing of the body, of our college community, as it were. The vision—or shall I say the *apparent* vision—may do us far more harm. We aren't dealing with facts any more."

This was the kind of thing about which Emil had been secretly apprehensive. Anderson was talking away, natural as the day is long, and the sheriff was afraid that he'd already begun to lose the drift.

"Not dealing with facts?" he asked.

"No, and I wish we were," Anderson replied. "Facts are easy to handle. But, in the case of the vision down there on the greensward, we have passed over into the realm of faith, or belief, where everything becomes much more difficult."

"You mean Bunny Hollman? Drawing all those people here on the strength of what she thinks she sees?"

"Exactly, Sheriff. You and I might cajole, argue, denounce, or persuade until our faces turn blue, but our efforts will have no effect upon a person who truly believes that an apparition is taking place in that pine tree. To complicate matters further, each person who comes to North Star seeks something different from Mrs. Hollman. The most simple-minded among them will aver that she is literally seeing the Virgin. The more sophisticated will claim that she is a vessel, a conduit, for forces abstract or symbolic, but they will also accept the legitimacy of her experience. There may even be those persons who possess, without being conscious of it, certain unusual—or shall I call them extranatural?—gifts. These people may experience bizarre perceptions of their own."

Emil was startled. Me? he wondered, amazed, thinking of the door, the fog, the jolt of electricity that had passed from Virginia and into him. *No, can't be. Nothing like that has ever happened to me in my life. Unusual experiences are out of my line. I never even won a Bingo game.*

"What you're saying then, Father," inquired Emil, "is that the more people we get down there on the golf course, the stronger their belief is going to be?"

"Aptly put, Sheriff. They will reinforce one another, both in numbers and in power of belief. It's happening already." He turned toward the window again. "Can't you *feel* it? Thousands will come here." He turned back and faced Emil. "Thousands. The believers. The curiosity seekers. And the troublemakers. Campus will be disrupted."

"And football revenues will decline," commented Vice-President Dexter.

"True." Anderson nodded soberly. "The season lies before us. If the campus is, in effect, cut off from easy access, football weekends will suffer. There will be requests for refunds. Sheriff, this university is neither the beneficiary of public funds, nor does it enjoy a splendid endowment, like the big private universities in the East. Student tuitions would never support us. We hover on the edge of red ink as it is. Only the sports program, and the national reputation that program has given us, allow North Star to survive with head held high."

Anderson paused and stared at Emil, his eyes slightly hooded, his expression ruminative. "Sheriff, what if I ask again that you and your men, armed with the force of law, go down there onto the golf course and remove everyone from campus?"

"Sorry, but I couldn't do it. There's no cause, at least not yet. No law is being broken and nobody's in any apparent danger. This is your land. If you want them out, you'll have to do it yourself."

Anderson and Dexter looked at each other.

"Why don't we just ask Charlie and Bunny to go somewhere else?" suggested Emil once again.

Rector Rex stood up, looking perplexed. "There are reasons why I can't do that. University reasons."

Emil had no idea what these "university reasons" were, and President Anderson appeared disinclined to explain them. Emil had the distinct impression that certain information was being deliberately kept from him, information about which Rector Rex was not entirely comfortable himself.

"What's your basic value, Dr. Anderson?" the sheriff asked.

The response was immediate. "Human reason. Rationality."

Emil nodded. Good enough. He got to his feet.

Anderson spoke. "You'll want to get started, I'm sure. Anthony Wiggins is waiting for you in the gym. He's our champion weight-lifter. And I'm happy to tell you that Vice-President Dexter succeeded in reaching Professor Torbert at his apartment in St. Cloud, and he's on his way to campus now. Coach Avano will make the three players available to you over at the stadium. The team is working out a few new patterns this morning."

"They just played yesterday," said Emil.

Anderson smiled. "Snopes is not one to let up." He exchanged a glance with Vice-President Dexter. "Fagin, would you please accompany Mr. Whippletree . . . ?"

"Oh, that won't be necessary," said Emil. "I'll find my way around."

"It's been my experience," persisted Anderson smoothly, "that two memories are better than one, especially where important conversations are concerned."

"Well, I'm sure you're right about that. But I've always had sort of a knack for separating the wheat from the chaff." He saw that the president really did want his aide to be present at the forthcoming interviews, but that was not the way Emil worked. He wasn't all that great as a talker, but he gave himself pretty high grades in the listening department.

"Good luck, Sheriff," said Anderson. "And don't forget: the reason for Miss Stanhope's murder will involve the killer's most deeply held belief."

"I won't forget," Emil said.

Emil crossed the green, hedge-bordered quad and climbed a rise of wide old concrete steps into the gym. A half-dozen guys were playing basketball, shirts versus skins, at the far end of the main court. He followed an arrow on a sign that said WEIGHT ROOM and when he heard *aaarrrrggghhh puff-puff-puff, aaarrrrggghhh puff-puff-puff,* he knew he was getting hot.

An elongated mass of muscle, naked except for a jockstrap, lay on a narrow leather bench, repeatedly lifting into the air what looked to Emil like an axle from the business end of an eighteen-wheeler. Gigantic steel discs at either end of the axle went up-down, up-down, up-down, until the torture ended with a final groan and the lifter carefully lowered the axle into brackets on the weight bench and rested beneath the burden.

"Mr. Wiggins? President Anderson said I'd find you here. I'm Sheriff Whippletree. Got to ask you a few questions."

The block of muscle got up from the bench and nodded matter-of-factly. Anthony Wiggins was equipped to be pretty casual about a lot of things. He wasn't that big a kid, height-wise, but every visible ounce of him—and all but a clump of heavy, hanging pounds *was* visible—was sweat-dripping muscle. Emil remembered that Brewster Titchell had referred to Wiggins as a "brain from Ely," which was a town Up North on the Iron Range. A very tough place, but not generally known as a hotbed of intellectual distinction.

Wiggins grabbed two towels, wrapped one around his waist, mopped his head and torso with the other. His face was very young, even cherubic, and it did not fit his powerful, handcrafted body.

Emil sat down on a pile of wrestling mats. Wiggins flexed and danced, cooling down, staying loose. "You're here about Alicia," he said. "I know. I'll be glad to aid you in whatever way I can."

Wiggins spoke with considerable authority, the detachment of intelligence that is sure of itself. If I'd had a son, Whippletree found himself thinking, I'd love one like this, especially for his strength, his sure self-knowledge of body and mind.

"Exactly what happened at that seminar on Friday night?" Emil asked. "And how well did you know Miss Stanhope?"

Wiggins draped the wet towel around his glistening shoulders and leaned against a Nautilus machine. "Frankly, Sheriff, Alicia was what is commonly known as a bitch-and-a-half. Are you familiar with the expression 'cock-tease'?"

"Yep. I guess so."

"Well, that trait describes a considerable portion of her rather dubious charms."

Johnny Pflüger had told an entirely different story, Emil reflected. His Alicia had been the real thing, hot and willing. "Sorry to see her dead?" he asked.

"Actually, yes. She was quite entertaining. Although the three Noble Norsemen in our seminar did not think so."

"Something specific happened during the seminar?"

"Yes. Gunnar Rutkow, who is a puppy-dog sort of giant, but not bright in the academic sense, confused the concepts of pluralism and secularism. Gunnar has confused simpler concepts in his time, but Lish was in a particularly mean mood—"

"She was mean?"

"She could be, and she was very proud of her mind. But I didn't think it was fair of her to attack poor old Gunnar and call him a stupid jock."

62

"What happened then?"

"Sheriff, you don't need me for that one! Rollins and Duffy sided with Gunnar, of course, and there was a brief shouting match as to who contributed most to North Star, the jocks or the grunts."

"Grunts?"

"Serious students. I guess you could call me a grunt, in spite of"—he gestured in the direction of the big weights—"in spite of the heavy artillery. But that exchange, which Professor Torbert terminated, was fairly insignificant compared to the other issue raised that night."

"Which was?"

"Which was Professor Torbert's accusation against Alicia and Brewster Titchell, Jr. I found it plausible, if bizarre, but the professor accused Lish and Titchell of spying on him. He said they'd secretly tape-recorded one of his lectures—it was about individualism in Western civilization, he gave it a few weeks ago—and passed it along to Professor Hollman, the department chairman. Torbert claimed that they'd cost him his job."

One *lecture* blew a man's position? wondered Emil. "Is that possible?" he asked.

"Oh, yes. Professor Hollman is a staunch conservative. It's been no secret that Professor Torbert does not share some of the chairman's most deeply held beliefs."

"Such as?"

"That only people with a college education ought to be allowed to vote. That nuclear weapons are therapeutic devices. That sex outside marriage is grounds for capital punishment."

"I see," said Emil. He'd read enough of Charlie Hollman's letters to the St. Cloud *Tribune* to know that these were, indeed, some of the man's pet verities.

Wiggins gave Emil a canny smile. "Professor Hollman's tenure committee met on Wednesday night and voted to terminate Dr. Torbert's contract, effective at the end of term."

Now Emil knew why the scheduled Wednesday-night seminar had been moved to Friday. He also realized he didn't know beans about the university business. Up until now, he'd entertained the vague but benign impression that a bunch of pretty smart people, more dedicated than most, read a lot of great books and then told what they'd learned to gaggles of eager students, and that everybody was fairly decent and accommodating. It appeared, however, that he was off the mark. If a guy could get canned for believing something to which a more powerful guy did not subscribe, then whatever the hell you happened to believe became pretty important.

"You said a committee voted Torbert down?" Emil asked the student. "Then he must have gotten a hearing from a number of different people?"

"There are three professors on a tenure committee. Charlie Hollman appointed them. In fact, he hired them. They owe their jobs to him."

"Check," said Emil. "A stacked deck. If the fix was in, though, why would Hollman have gone to the trouble of getting a tape of Torbert's lecture?"

"I am not completely sure that there was a tape. All I am saying is that Professor Torbert accused Lish and Titchell of making one and turning it over to Dr. Hollman. It is definitely in character, though, for Hollman to have come up with such a scheme. Another of his beliefs is that those in authority are permitted behavior for which subordinates would be condemned."

"Nice guy," said Emil. He had a flash of sympathy for poor Bunny, married to the man. "What'll happen to Torbert now?"

"I don't know. Do you suspect him of killing Lish?"

"I'll wait until I talk to the guy. By the way, where'd you go after the seminar on Friday night?"

Wiggins grinned. "So I'm a suspect too? All right. I went directly to the computer unit in the library. I'm researching my senior thesis, a statistical analysis of concept frequency in the works of Bacon, Bentham, Locke, Burke, and Hume."

"Sounds good to me," said Emil. He'd heard of bacon. "People see you there at the computer?"

"Of course. Besides, the record will show my access code as well as times of entry and termination. I was there until after two on Saturday morning."

Emil registered the information and stored it away. The iron-pumper was strong enough to break a big man's neck, to say nothing of a young woman's, but he was a good kid. Emil could tell. He was a good kid just as plainly as Johnny Pflüger was a bad one. Wheat and chaff. The sheriff had trusted his own judgment all these years and it hadn't let him down yet.

"Will there be anything else, Sheriff? I should hit the showers before my ligaments crystallize."

"No. Go ahead. Thanks a lot. Oh, wait. Couple of things. You know Diane Tiernan?"

"Sure. Why?"

"She's missing."

He watched Wiggin's face carefully. Mild surprise, maybe even a bit of shock. "It's the weekend," he said. "She'll probably show up."

"Glad to hear it. Have you ever met Mrs. Hollman?"

"Our visionary? Yes, once. At a reception for the history department. There is more to that lady than meets the eye, and if she ever gets out from under her husband's thumb, we might find out what it is."

Outside, squinting against the bright sunlight, Emil saw a young man jogging toward him across the quad. He steeled himself for the worst. This was a messenger, Dee-Dee had been found, and . . .

"Sheriff Whippletree?"

"My wife seems to think so."

"I understand you want to talk to me. I'm Dale Torbert."

Hell, the guy was young! When Emil thought "professor," he pictured either a skinny old guy with all kinds of brains but the wrong end of a necktie caught in his fly, or an eccentric like Charlie Hollman who knew everything, just ask him. But Torbert was as lithe as any athlete. He had blond, curly hair, cut short, a lean, tanned face, and clever blue eyes. He was wearing loafers, no socks, white slacks, blue blazer, and an ivory-colored dress shirt open at the collar. A handkerchief of pale-yellow silk flopped loosely from the breast pocket of the nifty blazer. Torbert looked in excellent shape, but his eyes were worried and tired.

"I tried to get here earlier, Sheriff, but the crowd and the cars held me up."

"I know. The vision. Tell you what, let's sit down on the steps here, catch a little sun."

"Whatever you say. I'm at your disposal."

They settled themselves on the warm stone. Emil took off his hat, enjoying the warmth of the day. Wouldn't last much longer. By October, there'd be a chill in the air, and come November, forget it, haul out the long johns, that's all she wrote.

"What do you think of Bunny Hollman?" he asked the boyish-looking teacher. If I had a son like him, he was thinking, I'd be smarter than I am. He could teach me things. But his own intelligence might cause him trouble. Some men would resent his natural quickness, others his looks.

"I've met Mrs. Hollman a few times," Torbert said, lighting up a low-tar cigarette. He offered one to Whippletree. Emil declined, opting instead for a wad of Copenhagen. "I don't know her well, hardly at all, but she seemed a little strange to me."

"How so?"

"Well, we were at President Anderson's Commencement reception last spring. It was very crowded. Most of the conversation was perfunctory, as it usually is at that kind of event. But Bunny recited some verses. She was very taken by them. In fact, I thought she might have written them herself, but they sounded vaguely familiar. I don't know."

"Verses? Like poetry?"

"Rather. Quite erotic too. All about men and women. I was surprised. She strikes me as more than a bit inhibited."

Yesterday, under the pine tree, Emil recalled, Bunny had said something similar to what Torbert was describing: ". . . *woman, soft and silken for the piercing . . .*"

"You think she's on the level?" he asked Torbert.

"With the so-called vision? I doubt it. Since you ask me, I'd say Charlie put her up to it. He's just causing trouble. He and Coach Avano have been feuding for years, and Charlie's finally come up with a monkey wrench to throw into the sports program. My illustrious chairman has long believed that all the emphasis on sports around here has prevented North Star from becoming a first-rate university."

"Is that true?"

"Sure it's true. But don't misunderstand. With Charlie Hollman, the obvious is deceptive. What he really resents is that Coach Avano is more important—and better known—than anyone on the academic faculty."

Torbert seemed to be relaxing. Emil decided to throw a rabbit punch. "Where'd you go after seminar Friday night?" he asked abruptly.

The professor didn't miss a beat. "Do you suspect me of killing Miss Stanhope?"

"Who told you about it?"

"I heard it on the radio."

"You want a lawyer, or something?"

"Of course not."

"Well, where were you this weekend?"

"In The Cities. I'm researching an article on early Midwestern settlements and I use the University of Minnesota library."

"You there all weekend?"

"Yes. Went down Friday night and drove back to St. Cloud this morning. Vice-President Dexter's call caught me just as I was entering my apartment."

"Where'd you stay in The Cities?"

"With a friend. Paul Barnes. He teaches at the U and lives in St. Paul."

Sounds plausible, reflected Emil, storing the name in memory. "And how do you feel about Miss Stanhope's fate?"

"If it had to happen to somebody, I won't quibble about the killer's choice."

"Understand she and Brewster Titchell were mighty handy with a tape recorder?"

"Yes, thank God."

"What?" Emil hadn't expected this response. "But I thought—"

"So you already know about my faculty wars? And you figured I'd be angry that Alicia and that Titchell twerp tape-recorded my allegedly heretical lecture? In which I made the damning case that all significant contributions to the intellectual history of the West, from Galileo to Freud, from Voltaire to Marx, have been resisted by the frenzied brainlessness of Orthodoxy—"

"Hey. Hold on. Give an old duffer a break."

Torbert laughed, a little embarrassed. "I guess I do get a bit full of myself sometimes," he confessed, in a straightforward way that Emil found charming. "But I wanted you to see the kinds of difficulties faced by someone trying to teach at a place like this. In the history department, we're supposed to teach The World According To Charlie Hollman. Now, don't get me wrong. He has a right to draw whatever conclusions that his own study and reflection suggest. But he routinely denies this same right to others."

"Who were the guys on the committee that voted you out?"

"Beauchamp, Binlow, and Bowers. A *troika* of dullards."

"How long have you been teaching here?"

"Two years."

"It took Charlie *that* long to figure out where you're coming from?"

"He just waited for something in black and white to convince the others that I'm in league with the devil."

"The tape?"

"Yes. Do you know that fat little fart actually went to the trouble of getting the tape transcribed and xeroxed for those three bozos on the tenure committee? Charlie is guilty of seriously unethical behavior, first in using the students to tape me without my knowledge, then in employing the transcripts against me in the tenure committee. So I'm going to petition President Anderson for an open hearing. I'm even thinking of suing Charlie."

The kid's a fighter, thought Emil, with a mixture of admiration and apprehension. He didn't want to see a sharp young guy like this get his life all bent out of shape by waging a futile war.

"What'll happen with Anderson?"

"I haven't the slightest idea."

"What I mean to say is, is the guy conservative like Charlie, or . . ."

"Or liberal like me? No one knows. He makes these brilliant speeches about freedom and education all around the country, but as far as I know nobody's ever petitioned him with a case like mine. We'll have our answer soon enough, won't we?"

We'll get down to Anderson's basic value for sure, Emil thought. "Has Rector Rex got the power to reinstate you?" he asked.

"Yes. He can overrule anybody on this campus, if he wants to. With the possible exception of Coach. That's a joke. I think. Anyway, I didn't kill Miss Stanhope, much as she deserved it."

Kid doesn't mince any words, thought Emil. A little restraint wouldn't hurt him. "Any idea who might've?" he asked.

"Not really. You might check on this new security guy, Lodge."

"Butch *Lodge*?"

"I don't know. Just a thought. I've heard that he's come on to some of the coeds."

"Alicia Stanhope?"

"Don't know. *She* did whatever she felt like doing, from what I hear. I'm pretty close to the students. They tell me things."

"Did you ever approach Miss Stanhope? In that way?"

The professor was startled. "Wait a minute! I don't . . . I wouldn't . . ."

"Calm down."

"Sorry."

Emil decided to drop the subject. He'd talk to Butch later. "How were the three jocks doing in your class?" he asked.

"Rutkow was flunking, Duffy was just getting by, and Rusty Rollins was doing surprisingly well. Why?"

"I understand President Anderson sort of dumped a lot of these players into the seminars."

69

"Yes, that's true. Most of them probably shouldn't be taking up the space. Sheriff, I feel sorry for some of these guys. They've been treated like heroes since maybe second grade, told that normal standards don't apply to them, given special dispensations whenever some difficulty arose. I know there's grade-fixing going on right here at North Star. Everybody knows it. Only two percent of all college athletes are ever going to sign professional contracts. Not even mentioning the injured, a lot of the rest'll have tough times."

"You ever flunk a jock?"

"Yes. Last semester. I had to give Gunnar Rutkow an *F* in History of Civ."

"Didn't that make him ineligible for football?"

"That's what I thought. So I went down to the registrar's office and checked his records. Somebody'd changed his grade to a *B*. I let the matter ride, though. I did what I had to do as a teacher, and I've got my own problems."

So have we all, thought Emil. He got slowly to his feet, unbending old joints. "Just one more question for now, Professor. I understand Diane Tiernan is a student of yours?"

Torbert gave Emil a sharp look. "That's right."

"She's my niece," Emil said, "and she's missing. You happen to know where she went after seminar?"

"Your . . . niece? Sheriff, how do you know she's missing?"

"No one's seen her all weekend. She was supposed to go home, but never showed up."

Torbert looked startled. "And you fear that because Alicia . . . oh, Sheriff, I'm sure it's nothing like that. I know these students pretty well, as I said earlier. There's probably a good explanation."

"That's what's been keeping me going," Emil said.

Emil got rid of his chaw in a wilderness of ivy next to the gym and ambled on over to Granitelli Stadium. He could see a big swatch of the golf course. Mass was being said. Emil heard young Father Ryder's chirpy ejaculations over a portable public address system, and the roaring responses of the thousands in the crowd.

For every thrust, a parry.

For every question, an answer.

But was that true? "I'm making some progress," he said aloud, to encourage himself. "I've already got three possible motivating factors."

Sex.

Campus politics.

Football.

"I really got the situation narrowed down," Emil muttered. "I'm right on top of things."

All the gates to the stadium were locked except one that was guarded by a pudgy giant with TEAM MANAGER stamped on his T-shirt.

"You must be the sheriff," he said, scrutinizing Emil. "Follow me. Coach said to bring you right in."

Locking the gate behind him, the sentinel led Emil at a pretty fast clip through a tunnel leading to the playing field. "This is pretty unusual," the kid called over his shoulder. "Coach is blocking out a new play. Hardly anybody ever gets to see something like that."

"I promise not to tell anybody," said Emil, struggling to keep up with the burly manager.

They came out of the tunnel and into the sweep of the stadium bowl. The team was out on the field, its members dressed in sneakers and shorts, T-shirts or tank tops. The players formed a tight semicircle around Coach Snopes Avano, who was explaining something to them.

Coach was dressed in a glistening white sweatsuit with red-and-blue piping—Norse colors—and he wore his trademark crushed cap with the polished visor. Tinted aviator glasses rested on his great hooked prow of a nose, and an unlit corncob pipe jerked up and down as he spoke.

"You guys had it easy yesterday," Snopes said, "and I figure you can take Notre Dame next Saturday, if you don't get overconfident. But the game we have to begin preparing for right now is Illinois, two weeks away. They were pretty tough last year. Remember, Rusty? They sacked you about a dozen times down there in Champaign-Urbana?"

A redheaded young man standing in the center of the semicircle ducked his head momentarily and grinned. Rollins, thought Emil. Handsome kid, open-faced, bare-chested, every line of his splendid young animal's body lean and honed.

Three scratches ran jaggedly down his left cheek.

Emil's awareness snapped to full alert. Johnny Pflüger had scratches on his right cheek. Type A blood had been found under the fingernails of Alicia Stanhope's right hand.

Quickly, he scanned the team. Rutkow was easy to find, towering head and shoulders above the others. He wore a Norsemen T-shirt cut off to expose a washboard-muscled midriff. A couple of angry red tears started just below his left rib cage and disappeared beneath the waistband of his jogging shorts.

Emil recognized Lem Duffy from his pictures in the *Trib* sports pages. His body was long, lanky, hard, his skin whitish. That body, along with thin, yellowish hair and gelid blue eyes, gave him an aspect of menace, of barely leashed violence. Emil was reminded of stock SS officers in old war movies. Someone had done a pretty thorough job of ripping up the skin on Duffy's left forearm.

"Assuming somebody settles that mess out on the golf course," Coach was saying, "we want to give the fans a good show against Illinois on Homecoming Day, don't we?"

The team answered him with a sudden, pagan roar of affirmation that resounded through the stadium, echoing down among the box seats and the bleachers.

"So I've come up with a play that I want to walk you through this morning. . . ."

Then Rusty Rollins noticed the sheriff standing there, caught Avano's eye, gestured. Coach broke off and turned. "Everybody take a lap," he said. "We'll get back to the play in a minute."

The players trotted over to the cinder track that ran around the playing field and broke into easy lopes. Avano approached Emil, looking very formidable for a fellow in his sixties. One-quarter

72

Chippewa, one-quarter Sioux, one-quarter French, and the rest indeterminate, he'd come off the Red Lake Reservation in northern Minnesota to achieve gridiron immortality with Charlie "Papa Bear" Halas in Chicago. Football was a sacrament to Snopes, sweat and liniment, body and blood.

Yet his greatest goal was almost certain to elude him. Rocco Granitelli, with those two hundred and two victories, seemed beyond overtaking. Still, Snopes would strive until his last breath to surpass that historic accomplishment. Emil wished him the best of luck. Although Coach might not have agreed, Emil figured that trying for something kept you going, whether you won it in the end or not.

Avano walked up to Emil. He didn't offer his hand, but nodded toward the team manager, who retreated immediately.

"Rector Rex said you'd be over," Snopes said brusquely. "Now, what we have to do is plan a way to get that Hollman woman off campus damn quick—"

"Hey, wait a minute," said the sheriff, "I'm not here about that."

"You aren't?"

"Didn't President Anderson tell you? I have to talk to three of your players. They were in class with the girl who got killed."

Avano jerked the corncob pipe from between his teeth. "Which players are you talking about?" he demanded.

"Rollins, Rutkow, and Duffy. President Anderson informed me that—"

"Well, I don't know what he told you, but he told me you were coming to see me about something important. I thought it would be about straightening out the crowd situation around here."

Either Coach misunderstood Anderson, Emil calculated, or he's protecting the Terrible Trio.

Avano confirmed the second possibility, without eliminating the first. "Sheriff, I want you to know that I voted for you last election, and I will again, but I've also got to tell you that I can't have my boys upset with these big games coming up, understand?"

"I just have to ask them a few questions, is all."

"You think one of them is involved?"

"I'm hoping one—or all—of them can help me figure out why the girl got killed in the first place."

Snopes was unconvinced. "What if I say no, you can't talk to them?"

"That'd just cause us all a lot of trouble," drawled Emil, meeting the peremptory stare from behind those tinted glasses. "I'd probably have to bring them into my office, that sort of thing. . . ."

Avano understood. "All right," he said, "but I'll want to be present."

"Sorry. I question them alone, one at a time."

"All right," Coach capitulated, "and just keep in mind that we're cooperating with you, in case we need you to cooperate with us on that Hollman business out there."

He stepped out onto the cinder track and flagged down the three players as they jogged by. Emil watched the faces of the young men as Coach explained why the sheriff wanted to see them. Rollins looked quizzical, and glanced over at Emil with interest. Gunnar Rutkow seemed suddenly afraid, his great bulk notwithstanding. Lem Duffy's craggy, asymmetrical face darkened, and his pale eyes began to smoulder dully.

Coach got his team back onto the field, where the players took up a loose scrimmage position, waiting for Emil's interviews to end so they could get to work.

Rusty Rollins came over first and sat down on the team bench next to the sheriff. He was a nice-looking kid, polite, well-spoken. This would be a good one for Dee-Dee, Emil found himself thinking. God, where *is* she, anyway?

"Understand you and your teammates had a little squabble with Alicia Stanhope during class Friday night?"

"Yes, sir," Rusty said. "I'm sorry about that. Best way to deal with that sort of criticism is to ignore it, I guess. But picking on Gunnar isn't fair at all. There's no better man than Gunnar when you're in a tight spot. Not everyone in this life has book smarts, isn't that right?"

"You said it there," replied Emil, smiling. "Know Alicia well?"

"Just from class."

"Anything you can tell me about her? About where you were Friday night?"

Rollins shook his handsome head, rich, red hair shining in the sunlight. "Gunnar, Lem, and I went right back to the dorm after seminar. Curfew was at eleven."

"Where'd you get those scratches on your face?"

"In the game yesterday. The Northwestern tackle got his hand under my face mask, darn it. And the ref didn't even *see!*"

"That's the way it goes," sympathized Emil, wondering what it was like to be so renowned so young. The only game he'd ever played was ice hockey, with brooms for sticks and a flat rock for a puck, when the creek on the farm backed up and froze over in the meadow. Fifty years ago. He had not been very good at it, either.

Lem Duffy was sullen, but forthright. "Yes, I knew Lish," he admitted. "We dated a couple of times."

"How'd you two get along, if you don't mind my asking?"

"Do I have any choice? Coach said I had to talk to you." He checked to see that Avano was out of earshot. "Lish and I made it, if you want to know the truth. But keep this between us, okay, 'cause things like that aren't supposed to happen in a place like this."

"You *made* it?"

"Sex, Sheriff. I wasn't all that hot for it but, I figured, why turn it down? It was there for the taking."

"When did this . . . happen? Where?"

"Last week. Down by the riverbank. Probably about where . . . where she . . ."

"I see. So the two of you got along pretty well?"

Emil was beginning to see that his initial impression of Duffy had been mistaken. Behind the threatening face, within the powerful body, was a twenty-year-old kid still trying to find his way into manhood.

"We got along pretty well for the time it took to make it. She never even let me get close to her after that."

"Made you mad, huh?"

Duffy's pale eyes met the old sheriff's inquiring gaze. "Sir, I never told a lie in my life and I'm not gonna start now. I liked the way she made me feel, but I didn't like her. I didn't like the way she dumped me, and I'm not sorry about what happened to her."

"Where'd you get your arm so torn up?"

"You see yesterday's game?"

"Just the last couple minutes."

"Then you missed when the Wildcat defender climbed all over me in the third quarter. I was in the end zone, just standing there waiting for Rusty's pass. Ref called interference. I bled for about half an hour, too. But no big deal. I've bled before and I will again."

"What do you think of Dale Torbert?" Emil asked on impulse.

Duffy thought it over. "Good man," he said. "Fair. I'm not the world's best student, but he's never put me down."

"Hell, Lem, you don't have to worry. From what I read in the papers, there are already about a dozen pro teams waiting to make you a rich man."

Duffy shrugged, and Emil found himself liking the lanky kid. "So what if I throw out my knee down at South Bend next Saturday? So what if I break my neck coming down wrong after a catch? Those scouts in the fancy suits won't even give me the time of day then."

Gunnar Rutkow walked reluctantly over to the sheriff, his expression, posture, and gait like those of a guilty kindergartener on his way to the principal's office: *Get me out of this!*

Emil tried to make him feel at ease. "Well, Gunnar, it's nice to see a Stearns County boy in a place like this."

The huge defenseman was from St. Augusta, south of St. Cloud, where even to graduate from high school was considered evidence of dangerous brilliance.

"Yuh," said Gunnar, slumping down next to Emil on the bench. "I didn't do it. I didn't kill her. I didn't even think of it."

"Relax, okay? No one's accusing you of anything."

Emil felt a little sorry for the boy. Obviously, he was not the brainiest guy around, and never had been. Until he'd come to college, it probably hadn't even dawned on him that his lack of "book smarts," as Rusty Rollins had put it, would ever be important. Not too many people read books in his hometown, and at Technical High, where he'd starred in football, brawn was all that had been necessary. But North Star was a new world, and Gunnar was smarting from the demands of challenges he'd never imagined to be important.

You crack through the line on Saturday and sack the quarterback, right? And you're a hero. It feels good. So how come in class on Monday or Tuesday some cute girl snickers when you walk in the door? How come the professor talks to you real slow, like you can't figure out what is going on? (Which is correct.) And how come skinny little wimps who were *absolutely nothing* in high school, who would practically run when they saw you coming, hardly ever even say hello when they see you now, and treat you like you *aren't even there?*

Emil understood all this, and felt a genuine sorrow for Gunnar Rutkow. If I had a boy like Gunnar, he thought, all I could tell him is, Play your big heart out, son, football is your one and only shot.

"I understand Alicia gave you a hard time at that last class?" he prodded. "Didn't know the difference between secularism and pluralism, did you?"

Rutkow reddened. He squinted, trying to think. "I memorized that after I got back to Valhalla," he said. "Now how did it go? Secularism is when it's not religious and pluralism is when—"

"No matter," said Emil. "I don't know myself."

"You don't know?"

"Nope. Ever date Alicia Stanhope, son?"

Gunnar's eyes widened. "Are you *kidding?* You know what she thought of me? She made no secret of what she thought about me."

"Wouldn't have minded it though, would you? Having a girl who looked like that?"

77

Gunnar looked away, embarrassed.

"How about Alicia and Titchell taping Professor Torbert? You know 'about that?"

"If that's true, it was a bad thing. A very bad thing."

"I thought Torbert flunked you?"

"So what? I had it comin'. But he never was mean to me, like some of 'em are, like Professor Hollman."

"Gunnar, have you heard what's happening on the golf course?"

"Yes, and I believe it, too. Soon's practice is over, I'm gonna go down there and pray."

"Two more questions and I'll let you go. How come you're still eligible when you got an *F* last term?"

"I don't know. Coach said there was a special rule and it's all right."

"And where'd you get those scratches?"

The huge footballer looked sheepish. "Couple of us guys was playing grabass in the shower room," he said. "It got out of hand."

Gunnar trotted back to join his mates. Emil waved at Coach Avano, who came over unenthusiastically.

"They're good boys."

"I already know that. I just hope you didn't disturb them with your questions. Once broken, concentration is difficult to regain."

"Could be. But now I need to see a couple of things from you. The Friday night sign-in sheets on all members of the team, and their physical records too."

"Their physical—what? Look, Sheriff, I've got a team to run and big games coming up. I can't be wasting my time—"

"I'd hardly think it's a waste of time to keep your boys out of legal hot water." Emil saw the Coach's eyes narrow behind the glasses.

"I know each of these boys like I know my own soul," he said, sticking the pipe back into his mouth. "If I didn't know you to be an honorable man, I'd feel an urge to knock you on your butt. You want that stuff you asked for, go get a warrant."

"I can do that," said Emil. Judge Brewster Titchell, Sr., loved to

78

give out warrants. Maybe not this time, however. Titchell was an avid Norsemen fan and a member of the North Star Board of Trustees, as was almost everybody who was anybody in Minnesota. President Anderson covered all the bases. "Mr. Avano," said Emil, "let's not make things difficult. There are certain things that I am empowered to check, okay?"

Snopes thought it over pretty hard. Emil couldn't tell if Coach was worried that one of his players might have been involved in homicide, or whether he was simply resisting any challenge to his authority over the team.

"Ellison! Schmid!" Coach yelled to his assistants. "Get them started on the drill. I'll be back in a minute."

He marched into the stadium, Emil trailing, down a granite-walled passageway, descending two white-tiled stairwells into the Norsemen's locker room. The place was spacious and even opulent, mirrored and shining and spotlessly clean. There was only the faintest trace of that wet-sweatsock odor characteristic of the athletic underworld. Avano's office, adjacent to the locker room, was also large, meticulously organized, without a hint of jumble or clutter. A large plastic container, three feet square, rested on the floor next to his desk. It was filled with tiny Nerf footballs, each signed by Coach with a magic-marker. A computer console, complete with a small video screen, took up a section of desktop, and Snopes invited Emil around to have a look. He began to press buttons. The Friday night sign-ins appeared onscreen: Rollins, 10:46; Rutkow, 10:48; Duffy, 11:07.

"Seems your tight end was a little late for bed-check."

"I've already covered that with him. He forgot to sign in, that's all. He has to do three extra laps per day as punishment. Sheriff, all boys are gonna screw up now and then. It's a good sign. Show me the perfect boy, and I'll show you somebody who's gonna go off the deep end one day."

It took longer to scan the medical records, mainly because Emil didn't want to let on exactly what he was looking for. It was also difficult for him to conceal a surge of agitated disappointment when he learned that Rusty, Gunnar, and Lem all had type A blood. He did not know Tony Wiggins's blood type, nor that of Professor Dale Torbert. But he'd met all five young men this morning, had liked them all, each in his own way, and would have been proud to have had any of them as a son.

"Thanks, Coach," he said, staying calm. "That'll be all for now."

Avano eyed him morosely, then took Emil back to the surface of the earth.

"Understand Gunnar flunked a course last term," said Emil.

"That's what I heard too," Coach shot back. "But when I checked the records, I found he'd gotten a B. There will always be vicious rumors about the mental wherewithal of athletes, I suspect."

Without a good-bye, Coach turned and went back to his waiting team. Emil hung around for a few minutes, standing on the cinder track, and watched the new play. He'd never played football and didn't know all that many gridiron tactics, but he knew perfection when he saw it. Lem Duffy was in motion toward the left sideline when Rusty Rollins took the snap. Rusty dropped back five yards, maybe seven. Lem was streaking toward the distant goal line, having already eluded three defenders. He was in the end zone. Rusty waited too long to throw. Lem was covered again. Then, with a feint, another, and canny blocking, the apparently besieged Rollins broke free, running even faster than Lem had. It would have been a certain TD, except Coach blew his whistle to save Rusty the effort.

"What do you call that thing?" Emil asked the team manager, who unlocked the gate to let him out of the stadium.

"That play?" The kid grinned. "Fool's Gold. You watched Rusty and Lem, didn't you? Look more closely next time. It's the blocking that makes it work."

Definitely, thought Emil, standing alone outside the mammoth stadium. But the sheriff was also overwhelmed by Lem Duffy's speed, almost as if the boy had been first in one place and then in another, never for an instant occupying the space in between, like those mystical components of atoms.

Could somebody that fast, he asked himself, have left the academic building, stalked and killed Alicia Stanhope down by the Sauk River, and gotten back to Valhalla by 11:07?

The answer was yes.

Whippletree set out across the golf course toward the praying throng. His mind was hard at work, which distracted him from the knowledge that he was pretty tired already, it was barely noon, and his heart was heavy.

Until he saw the girl walking toward him, carrying an overnight bag.

It was Dee-Dee.

Now don't go scolding her, he ordered himself, after first subduing an impulse to throw up his arms and shout in an ecstasy of relief.

But his anxiety returned when he saw her trudging along, downcast, her eyes red-rimmed and her usually shining honey-colored hair lustreless and even a little tangled. She didn't see him and would have walked right past him if he hadn't called her name.

"Dee? What's the matter?"

She looked up, startled, an accosted fawn. "Uncle Emil!" She did not seem entirely happy to see him.

"Where've you been?" He walked up to her, stopped, and took a look. She was wearing sneakers, faded blue jeans, and an old white pullover. She'd been crying. "Everybody's been looking all over for you!"

"I suppose because of Lish, huh?"

"You know about that?"

"I heard it on the radio, just this morning. I don't know what to say. I'm all . . . I feel like a shambles, or something."

"You haven't said where you've been." He held back the urge to add "young lady."

"I was . . . I was staying at my friend's house in town. Sally Batermann. You know the Batermanns?"

Emil nodded. A big family. Lived on the north side. And they did have a daughter named Sally, who was also a North Star student.

"She drove me back here as soon as we heard the news about Lish. I had to walk across the golf course, though, on account of all the people and cars blocking the road."

"Come on," said Emil gently, now that he knew where she'd been, "let's go to the cafeteria or someplace and get a cup of coffee. You look like you could stand it."

Her smile was half rueful, half winsome. "Thanks, but what I really need is a long, hot shower. Are you out here investigating the . . . ?"

"Yep. And I'm getting nowhere fast. Maybe you could give me a hand. You were Miss Stanhope's roommate, I've learned. When did you see her last?"

"Friday night, after class. I went home with Sally—"

"But you signed out for your own home. Your mom's been worried sick. Vice-President Dexter even called your house."

Dee-Dee looked stricken. "The school knows? That I signed out for home and didn't go? Ohmigod, that's an honors violation. I'll have to go before the Committee—"

"Look, it's your first offense. I hope."

Dee-Dee didn't say anything.

"Maybe they'll let you off easy."

"I hope," she said.

"Well, why *didn't* you go home?" he demanded.

"Because," she answered, in an uncharacteristically halting way. "Mom's been on my back a lot lately. I need a little space of my own these days. . . ."

Emil nodded, feeling shrewd. It was just as he'd suggested to Barbara. "So you didn't see where she went after class?"

"Alicia? No."

"And you didn't go for a walk down along the river, did you?"

"Uncle Emil?" she asked, surprised. "Why would I want to do that?"

"Just a point I had to get straight," he answered, thinking of the type O blood on the birch bark. "How did you feel when you learned that Alicia had been killed?"

"Awful. What do you think?"

"How well did you know her?"

Dee-Dee frowned. "Pretty well."

"Like her?"

A long pause. "Uncle Emil, I feel sort of . . . bad . . . about having to say this. I tried to like her. But it was hard sometimes."

"How come?"

"Well, she could be fun sometimes, she was very witty, but she could also be cold. And she had a pretty sharp tongue."

"Which I understand she used to tear into Gunnar Rutkow at the seminar?"

She looked quickly up at him. "You know about that?"

"Now and then I stumble onto a few things."

Dee-Dee smiled, beginning to look like her usual vibrant self again. "Oh, Uncle Emil! But I could have . . . I could have *slapped* her. Gunnar is a nice, harmless guy. In a way, the blame isn't all Lish's though. I mean, the way she was."

"Why not?"

"Her family's not like ours, Uncle Emil. I met her mother a few times, she's sort of la-di-dah, and her dad's some sort of important executive. He was always worrying that she'd do something to drag his name into the papers. They live in Edina."

Edina was an expensive Minneapolis suburb.

"So Lish had gotten into the habit of leading sort of a double life, know what I mean? She was even going out with some townie. They would meet at The Bucket, or she would sneak past Security by going along the river and he'd be waiting in his car down at the end of the drive."

"Did she sign out?"

"No. She said if you sign out, you have to sign in. I guess I was supposed to have reported it to Honors, but . . ."

"A roommate's a roommate. I understand. Did she date anybody on campus?"

"Mostly the guys here bored her. She toyed with a few of them."

"Like Lem Duffy?"

"Well, Lem was pretty mad when she dumped him."

"Do you know that they'd, ahh . . . ?" The sheriff was a little embarrassed. "Ah, that the two of them had . . ."

"It's all right, Uncle Emil," said Dee-Dee, with a little sympathetic laugh. "I'm a big girl now. Yes, I knew that they'd had sex. A date for Lish was having sex. She went out with Rusty Rollins too. Last year."

"Rusty Rollins? From what I've heard about Alicia, I'd hardly think she'd be his type."

"She wasn't. And he found out fast. She came home early that night."

"What about Gunnar?"

"He stared at her all the time, but he knew there wasn't any hope. Almost everybody took a second or a third look at Lish. And she wanted them to."

"Did that include Professor Torbert?"

Dee-Dee shook her head, amused. "She tried pretty hard to get his attention. I suppose a lot of girls do. He's so good-looking and intelligent."

"Professor Hollman doesn't think so."

His niece's eyes flashed darkly. "I hate him, Uncle Emil. Everybody hates him. He's a"—she thought hard to find something really bad—"he's a *Visigoth!*" she declared.

"Hold on, I'm just your old uncle, only know about planting corn and stuff."

"He almost gave me a B in African History last term. I had to cry to get him to change his mind."

"Interesting strategy. And here the family thinks you're just plain smart."

She touched his sleeve affectionately. "You won't tell them the truth, will you, Uncle Emil?"

"Look," he said, "you run along and clean up. I may have to talk to you again later. And if you need a character witness for the Honors Committee, I think we could scare somebody up."

"Thanks, Uncle Emil." She stood on tip-toe and pecked his cheek. "What are you going to do now?"

"Heading over to that pine tree and have a chat with the Virgin Mary. Maybe she can tell me who the killer is. Save me a lot of trouble."

They parted, but Emil turned and called after her. "By the way," he said, "you have a beau these days?"

Her laughter drifted toward him like music, and she winked. "Only you, Uncle Emil," she said.

Axel Vogel saw the sheriff approaching and trotted over to meet him. Mass had ended, but Father Ryder was leading the crowd of worshippers in a litany.

*"From the snares of false prophets . . ."*
  *"Oh, Lord deliver us."*
*"From the lure of empty visions . . ."*
  *"Oh, Lord deliver us."*

"What's up, Axel?"

"Sheriff, I found something. In the bushes near the road." The deputy fumbled inside his shirt pocket and withdrew a scrap of blue fabric, raggedly triangular in shape. He handed it to Emil. It felt slick and rubbery on his fingertips.

"Good work, Axel. I'll be damn surprised if this doesn't match the fabric found under Alicia's nails. Although I doubt if it came from Cowboy John's windbreaker." He nodded toward the crowd. "What's been going on here?"

The big deputy shrugged. "Not too fucking much. Bunny's over by the pine tree, like yesterday. Everybody's been praying."

"Everything peaceful and quiet?"

"Not so much as an angry word. But, Emil, some of these folks brought tents along with 'em. They got hibachis and bushels of food. Could turn into a bivouac. You find out anything?"

"Yep. College life is a lot more complicated than I'd thought. Bring the car over, would you? I'm going to see if I can have a word with Bunny."

Axel lumbered off and the sheriff shouldered his way through the crowd.

*"From the beguilements of Satan . . ."*
*"Oh, Lord deliver us."*

Emil caught sight of a KSTP-TV camera crew over by the pine tree. *Trib* reporter Roy Riley was talking earnestly to a soundman. Then Emil saw Sarah, kneeling among the crowd. She gave him a discreet little wave and a smile. He touched the brim of his hat, grinning back.

Bunny Hollman was kneeling between her husband and young Titchell. Her face was lifted raptly toward the pine, and her expression, just as it had yesterday, suggested the unmistakable evidence of physical delight. Professor Hollman saw Whippletree approaching and beckoned him over. Titchell glanced at Emil for a second, then looked away. He seemed sullen, angry, as if he blamed the sheriff for Saturday's unpleasantness.

"See, Sheriff," Charlie whispered, "what occurred yesterday was legitimate. It's happening again."

Emil dropped to his knees, old bones on cold ground, the better to converse. "Can we talk?" he asked.

"Yes, but quietly. It'll have to be here. I can't leave my wife."

"Suits me."

"Just a minute. The litany will be over soon."

*"From the snares of the hunter . . ."*
*"Oh, Lord deliver us."*

Father Ryder, an earnest, slightly chubby young man, stood before the portable altar, holding a thin, silver microphone. The altar was underneath the branches of the tree, which was surrounded by wreaths, bouquets, and vases bursting with blossoms. The priest's fervent cries and the mighty responses of the prayer pilgrims gave the occasion an air of timelessness and surreality.

The feeling was uncanny, powerful; its force grew within Emil.

86

He was overcome by a sudden, savage impression that this chant, rising toward the blue September sky, proceeded from the clattering jawbones of whitened skulls. He glanced around uneasily, seeking the reassurance of flesh and blood. There was Bart Bolthaus, who ran the five-and-dime. And Mavis Tuckerman, Doc Hallstrem's dental hygienist. And Dink and Ilsa Kufelski, who owned the Dippi-Freez ice cream franchise on West Division Street. And there was Sarah, fingering her rosary beads.

Emil felt much better, but he couldn't completely shake those premonitory jitters, nor discount President Anderson's remark that certain people would respond to Bunny's experience with bizarre perceptions of their own. *Twin silver rails raced along beneath fields of rolling purple fog, and somewhere at the ends of the earth was a light far brighter than the sun. . . .*

"Amen!" called Father Ryder.

The people answered him. Then, slowly, they got to their feet, conversing quietly among themselves. Charlie stood up too, and so did Emil. Brewster Titchell remained on his skinny knees, and Bunny did not stir. Her eyes were wide open. Emil saw the image of the white pine reflected in them.

"What did you want to talk to me about?" the professor inquired, looking slightly wary.

"I wonder if there's a good time for me to see Bunny?"

"What about?"

"Oh, just curious, I guess. This business is having some kind of an effect on me, and I want to discuss it with her."

The history teacher shook his big head lugubriously. "I'm afraid that won't be possible. She's very preoccupied. I'm sure you understand."

I'll have to get to her when Charlie's not around, Emil figured. "You're probably pretty busy yourself these days," he said.

The professor sensed something unstated in Emil's tone. "How's that?" he asked, with a cautious, appraising glance.

"Well, for starters, I heard that Dale Torbert is planning to sue you."

Charlie's eyes narrowed. He lost a little color. "Oh, I doubt that," he said.

"No. He seems pretty angry about something. I think it has to do with an illegal tape-recording."

Hollman reddened, a flush of sudden anger. Emil saw Brewster Titchell giving the professor a brief, shaky glance.

"Yes," the sheriff went on, sort of pleased with the pious innocence of his tone, "Torbert is going to bring the issue to President Anderson's attention. And there was something about transcripts too."

A big vein throbbed into action at Charlie's left temple. "That is all a smokescreen, Sheriff. It's sour grapes on the part of a man who couldn't meet the high standards of his department. No sane person would question the decision of a responsible tenure committee, nor hope to override it. But I assure you that there was no such tape recording and there were no transcripts."

"You're certain?"

"Absolutely."

"Gee, that's too bad. I was working on a theory that Torbert killed Alicia—or that somebody loyal to him killed her—in revenge for her role in making the tape."

Emil watched Hollman, and saw that the little scholar did not at all dislike the idea that Professor Torbert might be a suspect.

"He could have killed her for another reason, too," offered Hollman helpfully.

"You can be sure that I'll pursue every lead."

Charlie glanced over his shoulder, then turned back to Emil and spoke in a lowered voice. "I have reason to believe," he said, "that Dale Torbert is of questionable moral character. Lascivious, if you will. I have seen him gazing lustfully at the coeds."

"Men look at woman and vice-versa," said the sheriff. "It's sort of in the nature of things."

"Sheriff, please do not be disgusting at a time and place like this. I have never gazed lustfully at any woman, including my wife."

Emil remembered that the Hollmans had no kids, and stole a

glance at Bunny. If her face didn't show *the look*, he'd eat his hat right here. When he and Sarah were young and just married, going at it more than they'd been led to believe possible, Sarah had always gotten that certain sweet look on her face, her eyes filled with something like pain but not pain, her skin a fiery rose, her lips parted for a cry like a sob. Emil adored that look because it meant that Sarah, whom he cherished, was as happy as his full passion could make her.

"All I said was that it's the nature of things, Charlie. Could you be more specific?"

"All I know is that Miss Stanhope informed me he'd made advances toward her."

"I wish she were here to corroborate that." Emil decided not to tell Charlie about Alicia's dubious reputation in the morals department. In spite of what he'd learned from Dee-Dee and the others, she'd been just a kid. Kids make mistakes. "Only reason I brought up the matter of the tape," Emil drawled, "is because I want to head off the next killing if I can."

"The next . . . ?" gasped Professor Hollman.

"Sure. I may have this wrong, of course, but if Alicia and you, Brewster, were in on the tape deal together, and if the murder relates to the tape, well, I figure you're the next who ought to be ready to greet St. Pete."

Junior had been listening, of course, and the way his terrified eyes sought Charlie's, the reflexive manner in which the professor's head snapped toward the younger man, proved to Emil that Hollman was lying through his teeth. There had been a tape. And there were transcripts.

"We shall see . . ." the professor managed, his usual self-certainty a little the worse for wear.

Then the KSTP-TV cameraman moved in for a close shot of Bunny.

"*The lance of man is ivory,*" she cried out suddenly, in yesterday's eerie voice, "*and woman's cave is all sweet velvet to the bone.*"

Those near her, Emil included, fell silent. Their expectant still-

89

ness communicated itself to the rest of the crowd, so almost everybody heard Bunny proclaim, in a ringing voice of ecstasy and wonder, *"Our Lady is about to speak!"*

A hush, charged with currents of alien power, spread across campus. The Sacred Steeple pierced blue sky; metal folds of Jesus' robe seemed to move and flow in sunlight. A sense of unearthly imminence descended upon Emil, cloaking his awareness like a fall of dew.

*"I see her,"* shouted Bunny, from the depths of her trance. *"I see her face plain as day. Oh, God! Oh, Blessed Mother!"* she cried in a holy sob.

"It's a miracle!" someone said.

*"There is a light shining all around her, and her gown, it's beautiful, it's like the sun, and there is a halo of diamonds around her golden hair. . . ."*

Everyone was staring at the tree, transfixed. Emil looked too, but in spite of the tingling across his scalp, and the sense of something wild and strange riding the very air, he saw only the gray trunk and green, needled branches of the pine tree.

*"Is Bart Bolthaus here?"* asked Bunny. *"Our Holy Mother has a message for Bart Bolthaus."*

"I'm . . . here . . ." faltered the lanky manager of St. Cloud's five-and-dime. He rose from his knees, almost stumbling, looking as if he'd just been summoned to be shot.

*"Bart, the Virgin says that your son, Toby, is in heaven, and that he forgives you for not fixing the brakes on the Pontiac coupe."*

Bolthaus, a man of about fifty, burst into tears. Emil knew Bart fairly well. Played cards with him when the Knights of Columbus held poker nights. He also knew that the man blamed himself for his son's auto crash. But Emil, who had practically peeled Toby Bolthaus from a concrete abutment along I-94, ascribed greater blame to a blood-alcohol level of .21, a fact that he and Doc Divot had decided not to make public. What point would there have been? The poor kid was dead.

And in heaven.

Bolthaus's relief was total. He had probably never been happier in his life than he was now, hearing the message Bunny had conveyed to him, falling again to his knees with joyous sobs.

"*And Mavis Tuckerman?*" cried Bunny in that unearthly voice. "*Mavis, are you here?*"

"I kneel before you, Blessed Mother," answered the dental hygienist. In the tension of the moment, she tore apart her rosary. Beads scattered everywhere, a tiny shower of tinted plastic hail.

"*The Virgin knows that you have been searching everywhere for the diamond earrings that belonged to your dear, departed sister, Hilda. She wants you to have them, and you will find them in the false bottom of the cedar chest by the bay window in Hilda's bedroom.*"

Mavis managed a strangled cry, a combination of fear and awe, then got up and moved through the crowd, presumably toward her car, St. Cloud, and the cedar chest with the false bottom.

Bunny continued to stare at the pine tree, silently now. Then a look of tragic disappointment appeared on her face.

"*The Virgin says that our prayers have been insufficient. Her Divine Son has no messages for us today.*"

A mournful *ohhhhhhhhhhh* rose from the listeners in response to this news. Mrs. Hollman began to get to her feet. The look of physical ecstasy on her face was fading, but she was still very much in the grip of something that suffused her flesh with soaring pleasure. She faltered. She fell. The crowd, watching, cried out in fear and alarm.

"What happened?"

"Bunny's dead!" someone shrieked.

People pressed forward, a mob reflex, in awestruck concern. Emil, right next to Bunny, judged that she'd merely fainted, just as she had yesterday at the conclusion of her vision.

"She's all right, she's all right," he shouted facing the throng and lifting his arms into the air. "Just get back now, all right? I need your cooperation." Then he turned back to Bunny and bent down to help Charlie loosen her clothing.

"Oh my God," Charlie was saying. "Bunny, talk to me."

"Get away from here, Sheriff," shouted an agitated Brewster Titchell, who had not learned yesterday's lesson too well.

Axel managed to shoulder his way through the crowd. He too bent over the fallen woman. "What's goin' on here?" he wondered, eyeing the young man. "Anything I can do?"

"Charlie," said Emil, "get that kid out of here before he screws up again."

The professor stood up and stepped between Titchell and the deputy. Emil loosened the collar of Bunny's dress and patted her cheeks lightly. She was stretched out on the grass. Her lips began to move. Emil lowered himself further, pressing his ear to her mouth.

*"Minnesota will beat the Broncos this afternoon,"* he heard her gasp, *"fourteen to thirteen."*

My ten-dollar bet! he thought.

She opened her eyes and began to come around. A kind of sleepy joy showed on her face, the expression of a woman who has just coaxed from her dazzled flesh all the hoarded delight it possessed.

"It's all right, folks!" Axel boomed, addressing the crowd. "Mrs. Hollman is fine. Just move back and give us all a little room."

Axel was pretty intimidating. The people began to comply, but Brewster Titchell, Jr., who'd been addressing Charlie in angry hisses, and who was obviously even more susceptible to the mood of the vision than Emil had suspected, suddenly lost control of himself.

"I won't be moved away!" he shouted in a high-pitched tone of outrage. "*You* get out of here!" he said to the sheriff.

Emil was still kneeling over Bunny, completely unready for an assault, so when Brewster stepped suddenly toward him, stuck out his thin arms and pushed, the sheriff, caught off-balance, fell sideways onto the grass. Startled but unhurt, he looked up to see the furious kid clenching and unclenching his fists, as if he'd won some big fight. Emil also saw a smirk of satisfaction on Professor Hollman's fleshy face, before Charlie found the wit to veil his expression.

92

"Hey!" roared Axel, when he saw what Titchell had done. "Sheriff, you all right?"

Emil got very slowly and deliberately to his feet, gazing at Brewster. "I'm all right," he said, "and this time I've had enough. Brewster, my boy, you're under arrest. We're going to give you an educational tour of the Stearns County Jail."

"Way to go, Sheriff!" Axel said.

"But he didn't mean it!" cried Charlie, seeking to mediate the situation.

"He didn't mean it yesterday, either. First time, shame on me. Second time, shame on you. Axel."

With a pleasure that was perhaps excessive, Deputy Vogel grabbed Brewster around the shoulders and got one of his arms behind his back. Titchell let out a little cry, too startled and embarrassed to do much of anything else.

"I'll take him over and put him in the car," Axel said.

"Charlie," said Emil, as the deputy hustled Junior off through the crowd, "what are you up to, anyway?"

"What do you mean, 'what am I *up* to?'"

Bunny was on her feet now, looking dazed and bewildered. Even if her visions were self-induced, Emil reasoned, their effect upon her was genuine and profound.

"I mean what's this all about? President Anderson and Coach Avano are worried that the whole campus is going to be disrupted."

"They are, are they?" Hollman could not conceal his satisfaction.

"Bunny," said the sheriff, turning toward Mrs. Hollman, "how about if I talk to you later? I could stop by your house."

"She's very tired," snapped the professor. "Aren't you, dear?"

"I don't know . . ." Bunny said, still in the grip of her experience, "I guess so . . ."

"We're going to get you home now," declared Charlie, taking his wife's arm. The surrounding crowd and KSTP-TV watched the two of them walk away.

While Emil was making his way to the patrol car, a couple of outlanders in the crowd—outlanders were those who hadn't spent their entire lives in Stearns County—awarded him with a few catcalls about "tough guy" and "unbeliever."

"Don't let it bother you," soothed Sarah, appearing beside him and slipping her hand into his. "I thought you did fine. Wasn't it wonderful, though? Bart Bolthaus is telling everybody that nobody in his whole life ever lifted a burden from his shoulders like the one Bunny removed when she said that thing about the brakes. And Mavis has been looking for those diamond earrings ever since her sister died two years ago."

"We don't know if she found them yet, though."

"She will," said Sarah, convinced.

"I wouldn't have thought you'd buy a deal like this so quickly," Emil wondered, looking at her.

"Well, maybe I do and maybe I don't. But the whole thing just made me feel so *good.*"

"We'll talk about it later," he said. "I have to get back to the office. The Stanhopes will be arriving pretty soon."

"Who was that young man I saw with Axel? It looked like he was under arrest."

"He is. That's Judge Titchell's kid."

"Oh, Emil! Is it serious? Did you have to do it? You and the Judge don't see eye-to-eye now, and if—"

"Honey," he shushed her, "I already gave that whippersnapper one break. And I'll *never* get along with the judge. We're just different. I'll only hold the boy until his dad shows up to sign him out. Maybe it'll turn out to be a lesson for them both."

They never kissed in public, so she squeezed his hand, he squeezed back, and they parted.

Titchell sort of blubbered all the way into St. Cloud, but he didn't beg for leniency, or even sympathy, for which the sheriff gave him credit.

"Farley," Emil ordered, when they brought Junior into the office, "fingerprint this guy and lock him in the cell next to Pflüger. Give him a chance to see how the other half lives. Then I want you to get on the phone to a Paul Barnes, lives in St. Paul, and find out if Dale Torbert stayed with him this weekend. When the Stanhopes show up, give them coffee. I've got to run over to Doc Divot's house. I'll be back in a little bit."

He took the old St. Germain Street bridge to the east side, the Mississippi low and slow this time of year, and headed north on Riverside Drive. Divot lived in an old but spacious and pricey brick manse overlooking the river. Emil found Doc on the patio in back of the house, reading the Minneapolis *Star and Tribune* and nursing a gin and tonic.

"Want one?" Doc asked, holding the drink aloft.

"Can't. I'm working."

"That's why I quit surgery," said Doc, taking a swallow. "When your scalpel slips in the coroner's trade, it doesn't make any difference. What do you want?"

Emil gave him the scrap of fabric. "Could be important," he said.

"Dammit, you want me to check that out now? I'll have to go over to the lab, and the Vikings–Broncos game'll start pretty soon on TV."

"I'll mention your name when Roy Riley does that big story about me solving the case."

"What do you mean? Butch Lodge is already saying that he's got everything under control."

"What?"

Doc riffled through the Minneapolis paper and showed Emil a small story headed DEATH ON CAMPUS. Lodge had stated, to a Twin Cities reporter, that his ace sleuthing talents had led to the arrest of one John Pflüger. "All signs point to this man's involvement," the security boss was quoted as having said.

"You making any progress?" asked Doc.

"Hard to say. I've got Titchell's kid locked up, though."

He explained the situation. Doc thought it was funny. "Old

Brew is gonna throw a fit when he finds out. You really gone and done it this time, Emil."

"Maybe so, but the boy got me riled."

Divot shook his head. "Remember the time that Protestant was elected mayor of St. Cloud, and Titchell circulated a petition for recall, claiming St. Cloud was a Catholic town and the new mayor didn't represent the majority? He might do the same to you for arresting his only begotten son."

"I'll have to take my chances, won't I? Anyway, I'd appreciate a quick job on that fabric."

"Oh, all right. I'll give you a call later. By the way, are we gonna participate in the deer-hunting season this fall?"

"I don't know. I'd like to. But Sarah and I took that 'roots' trip to Europe, for all the good it did, and I want to go to the Rose Bowl. Cash is a little tight."

"Well, make a decent bet with Wienie, and you'll be in clover."

"With my luck?" said Emil.

On the way back to the office, he stopped at the Batermanns' house on the pretext of thanking Sally for giving Dee-Dee a ride out to campus. All young girls looked incredibly pretty to him, and Sally was no exception with her tight jeans and long flowing hair.

"It was nothing, Mr. Whippletree. I had no plans and she just showed up on the doorstep."

"Oh? What time was that?"

"About eight this morning."

"Is that right? Well, thanks a lot."

Whippletree left the Batermanns' house confused, and a little hurt. Dee-Dee had lied to him. She had not spent the weekend with Sally. Question now was, where *had* she spent it?

Returning to the office, he learned that Mr. and Mrs. Stanhope had not yet arrived, and that Cowboy John was incensed to have Titchell, Jr., in the cell next to him.

"This guy's a wimp, Sheriff," Pflüger complained. "It's written all over him. I got my reputation to think about."

Titchell, who'd made his one phone call, had learned that his father was down in The Cities attending the Vikings–Broncos game. That meant he'd be in jail all afternoon, at least, and he was too dispirited to do anything except lie on his bunk and stare at the gray, concrete ceiling.

"That's Judge Titchell's kid," Emil told Pflüger. "You'll be arraigned before the judge tomorrow morning for that theft at Heffner's station."

Cowboy John's eyes glittered as he processed this information. "Hey, kid, you want a cigarette?" he asked Titchell. "We might as well be friends since we're gonna have to spend the afternoon together."

Emil left the cellblock, closing the door behind him.

"Sheriff, you wanted some information on a Paul Barnes?" said Farley. "I think I got it."

"Shoot."

"Barnes has been out of town for two weeks, on an archeological dig in Arizona. I talked to his wife. Said her name was Sandy. She was a little reluctant to talk, but she said, yes, Dale Torbert stayed with her over the weekend."

"That might mean . . ."

"Think Torbert might've been playing around? Mrs. Barnes did seem very uncomfortable over the phone."

"Well, that's her problem. It means Torbert's got a good alibi, though." Emil recalled that Charlie Hollman had cast some aspersions regarding Professor Dale Torbert's moral character. Maybe Charlie was actually right.

Emil walked into his office, sat down behind his desk, and put his boots up. He helped himself to a chaw and tried to figure out where to go from here. Pflüger didn't kill anybody, he thought. Torbert might've been in bed with Mrs. Sandy Barnes all weekend. In any case, his whereabouts are covered. Tony Wiggins, the weightlifter, was in the computer room at the library. That leaves the three football players, each of whom had been involved in that seminar argument with Alicia. And Dee-Dee.

Who'd told him that she hadn't really cared for Alicia Stanhope all that much.

"Hey, Emil," Axel boomed, sticking his head around the doorjamb, "Roy Riley's here. He wants to know if you have any comments for tomorrow's edition of the *Trib*."

"Comments about what?"

"He says anything will do. Pflüger. The murder. Those three jocks. Bunny Hollman's visions."

Emil spat into the cuspidor next to his chair. "Tell him no."

"Oh, come on, Sheriff," said Riley himself, appearing behind Axel's bull-like shoulder. "What's going on? Did you talk to those jocks yet? How come Pflüger's under arrest?"

"Okay, Roy, here's your interview. I'm not sure what's going on. Yes, I talked to Rollins, Rutkow, and Duffy. And Pflüger's in here on a theft charge."

Axel herded the protesting reporter away. Whippletree had just concluded that he'd better set up detailed interviews with the three footballers when Farley appeared in the office doorway.

"Sheriff, there's an awful big car just pulled up out front."

Emil shot a bull's-eye into the spittoon, got up, and ambled over to the window. A long black Mercedes was parked at curbside in front of the jail and a blue-uniformed chauffeur was hustling around to the back door. A moment later, two figures emerged from the cushioned luxuriousness within. One of them, a tall, elegant woman in a splendid peach-colored dress, staggered a bit. She was steadied by her companion, a lean, iron-haired man wearing a suit that couldn't have cost much more than the sheriff's monthly wage.

Emil met the Stanhopes at the door and showed them into his office. He'd placed his two best straight-backed chairs out in front of his desk, and the bereaved parents took seats. Mrs. Stanhope's eyes were dry, but her face seemed on the verge of cracking into a hundred pieces. She stared at Emil's cuspidor, her expression revealing sudden horror when she realized what it was. He wished he'd had the forethought to slide it into the closet.

Robert Bruce Stanhope was looking at the sheriff with undisguised disappointment, and Emil knew exactly what the man was thinking: *This old country hayseed will never be able to find my daughter's killer.*

"We are calling on you, Sheriff Whippletree," he began, in crisp, lawyerly tones, "to apprise ourselves of the direction and progress of your investigation to date."

"I've made a solemn promise to see justice done, sir, I can tell you that. You can count on it."

Stanhope seemed unconvinced. "Have you ever had a case like this before?"

Emil felt more hurt than offended. The guy had lost a daughter—Emil knew *that* pain only too well—but even under the circumstances, he figured he had a right to some confidence.

"I've had a couple of homicides, yes," he said. "Took me a little while, but I got them solved."

Stanhope was unencouraged. "And what have you done so far?"

"Well, I've been interviewing the people who saw your daughter last."

"I'm afraid that's not good enough," came the man's response, as his wife nodded sadly. "Now, I'll tell you what to do. Obviously, the animal who did this was strong enough to carry Alicia from the dormitory and into that ravine by the river. She would never have gone to a place like that on her own. She had *not* signed out and she would *never* have left campus without so doing. Furthermore, that *bastard* . . ."

Mrs. Stanhope sighed.

". . . might have been a member of the football team. I know for a fact, because my daughter told me, that she was recently the object of unwanted attentions from a certain Lemuel Duffy. Now, my daughter was intellectually refined, she's had the best of everything, and Professor Hollman has assured me that she would have had nothing to do with a mere athlete. I suspect Duffy resented this, and acted according to the impulses of his nature. Why hasn't he been arrested, might I ask?"

Emil held up his hands. The Stanhopes, like many who are victims of great and complicated tragedies, had already devised a perfect explanation, complete with villain.

"I'm sorry, but I haven't got enough evidence yet to—"

"Then *get* some," snapped Stanhope, leaning forward in his chair. "Get some, or I'll want to know the reason why."

Emil's temper flared, but he held it in check.

"And if North Star tries to cover this up, just because there may be football players involved—" Stanhope continued.

"Wait!" said Emil. "Hold on a minute. Where'd you come up with that?"

"Professor Hollman suggested that it is a possibility," said Mrs. Stanhope, trying to keep her eyes away from the cuspidor. Emil felt a need to spit, too.

"I've spoken to President Anderson several times," he said, "and I can assure you that nothing could be further from the truth. The university is going to help in every way it can."

"Well, we'll be watching this *very* carefully," Stanhope said. "I can hire investigators of my own, if need be."

"I'm sure you can. But please give me a chance. I know my county. I'll get to the bottom of it."

"I hope so," said Mrs. Stanhope, without much conviction.

Stanhope rose. "We'll be leaving now, Sheriff. I've arranged for a hearse to pick up . . . Alicia . . . at the morgue. We'll be going home to Edina, but I'll be in close touch."

The sheriff stood too. He forced himself to swallow some tobacco juice, and it didn't go down any too smoothly. "If I could make a suggestion . . . ?" he began.

"I'll listen to anything," replied the other man.

"President Anderson told me he'd offered to hold the funeral in the university church. Can I ask you to go along with that?"

"What?" asked the woman.

"Sheriff, my daughter was *killed* on that campus," Mr. Stanhope protested, with barely concealed outrage. "Surely you can understand how we feel?"

"But I think it might help to smoke out the killer."

"Sheriff, do you have any reason for saying this?"

"No. I don't. But isn't it worth a try? There are a lot of wild emotions in a case like this."

"And you think the killer will attend the funeral and give us some kind of a sign?" Stanhope looked disgusted. "That kind of thinking is as old as the hills. If I were a killer, I'd make it a point *not* to attend."

"So we'll also see which of my tentative suspects doesn't show up."

Stanhope thought it over. He and his wife exchanged a long glance.

"I'll take care of all the arrangements," Emil offered.

The man slumped back down into his chair, all the hard self-certainty suddenly gone. "All right, Sheriff," he managed, "we'll find the strength to bear it somehow."


Parents are protected by what they don't know, thought Emil, watching from his office window as Mr. and Mrs. Stanhope walked back toward their limousine.

Roy Riley approached Mr. Stanhope and asked a couple of questions. Whippletree saw the bereaved father gesturing energetically, perhaps angrily, before getting inside the car.

There was a lull in the office after that. Emil was suddenly hungry as hell, so he sent a more-than-willing Axel out for burgers, fries, shakes, and coffee from The Restaurant on Germain. Almost every town in the Middle West had a Main Street. Except St. Cloud. Here it was St. Germain. That was class.

Axel brought back the eats and everybody chowed down. Pete Poll turned on the TV. The football game in Minneapolis was well along.

"It's Vikings fourteen, Denver thirteen," shrieked the announcer, "with two minutes to go."

Emil, who'd been slouching in a chair and sipping coffee, sat up straight. "What'd he say?"

"Looks like we'll finally get one," observed Axel. "How much you gonna win today, Sheriff?"

But Emil wasn't even thinking about money. Bunny's prediction was on his mind. The Vikings had the ball and they were playing it safe, the quarterback taking the snap, falling on the pigskin, running out the clock.

First down. A minute and twenty to go.

Second down. Fifty seconds. Fans were pouring out of the stadium already.

Third down. And the place erupted in cacophony and chaos.

101

Somehow, the center's snap got away, squirted through the quarterback's fingers. Emil leaned toward the screen, saw the football bounce once, crazily, and veer into the outstretched arms of a Bronco lineman. The player stood there for a split second, too surprised even to realize what had happened—he was not alone—then he plunged forward through a gaggle of baffled Vikings, running like a madman. Nobody laid a finger on him.

TD Denver.

"Too bad," said Axel Vogel. "Try again next week, hey, Emil."

"Why don't you quit betting for awhile, Emil?" said Farley. "I think you're jinxin' the Vikes."

The sheriff didn't say anything. He didn't have any words. How could Bunny Hollman have come so close? Again? How could she have come so close if she didn't have some sort of pipeline to Something or Someone Somewhere?

Hell, maybe she did.

"Emil!" cried Sarah excitedly, when he arrived home for dinner, "you'll never guess what happened."

"I guess not. So tell me."

"The news is all over. Mavis Tuckerman rushed home from campus after hearing what Bunny'd said about those diamond earrings."

Emil helped himself to a Cold Spring beer from the fridge. "Yep?"

"She went right to the cedar chest by the bay window. It did have a false bottom. She'd never known. And in it were the earrings her sister, Hilda, had promised her years ago. Hilda's been dead for almost two years, too. Isn't that amazing? Isn't that *wonderful?*"

Emil swallowed, burped, scowled.

"Well, isn't it?" Sarah demanded.

"It sure is for Mavis. I expect diamond earrings don't come cheap these days."

"Oh, Emil! I'm so excited. This means—"

"If you think Bunny is in contact with heaven, I wouldn't bet money on it."

Sarah almost got angry. "Oh, Emil! Sometimes you just have to accept what's right in front of your eyes. You have to believe!"

"And here I thought you were an old Stearns County girl, didn't go off head over teakettle about shenanigans like this."

Sarah hesitated, giving him a long, serious look. Her voice, when it came, was very soft. "I've been thinking of asking Bunny about Susan."

Now it was Emil's turn to pause. "Oh, honey, don't torture yourself"—he meant don't torture *us* —"by opening that up."

"*. . . I already told the man the story, Daddy, but he says he's just pretending . . .*"

*. . . and she had not seemed afraid . . .*

*. . . where the twin silver rails ended in a wilderness of life and time . . .*

"The church teaches that we live forever," Sarah told him. "Who is to say that Bunny Hollman is not an intermediary between us and heaven? Don't the earrings prove it? Sometimes a person has to accept the truth, especially when the evidence is overwhelming."

"Only overwhelming evidence I want is the kind that'll find and convict a killer," Emil replied, heading for his favorite living-room chair to drink his beer and skim the Sunday paper.

They had turkey pot pies and cole slaw for dinner. Doc Divot called to say, yes, the scrap of blue fabric was the same material that had been found beneath Alicia Stanhope's left-hand fingernails.

"Pflüger agree to a blood test yet?" he asked.

"Nope," said Emil. "I'll talk to his lawyer in the morning. Tricky Ricky Stein has got to be smarter than Cowboy John."

He was just about to dial the university in order to tell President Anderson that he'd persuaded the Stanhopes to hold the funeral Mass there, when Vice-President Dexter called.

"Hello," said Emil, giving him what he thought was welcome news. Dexter acknowledged it, but went on to something else about which he was considerably wrought.

"Sheriff, did you speak with Mr. Roy Riley?" Dexter demanded.

"Sure did. Something wrong?"

"It certainly is. I heard on TV a few moments ago—and Mr. Riley assures me I shall read the same in tomorrow's newspapers—that you have questioned Rollins, Rutkow, and Duffy about the . . . the incident."

"Well, I did."

"But the story sounds as if they are prime suspects. Sheriff, do you know—do you really *know*—how damaging this is going to be to the university? President Anderson is furious. Now we must deal with this, placate Coach Avano, handle the crowds Mrs. Hollman is attracting, *and* treat the very serious charges that Professor Torbert has leveled. Sheriff, is it possible for you to clear your activities with the university from here on out?"

"Clear *my* activities with . . . ? Wait a second, here. Let me speak to President Anderson, please."

"I'm afraid that won't be possible. He's had to fly to Washington, D.C. He's testifying this week before an educational subcommittee in Congress. But he'll be in constant touch with me."

"So will I," said Emil, "so will I. Looks like you have a little on-the-job training coming up."

"And I welcome it," Dexter said.

News that three nationally known football stars from famous North Star University had been questioned in connection with the perverse abuse, rape, and murder of a beautiful young woman made headlines across the country. President Anderson, arriving at the Capitol on Monday morning for crucial hearings on educational funding, smiled into a thicket of hand-held microphones and said, "Now, fellows, you go back and check your facts. When the complete truth is made know, as I have every confidence it shall be, we will see these baseless rumors laid to rest."

Coach Avano phoned Emil before the sheriff had even gotten

out of bed. "I just want to let you know where I stand," he told Whippletree, fairly calmly, considering. "The harm you've done to my boys is incalculable. They are off-limits to you from now on, and the university is backing me up."

Emil was still half-asleep—Sarah, beside him in bed, was barely stirring—but he was waking up fast.

"The university?" he yawned, running a hand through his tangled salt-and-pepper hair. "You mean Vice-President Dexter?"

"No, I mean Rector Rex," said the Coach. "You may have made an honest mistake in blabbing to that reporter, but you ought to have known better. I've got big games coming up, and the university depends on me and my boys. Be careful from now on. People believe North Star is something special, and that makes us more than we are."

"Now, look—" began Emil, in an attempt to tell the angry coach that he *had* to talk to the players again. The piece of fabric that Axel had found demanded continued investigation. But Avano had already hung up.

"Whew!" said Emil, sitting up and putting his feet on the floor.

"What was that?" Sarah asked, slipping a robe over her nightgown.

"Bad news, I think."

He was eating his usual breakfast of porridge with honey, unbuttered wheat toast, and coffee, when he heard the thwack of the St. Cloud *Tribune* on the front porch. Sarah went out to get it, scanned the headlines, and handed it to him with a stricken look.

"If Coach was upset before," she said, "wait'll he gets a look at this."

GABRIEL'S GUARDS ARRIVE IN COUNTY
*Canadian Group Devoted to Virgin*
by Roy Riley

A group of religious pilgrims from the province of Quebec, in eastern Canada, arrived in Stearns County Sunday evening. They came in a caravan of buses, cars, and vans, came in a caravan of buses, cars, and vans, driving nonstop across Canada and south into Minnesota after hearing radio stories that a St. Cloud woman, Mrs. Bunny Hollman, was reported to have seen the Virgin Mary in a vision.

The Guards, 120 in number, take their name from the Archangel Gabriel, and have sworn eternal devotion to the Mother of God. They dress in quasi-military fashion, brown uniforms and brown berets, and claim to have received a Papal Charter of Organization from the late Pope Pius XII in 1950. The Guards have set up camp on the golf course at North Star University. Their leader, Jacques LaBatt, interviewed briefly outside the home of Dr. and Mrs. Hollman last night, said he had brought his men here "to protect Bunny Hollman from mockers and unbelievers, to guard the holy place at which our Blessed Mother has appeared, and to serve notice on a sinful world that there are men still willing to crusade for Faith.

Emil recalled Father Anderson telling him that a group of pilgrims had contributed to disruption at the site of another vision in New York ten years earlier. How lucky can I get? he thought.

Riley went on to report that Jacques LaBatt, who claimed to be a former seminarian and was now a used-car salesman in Quebec City, seemed "particularly strong-willed" and "disinclined to discuss his motivations or intentions with this reporter."

Uh-oh, thought Whippletree. He knew Riley pretty well, had been round and round with the reporter about the countless petty crises and scandals that colored local politics, and he realized that Riley was attempting to tell everybody: *LaBatt is trouble!*

Conflict was also portended by Charlie Hollman's letter to the *Trib*, which was black-bordered on page one.

Dear Sir:

*Of the many lessons that History teaches, perhaps the most important is this: Those too blind to perceive opportunity cannot seize it and win the day. Understanding that we work God's will on this earth, we are nonetheless painfully aware of reading His will "through a glass darkly." And that is why, at rare times in our passage to eternal union with Him, He sends signs so clear that even a tiny child could grasp them. To wit: the blessed experiences currently gifted to my beloved wife.*

*May I be frank? North Star University stands at a momentous crossroads. Will it turn down the pathway of hedonism and liberality, of escapism and frivolity, where all notions are countenanced but none are revered? Or will it renounce, once and for all, the siren songs of popularism and popularity, and take up the banner of the One Eternal Truth in which cause it was (I certainly remember and surely you recall) founded?*

*In the appearance of Our Lord's Mother, we have our answer and our sign. Now is the time for all of us who love the University, who believe and practice age-old Truth, to stand up for what is right.*

> Charles Z. Hollman, Ph.D.
> Chairman
> Department of History

"What does all this mean?" asked Sarah, reading the paper while Emil finished his breakfast. "We don't need outsiders to protect Bunny. And Charlie writes as if there's a war coming."

"Father Anderson picked the wrong time to go out of town," Emil said.

"I'm sure he had to go."

"Well, hope he hustles back. North Star is goin' to need somebody strong at the helm. Dexter has too much ambition and not enough experience, which is a danger right there, and I haven't come close to figuring out Butch Lodge yet, except that he wouldn't mind wearing this badge." He patted the big old star pinned to his left breast pocket.

"No," said Sarah, "they'll retire that badge when you're through."

When I'm through," he mused. "Yep. The last of the Whippletrees."

Emil left the house and climbed into his car, intending to drive directly to the office. But, on impulse, he turned north instead of south, and cut up Eighth Avenue. Scatterings of tinted leaves lay lightly upon wide old sidewalks and deep thick lawns. Children, schoolbound, swung their new September lunch boxes, walking slowly now that summer was over. A woman stood in the doorway of a green clapboard house, looking down the street. She was young, very pretty. Her face showed a mingling of pride and worry. Just sent a young child off to school, Emil guessed. First grade, probably. Adults thought that sending kids off like this, year after year, prepared the children for the final leave-taking at maturity. But that wasn't it at all. Parents just fooled themselves. All the little departures, day after day, year after year, made an adult's pain less (just a tiny bit less) on the day that last leave-taking came.

A young man appeared behind the woman. He put his arm around her waist. She pressed her head against his shoulder. They stepped inside the house and closed the door. Emil drove to the corner, turned right, and slowed down as he approached the Hollmans' yellow-shingled Cape Cod. Charlie's Datsun was in the driveway. A string of cars was parked along the curb. Every car had a Quebec license plate.

The Hollmans' lot was narrow and their house small. However large North Star's conception of mankind's origin and destiny, salaries paid to professors encouraged the alleged virtue of self-denial. The paint on Charlie's house was peeling and cinch-bugs ruled his unkept lawn. Professor Hollman believed that he represented the ideal of North Star. But, in comparison to his paltry eighteen thousand, Coach Avano hauled in upwards of a hundred grand (if not more), promo deals and assorted tie-ins not included. Yet the university remained in the black only because of Coach and the boys, which meant that Charlie could count on the pittance supporting his genteel poverty.

Emil spotted the two men as he swung in behind the Datsun and slipped the gearshift into park. They seemed to rise out of watchful crouches on either side of Charlie's front steps. Gabriel's Guards. They came up off their haunches like angry young lions at the sight of his car, but a glimpse of his badge when Emil stepped out of the Ford had the effect of a trainer's whip. They did not shrink back but their eyes showed grudging caution.

"Howdy, boys," said Emil, walking across the small patch of ratty grass toward the front door. "Bunny home this mornin'?"

One of the men touched his brown beret, almost a parody of a salute. A small plastic cross was pinned to the headpiece, like a badge of rank. "*Bonjour*," he said. "What reason you come?"

"I'm the one could be asking *that* question." Emil grinned, slouching up the steps and ringing the bell. The men watched suspiciously, eyeing the .38 at his hip.

Bunny herself opened the door. Her face showed its usual blend of tension and obscure worry, and in her eyes Whippletree saw signs of a bewilderment that was much like fear. "Emil!" she exclaimed, happy to see him. She opened the door quickly, glancing fretfully at the Gabriel's Guards on the front step. Emil entered the little house.

"Think maybe we might chat a moment?" he asked.

Before she could respond, Charlie came over. "We really don't have much time today, I'm afraid."

"It won't take long, Professor."

"Come in, Emil," said Bunny. There was a note of pleading in her voice. She wanted him there.

Charlie glared at his wife. Bunny led Emil into the living room, cluttered with bric-a-brac, a tired old sofa, and several overstuffed, mismatched chairs. The Salvation Army was no stranger here.

109

The stranger sat in one of the chairs. He wore a Guards uniform, belted tightly at the waist, which enhanced a sleek, Whippetlike leanness. Black hair was slicked back with oil, making it appear as if he were wearing a leather helmet. His face was narrow and tanned, not unattractive, but his black eyes were unsettling beneath bushy brows. Emil knew he'd seen identical eyes somewhere before but, memory searching, he couldn't recall exactly where, or to whom they had belonged.

"Sheriff," intoned Professor Hollman, "I'd like you to meet Mr. Jacques LaBatt. Mr. LaBatt, this is Emil Whippletree."

Bunny stood anxiously to the side as the two men met. Emil surmised that LaBatt's presence troubled her. Hell, it troubled *him*! Shaking the man's long, strong hand—LaBatt chose not to rise for the encounter—Emil looked closely into those onyx-hard eyes. They permitted no entry into LaBatt's soul, but projected an implacable, unyielding mercilessness. Emil thought of the shotgun-wielding maniac in the alley behind the Hannorhed Bank. But, no, he had not seen that man's eyes. Someone else . . .

"It is a pleasure to make your acquaintance, Sheriff," said LaBatt in accented English. *"Eet ees a ples-your . . ."*

Quite obviously, he did not think it was that, nor did Emil. Riley was right, this guy is trouble, he thought. Nobody invited him to sit down, although he had the feeling that Bunny wanted him to stay a bit. So he flopped down onto the sofa. "Got a cup of coffee handy, Bunny?" he asked casually, and, as if he didn't know, "What brings you to these parts, Jacques?"

LaBatt's frightening eyes flickered darkly. "Worship," he said.

Mrs. Hollman had scurried out into the kitchen. Charlie checked to make sure she was gone, lowered his voice, and said, "Mr. LaBatt and his men have come from Quebec to pay homage to the Virgin."

LaBatt nodded.

"That's nice," said Emil. "Where you planning to stay?"

The Guards' leader did not like questions. "We have erected our tents on the university campus," he explained, too slowly and too politely.

"That's okay with North Star?"

"No one has said a thing in protest."

Emil shrugged. "How long you planning to stay?"

LaBatt smiled for the first time. It was not a pleasant thing to see. His mouth tightened horizontally. There was a glimpse of strong-looking but yellowish and pointed teeth. "As long as is required," he said.

"The Gabriel's Guards are devoted to the ideal of our Holy Mother," Charlie pointed out. "They journey around the world on pilgrimages to places associated with Our Lady."

"I think (*I theenk*) there is no law against such a thing in your county?" said LaBatt.

"Not a'tall, not a'tall."

Bunny brought in a cup of coffee, chock full of cream and sugar. Emil always took it black, but sipped without complaint, keeping his eyes on LaBatt, who stared back with that peculiar gaze Emil could not place. The Guard had an ascetic's face and body, but there was a hint of violent hunger in his eyes, of total dedication.

"Read in the paper that you studied for the priesthood," Emil said.

LaBatt stiffened. "That is correct."

"Weren't cut out for it? Or vice-versa?"

The man flared. "I do not discuss personal matters."

"Sorry. Just curious."

"I left the seminary to marry," LaBatt offered, apparently realizing that Emil was drawing suspicious conclusions about him.

"Wife come here with you?"

"The Guards are all male, Emil," Charlie pointed out, quite pleased with the fact, too.

"Must sell a lot of used cars, being able to finance big trips and all," suggested Emil, setting his cup down on the coffee table.

Flashpoint. LaBatt jumped to his feet and stood over Emil. "I am a guest in this house, am I not?" he cried, looking toward Charlie for corroboration. "I have come here to offer my services

111

in a holy cause. I intend only what is right, and I think I need not bear these snide insinuations—"

"Hey, hold on," said Emil, getting to his feet and facing the man. I think I could take this guy if I had to, he figured, but it'd be close. "Wait a minute. I was just asking some courteous questions. We're downright hospitable here in Stearns."

Bunny looked stricken. Trouble was the last thing she wanted in life. Whippletree didn't want it either, but he'd taken his reading of this Guard, and he did not like what he'd seen at all. "Guess I'll be seeing you all out at campus," he said, heading toward the door. "Thanks for the coffee, Bunny."

LaBatt and Professor Hollman stayed where they were, but Bunny hurried after him.

"Everything all right with you?" he murmured, as they stood for a moment in the doorway.

She hesitated. "Yes, I think so."

The two Guards out front were watching carefully.

"Anything you want to talk about?"

She shook her head and smiled weakly.

"All right. But you know where to find a friend if you need one."

He listened to the news on the radio as he drove south toward the office. More trouble between Iraq and Iran. And Emil knew where he'd seen LaBatt's eyes before. In pictures of Ayatollah Khomeini.

Going to be one hell of a day. Deputies Poll and Vogel were standing around, slurping coffee. Alyce, already frazzled, was handling the phones.

"Sheriff," she groaned, looking up as he came in. "All kinds of people are calling to ask if you've solved the murder yet."

"You can tell 'em no."

"And Judge Titchell wants you to call him back right away. He's over in his chambers at the courthouse."

"He didn't put up bail for his kid?"

"No, he says he's got to talk to you. Something about a special arrangement."

"Huh! Doesn't that sound just like him? Let's wait until he calls again."

"Think that's wise, Emil?" Vogel opined.

"Junior have breakfast yet?"

"Sure, Sheriff."

"Then he's already cost the county for this morning, hasn't he? We can bunk him 'til noon at no charge."

"Well," said Alyce, reaching for another ringing phone, "you certainly got up on the wrong side of the bed, didn't you?"

This was not a call about the Stanhope case, because Alyce started jabbering to somebody about a bridal shower that had apparently taken place over the weekend. Emil kept remonstrating about the inadvisability of personal calls during business hours, without success. In a small town like St. Cloud, where everybody was into everybody else's business, there was probably very little information that could be considered personal.

"Oh, Sheriff," said Pete Poll huskily, looking as if he'd had a couple of shots already, "Pflüger's lawyer is waiting in your office. We didn't think you'd mind."

"Nope," said Emil. "Nothin' in there that even a lawyer would want to steal."

"Well, good mornin' there, Ricky," he greeted Apple Valley's leading—and only—attorney. "Looks like your most devoted client has gone and done it this time."

Stein, who'd been standing over by the windows and looking at the courthouse—probably wondering whether he should make his bid for elective office before or after he went broke in the practice of law—turned to give Emil a beaming, confident smile. He always wore a three-piece suit with a silk handkerchief in the breast pocket, an affectation considered to be a sure sign of pederastic tendencies by half the population in Stearns County. He'd earned his degree at night school in The Cities and had won the nickname "Tricky" by a talent for complicating his clients' cases until even he couldn't figure out what was going on.

"Emil," he said expansively, "Mr. Pflüger has agreed to take that blood test you asked for."

"He has?" Emil sat down behind his desk, leaned back in the

113

swivel chair, and put a chaw between cheek and gum. "Wha
brought about that sudden change of heart?"

Stein pulled up a straight-backed chair and straddled it cav
alierly. "Look," he said, winking, "can we deal?"

"Don't know that you've got much to deal with, but I'm listening."

"Great. See, Emil, it's this way. It's to your advantage, too.
arrange with Judge Titchell to get Johnny's arraignment post-
poned. This gives you time to get the blood test run. You can'
charge him with the murder anyway."

"I wasn't going to, but why can't I?"

"Because he and Byron Tillman were robbing Norb Heffner'
gas station at the time of the homicide. They vouch for each othe
on it. Meantime, we get Norb to drop charges against both o
them in return for restitution of the appropriated property."

"You mean the stolen property, don't you?"

"Well, I wouldn't put it in exactly those words."

"Why in hell would Norb want to go along with your . . .
plan?" He'd almost said "scheme."

"Because why would he want to have to drive in to St. Cloud,
maybe a dozen times, just to lock up Pflüger for a couple o
months? You know how trials drag on."

"You've spoken to Norb about this?"

Stein grinned. "I hoped you'd do that."

"Me? Why?"

Stein ducked his head sympathetically. An old duffer like Emil
just had a hard time keeping up with shrewd legal reasoning.
"Because that's what you do for us, in return for our agreeing on
the blood test. You want it as soon as possible, right? To eliminate
a murder suspect? As I said, Sheriff, it's all to your advantage. No
benefit to you, is there, in putting Johnny in the reformatory?"

Emil thought it over. "Well, I guess you're right. If I want tha
particular satisfaction, he's sure to provide me with future oppor-
tunities. Okay, you talk to Titchell about the arraignment and see
Poll out in the office for the blood test. Alyce," he yelled, "get me
Norb Heffner on the phone, will you?"

Old Norb, with whom Emil had shared a marginally profitable moonshine business back in the early forties, had to be one of the most luckless men in Stearns County. When it had become clear that I-94, the big new superhighway, was going through, Heffner had started buying up land. His big dream was to build a gas station at one of the exits, and say good-bye forever to the little one-pump shack in Avon from which he wrested a mean life. He worked hard, even paid bribe money, for secret information from the Highway Department. They told him exactly where the exit was going to be. He bought land right there. Then they told him that the exit location had been changed. He bought more land. In the end, he owned five hundred acres of practically useless land, not one square foot of which was less than a mile from the exit that was actually constructed.

"Norb's on the line now," Alyce called.

"Hey, Norb! How you doin'?"

"I hear you caught that asshole, Pflüger. Good goin'."

"That's what I'm callin' about." Emil explained Stein's proposed deal, along with the alleged advantages all around. Norb saw the point. He would be more than happy to get his tires and oil back and call it quits.

"You know anybody wants to make use of some prime real estate?" he asked before hanging up. "Any purpose. Any price."

"I'll keep my ears open," Emil promised.

"Associated Press on the wire," Alyce yelled.

Big stuff. Emil groaned, cleared his throat, and picked up the phone. "Hello?"

"Sheriff Emil L. Whippletree?" The L. was for Lawrence. The voice was familiar.

"Riley?"

The *Trib* reporter laughed. "Just getting you in practice for the big leagues, Emil. Your name was mentioned in *The Washington Post* this morning."

"You're kidding?"

"Nope. Rector Rex told reporters in D.C. that the murder was going to be solved very soon. He said you'd promised to get it wrapped up quick."

"I said I'd solve it. I didn't say fast."

Emil did not like what he was hearing. Anderson was putting a lot of unnecessary pressure on him, and the North Star chief was not one to speak or act without calculation.

"How *are* you doing?" Riley pressed. "What about Cowboy John?"

"He's agreed to take the blood test. Call back later."

"The football players? That's what Anderson is worried about. It's big news, and not good for the university."

"I can't help that." He did not tell Riley that he planned to search the players' rooms, seeking to find a garment from which that scrap of blue fabric had come.

"Meet Mr. LaBatt yet?" Riley wanted to know.

"Guy's a nutso, if you ask me."

Riley hesitated, then said, "Emil, I'll give you some information that might help you, if you promise to keep me clued on developments."

"Info about what?"

"About LaBatt. I did some checking."

"What'd you find out?" Emil asked.

"LaBatt was charged with murder. In Quebec last year. He was supposed to have killed his wife, Michele. It was a strange sort of rape-homicide. Very quirky. The perpetrator left a crucifix jammed up her—"

"I get the picture. But LaBatt got off?"

"Couldn't touch him. She was killed in their mansion, but there wasn't a print or a clue, and some of his Guards swore he'd been on a prayer retreat with them at the time."

"Did you say 'mansion'? I thought the guy was a used-car peddler?"

"That's true, but misleading. It was the only job he ever held . . . for about three months, just after he left the seminary. Automobile dealerships are one of the family sidelines. They're flush, the LaBatts. Jacques forsook fortune, though, and entered St. Anselm's, a big religious place up there."

"But they booted him out?"

"No. He left. Apparently he thought the seminary was corrupt, their brand of religion impure. He's a fanatic, Emil."

"Do tell. So he got married?"

"Legally, if not physically. The woman had instituted divorce proceedings just before she was killed. On the grounds that certain things she had expected were not forthcoming in the relationship. Or shall I say upcoming?"

"I get you," said Emil. He was wondering if, somehow, Jacques LaBatt could have been in Stearns County, on the North Star campus, late Friday night.

"You getting any help from North Star?" Riley inquired.

"Not enough," said Emil, hanging up.

Alyce was standing in the doorway. "Sheriff, while you were talking to Riley, Judge Titchell called. He wants to see you over in his chambers."

"He does, does he? Well, I don't feel like walking all the way across the street and climbing the courthouse steps. Get him on the phone."

"This is Brewster Titchell."

"Mornin', Judge."

Titchell's voice, as always, was thin and precise, with just a faint bit of resonance lent by the echo chamber of his big nose. "Emil, come on over and have a cup of coffee with me."

"I'm really pretty busy this morning. Have to leave in a little while for the funeral out on campus."

"Tragic thing." Titchell paused, then decided to plunge ahead. "Emil, exactly what did my boy do to get you all wrought up like this?"

Emil told him.

"Hell, he's just an excitable kid. And he's very close to the Hollmans. He got carried away, is all. Whyn't we just expunge the record of his arrest and let him go? It'll never happen again."

The dogmatic old judge, who'd thrown the book at poor retarded wino Paulie Meyer for pissing behind a tree in Hester Park, who'd jailed Delbert Ebenscheider for (probably mistakenly) sell-

117

ing a retread as a new tire, wanted Emil to alter the records of his office? The sheriff was offended, and he said so.

"Emil, you've got me all wrong. I'm just talking as a father now. Maybe you don't know how that feels, but . . ."

"I know how it feels, all right."

". . . but think of the kid's permanent record. He wants to go on to law school, you know. Follow in the footsteps, and all. An arrest on his record! Think of it. Emil, I'm pleading. Isn't there anything you can do?"

The sheriff felt himself softening. "Judge, I can let him go, but I can't change the record."

"Oh, dammit, Emil! You ought to be out hunting up that killer, not harassing a fine young man."

"Look, Brewster," Emil said. "Could you give me a couple of hours on this? I'm sure I could find my way clear to work something out."

The judge sighed. His only-begotten son left to languish for yet a longer spell in the clink. "All right. I'll take you at your word. I've got to run anyway. That jerk from Apple Valley is waiting in my courtroom. But just one thing on another matter. You know North Star?"

"Of course I do."

"I know that. But I'm referring to the Stanhope deal. Try and make sure the university doesn't suffer, okay? I'm on the board of trustees, you know, and Rector Rex called me just before he left for D.C. He asked me to talk to you about this. North Star means an awful lot to a lot of people, and it won't do anyone any good to drag its name in the mud. You catch my drift?"

"Gotcha," Emil said, wondering how many other VIPs Anderson had called.

All four deputies were in the Day Room when Emil stalked out of his office, bound for North Star. They were staring at some news show on the TV.

"Poll," said the sheriff, "you come along with me." Leaving the alcoholic deputy in the office too often left him near the constant

118

temptation of the Courthouse Bar and Grill across the way. "Axel, you too. Farley, you drive out to Holdingford and get a statement from that guy whose combine was stolen. Gosch, you stay here and keep an eye on our prize guests back there in the cellblock."

The men nodded and started shuffling around. Gosch reached to turn off the TV.

"Hold it a minute," Emil said. The screen showed an ornate, imposing, and somehow familiar chamber, jammed with well-dressed men and women. As the camera panned the vast room, Emil recognized, from the televised Watergate deliberations, among others, the U.S. Senate Hearing Room. At a long table in front of the room sat a number of politicians, some of whom Emil knew by sight, and facing them across a small distance, himself seated behind a thick, polished table, was President Rexford Anderson. Greetings were exchanged between the senators and their serene, impressive witness. Anderson requested permission to commence the proceedings with a prepared statement. Approval was granted in a courtly, orotund and rather obsequious manner by some Southern pol who appeared to be head honcho, and President Anderson began.

"Mr. Chairman, members of this committee, distinguished guests, ladies and gentlemen . . ." He began brilliantly to summarize the purposes of education in a free society, and the particular financial needs of private universities struggling to survive in a nation sworn to separation of church and state. Anderson played with American beliefs like a fine musician plays his instrument. He used his eloquence to bring plausibility, if not credibility, to everything he said. Emil was almost certain he heard Rector Rex declare that the U.S. Constitution dealt unfairly with North Star, but the president executed the verbal equivalent of sleight-of-hand, finessed, and returned to higher ground. "We seek," he concluded, "an educational institution in which full freedom of inquiry prevails, in which the truths of our fathers are held sacred, and in which young people contribute to the community through the utilization of their physical abilities. . . ."

Emil was somewhat awed. In one fell swoop, Anderson had

119

managed to incorporate the main beliefs of, respectively, Professor Dale Torbert, Dr. Charlie Hollman, and Coach Snopes Avano. But, if he were forced to choose, on which of those beliefs would Anderson himself hang his hat?

Butch Lodge flagged down Emil's car as the sheriff and his deputies drove onto campus.

"Mornin', Emil. What's the good word?"

"Ask me later when the funeral's over. It won't be easy. How about yourself?"

"No complaints yet. These Canadian guys are a little spooky, but they've been pretty helpful so far."

Whippletree took a look. There was a good-sized crowd of worshippers, several hundred at least, kneeling in prayer on the golf course. They formed a well-ordered semicircle around the pine tree. Gabriel's Guards, in uniform, were busy making sure that arriving cars parked off the roadway, and more of them stood, like sentinels, along the borders of the growing crowd.

"They set up tents in the woods on the other side of the golf course," Butch explained. "Dug latrines and everything, just like in the army. What do you make of that?"

"Well, I don't know. You meet LaBatt?"

"Nope."

"You will soon enough. Got the murder case solved yet?"

Butch leaned into the car and spoke softly. "If Pflüger didn't do it," he said, "I'd spend more time on Torbert. So he says he was down in The Cities over the weekend? So what? He could have killed Alicia before he left. You think of that?"

Mutual admiration society here, Emil thought, recalling Torbert's mention of Butch as a possible suspect. "Check it out, Butch," he said. "Might be something there."

Then they drove to the parking lot behind the Sacred Steeple and got out of the car. The hearse and several limousines were already in front of the church. Students were arriving and entering the church in small, subdued groups to pay last respects to a class-mate. Put me back into the earth on a rainy day, Emil thought. The northern sky, especially in fall, was a rich, dark blue, glorious and compelling. The sun, warm above Minnesota fields and trees, heightened the scents of living things. Emil smelled wheat, corn, old clover and—climbing the granite steps into the university church—a musky whiff of perfume. He'd been thinking that it was not right for anyone to be buried on such a gorgeous day, but that wafting fragrance stilled his melancholy reverie. He stopped abruptly, there on the steps.

"Something wrong, Emil?" Axel Vogel asked.

Emil glanced around as the students climbed past him, sober young men in jackets or sweaters, sad, lovely coeds in dark dresses with scarves or kerchiefs covering their glossy hair. He had smelled, for just an instant, the same scent that had been on the shred of nylon found at the murder site. It was gone now, though.

"No," he said. "Let's go inside."

The campus church looked fairly traditional from the outside, with the steeple, vaulting roof, even a suggestion of buttresses in its superstructure. Modified Prairie Gothic. But the interior was ultra-modern, spacious and glittering, steel and glass. A gigantic cross, thirty feet in height, hung above the high altar. The organ with its hundred pipes, created in Vienna to President Anderson's exacting specifications, played quietly, mournfully, as the lawmen made their way to the front of the church and slipped into a pew behind Mr. and Mrs. Stanhope. She was weeping quietly into a white silk handkerchief. Mr. Stanhope half-turned. Emil shook his hand.

"I hope you get something out of this," he said to Emil. "I'm not sure I can endure it."

"We're on the right track," he replied quietly, thinking of that telltale whiff of perfume.

A little prayer wouldn't hurt either, he thought, so he said one. Alicia Stanhope lay in an open bronze casket upon a flower-encircled catafalque before the altar. Emil wished there were not quite so many blossoms; their fragrance might impede an idea that came to him suddenly. Was the thought an answered prayer? Too soon to tell. He slipped out of the pew, and found Vice-President Dexter in the vestibule. Dexter was to give a brief eulogy on behalf of the university.

"I'd like to ask a favor," said Emil. "When the funeral is over, could everybody file by the casket to pay last respects?"

"Everybody? There's a big crowd out there . . . ah, you have a plan? I see. All right, I guess it's worth a try."

Emil thanked him, and went back to his pew. "Where'd you go?" asked Axel in a husky whisper.

"When the service is over, I want you and Poll to head out to the steps on the double. Keep an eye on people, and see if you can pick out a girl who wears extra heavy perfume."

"*What?*" wondered the big deputy.

"I'll stay up here by the coffin."

Then the funeral began, with the Stanhopes crying quietly, the husband's arm around his wife. Emil could not help but remember another husband, another wife, in the front pew of a little country church, way back there in the spring of 1941. The coffin had been a lot smaller than Alicia Stanhope's, but the suffering was the same, and so was the dream that had died.

March of 1941. Night. He and Sarah slept downstairs, in the big bedroom just off the porch. Upstairs, in a room with a window overlooking the porch and the Mississippi Valley, Susan had her little bed, her toys, her pictures on the wall, and boxes of mysterious treasures that only she could properly evaluate. It had been raining for days, the river had been rising, but that night Emil had come home, dead-tired after days of sandbagging, to hear Sarah say, "I think she's crested. The danger's over."

But while they slept the river rose and kept on rising. Emil awoke to a strange, gurgling sound, juxtaposed against the steady, distant thunder of the river itself. He fumbled for matches to light the kerosene lamp—no electricity until after World War II—and when he failed to find them he sat up and swung his feet over the edge of the bed.

Into water. The house was flooding.

He could not remember if he'd screamed or not, but then Sarah was awake and they had lit the lamp, which cast strange, frightening shadows on the water that was rising in the room.

Upstairs, Susan slept.

Emil had been a strong man then, and Sarah a young woman. They waded through the bedroom and raced upstairs. Susan was asleep, but as they stayed in her room, trying to gauge the progress of the flood, she stirred, rubbed her eyes, and sat up.

"What's the matter, Daddy?"

"Nothing, honey, go back to sleep. We're here and you'll be fine."

But it was not nothing. The water was coming up the stairs now, and a mighty current washed against the sides of the old farmhouse. If it reached the second story, they would have to get out.

But where could they go?

Rain battered against the wooden shingles of the roof. The ebb and sob of the throbbing wind drove into the house. And the killer river kept on rising. When the water reached the second floor, the three of them dressed and climbed out onto the roof of the porch. And when the water rose still higher, they crawled up onto the steep roof of the house itself, huddling there, listening to the water, bracing against the wind, Emil holding onto Susan . . .

. . . holding onto Susan, when either *she* twisted in his grasp or, overcome by a moment of fatigue, *he* let her go.

. . . and she was sliding down the slippery shingles and into the black, roiling waters of abyss.

In all of the years that had come and gone since, Emil still did not want to face what had happened on that roof, except that his body had betrayed him, betrayed Susan, and his love had not been enough to save her.

Without acceptance, no redemption. Without certainty, no peace.

The church was filled with muffled sobs as Dexter stepped forward to speak.

Emil broke off his doleful reminiscence, and looked discreetly around. He saw Dee-Dee kneeling in a pew across the center aisle, wiping her eyes decorously. Whatever she'd thought of her late roommate, her tears were real enough, her eyes were red. Professor Torbert, a couple of rows behind Emil's niece, leaned forward, his head in his hands. Was he thinking of Alicia? Or of his approaching battle with Charlie Hollman? The Terrible Trio sat together. Gunnar seemed the most affected by the occasion, but Rusty and Lem didn't look too happy either. Emil also saw Roy Riley, over at the far side of the church, trying to make his two hundred pounds look unobtrusive.

"Those who wish to do so," Dexter told the assemblage, "may now file past the casket and pay final respects."

Emil and Mr. Stanhope exchanged a hopeful glance. Poll and Vogel left the pew and headed for the back of the church. Emil got up too, and slid into the front pew beside the Stanhopes. He was about ten feet from the coffin, and everyone in the line now forming down the wide center aisle would file directly past him.

It was slow going, what with all the students, and Mr. Stanhope leaned over to whisper in Emil's ear. "Really, Sheriff, do you think this will do any good? I'm worried about my wife."

"I'm sorry," Emil replied. "There's no way to call it off now."

He sat there, hoping. When Dee-Dee passed him, he reached out and touched her hand. She seemed surprised to see him, an awkward moment that ended when she managed a tiny smile. Torbert, behind her, just nodded. Their moments before the casket were brief.

More people filed past: students, teachers, friends. The sobs were muted, the last glimpses hasty.

Then Emil caught the scent, unmistakable in its muskiness even against the heavy fragrance of funeral flowers. He half-turned in the pew. Several young women were walking past him now, and he was sure that one of them wore the scent. But which one? Was it the dark-eyed, slender girl with a beauty mark on her left cheekbone? Or the cute, petite young lady with hands folded piously beneath her full breasts? Was it the rather formidable redhead, with a sleek, long-limbed body that might belong to a model or an athlete? Or the blonde wearing a white headband, demure in a dress wholly inadequate to its purpose, who sniffled into a handkerchief?

The girls filed past the coffin, followed by Rusty, Gunnar, and Lem. Emil swore to himself. He wanted to get up and follow the four girls out of the church, but he also needed to remain here and check the reactions of the Terrible Trio.

Emil felt Mr. Stanhope stiffen beside him as the football players approached his daughter's coffin. Rusty Rollins stopped for a moment in front of the casket and made the sign of the cross. His red hair, closely shorn, glowed in the sunlight that came through the tall glass windows of the church. Broad shoulders in an inexpensive woolen jacket tapered to lean hips, powerful legs in polyester slacks, perfectly creased like the edges of knives. Rusty moved on. Then Gunnar shuffled up to take a last look at the girl who'd ridiculed him only days earlier. His big, wide face was hot and flushed. He seemed on the verge of tears. Self-consciously, he dropped to his knees in front of the open coffin, rested one huge hand on its edge and—Emil was sure—slipped something next to the body.

Mr. Stanhope nudged him with an elbow. "I think that young man . . . wait, here's Duffy . . ."

Gunnar was back on his feet now, stepping slowly away from the casket, his eyes still on Alicia's face, forever locked in loveliness and death. Lem Duffy had removed something small, square, and black from the pocket of his plaid sports jacket. He was lifting it toward his face. For a long moment, Whippletree had no idea what was happening—Lem's action was so unexpected and bizarre under the circumstances—but then Emil realized that the lanky tight end had a camera. And he was snapping a picture of Alicia Stanhope.

The dead girl's father saw what was happening. With a strangled cry of pain and outrage, he pushed past Emil, lurched out of the pew, and flew at Duffy, grabbing him by the shoulders. "You son of a bitch!" he shouted, smashing the bewildered young man down onto the polished granite floor of the church. Mrs. Stanhope screamed. Vice-President Dexter, who'd been standing inconspicuously off to the side of the altar, rushed forward.

"Hey, wait . . ." grunted Duffy, under attack. His camera skidded beneath the front pew. Mr. Stanhope, half on top of the football player, pounded him with unaimed, windmilling blows, some of which struck Duffy in the head and about the chest. Gunnar just stood there.

"You *bastard!*" sobbed Stanhope, hitting and hitting.

"Stop it!" Duffy said then, his voice curt, taut.

Emil was on his feet now, moving forward to pull the executive away from Duffy, but his aid was not required. Lem collected his wits and strength, twisted once, twice, and threw Mr. Stanhope off him. Then, with that incredible speed Emil had witnessed in Granitelli Stadium, the tight end leaped to his feet, reached down, caught Stanhope beneath the armpits, jerked him upright, and immobilized him with a hammerlock.

Stanhope sobbed in fury and frustration.

"Lemuel!" cried Dexter.

"Let him go, Duffy!" snapped Emil.

Lem's eyes were narrow and cold, his face as hard as any Emil had ever seen. He seemed disposed to yank Stanhope's arm from its socket. But he looked at Emil, read authority in eyes and badge, and slowly released his victim.

"What kind of stunt were you trying to pull?" Emil asked Duffy, as Mrs. Stanhope wailed and the people on line gaped.

"It's . . . it's my hobby," the jock explained nervously. "I take pictures of everything . . ."

"That's the truth," offered Gunnar. "He takes all kinds of pictures. . . ."

"You two put together don't have the good judgment of a hill of beans," Emil said. "Now go back to your dorm and wait. I'll want to talk to both of you, and to Rollins."

Duffy dropped to his knees, retrieved his camera from beneath the pew—Emil was afraid that Mrs. Stanhope might stamp on his hand—and slunk out of the church with Gunnar on his heels, a chastised greyhound trailed by a baffled St. Bernard.

"I can't tell you how sorry we are . . ." Dexter said to the Stanhopes.

"Get everybody out of here," cried the bereaved father. "Nothing has been accomplished by this," he said accusingly to Emil. "You've only caused us more heartache."

There wasn't much that Emil could say. For a moment, he watched the people leaving the church—Roy Riley was in the crowd—then stepped up to the casket. Inside, partially concealed by the folds of Alicia Stanhope's ivory-colored burial dress, was a tiny Nerf football, which Gunnar had placed there. Whether the totem was the last offering of an innocent, sentimental kid, or a more sinister talisman of a strange nature, the old sheriff did not know. But, unseen by any of the others, he picked up the football and slipped it into his pocket. Gunnar and Duffy had acted in a manner so unusual, so shocking, that anyone would have to wonder about their basic motivations.

And Whippletree was wondering very hard.

The funeral director and his assistants were hovering now, so Emil left the Stanhopes with their daughter and walked outside. He met Axel and Poll out on the steps.

"What the hell happened in there, Emil?" Axel wanted to know.

"I'm not sure. You boys learn anything?"

"We was a little embarrassed, Sheriff," reported Poll, ducking his head. "It's not easy hanging around and sniffing girls. It's hard to stay cool in a situation like that. But a couple of 'em did seem to be wearing a little more smell than absolutely necessary."

Vogel nodded in sober agreement. "There was this one with, like, a little mole or something on her cheek . . ."

"Go on," said Emil. He remembered her.

"And another one, a blonde. God, Emil, she had a body that didn't quit. She had one of them headbands on, too."

That was the girl who'd been crying into her handkerchief. She'd been pretty well built, her voluptuous, blooming young figure trying to find a way out of its dress.

127

"See where they were headed?"

"Well, they walked out of church together, but they didn't talk to each other or anything. The dark one drifted on over toward the cafeteria. The bombshell stood looking around for a little, like she didn't quite know where to go, and then headed down toward the golf course."

"We've got to check it out," Emil said. "You boys go over to the caf and see if you can find the brunette. Bring her to me if you do. I'll check the golf course—maybe the blonde went down to the pine tree—and later we'll interview the jocks at Valhalla. Got that?"

"Yup, Sheriff," said Poll. He and Axel trudged off. Emil waited a moment to watch Alicia's coffin being loaded into the hearse for its journey south to Edina. Mrs. Stanhope was already in the limo and he didn't trouble her further, but he had to say good-bye to Alicia's father.

Stanhope shook hands reluctantly. "I don't think you're the man for this job," he pronounced coldly.

Dexter, standing next to the hearse, listened with interest.

"I'm doing all I know how," said Emil in his own behalf. "I made your daughter a solemn promise to find her killer, and I will."

"There'd better be some action fast, or I'm bringing in my own private investigators."

Emil was not sure but he thought he saw a look of quick, acute anxiety appear and disappear on the vice-president's smooth face.

Stanhope lowered his voice. "Even if there's a trial," he said, "there'll still be pain to bear. I got the information out of that coroner of yours, Divot. I know what that maniac did to my little girl. Such hideous perversion, the football . . ." His voice trailed off. He slid into the limousine beside his wife. "There's never any end to things like this, is there?" he asked bleakly.

Emil said nothing. The only thing he could have said, honestly, was no.

The crowd on the golf course had grown during the short time taken up by the funeral. A long line of buses was parked up and down the drive, bearing license plates from Minnesota, the two

Dakotas, Iowa, and Illinois. There was even one from Kansas. Were the lives of people so bleak, their need to believe so strong, that the mere hope of touching something or someone out of the ordinary caused them to pull up stakes and wander, like gypsies of the spirit?

Emil saw Bunny Hollman, looking almost pretty in a bright, flower-print dress. She was kneeling beneath the pine. Charlie was with her, leading a rosary in his deep, liquid baritone, and Jacques LaBatt was there as well, thin as a knife, ramrod straight. The three were surrounded by Gabriel's Guards. A Minneapolis TV crew stood outside the circle of guards, using a long-stemmed sound-boom to catch Bunny's voice, should she begin speaking. Roy Riley was standing with the members of the television crew. There were over a thousand people in the crowd, which Emil scanned in search of Sarah.

"Lookin' for somebody, Emil?" asked Butch Lodge.

"Yep. A blonde. Mighty pretty, and wearing a white headband."

"This is Minnesota, Emil. We got all kinds of blondes. Matter of fact, I did see one that caught my eye."

Butch gave a brief description. Emil realized he was talking about Dee-Dee.

"Nope, that's my niece. Then it occurred to Emil that the girl's hair was probably bleached, which Dee-Dee's certainly was not.

"Your niece?" exclaimed Butch. "Emil, I didn't know good looks ran in your family."

"Sure didn't get it from me, I guess."

Butch laughed ruefully. "Lot of good looks are. My third ex-wife, Trudilynn, was the best-looking of the lot, and she treated me the worst."

"See where Dee-Dee went?"

"Nope. I saw her come down from the church, followed by that Torbert fellow. He caught up with her, they talked for a little bit, then they joined the crowd, I think."

"Torbert?"

"One and the same. I wouldn't be too happy if a guy like that, who might've done murder, was hanging around with any kin of mine."

The rosary had concluded now; the crowd had fallen silent. It occurred to Emil that, on past occasions, Bunny's visions had come, very conveniently, when there were few distractions, when she had command of the crowd's attention. She did not suddenly, in the middle of prayer or rosary, speak of Mary's presence.

"*Man's gourd is bursting, filled with golden seed . . .*" cried Bunny then, into the microphone that Charlie held.

"*. . . his staff is long to sow the swelling fruit.*"

"Emil," wondered Butch, as he looked over toward the pine tree, "that woman sounds like she's in the middle of getting—"

"I know," said the sheriff.

"*Woman's ache is great in emptiness, her body sweet to tantalize. Be filled, all bellies, stroke the flowing root . . .*"

It was barely perceptible at first, like the single beat of a swallow's wing, the trembling of a spider's web. But Whippletree felt the quickening of his pulse. The hallucination of reality mingled for an instant with the world of dreams and glory, dreams and doom, and he felt the flutter of diaphanous curtains part before the dawn. Wind moved since forever among the pine forests, in the hills. God's breath touched the holy fields of time. Now he heard the pealing bells of eternity, blades of grass singing, leaves of trees beating like drums. Jesus raised his arms, beseeching heaven. The Sacred Steeple soared into blue sky. Then every sound receded to a silence profound and shimmering. Susan was here. Susan was with him, *in* him. Susan, his daughter, was all about, in every living thing.

"*Our Lady is about to speak!*" cried Bunny Hollman, and the great mass upon the golf course sobbed once in holy terror, blessed awe, gazing up toward the pine tree, each worshipper's deepest yearnings poised for a moment in the lambent vortex of sacred and profane.

Bunny Hollman began panting into the microphone. Emil, whose being was drugged with the memory of his daughter, still possessed enough consciousness to sense in Bunny's gasps the reflexive aftermath of sensual release.

"*Our Lady says her Divine Son is disappointed in us . . .*"

130

Many in the crowd moaned. Some began to weep.

"... *we have not shown sufficient faith. We have not prayed enough* ..."

"No! No!" came the crestfallen wails.

"Do you see her?" someone cried. "Can you see her face?"

It seemed a long time before Bunny answered. "*Yes, I see her!*" she exulted. "*And behind her I see ... I see an angel. Who is it? Wait ... I do not know ... no, the Virgin is telling me ... It is the Archangel Gabriel!*"

An exhalation of wonder rose from the crowd. Jacques LaBatt stood straighter than before.

"What does he look like? What does he look like?" came the cries.

"*His wings ... his wings are like beaten gold ...*" faltered Mrs. Hollman. "*He looks like ... Robert Redford ...*"

"Jesus, Emil," Butch Lodge said. "Robert Redford and the Virgin Mary are sure going to louse up the football season."

"I can't see *anything!*" some woman wailed.

"*Is Emil Whippletree here?*" Mrs. Hollman asked.

Emil was too stunned to say anything, but several people in the crowd attested loudly to his presence.

"*Emil,*" said Bunny, in the eerie, unearthly voice of her visions, "*Our Blessed Mother wants you to know that Susan is safe and happy in heaven. She twisted away from you on the roof. You did not let her go.*"

Whippletree ceased breathing, his body, his very soul seized by a joy so powerful he was afraid it would drive him to his knees. How could Bunny Hollman know the cause of the pain that had tortured him all these years since Susan's death? He heard a woman weeping in the crowd, and knew that it was Sarah.

"*On the day of judgment, Emil, you will find your little girl,*" Bunny continued. "*Susan will meet you in glory at the edges of the world.*"

Whippletree almost gave way to tears, which would have been composed partially of ecstatic relief, partially of pain. How could a message such as Mrs. Hollman had given, even if it proceeded

131

from heaven, set his life aright, or redeem decades of agony? But he held on, he remained in control of his emotions. The television camera had shifted to him; people were taking his picture with instamatics.

"That is . . . that is all . . ." Mrs. Hollman cried then, "the Virgin and Gabriel are leaving, they are fading . . . there is to be no word from Christ, Our Savior . . ."

A sudden gust of wind seemed to chill the air, or perhaps it was only the profound disappointment of the prayer pilgrims, failing once again to muster sufficient piety to elicit a word from God.

Whippletree was not surprised at the sudden commotion around Bunny. She collapsed, just as she'd done before at the conclusion of her experiences. Charlie and the Guards bent over her, LaBatt too. "She's all right, she's all right, everybody stay back," Charlie called. The TV camera saw it all.

Sarah came rushing over, tears in her eyes. Whippletree took her into his embrace. "Oh, Emil, oh, Emil . . . !" was all she could say.

People were watching them, standing a small distance away, reverent in their bearing. Had he been anyone but Emil Whippletree, had he possessed a nature different from his own, with its tender yet skeptical frontier soul, the sheriff might have been overcome with belief, or at least a need to believe, in the message Bunny had conveyed. But he was only Emil, and so he thought, *It has to be some trick, doesn't it? It can't be this simple.* And he wondered what an educated man like Rector Rex would think.

"Did you talk to Bunny?" he asked, still holding his wife, who cried tears of joy that dampened his uniform shirt. "You said you were going to mention Susan to her?"

"I thought about it, but I didn't," Sarah said. "And I'm glad. If I had, then we'd suspect that what she said today was . . ."

"Bogus," Whippletree finished. "Look, are you all right . . . ?"

Sarah nodded and stepped away from him. "I'm better than I ever was."

"Well, you go home. I've got a lot of stuff to do."

Tanys Voorde and Bertha Benoit, Rosary Society members, approached Emil excitedly. "I took your picture, Emil," said Tanys, handing him the print from an instamatic. "Do you know how blessed you are?"

Emil stared, with some puzzlement, at a snapshot of himself. The pine tree was in the background. All over the picture were jagged marks, like flashes of light.

"So?" he asked.

"That's a sign!" Bertha exclaimed, disappointed that he didn't understand. "Those little squiggles are heavenly rain, falling all around. They're in every picture we've taken of Bunny, and now they're in your picture too!"

"You check your camera?"

They regarded him, and his sacrilegious unbelief, with distress.

"Sheriff Whippletree, could I have a word with you, please?"

It was the television reporter, with his cameraman and sound man.

"Only off the record," he growled. Behind them, he saw that Charlie and a half dozen of the Guards were taking Bunny away.

The reporter looked disappointed. He gestured to the cameraman, who lowered his machine. "How did it feel to be signaled out like that?" the reporter asked.

"I don't want to talk about it. Personal thing."

The reporter nodded understandingly. "How is the murder investigation progressing?"

"Can't comment right now."

"Mr. Riley, of your local *Tribune*, says there was a scuffle between Mr. Stanhope and one of the football players. In church. I understand you broke it up?"

"I'm not making any comments. Tell me, did Mrs. Hollman say something when she collapsed? Something the crowd wouldn't have been able to hear?"

The members of the TV team looked at one another. "Yeah, I guess she did," the sound man admitted. "I got it on tape, I think, but it didn't mean much to me."

"Well, what was it?"

"Wasn't too clear. Something about Norsemen, then some numbers. Twenty-four and twenty."

Was this Bunny's prediction for the North Star–Notre Dame game on Saturday? The Norsemen were supposed to beat the Fighting Irish by four points? Well, she'd been wrong twice before, but very close both times.

"Mean anything to you, Sheriff?" the reporter asked.

"Not a thing," said Emil.

Jacques LaBatt strode toward them as if he owned the whole campus and most of Minnesota. He stopped in front of Whippletree. "*Now* do you believe?" he demanded, his eyes glinty and fierce.

"Haven't made up my mind," answered Emil truthfully.

The reply, honest though it was, served merely to exacerbate LaBatt's already unyielding, choleric nature. He flushed darkly in anger, the blood evident even beneath his deep tan.

"Whyn't you fellows interview Jacques here?" Emil said to the reporters. "I understand he's had some experience with homicide up there in Quebec."

The leader of Gabriel's Guards stared at the sheriff, first with horror, then with arrogant contempt.

"You are so *common!*" he pronounced. "You are pathetic." He pronounced it *pa-thet-ique.*

Emil left LaBatt there with the reporters, knowing he'd earned the man's enmity. What the hell, he figured, I guess I had that from the moment we laid eyes on each other at Bunny's place. It was true. There were certain types of people he would just never get along with.

Emil's deputies were coming down the walk from the cafeteria. The three men met at the entrance to Valhalla.

"I see you didn't find the girl," Emil said.

"No, we found her all right," replied Pete Poll. "But she said she had to go to class. She wasn't the one you were looking for anyway."

"Didn't wear a heavy scent?"

"None at all. We asked her about it. She said the girl sitting next to her at the funeral wore something heavy, though. Said she'd had a hard time breathing, too. It was the blonde with the big bazooms."

"Student here?" asked Emil.

"We asked her that," Axel replied. "She didn't think so. Said no North Star girl would be caught dead smelling like that."

Emil frowned. A townie out here for the funeral? He didn't know what to think. Had this sweet-smelling girl killed Alicia Stanhope? Moreover, who was she and how was he going to find her?

"You guys bring the car over to Valhalla. I've got to see Coach."

The athletes' dorm was a modern, granite building with tall, thin, slitlike windows. It looked as impregnable as a fortress, but Emil walked right in. Avano's office was just inside the entrance. Emil recognized Snopes' bespectacled, middle-aged secretary, Olga Berquist, whose husband, Lars, drove a sanitation truck in St. Cloud.

"Hi, Olga. Got to see Coach."

She stared at his badge, looking doubtful, caught between the twin authorities of law and boss. But she pressed a button on the intercom and announced him.

Avano appeared, looking angry and suspicious. "I told you on the phone this morning—"

Emil cut him off. "I'm here to see the Terrible Trio and to take a look at their rooms."

"You've already talked to them. At the stadium yesterday. And their rooms are private property."

"You're not going to make me do this the hard way, are you, Coach?"

"You're damned right I am."

"Why?" Emil asked.

Coach paused a moment, glanced at Olga, then motioned Emil into his private chamber. It was almost identical to his office beneath Granitelli Stadium, with the desk, files, big-screened computer, and box of signed Nerf footballs.

135

Snopes did not invite Emil to sit down. "Let me tell you a story," he said, glowering from behind his tinted glasses and lighting his corncob pipe with jerky movements. Emil recognized the aroma of Captain Black. "Everybody knows I broke into football with the Chicago Bears," Coach said, "and they think they know that the rest is grand history. But it wasn't like that, not all the time. After a couple of good seasons, I went to Charlie Halas and asked for a little more money. It didn't amount to much, maybe five hundred bucks per season. I'd led the league in rushing. I was pulling in thousands of fans per week. I figured I deserved a raise. But you know what Halas did?"

Emil shook his head.

"He threw my ass out on the street! For two years I was out there in the cold, losing some of the best playing time of my life, giving exhibitions and hanging around. He had it fixed so I couldn't play with any other team. So finally I had to come crawling back to him, hat in hand. It was either that or give up football, and giving up football would have been like dying. I might as well have gone out and bought a coffin."

"I never heard that story," Emil said.

"People only remember the good stuff. But the experience stuck with me, and I vowed that if I ever got to be a coach, I'd back each and every one of my players. In everything. To the hilt."

"I can understand that," said Emil.

"Anyway," said Snopes, "the boys aren't here. They left to attend an all-State sports banquet with Governor Bauch in St. Paul."

"I'll have a look at their rooms then."

"Off-limits. President Anderson's orders."

"He never told me anything like that. He said he'd cooperate in every way."

"He's changed his mind."

"I'll have to hear that from him."

"You go ahead and do that. He'll tell you."

"I'll be back."

"Any time," said Avano, blowing a cloud of smoke.

"Hope that banquet doesn't distract the boys too much," said

Emil, leaving. "But I hear you're favored over Notre Dame by four points."

"Is that right? Makes no difference, just as long as we win. Which we will."

"Take care of yourself, Olga," called the sheriff, as he walked out of the office. "Say hi to Lars for me."

"*Ja*," she replied.

Axel and Poll were waiting outside in the car, listening to Waylon Jennings on the radio. "How'd you make out?" Axel wanted to know.

"Not too well. Guess I'll have to get a warrant."

"From Judge Titchell? Never happen. He's in too tight with NSU."

"We'll see," said Emil, his mind working on a maneuver. It wouldn't be the noblest thing he'd ever done, but a fellow has to make some compromises every now and again, or he's going to be flat on the pavement with the steamroller grinding down the block.

They headed back toward St. Cloud. Axel noted that it was a little after twelve o'clock. Poll agreed. Axel said it was five past twelve and getting later every second. Poll said, yep, Axel was surely correct as to the time. Emil, contemplating the wilderness of intangibles that faced him, finally got the message.

"You boys aren't hungry, are you?" he asked.

"Well," admitted Axel slowly, "I guess I could stand a bite. That is, if you really want to, Sheriff?"

They pulled into Bunyanland, an amusement park and restaurant just outside of town. Named after Paul Bunyan, Minnesota's mythological lumberjack, the place had something for everybody. There were rides, games, and a playground for the kiddies featuring a twenty-foot-tall figure of Paul himself. He could swing an axe, which split a false log in half. He could lift the log above his head. And he could say, "Hello, boys and girls. I'm Paul Bunyan and this is my blue ox, Babe."

Next to Paul stood a mammoth plastic ox, which did not move at all, but out of whose mouth came a recording of what, to Emil, sounded like a cow in a terminal ward. In the early days of Bunyanland, Manager Luther Proctor had acquired a real live bull from a local farmer, which he'd painted blue and tethered in a pen next to the merry-go-round. The county ASPCA was in the process of suing on behalf of the humiliated quadruped when it broke loose one night, rampaged through the penny arcade, destroying the Pac-Man and Starfighter games, then demolishing the wishing well, and finally goring Paul Bunyan himself. End of a live Babe.

There was a snack bar for children too, and a small sit-down restaurant, Timbers, for anybody who liked, and there was also the Boom-Boom Room, where liquor was served, full-course meals were purveyed, music and dancing were featured. And where not a few assignations, discreet or otherwise, had been plotted.

Neither Emil nor his men wanted a "Brawny Bull," which was a beef hot dog with chili sauce, from the snack bar. They walked into the thickly carpeted vestibule that separated Timbers and the Boom-Boom Room. Emil was in a quandry. He wanted a beer and a roast-beef sandwich. And he knew Axel would opt for the kind of big meal he could only get in the barroom. But if they went in there, Poll would start getting sweaty-palmed and dry-tongued and discombobulated merely from the sight of all those bottles behind the bar.

"We haven't got much time," he said, accurately, and turned reluctantly toward the Timbers entryway. Then, there in the vestibule, he caught a whiff of heavy scent. No mistake. "You two go in and get us a table," he ordered.

It was Monday. Not many people were around. Emil saw some potted palms, an unattended coatcheck room, and the twin doorways to "Pointers" and "Setters." He selected a Bunyanland brochure from a rack on the wall and took up a position near the "Setters" door. Nobody went in and nobody came out. Giving up, he reconnoitered the barroom, unpatronized at this early hour. And, when he entered Timbers and sat down with his deputies, he saw that neither of the two waitresses on duty looked remotely like the girl he'd seen—and smelled—at the North Star church.

Emil had his roast-beef sandwich with coffee, which was all right but not ideal. Axel devoured three club sandwiches. Poll managed on a plate of French fries and five bottles of Coke.

An excited little crowd had formed around Paul Bunyan when Emil and his deputies left the restaurant, and the reason was quickly obvious. The lumberjack's mechanism had run amok. Paul could no longer swing his big axe, but only hoist the fake log over and over. The recording had gone out of whack too, and every time the log was raised, Paul grinned and said, ". . . ox, Babe . . . ox, Babe . . . ox, Babe . . ."

"He keeps lifting that thing, he's gonna herni-ize himself," Axel guffawed.

*Lifting!*

Emil remembered.

Tony Wiggins, the formidably intelligent weightlifter, had not been at the funeral.

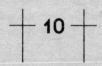

**10**

"Where is everybody?" wondered Emil, when he got back to the office and saw Alyce alone there with the phones. "Farley and Gosch go to lunch? One of 'em should've stayed—"

"No, no, it's all right," explained the secretary, "they're out on a call. At Professor Hollman's house."

"That's St. Cloud Police jurisdiction."

"I know. But the cops called for back-up support. There was some sort of a dispute between the Gabriel's Guards and home-owners along the Hollmans' street. About blocking driveways with parked cars."

"Wouldn't be surprised," Emil grumbled darkly. More trouble. Now, however, he had other things on his mind. His usual style of working would have been termed slow, if not lackadaisical, by an efficiency expert, but Emil knew that most people spun their wheels much of the time. He got things done when he wanted to.

"Alyce, what's the story on Pflüger?"

"Test showed blood type B, Sheriff. Heffner's dropped his charges. Tricky Ricky's straight with Judge Titchell."

"All right. Axel, kick Cowboy John out of here before he costs us for lunch. How's Junior doing?"

"He didn't eat his breakfast," Alyce said. "And I heard him telling Johnny Pflüger that if his dad abandons him, he's prepared to end it all."

"Pretty dramatic. I'll settle things with the judge in a bit. First get me Vice-President Dexter on the phone."

Emil went into his office and sat down in the old swivel chair, which screamed like a lost soul under his weight. Brewster, Jr., was his hole card in the plan-of-attack he'd decided upon.

"Dexter's left for The Cities," Alyce called from the Day Room. "He's attending a sports banquet with—"

"I know. The governor. Then put me in touch with Rector Rex in Washington, D.C. Leave a message that I want to talk to him pronto about a matter of life and death."

Judge Titchell called while Alyce was busy trying to contact the Great Outside World. "Well, what about my boy?" he wanted to know.

"I guess he's on a diet. Or he doesn't like my chow. Good chance he'll be free to buy his own lunch. Got something pressing now. Get back to you in a minute."

Cowboy John came in to thank Emil for the stay and say so long. "Guess you had nothing on me," he crowed.

"Give it time, John."

Cowboy John sauntered out, his engineer boots clomping on the floor.

"Sheriff!" hissed an awed Alyce. "It's President Anderson on line two."

"Well, howdy there, Doctor," drawled Emil. "Saw you on TV this morning."

There was a slight pause. "I thought this was a matter of some urgency," Anderson said then in his mellifluous, controlled voice. "I'm lunching with Senator Durenberger, and—"

"Oh, sure. I understand. It's just that the case compels me to inspect the rooms and personal effects of Duffy, Rollins, and Rutkow. But Coach won't let me into Valhalla. He said you wouldn't allow it."

"You might have taken this up with Vice-President Dexter," Anderson said.

"Out of town, just like you," said the sheriff. "Now, can I get in that dorm to do my job, or not?"

"Of course you must do your job, Sheriff. You may so inform Mr. Avano."

"He seems confused about this. Think you could give him a call and straighten things out?"

For the first time since he'd met the president, Emil sensed negative emotion in Rexford Anderson. He perceived it, minute but undeniable, over the phone and across the miles.

"Have no doubt, Sheriff. Sosthenes Avano will do as I direct."

"Glad to hear it," said Emil, signing off. He dialed Avano himself, after waiting about five minutes to allow time for Rector Rex to call the coach.

"He's not in, Emil," explained Olga Berquist, Snopes' secretary.

"Don't lie to me, Olga." The sheriff laughed. "You're too honest to do it right."

"I'm sorry, Emil. But that's what Coach told me to say."

"Did he just get a call from Washington, D.C.?"

"Why . . . yes. How did you . . . ?"

"Have a nice day," Emil told Mrs. Berquist. Dammit! he thought, hanging up. Am I getting the royal runaround or am I getting the royal runaround? He could understand how Coach and Anderson must feel about their players being under suspicion. Emil didn't like it any better than they; those young men might well have been like his own sons, if he'd been fortunate enough to have any. But couldn't the president and the coach realize what he had to do as a lawman? And why couldn't they discuss things outright?

"Get me Judge Titchell," he called to Alyce.

"All right, Brewster my friend," he said when the judge answered, "I get warrants to search three dormitory units at North Star, and you get one young man with not even a mention of his name on the blotter."

Wary pause. "These would be the rooms of those football players? On what do you base your request?"

141

"Bona fide material evidence."

"Skip the Latin. Such as what?"

"Something I can hold in my hand."

"You'll have to tell me what the material evidence is before I issue warrants."

The scrap of weatherized blue fabric that Axel had found near the Sauk River was one of Emil's few leads. Given Judge Titchell's strong bonds to the university, and Emil's increasing dismay over Anderson's ambiguous behavior, he wasn't disposed to waste ammunition.

"A warrant on those terms," Titchell was saying, "is a horse of strange color."

"Losing a blotter sheet isn't something that happens often either, at least not since I've been on the job."

"Let us congratulate ourselves on high ethical standards," the judge said sarcastically. He was thinking things over, not happily. "How's my boy doing?"

"Considering suicide, I believe."

"Goddamnit, Whippletree—"

"Hold on. You haven't even come across the street to see him."

"I know. But how would it look?"

"How do you think it'll look when he appears in court and Riley writes the story for the *Trib?*"

Titchell capitulated. He cherished his reputation. A line of bad ink in the local press was, to him, like the indelible mark of a mortal sin upon his soul, which even Purgatory would be powerless to burn away.

They struck a deal. Titchell, Jr., was, for the moment, free on his own recognizance. Emil would get the warrants "within twenty-four hours." When he recieved them, the judge could have, and do whatever he wished with, the blotter on which his son's outlaw escapade was writ small.

The rest of the afternoon passed quickly. Young Brewster left the jail in a high, proud dudgeon that began at the moment Emil unlocked his cell door. He had, apparently, been tempered by fire, strengthened by persecution, ennobled by suffering. Galileo, Gandhi, Solzhenitsyn, and Brewster Titchell, Jr.

Farley and Jamie Gosch returned from the north side to report that all was quiet on the Hollmans' street. The Gabriel's Guards, all but two standing sentinel in front of Charlie's house, had gone back to campus.

Emil dodged a phone call from Roy Riley.

Late in the afternoon, Axel Vogel rushed into the sheriff's office. "I just heard it over the radio, Emil. A bunch of women in Indiana are planning to picket Saturday's game between the Norsemen and Notre Dame. They're calling our Terrible Trio rapists and murderers. They're asking if we don't have any law up here, or what?"

"Holy mud," replied Emil. He called Doc Divot and said it was a damn fine time of day for two good men to sample strong drink.

They met about fifteen minutes later at the Courthouse Bar and Grill. Ethan "Wienie" Pappendorf, the bookie, was already there, sipping a boilermaker (draft beer to which a shot of bourbon had been added) and going over accounts. Wienie was small and wiry, with a largely self-promulgated reputation for cunning.

Emil sat down at the bar on one side of the bookie, Doc Divot on the other. A gang of courthouse regulars was already there, too, drinking up a storm, talking crops, politics, pennants, and watching a "Leave It to Beaver" rerun on the TV in the corner above the pinball machine.

"Thanks for the action, Emil," Wienie said.

"How's that?" asked the sheriff, ordering a couple of bourbons for Doc and himself.

"Everybody in town's bettin' on your murder case. Odds are seven to one against your getting it solved by Christmas."

"Ouch," Emil said.

"I don't like it either," the bookie sympathized. "But we're dealing with reality here. This is science. This is empirical data."

"What's that?" Divot asked, downing his shot. He called for another, and a beer to chase it.

"You wanna know the odds on Butch Lodge running for sheriff next election?" Wienie prodded.

"That won't be 'til next fall."

"I'm just talkin' street odds. I'm talkin' word-of-mouth. Three to one Butch runs."

"What's the story on that guy, anyway?" Doc asked. "Sometimes I like him, and sometimes I don't know what the hell to think."

Emil realized that he felt the same way, but he didn't say anything.

Wienie looked quickly over his left shoulder, then his right. Nobody there. "You wanna know the lowdown on Butch? And you didn't hear this from me. But I got it straight from his ex-wife, Trudilynn. She's a client of mine, an' so is her new husband, T.R. Butch, she said, is a guy with great wind-up and no delivery." He looked squinty-eyed at sheriff and coroner. "You get me?"

"Hell, Butch ain't no fag," Doc said, lapsing into the vernacular in honor of his surroundings.

"Trudilynn didn't mean he was a . . . like that," Wienie explained delicately. "If that woulda bothered her, why in hell would she have married a jerk like T.R?"

Emil and Doc had a laugh on that one. T.R. Steinhaus, the oft-married local playboy, had taken his father's thriving Lütefisk business and, by dint of natural talent, turned it into a red-ink enterprise.

"No, what she meant," Wienie continued, "was that Butch appears to be something he isn't."

"Those ribbons and medals he wore on his uniform in that *Trib* photo I saw couldn't have been fakes," Emil said. He was beginning to feel the first warm pleasant rush of the bourbon, a patina, a glow to hold the day at bay.

"Naw, that boy was a fuckin' hero in 'Nam," agreed Divot, ordering a third round.

"You guys ain't *listenin'* to me," Wienie protested.

"You workin' for E.F. Hutton all of a sudden?" Doc said. He and Emil laughed again.

"We better slow down," Emil said.

"What I *mean*," the bookie persisted, "is that Butch doesn't deliver over the long haul. He goes to pieces. He's strong, and he may even be pretty smart. He did the individual things that got

144

him his medals. But he's not certain who he's really supposed to be, and he kind of peters out . . ."

Doc and Emil howled.

"Look, if I can't talk serious to you bastards . . ."

"Okay. Okay, Wienie," Emil said, wiping his eyes, aware that some of the regulars were staring, wondering why all the hilarity with a murder to solve and a big crowd hassle at North Star. "Okay, we get you. But if Butch is like you say he is, how come people are thinking of him as the next sheriff?"

Wienie looked away, and swigged his drink. Emil understood. He didn't seem to be doing all that hot right now, and Butch seemed like a good alternative.

"What the hell, I got to quit sometime," he said. In my own good time, he added to himself.

"Vikings against the Raiders Sunday," noted the bookie, dismissing the vagaries of Butch's personality. "You two want in?"

"Sure," said Emil.

"I s'pose," Doc allowed. "What's the story on the Norsemen–Notre Dame game Saturday?"

"No spread yet, but speaking as a fan I'd say it'd be a pretty close game," Wienie replied.

Yeah, thought Emil, twenty-four to twenty. "Say, Wienie," he said, "when you get the numbers, let me know. I might want in on that game. Remember, I got to finance that trip to the Rose Bowl, and it's not likely I'll get a raise in pay from the county anytime soon."

They took it slow with their third round—three was Emil's limit anyway—and wondered whether Alf Laundenbush, the bartender, would dispense a good-luck drink in gratitude for their loyal patronage over the years. Odds against this happening seemed staggering, since he'd never done it before.

Emil was just about to leave when Johnny Pflüger swaggered in, cocky as ever, free as a bird. He was trailed as usual by his feckless buddy, Byron Tillman.

"Drinks for everybody," Cowboy John proclaimed. He took a barstool next to Wienie and sent Tillman over to the jukebox.

145

*"Drove a pickup truck, packed a shotgun . . ."*

"You want one on John, Sheriff?" Alf was asking.

"Why not?"

Wienie and Doc shrugged agreeably. "Thanks, John," the bookie said.

Pflüger had been celebrating for a while already. He wasn't drunk, but his voice was loud and his eyes were unnaturally bright.

"I just wanna tell you, Emil, no hard feelings," he proclaimed.

"You told me that before."

"And I meant it. And I meant it. You know, though, there's just one thing that really pisses me off."

"What? That Norb Heffner got his tires and oil back?"

"No. It was how those snooty bastards at North Star tried to hang the rap on me. Just because I ain't educated with books and stuff doesn't mean I ain't smart. Anybody will tell you: it's not what you know, it's what you do with what you know, get me?"

"I think so," Emil nodded, trying to keep a straight face.

"I agree with John on that," said Wienie soberly.

"See!" John gloated. "Here's a man who knows the score. Ha ha. Get it? Knows the *score?*"

"We get it," said Doc.

"Yeah, an' anyway, where does North Star get off, throwing us townies off campus and stuff? Or I guess it's only *certain* townies, like me. There's others I could name that hang out there, and nothing seems to happen to them. It's prejudice, that's what I call it."

Emil, who'd been listening to this dull-witted raving and wondering how the human race had gotten as far as it had, turned suddenly toward Pflüger.

"Other townies? Who?"

"Well, there's one I know that goes there all the time. She sneaks onto campus and hangs out there. Huff is her name. Muffy Huff. I scrogged her a coupla times—"

"Why does she hang out there?"

"Hell, I don't know. Ask her."

"Maybe I will. Where can I find her?"

Cowboy John downed a double shot of Guggenheimer's and demanded another. "Find her?" he said. "That's easy. She works out at Bunyanland. Sometimes as the coat check girl and sometimes as a waitress in the Boom-Boom Room. You can't miss her. Bleached hair, built like a brick shithouse, and wears this perfume that's the sweetest thing God ever made since day-old pussy."

Emil scooped some of his change from the bar and walked over to the pay phone next to the men's room. He *knew* he'd smelled that perfume in the vestibule outside the Bunyanland restaurant, and now he figured it'd come wafting out of the coat check room. This Muffy Huff girl hadn't been there at the time, Emil was sure, but a strong scent tends to linger. He dialed Bunyanland.

Some lady with a chirpy little voice told him, "It's Muffy's day off. She'll be in at about eleven o'clock tomorrow morning."

The Greater St. Cloud telephone directory did not have a listing for Muffy.

Damn, thought Emil.

When he returned to the bar, with the intention of asking Pflüger a few questions about Miss Huff, he saw that Cowboy John and his worshipful sidekick had left in pursuit of other adventures.

"So!" said Sarah, sniffing the air when she greeted Emil at the door, "you and Doc have been conferring again. Quick. Come into the living room. I think there's going to be something on the news. I was in the kitchen and I heard North Star mentioned."

Dan Rather stared at Emil and said, "Is it possible for medieval faith to thrive in these rather cynical, sophisticated times? Is it conceivable that a prayer meeting can outdraw a major college football team? For answers we go now to the campus of North Star University, near St. Cloud, Minnesota. . . ."

Bunny Hollman appeared on screen, kneeling beneath the pine tree.

"That was this morning," Sarah said softly, putting a hand on Emil's shoulder.

"This is Bunny Hollman," explained the reporter in a voice-over. "She claims to have seen the Virgin Mary three times, and has relayed messages that she says are from Mary to believers who arrive in increasing numbers daily. . . ."

The camera panned the crowd. Emil saw himself standing there. The crowd seemed huge, fully twice as large as it had actually been. Yet—face facts—it had been pretty damn big anyway.

"University officials, who declined to be interviewed, are downplaying the effect of these prayer groups, but Coach Sosthenes Avano of the nationally renown Noble Norsemen was less reticent."

Snopes appeared on screen, minus his pipe but looking eminently combative. "Sure I'm concerned," he growled at the camera. "We have an army of fans that come here for every game. Frankly, I don't think there's room here for two armies. . . ."

Next, Gabriel's Guards were shown surrounding Bunny as she prayed. Jacques LaBatt's fanatical eyes burned out of the TV screen.

"*Yes, I see her!*" Bunny was heard to say, in that strange, passionate, utterly believing voice. "*And behind her I see . . . I see an angel. . . .*"

"Two armies?" the reporter asked rhetorically. "Perhaps not. But there is certain to be conflict here in the Upper Midwest as believers struggle to order the priorities of heaven and earth. . . ."

"Thank God he didn't mention the murder," said Emil, easing his big frame into his rocking chair. "That'll come, too, if coverage continues."

"I thought you looked sort of . . . nice on TV," Sarah said.

"Hell, they only showed me for half a second. What's for dinner?"

"Lamb chops and rice. Emil?"

He had turned off the television and was reaching for the *Trib*. "Yep?"

"On TV. Your face looked as if you . . . believed?"

She was referring to Bunny's message about Susan. Emil didn't have the strength to face it just now. Or, more accurately, didn't have the emotional wherewithal to examine the feelings that Mrs. Hollman's words had stirred in him.

148

"There's no harm in what she said," he allowed. "I just wonder how she got such personal information. You sure you didn't say anything to her? You were thinking of it."

Sarah dropped to her knees next to the rocking chair and took his hand. "Emil, I think she is in touch with . . . something. Maybe not Mary, but *something!* Think of Mavis Tuckerman's earrings. And the Bolthaus boy, Toby. And now Susan . . ."

"If you want to believe it, no harm in that."

"Bunny is making people *happy*, Emil. Is that bad?"

"I never said it was." He began to read a story about the forthcoming bumper corn crop. He always read harvest news with interest. It was the farmer in him.

Sarah went out into the kitchen to finish making dinner. Emil completed the corn story and sat there in the rocker thinking. He had always believed that there was a logical explanation for everything, no matter how irrational or peculiar the event in question might appear. If there were no Whippletrees in the world, himself excepted, it was because they had died out. Just as I will, he groused. If Bunny Hollman suddenly started spouting pagan verse and having what amounted to public orgasms, something in her brain or body must be off the track. And, if that were true, then the messages she purported to be receiving from heaven were—obviously—just weird mental twitches produced by abnormality.

Obviously.

Obviously?

Then how did she know such detailed, private information? That Emil had never shared with anyone but Sarah?

He felt a hot tear form in the corner of his right eye. Because he knew, in the depths of his secret soul, that his fatigue-ravaged body had betrayed him there on the rain-battered roof in 1941. *He* had failed. *He* had weakened. *He* had lost his grip on Susan.

And he had never told Sarah that.

They spent a quiet evening. Sarah worked on her burgeoning family tree, painstakingly applying recently acquired calligraphy skills to massive oaktag panels. Emil sat in the living room, jotting on a scratchpad.

149

*Girl dead—who did it?*
*Univ. thinks Pflüger. No way.*
*Butch thinks Torbert—get his blood test.*
*Torbert thinks Butch—get his blood test.*
*Hollman thinks Torbert—call Mrs. Barnes in St. Paul.*
*Suspects, other: Duff, Roll, Rut.*
*Muffy Huff saw?*
*Dexter, Rex—why so difficult?*
*LaBatt? Bust his head for blood sample. (ha ha)*
*I think . . . Wiggins? Computer alibi.*
*I think . . .*

"Can't think a damn 'til I find Muffy Huff," he muttered.

"What's that?" asked Sarah, looking up from her labors at the dining-room table.

"Time for bed," he answered.

Love has more seasons than the year does. The fever of raw passion, which had colored their early nights, was diminished now, banked but not extinguished. Sparks still flickered, embers glowed. Flesh upon flesh, sweet as ever, could stir the flame again. Emil no longer experienced the vast throbbing flows of his youth, but the long, slow rush was just as intense in its pleasure, he and Sarah breathless as always when need became peace.

"Oh, by the way," she said, drifting into sleep beside him, "that investment man, Ethan Pappendorf, called again today."

"Right. I spoke to him. Think I might do a little business with him pretty soon."

Saturday. Twenty-four to twenty. Bunny had to be right at least once. It was in the odds.

In his office next morning, Emil shut the door for a while and spent almost two hours reading the portions of the county charter that dealt with the sheriff's office and its role in law enforcement.

He'd never actually gone through the whole thing before, at least not word by word, and he was pretty surprised by the latitude some of the codicils gave him during times of emergency.

While he studied, Alyce, according to his instructions, had also been busy. "Sheriff," she informed him, when he rambled out into the Day Room for a cup of coffee from the machine, "I found out that stuff you wanted to know. Tony Wiggins, that student, has a rare Rh factor blood type. Professor Torbert is type A."

"You're sure?"

"I spoke to him myself. He wondered why we wanted to know. I didn't tell him. I just said it was part of the investigation."

Wonder if he's telling the truth, Emil mused. "How did he sound? Was he cooperative?"

"He was real polite, if that's what you mean. And Sheriff? Judge Titchell's secretary called. She said there might be a bit of a delay on those warrants you wanted."

"Jamie," snapped Whippletree.

Deputy Gosch, who was at a desk in the corner reading pamphlets designed to prepare him for a promotional exam, looked up. "Yeah, Emil?"

"Trot on over to the courthouse and tell Titchell's girl that Roy Riley is clamoring for the blotter. He uses it to write his weekly county crime story. Maybe that'll speed things up over there." He picked up his hat and headed for the door.

"Where you goin', Sheriff?" asked Alyce.

"Got a date with a blonde at Bunyanland."

"Emil!" cried the literal Alyce. "Does Sarah know?"

Emil climbed into Stearns County One, left the parking lot behind the jail, and drove out of town. A front had moved in from Canada during the night. Low, gray, slow-moving clouds covered Minnesota. Thin patches of fog drifted above wet pavement, sodden earth. The rain came down chilly, steady, and light, a daylong drizzle. Emil turned the heater on to low, taking a hint of chill out of the car. Be Thanksgiving in just a couple of months.

151

Hard to believe. How fast time passes. Whistling to himself, Emil arrived at Bunyanland just before noon.

There were hardly any cars in the lot, a rainy day like this, and the amusement area was deserted except for a technician in a blue slicker, who swore fervently but quietly as he attempted to repair big Paul's mechanism. Merry-go-round horses pawed the mist; metal bump-'em cars glistened with raindrops, like icy bottles of pop on a hot day.

There was no one in the coat check room, nothing in it but a few umbrellas, some jackets and coats, and the telltale scent of musky perfume. Emil glanced into Timbers and saw a gaggle of Gabriel's Guards drinking coffee at a long table. They didn't see him, which was just as well, nor did he see the blond girl who had been at the funeral.

Then he walked into the Boom-Boom Room and saw his niece, Dee-Dee Tiernan, sitting alone at a table in the corner. Except for the bartender, busy polishing glasses, there was nobody else around. Dee-Dee appeared to be lost in thought. She didn't see him until he was only a few feet from her table. She looked up with a smile that seemed strangely expectant, then let out a startled "Uncle Emil!" Her eyes darted quickly around the barroom, as if she were looking for something, maybe a way out. Then she smiled again, a little shivery and tentative—he thought—at the corners of her lovely mouth.

"What the hell is this?" he growled good-humoredly. "You playing hooky, or something?"

"No . . . no, I just don't have morning classes today, and I wanted to get away from campus for a little while."

"Right," he said. "I understand. The whole thing is pretty upsetting, isn't it?"

Dee-Dee nodded in assent. She kept glancing around nervously.

"How'd you get here?"

"I took the campus bus that goes to St. Cloud. The driver dropped me off here."

"Well," he said, looking around for signs of Muffy Huff, "how about we have some lunch and I'll take you back to NSU?"

"Oh . . . that's . . . thanks, but that's fine. I just . . . finished."

Emil glanced down at the table. Two place settings were in order, except for a teaspoon she'd been spinning slowly as they talked. Coffee cups rested upside-down in saucers. Even the Boom-Boom napkins lay perfectly curled in their plastic rings.

Something's wrong, he realized, debating for a moment whether to intrude upon ground where he might not be needed, much less wanted. Concern decided for him. "Diane," he began, addressing her formally for probably the second or third time in history, "you know if you need me for *anything*, ever, and in absolutely the *strictest* confidence, you just come tell me. . . ."

She was nodding, not meeting his eyes. Sure, he'd always known that kids go through stages, kids change. Adults do too. But, in the fabric of most lives, and barring unbearable catastrophe, the thread runs through. People remain *themselves*.

Dee-Dee did not seem herself.

". . . you don't want to talk about something with your ma, all right. You don't want Aunt Sarah to know, fine. And I swear I won't push in if you don't want me to, but if you need somebody to talk to, you just call."

The double doors that led to the kitchen were located just to the right of the bar, where the beer taps dripped. One of them swung open now. A waitress came through, carrying a pot of coffee on a tray. She wore a black, short-skirted outfit, showing strong, tanned legs, and a tuxedo-type top with white shirt front and a little black tie, the formality of which did nothing to obscure the full, proud swell of her breasts. Her hair, in the gloom of the Boom-Boom Room, glowed softly. She wore a headband that partially covered her forehead. Her eyes were not innocent, but a little sad, her face pretty, sweet, vaguely vulnerable. She had a nice, open smile. There was a dreamy air about her, as if her mind were someplace else.

Emil smelled the perfume even before the waitress reached the table and set down the coffee pot. "Miss Huff?" he asked.

She looked down and saw the badge on his chest. Her mind came back, right away, from someplace else.

Whippletree knew fear when he saw it. Not good. He had to talk to her, and people who are afraid don't reveal themselves easily. Moreover, Dee-Dee was here too, and her behavior troubled him. Something was going on.

"Well, here comes the bus," said his niece, almost with relief. "I've got to run." She pulled her beige trenchcoat tight and stood up. Through the rain-streaked windows at the opposite end of the Boom-Boom Room, Emil saw the red-, white-, and-blue North Star bus rolling up the highway. It made the trip between town and college every hour, from eight in the morning until ten at night.

"Nice talking to you, Uncle Emil," Dee-Dee said in farewell. She practically jogged out of the restaurant.

"Hey, what about the coffee . . .?" the waitress called ineffectually. She looked at Emil and shrugged. "Some people," she said. "Oh, I'm sorry, you're her uncle . . . ?" She made a move to pick up the coffee pot.

"Hold on a second," he said, touching her hand. "I wouldn't mind some of that. Do you have a minute?"

"I'm pretty busy," she said, looking away. There wasn't a sound, save for the clinking of glasses behind the bar.

"Yep, pretty busy in here," Emil commented. "Sit down for a moment, will you, please?" He added a small edge of authority to his voice. A few beads of perspiration had appeared on her forehead, at the edges of the headband.

"I think I can help you," Emil added, gently now. "You might need it, too."

Muffy peered at him doubtfully, still fearfully. Reluctantly, she sat down across the table from him, on the edge of the chair as if to assure a quick escape.

"Hey, Muff!" called the bartender, in mild warning. Bunyanland apparently discouraged the appearance of fraternization with customers.

"It's okay," said the sheriff, turning and showing the badge.

"Oh, Emil! Sorry, I didn't know . . ."

Whippletree turned back to the jittery Miss Huff. "I just want to ask you a couple of questions."

He saw her bracing herself.

"Nice perfume. How long have you worn it?"

She seemed startled, and smiled in nervous relief. Was this old codger making some kind of a pass? "Bombay Musk. Coupla years now. You like it?"

"Sure do. And I bet the boys do, too."

Muffy smiled, pleased, and touched her hair. She had relaxed a little.

"I like your headband, too," he went on disarmingly. It was glistening white. "What do you look like with it off?"

Her eyes widened. She leaned away. "What is this, any-way . . . ?"

Bingo, thought Emil. "I think I found some of your blood on a tree trunk," he said. "How bad is the cut?"

Muffy turned away. Her face was white.

"It's all right," he said quietly. "You have to help me. What did you see along the river Friday night?"

"Nothing," she managed, but the show of uncertain defiance was short-lived.

"Come on, now," Emil said, pouring them both a cup of coffee. "For the moment, this is strictly between us. I think you saw what happened to that college girl. What were you doing out there any-way, that time of night? You attend NSU?"

"No," she answered, surprising him with her vehemence. "Do I look like the type of girl who'd go to college?"

"I didn't know there was a type." He smiled. "You look fine to me."

She smiled wanly.

"You from St. Cloud?" he asked.

A nod.

"Looked you up in the phone book."

"I don't have a phone. I stay in a room in a private house." She gave a name and a west-side address. "I'm trying to save all the

155

money I can," she said. "I want to get out of here and make something of myself."

Muffy examined him, deciding whether or not to continue. She seemed to make a private judgment in his favor.

"You see, Sheriff," she said, "my parents divorced when I was real little. Neither of them wanted me, so I was placed in the St. Cloud Children's Home. I was there until sixteen, two years ago. I just graduated Apollo High last June. I liked school, too. But there was no way I could afford college. Not now, anyway. But sometimes I just go out to North Star and pretend I'm a student there. Nobody seems to mind. I go to the cafeteria. I read in the library. I've even gone into some of the classes and listened. I know lots of stuff. I read and study on my own, sort of. I almost got a B-minus average in high school. I even like poetry. DeVilliers, especially."

Emil's heart went out to her, a pretty, young lady with big, good dreams, but no way to realize them just now. *He* certainly hadn't read anything by DeVilliers, whoever that was. "I'd fit right in," she was saying, with a poignant pride that was also a bit sad. "I bet I could."

"So what were you doing there Friday night?"

"There was a mixer. You know, a dance? In the student lounge in Cuthbert Center . . ."

Her voice trailed off. He understood. She'd been trying to pick up a college man. Well, nothing wrong in that, and it sure beat hanging out at The Bucket with the likes of Cowboy John.

"But I missed the last bus to town," she continued, "and I didn't want any hassle with Security, so I took the river path. I was going to hitchhike back to St. Cloud. Or walk."

"Dangerous."

"I've done it before."

"Thought you worked evenings?"

Muffy glanced guiltily at the bartender. "I called in sick," she whispered. "Please don't tell."

Emil nodded and sipped some coffee. Muffy's hands shook when she lifted her cup.

"So what did you see along the river?" he asked slowly.

She looked up at him with a glint of desperation in her eyes. "Sheriff, I'm afraid. I think . . . I think the killer might have seen me."

"So you *did* see the murder?"

She bit her lip and nodded jerkily. "Not close up. But I saw."

"Tell me all of it."

Muffy tried, without great success, to compose herself. "Well, I left Cuthbert Center and I was walking along the river, like I said, and then I saw a girl walking up ahead of me. She seemed to be in a hurry. I was too, but I slowed down so she wouldn't see me. Then"—she grimaced—"I saw this thing or person that jumped out of the bushes in front of her."

"But you didn't see a face?"

"No, I wasn't close enough. But whoever it was had on some sort of parka or cape. The girl stopped. 'Oh, it's you,' she said, and laughed."

Alicia Stanhope had recognized her murderer, Emil realized.

"He said something I didn't quite catch," Muffy continued.

"He?"

"Yes, it was a man's voice. An angry sound to it. But the girl didn't seem worried. She said something like, 'If that's all you want, here it is . . . and, Sheriff, I swear that she started to unbutton her blouse. Her back was toward me, but that's what it looked like."

"What happened then?"

"A lot of things. And very fast. He leaped at her and they both fell down. That's when I dove behind the tree. When I looked again, he was choking her, I think. She was trying to yell, but nothing came out except a"—Muffy shuddered—"a terrible gurgle. She was fighting. I've never been so scared in all my life. I heard some small snaps, like branches breaking . . ."

Alicia's wrists, thought Emil.

". . . and then a . . . a dull, horrible cracking sound . . ."

Neck.

". . . and after a little while he stood up and looked at her."

"Then he went away?"

Muffy covered her eyes with her hands. "No. He bent down and tore away her clothes. Then he took something out of the pocket of this overcoat, or whatever he had on, and he seemed to shove it in her . . . in her mouth . . ."

"I know."

"And after that . . . after that he opened his coat. He was naked underneath. He was"—she dropped her eyes—"hard. Then he reached into his pocket again, I don't know why, I wasn't that close, but he seemed to be . . . sort of . . . *playing* with himself . . ."

Slipping on the condom, Emil figured. "Go on."

". . . and then he went down . . . I mean, he laid on top of her, and . . ."

"I know."

"It didn't take him long. When he got up again, I thought everything was over. All I'd have to do was stay quiet and he'd go away."

"He waited around afterwards?"

"Yes. And the strangest thing happened. Flashing light seemed to come out of his eyes. It happened at least two or three times. I was blinded and I didn't see anything clearly for a minute. When my eyes focused again, I saw that he was staring in my direction. I was sure he'd seen me, with all that light . . ."

"You're sure the light came from his *eyes?*" Emil asked doubtfully.

"Or from his head. It happened. I didn't imagine it."

Emil took a long swallow of now-cold coffee and thought about what Muffy had just said. Light did not just shoot out of a normal human being's *eyes!* "Maybe he wore glasses that reflected in the moonlight?" he suggested.

Muffy held her ground. "No. The light was bright and blinding."

Well, I guess what we have here, with the murder and perversion, is *not* a normal human being, Emil decided. Question was: how *abnormal?* Question was: how *human?* He let his imagination run on for a moment, as Miss Huff shifted nervously in her chair.

Whippletree's perceptions had been subtly distorted since Saturday, when, at the time of Bunny Hollman's first vision, he'd sensed on the golf course, in the very air, an undercurrent of alien force, felt the presence of a powerful yet impenetrable reality just beyond the borders of cognition. He was fully aware of what he'd experienced—as certain of its reality as Muffy Huff was of "flashing lights"—but he could not explain it according to any rules or laws or precepts known to him. And, sitting there in the Boom-Boom Room, it occurred to Emil that Alicia Stanhope might have met her end at the hands of an evil as transient and untraceable as the gunman in that alley behind the Hannórhed bank. If Bunny saw citizens of heaven, what—or who—did others see?

No, he decided wearily, the basic rationality of his Stearns County soul again ascendant, there's nothing supernatural here. A *man* of flesh and bone and breath and beating blood killed Alicia.

And I've got to find him.

Before he kills again.

"What happened next?" he asked Muffy.

"He disappeared."

"The killer *disappeared?*"

"Yes. One moment he was there, the next he was gone."

Probably ducked into the bushes and crawled up the embankment, Emil guessed. "What did you do?"

"I waited a long time. I thought he might still be around. But I didn't hear anything, so I ran. I made it down to the highway, started walking toward St. Cloud, and flagged down the first car that went by."

"Who was in it?"

"Some young guy. Nice-looking. He was from North Star, I think. I noticed he had a faculty parking permit on the windshield of his car."

"Make of car?"

"Something European. A sports car, I think. They all look alike to me."

"Did the fellow have short blond hair? Handsome type?"

Muffy nodded.

Emil wondered what kind of car Dale Torbert drove. Maybe Butch Lodge was right about the professor after all. "Weren't you afraid to get in the car with a lone man? What did you talk about during the drive?"

"We didn't talk about much of anything. I was too upset. And I wouldn't have turned down a ride from anybody, not after what had happened."

"Not even if he was the killer?" Whippletree suggested.

Blood sank away beneath Muffy's skin. Her face seemed for a moment like a death's head as she realized what Emil was implying.

"No! He was a nice guy. I would have settled for being dropped off here at Bunyanland, even if my boss would have fired me for lying about being sick, but he drove me right to the house I stay at."

"Nice-looking girl like you? He wasn't curious as to why you were hitchhiking at that time of night?"

"If he was, he didn't ask."

Emil put together what he'd learned from Muffy. He knew now what had happened to Alicia that night, in its exact sequence, and he knew that a man, naked beneath some kind of overcoat, had done the killing. Whippletree thought of the scratches on Rusty's face, Gunnar's torso, Duffy's arm. Could Alicia, in her death struggle, have gotten a hand up Duffy's sleeve and torn his skin?

Yes, he decided.

"Why didn't you tell somebody about what you'd seen? Why didn't you call me?"

A tear appeared at the end of Muffy's long, mascaraed lashes. "Sheriff, I was *afraid*. I still am. I think he might have seen me when those lights flashed. Besides, I've had nothing but bad times most of my life. I want to get out of here someday, and start all over with a clean record."

"Where are you going to go?"

"To The Cities. Where does everybody go when they leave here?"

"But if you were so scared, why'd you go to the funeral?"

She dried the tear with a napkin. "There'd be a lot of people around. I'd be safe. And I thought I had to pay her back, sort of, for being such a chicken."

"You're not that," he said. "You didn't do anything a hundred others wouldn't have done, given the circumstances."

"Do you think so? Really?"

"Sure. And you can prove you're courageous by helping me out. Let's say I release information to the effect that there was a witness. . . ."

Muffy did not look at all courageous now. "And mention my *name?*"

"Not right away. Maybe we won't have to. It's just an idea to smoke the killer out, so to speak."

"Oh, Sheriff, no, please . . ."

"Well, I guess I'm not ready to do something like that anyway. Would you think about it, though?"

Muffy didn't say yes but she didn't say no. Emil stood up. "Thanks," he said, "for your help."

Muffy stood up too. She really had a gorgeous body, and, in spite of his years, Whippletree felt the warmth of physical response.

"One more thing," he said, tossing a couple of bills onto the table. "What did my niece have for lunch? I should probably pay for that. She left in a hurry."

"Lunch?" asked Muffy, mystified. "That girl? She didn't have lunch. She just ordered a pot of coffee and left without drinking any of it."

Funny, thought Emil, leaving the restaurant and walking to his car. A whole pot of coffee? And then running out. Dee-Dee was a level-headed girl, not given to erratic behavior. Maybe she was even more upset than she'd appeared.

Gabriel's Guards were gone now, but Emil noted that the mechanic was still there. He'd given up temporarily in discouragement—Paul Bunyan's electronic entrails were spread out on a canvas—and was leaning against Babe the Blue Ox, smoking a cigarette. His ineffectual blue slicker was soaked with the drizzle that continued to fall.

"How goes it?" Emil asked in passing.

"Not so hot."

Same with me, thought Emil. The radio was squawking when he got into the car.

"Whippletree here."

"Oh!" It was Alyce. "Sheriff, I've been trying to reach you. Judge Titchell sent over those warrants. You can search those rooms in Valhalla now."

"Okay, Alyce, good going. Send Farley and Poll out to campus with the documents. I'll meet them in front of the dorm." He glanced at his watch. It was a few minutes after one o'clock. "Tell 'em in about an hour. I've got somebody else to see first."

"Right, Sheriff."

Emil drove to campus over the rain-slick highway and turned in at the football-shaped "Noble Norsemen" sign. At first glance, it seemed to him as if the golf course had been covered by a vast, black tarpaulin, but then he noticed a slow, unrhythmic undulation, and, driving closer, saw thousands of people standing under umbrellas in the rain. Many others knelt bareheaded, praying, doing penance, atoning for God knew what, yet all the worshippers attesting to the strength of their belief.

Emil moved slowly up the drive toward Jesus and the Sacred Steeple. The pine tree was ringed by a motionless cordon of Gabriel's Guards, an honor watch around the site of mystery. They wore military-style ponchos, and with their position and bearing, formed an unobtrusive but very definite barrier between crowd and tree. Emil saw neither Jacques LaBatt nor Bunny Hollman. The worshippers seemed not so much to be waiting today, but standing in trembling vigil.

Whippletree shuddered, not knowing why. The chill of the day, gray sky, branches of the pine bent beneath rain: these cast in ominous light the patient, brooding mass, the unpredictable standing tribute to the unfathomable.

Emil drove on. He parked the car, asked directions first of a fresh-

162

man wearing an initiation beanie, then of a professorial-looking, dapperly dressed man with a crew cut, and wound up in Tobias Hall, where faculty in the College of Arts and Sciences had offices. The building directory informed Emil that *Torbert, Dale N., History*, was in 201 C, so he climbed a flight of steps, ambled down a corridor, and found the appropriate doorway. He was just about to rap on the door when he heard somebody crying softly.

"What should I do now?" a girl asked, between sobs.

"First of all, don't worry." It was Torbert's voice.

"You're my faculty advisor."

"I am that," Torbert said, with an intonation Emil could not interpret clearly.

"Do you *believe* this is happening?" the girl asked tearfully.

Torbert's lack of response was an affirmation.

Emil did not know what *was* happening, but he certainly didn't want to intrude upon an obviously tense academic conference, so he retreated some distance down the corridor and read notices on a bulletin board, waiting for the student to depart. Students with the ability to type were offering their services. Rides were sought to South Bend, Indiana, for Saturday's game with the fabled Fighting Irish. Somebody wanted to sell a textbook called *Methods of Non-Parametric Statistics*.

"I can understand why," Emil muttered.

The man with the crew cut who had directed Emil here came striding up the hallway. His walk was brisk, self-important, his demeanor bright and chipper.

"Sheriff, you passed Torbert's office," he said. "It's back that way."

"I know. He's busy now."

"Suppose he is. These days." The tone was half amused. Half contemptuous. Emil didn't care for it. The man disappeared into 204 A.

Curious, Emil went back and checked the directory again. *Beauchamp, George N., History*. Emil dropped a bucket into his memory well. Right. Beauchamp was one of the three professors on Dale Torbert's tenure committee. Obviously not a compassionate type, the sheriff decided. The young teacher wasn't going to get much sympathy from that quarter.

Emil took a quick pit-stop in the men's room at the end of the second-floor corridor, and just as he was coming out, he saw Dr. Torbert's office door open, saw his niece leave hurriedly.

Dee-Dee had been the girl crying in there? Suppressing an impulse to call to her, he waited until she'd gone down the stairs, then approached 201 C. The door was slightly ajar. Torbert was slumped over his cluttered desk, head in his hands. Emil rapped on the door.

"Yes? Come in."

Emil edged into the office. "Sorry to bother you. Got a minute?"

The professor stood up slowly. He looked good in a well-tailored charcoal-gray pin-striped suit, and his hair was bright as a jonquil, but there were dark circles under his eyes.

"Wasn't that my niece who just left here?" Emil blurted, a little worried himself. "What's the problem?"

Torbert pulled up a chair for the sheriff. Both men sat down.

"Miss Tiernan has been summoned by the Honor Committee," the professor said. "There'll be a hearing next Friday. She apparently violated sign-out regulations."

"Is that so awfully bad?"

"It can be, if a student doesn't offer an explanation as to his or her whereabouts. Moreover, Vice-President Dexter has taken a personal interest in the matter."

"That's unusual?"

"Rather. The committee is comprised of students elected by their peers, and a faculty advisor. The administration reviews all findings, of course. But it's very rare for a top administrator to be at the actual hearing."

Emil experienced one of those hunches of his, which were seldom wrong: Dexter's interest in Dee-Dee might just stem from the fact that Whippletree was her uncle. He didn't care for the inference.

"I'm her advisor," Torbert said. "That's why she came to me."

164

"What did you advise?"

"Well, it's complicated. She could probably get off with a warning, if she made a clean breast of things, so to speak. But there's a principle involved here, too. She's of legal age. What she does with her private time might not necessarily be university business."

"I see," said Emil, reserving judgment. "Anything I can do to help, count on me."

"Thanks. I wish there were. We'll see."

"How's your own situation?"

Torbert spoke sardonically. "The administration will 'entertain' my charges against the Tenure Committee next Friday as well."

"How does that work?"

"Very grandly. Representatives of the Faculty Senate, the Faculty Judiciary Committee, and the ad hoc Committee on Professional Ethics will listen to me make my case against Charlie Hollman regarding those tapes and transcripts. Either Dexter or Anderson will chair the session."

"And then everybody votes?"

Torbert laughed and ran a hand wearily through his close-cropped hair. "You've lived under democracy too long, Sheriff. Those faculty advisors are powerless. Put most of our people on committees, they're honored. They think they've got real clout. But the administration holds the reins."

"Who do you stand a better chance with? Dexter or Rector Rex?"

"Neither. But if I walk into that hearing and see Dexter in the chair, I might as well save my breath. Anderson makes all the decisions of course, whether he's on campus or not. But if it's bad news that's going to come down, you can bet Rector Rex will find a way to be absent. He's splendid that way. It's an executive technique that's stood him in good stead for over forty years."

"I think I see what you mean," said the sheriff. Decisions were being made to hinder Emil's investigation, decisions that could only come from Anderson.

"It's not necessarily more effective to strike from a distance,"

Torbert was saying, "but it makes counterpunching a lot more difficult for an opponent. In this case me."

Me too, Whippletree realized. "You don't seem too confident," he observed.

Torbert laughed and lit a cigarette. Emil felt like a chaw, but refrained. There was no place to spit.

"Hollman denies there *is* a tape," said the professor, exhaling. He sought an ashtray amid the piled books and papers on his desk, gave up, and flicked a length of ash into the wastebasket. "My only hope is to get my hands on one of the transcripts, to prove the bastards actually went that far to frame me. I mean, even with a transcript, I might be dead. But at least I'll have something to use against them if I want to pursue a legal case. My only hope, if Anderson turns me down, is to have some embarrassing ammunition to employ against them. Rector Rex will do some hard thinking if his beloved NSU stands to suffer being held up to public scrutiny."

Emil thought, once again, of the president. If freedom of ideas were his basic belief, he would side with Torbert, wouldn't he? If the university were most sacred to him, how would he react? Compromise was a time-tested administrator's gambit, and Anderson knew all the moves. If, however, the president's secret soul lay in another area, then what? The whole situation was up for grabs.

"You think those three professors have the transcripts?" Whippletree prodded.

Torbert took a deep drag and crushed out his cigarette. "Hard to say. Binlow told me, point-blank, that he'd never seen one, although the bastard had it right in his hand at my tenure hearing. Bowers said he lost his copy. Beauchamp is being cagey. He doesn't trust anybody, so he might be holding onto the thing for insurance."

"Nice group of guys."

"You've noticed." Torbert seemed to brace himself. "Anyway, Sheriff, I doubt you've come here to discuss faculty politics. What can I do for you?"

Emil nodded. "I do have to check on a few things, and forgive me if I go over old ground. But when did you say you left campus Friday night?"

"Right after seminar."

"Directly afterward? The very next minute?"

"Well, no, of course not. I stopped back here at the office first and dropped off my lecture notes. Then I went to my car in the parking lot."

"How long did all this take?"

Torbert shrugged. "I really didn't notice. It might have been twenty minutes. Certainly no less."

That does give him a small out, the sheriff figured, but not much of one. "What kind of car you drive?"

Torbert seemed surprised. "A BMW. Why?"

"Sports-type car?"

"Yes, it is. Six hundred and thirty-three CSI."

"I wouldn't know about that. Something like a Honda or a Datsun?"

The professor smiled. "Not quite. But I guess they all look alike, don't they?"

"Sure do at my age. Recall picking up a young lady who was hitchhiking that night?"

Torbert's eyes narrowed. "Yes," he said. "She was alone on the highway. Something wrong in that? I didn't *touch* her. We hardly spoke."

"Hold your horses. This isn't an accusation."

"All right," said the younger man. "It's just that I've heard all this stuff that Charlie Hollman is spreading around about my morals, or lack thereof."

"I understand. But you yourself seemed to suggest that Butch Lodge has a roving eye."

"Well, he does, as far as I know."

"Butch seems to have an alibi for Friday night."

"So have I. I dropped that girl off at her house, just as she wanted, and then I drove to my friend's place in St. Paul. Paul Barnes. I told you."

"The girl says she wanted to be let off at Bunyanland. And your friend is out West on some sort of archy-logical deal."

Torbert paled, and lit another cigarette.

"It's okay, though," drawled the sheriff. "His wife, Sandy, says you were there, all right."

"She and I are *just* friends. If you're suggesting . . ."

"Nope, I don't do much of that," Emil allowed. "People who go around making suggestions all the time wind up being just too damn unpopular to stand."

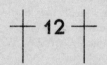

## 12

Farley and Poll were in Snopes Avano's outer office, jawing with the coach's secretary, Olga Berquist. She looked worried.

"You got 'em?" Emil asked.

"Right here," said Poll, holding up a thick manila envelope. "But Olga says we can't get in. No way."

"Where's Coach, Olga?" asked Whippletree.

She looked this way, then that way. "He's in the auditorium with the team. They're watching the videotape of Notre Dame's last game."

"Better go get him."

"Emil . . ."

"Look, those rooms are going to be searched. I can go up and do it right now, but I want the players there while I do it. I'm not some kind of barbarian, goes poking around in a guy's private stuff when he's not around."

Mrs. Berquist got the point.

"I can't believe this is happening," said Benny Farley, after the unhappy Olga had left to summon Coach.

"What? That we're executing some warrants?"

"No. That I'm gonna meet Snopes Avano. He's more famous than"—Benny sought a worthy comparison—"than Bob Hope."

"Well, I wouldn't ask him for his autograph today. I doubt if he'll be in the mood."

He wasn't. "I thought I told you—" Snopes began, raging already even as he was coming through the door.

Emil held up his hand. Coach was not wearing his hat today, and the sheriff was surprised at the whiteness, the thinness, of Avano's hair. The famous athlete was getting old.

"Got to be done," said Emil, matter-of-factly. "Got to be done, and gonna be done." He opened the manila envelope and displayed the warrants. "I didn't want to do it this way, as you know. You want to read these?"

Snopes waved away the offer in disgust. "Emil, you're the one who's going to have to pay the bill for this."

"Don't you think I know that? Send the boys up to their rooms."

Gunnar, Lem, and Rusty had adjacent quarters on the fourth floor, with big plate-glass windows that looked out toward the stadium. Each room was similar, with lightweight, pale-blue drapes, deep-blue, heavy-duty carpeting, a bed, some chairs, bookshelves, large closet, and a small shower and toilet in a cubicle just to one side of the door. But each room was different in that it reflected the personality and interests of its occupant.

Rusty was sitting on the edge of his neatly made-up bed when Emil entered. He stood up quickly, like a cadet coming to attention for inspection.

"You could have come up here any time, Sheriff," he said, smiling a bit nervously and offering his hand. "It's just that I guess Coach felt . . ."

"No matter, son. This won't take long."

He surveyed the room at a glance. Rollins was a well-ordered and squared-away kid. His books were lined up neatly on the shelves, along with a couple dozen trophies—probably about one-tenth of those he'd won since kindergarten. His desk was loaded with texts and notebooks, but they were stacked carefully. A long rank of file-folders, each bearing an index-tab, stood between bookends near the reading lamp, and his typewriter was shrouded by a plastic dustcover. A collapsible ironing board slanted against the wall behind the desk, and a small electric steam iron rested end-up on the window sill. There were two pictures on the wall. One, a group portrait of—Emil counted—fifteen people. The second, the graduation photograph of a very pretty girl.

"This isn't your sister, is it?" Emil grinned.

"No, sir," said the quarterback, ducking his head slightly. "That's Jennifer. She's the girl back home."

Whippletree took a closer look. Jennifer had long, reddish hair and bright green eyes. Her smile was flawless. She was beautiful in an innocent and unrefined, country sort of way.

"Where you from, Rusty?"

"Sleepy-Eye."

Farm town. Southern part of the state.

"See much of her? You up here and she down there?"

"Not as much as I'd like. There've been some problems, I guess. She hasn't gone to college. Couldn't afford to. She's from a big family, like mine."

Emil looked at the other picture. Father, mother, and kids. The parents, the sheriff could tell, were farm people, staring into the camera unsmilingly and a little self-consciously. Rusty was the oldest—or at least the tallest—offspring. The rest of them, boys and girls, ran on down to a toddler about two years of age.

"Without the football scholarship, I couldn't have gone to college either," Rusty said. "It's been hard on me—on Jenny and me—but it'll be worth it in the end."

"Hmmmmm," said Emil, "good luck. Education can get pretty expensive, no denying."

"I economize in every way I can," said the quarterback, with a kind of abashed pride. "I even do my own laundry and ironing."

"Mind if I look in your closet?"

Rusty opened the door for him. There weren't many clothes inside. One sports jacket, which Emil had seen Rollins wearing at the funeral. A green nylon windbreaker, with a name tag neatly affixed to the inside of the nape. Five dress shirts, similarly tagged, were on hangers next to the windbreaker. Four pairs of slacks,

170

perfectly pressed, hung in the closet, too. On a shelf were several sweaters and a small pile of soft-collared sports shirts. Rusty was wearing a pair of freshly laundered chinos and a red sports shirt with a polo player on it. He had on a pair of sneakers, of which there were two more pair on the floor of the closet, along with brown dress shoes with trees inside. Emil did not see an overcoat or a slicker, or even a blue coat or jacket of any kind.

Feeling a bit embarrassed, Whippletree next checked the desk drawers and ran his hand between the mattress and bedspring. It had occurred to him that the killer may have been wearing rubber gloves, portions of which Alicia could have clawed away during her death frenzy.

Rollins stood there in the room while Emil made his investigation, showing discomfort only when the sheriff went into the toilet and checked the shaving kit.

"Got to do it right," said the sheriff apologetically. He'd found nothing of use here, and he knew it. "By the way, what'd you and Miss Stanhope do that time you took her out?"

Rusty looked puzzled. His reply was swift. "I never took her out."

Emil was sure he recalled Dee-Dee saying that Rollins and the dead girl had had at least one date. Perhaps he was mistaken. "Must have gotten some things mixed up," he said, thanking the quarterback and moving on to Gunnar's room.

The huge lineman was sweating profusely, large, wet circles visible beneath the armpits of a blue workshirt. He was pacing back and forth when Emil entered his room, and turned to look at the sheriff with enormous, frightened eyes.

"This won't take but a minute . . ." Emil began. Then he got a look at the room. It was an odd mixture of clutter and care. Rutkow's bed was unmade, his clothes—blue jeans and shirts— were tossed haphazardly over chairs and windowsills, and several generations of sweatsocks were scattered across the floor and underneath the bed. The desk was a jumble of books and sports magazines. In contrast, arrayed impressively upon the bookshelves, were models of every kind: airplanes, racing cars, warships. A model of

Lindbergh's *Spirit of St. Louis* spun slowly from a hook in the ceiling, and on a small table in the corner of the room was the figure of a football player, constructed entirely of glued-together toothpicks. Under one toothpick arm, the player carried a little Nerf football.

"Do this yourself?" Emil asked.

Rutkow tried to say yes, but gulped. He nodded instead.

"Nice work."

"Models are my hobby. They relax me."

"Did you know that Alicia was found with a little football just like that one jammed in her mouth?"

The big jock's face went pasty-white. Emil was afraid he was going to faint.

"Why'd you slip one in her coffin, Gunnar?"

"I . . . I . . . meant it . . . affectionately. I felt bad for her, even after what she'd said about me. You're supposed to let bygones be bygones when somebody dies."

"Okay, Gunnar."

The closet showed more clutter. Rutkow's duffel bag, with "Gunnar" scrawled on it in magic-marker, lay open on the floor. There were more sweatsocks in it, and underwear, and an old pair of jogging shoes. Gunnar had made an attempt to hang his shirts and slacks, but they were in wild disarray. No name tags for him: again, "Gunnar" was written inside the garments.

"The laundry needed my name," he explained. "Those darn little stickers kept coming off on me."

Whippletree completed his inspection of the room but found nothing worthy of note—nothing that he was looking for. Gunnar owned an old tan trenchcoat and a big blue woolen overcoat that Paul Bunyan could have gotten lost inside. Rutkow sagged with sweaty relief when the sheriff made his departure.

Duffy, in contrast to his teammates, was cool, sullen, self-possessed. His quarters had a recently straightened-up look. There weren't many books evident, but there were cameras of all shapes and sizes on the bookshelves—Polaroids and Minoltas, Hasselblads and Fieris, foreign and domestic makes—and almost every inch of wall space was covered with pictures that Duffy had taken. Apparently, his picture-taking was quite serious, and he was very good. The sheriff was particularly drawn to an enlarged shot of the statue of Jesus. It had been taken at night, in color, and the eerie meld of light and darkness conveyed an aspect of sinister power. The great bronze arms, upraised, seemed wildly triumphant, the statue's face alive.

"I call it Triumphant Jesus," said Lem, noting Emil's interest. "Took it last week. I'm gonna enter it in a national contest."

"Sure catches the eye. You do your own developing and enlarging?"

"Sure," said the tight end emphatically, as if the query had been an insult.

"Just be careful about where you take your shots."

Reluctantly, Duffy offered an apology for snapping Alicia in her coffin. "It was dumb of me, I know. But I never had a picture like that, and—"

"What? Of an old girlfriend, dead?"

"She wasn't no girlfriend!" Duffy snapped. There was something in his eyes, whether meanness or hurt Emil could not interpret. "Like I told you before, it was a few quick bangs. And if she hadn'ta come on to me like she did, it never would have happened."

Emil noted, in the top right-hand desk drawer, five little Nerf footballs, but he made no comment. He found no rubber gloves, nor any garment made of blue waterproof fabric. Duffy's closet was interesting only for the fact that his shirts were not tagged with his name.

"I got to do it one of these days," he said. "But it's early in the year. I haven't sent any clothes to the campus laundry yet."

"Just write your name on everything with a magic-marker, like Gunnar does," Emil suggested.

Duffy actually laughed. "Gunnar is good with shortcuts," he said. "But he hasn't figured out that the ink is gonna come out sooner or later."

"Everything comes out sooner or later," said the sheriff pointedly.

Still, nothing that he'd been looking for had turned up in his search, and it was with a combination of embarrassment and relief that he made his good-byes to Coach.

"There, you see?" Avano said, with no small amount of his own relief. "Didn't I tell you? Those boys are terrific, each one of them. So is everybody on my team, and every team I ever coached."

"Good luck in South Bend. I guess you're counting on a big win to tune up for the Illinois game?"

"We'll cream 'em," vowed Coach. "You know, what makes me mad is I heard the spread is only gonna be four points. Can you believe that?"

Twenty-four to twenty, Emil thought. Bunny's prediction.

"Not that all of us are betting men," he added, winking at the sheriff. "Anyway, by next week I'm sure you'll find a way to get all those praying weirdos off campus so we can get back to business around here."

"We gonna arrest anybody, Sheriff?" asked Poll, who was waiting with Farley outside Valhalla.

"I guess not today. You boys go back to the office. I want to have a talk with my niece before I leave."

He didn't know where Dee-Dee might be at this time of day, but he figured he'd try Halston Hall, the big women's dorm. It was still drizzling and he had no umbrella, so he walked across campus as fast as he could, which was not all that fast these days. The trouble with getting old—*one* of the troubles—was that your mind remembered how easy and pleasurable it had once been to do all kinds of things, but your damn body had forgotten almost everything.

Students, alone or in groups, hatless or hooded, were hurrying every which way across campus, young people on journeys into the unreadable future. Youth was the vehicle with which to reach the future. Hope was the fuel.

The arms and head of Triumphant Jesus were obscured by fog today. Emil glanced at the statue as he hurried past, remembering Duffy's powerful, alarming picture. On the night he'd taken the shot, the light must have been just right, because a flashbulb wouldn't have . . .

Flashbulb!

Then he knew. The strange bursts of light that Muffy had seen on the night of the murder had been flashbulbs going off.

The murderer had taken pictures of his victim!

The coed on duty at the desk in the lobby of Halston Hall was, Emil thought, somewhat overawed by his badge and holstered .38, and she hastened to call Dee-Dee's room. Still, it took Emil's niece almost ten minutes to make her appearance. The reason for this delay was obvious in a freshly applied coat of makeup that did not quite manage to conceal traces of pinched, beleaguered tension. Dee-Dee's eyes were tired, and her lush, honey-colored hair could have used a good shampoo. But the sheriff, as always, was inordinately happy when he caught sight of her, striding toward him out of the depths of the dorm. They still had dorm rules here at North Star; a young woman could retreat and be alone if she wanted to. Judging from Dee-Dee's greeting, being alone might have been what she'd preferred just then.

"So we meet again, Uncle Emil," she said tonelessly.

"What do you think, that I'm following you around?" he replied, too expansively, as she led him to the first-floor lounge, with its couched conversation-pit and fake fireplace. They sat down side by side on a maroon leather couch.

"Did Mom send you to talk to me?" Dee-Dee demanded.

"Barb? No. Why do you think that? Have you had another squabble or something?"

"No. Not another one. The same one."

"About what?"

"Nothing in particular," she said evasively. "She just wants to know too much."

"So do I," he admitted. "I'm worried about you."

Dee-Dee's eyes glazed briefly with a teary film of tenderness.

"Maybe we ought to get this out in the open, whatever it is," Emil said. "Why did you leave Bunyanland so hell-for-leather? What were you doing there, anyway? And, although I wasn't eavesdropping, I had to see Dr. Torbert, and I couldn't help but overhear you crying in his office."

She seemed startled that he'd been there. "I might get kicked out of school," she informed him. "I guess that's reason enough to be upset."

"Sure is. But why are they being so hard on you?"

"Because I . . . because I won't tell where I was over the weekend."

"Any reason you can't? Any reason you don't want to?"

She bit her lip and looked away.

"I sure as hell won't tell anybody," he said, with gruff tenderness. "Why, back when I was courting your Aunt Sarah, I didn't bring her home once 'til two in the morning. Her pa was waiting out there on the porch, fit to be tied. If he'd owned a shotgun, he would have had it with him, too. Sarah had come up with the story that a tree had fallen across the road, and that I'd had to go borrow an axe from a farmer and chop up the tree before we could get on our way again. She said we had to stick to that story no matter what, because it was just unbelievable enough for her pa to buy it."

Dee-Dee was looking at him with affectionate amusement now. "Did that really happen, Uncle Emil? Or are you just trying to make me feel better?"

"Both. But it's true. That is, about the story we made up and sold your grandpa. Of course, what we'd really been doing is necking in the woods by Grand Lake."

"So you've guessed."

"Wasn't hard. I guess it didn't dawn on me right off. Any more than you'd picture me and Sarah getting all hot and bothered in prehistoric times."

Dee-Dee smiled, then frowned. He saw a serious, woman-face in the expression, beneath her blooming youth. "I . . . we weren't just necking in the woods, Uncle Emil."

"Figured that too. Who is he?"

"I'd . . . rather not say . . . for now."

"That's your business. All's I want to know, is he a good man?"

Her lovely face glowed. "Oh, Uncle Emil, he's the best! I just love him so much. But . . ."

Emil imagined some suave jerk who'd pulled the wool over Dee-Dee's eyes as he pulled the clothes off her body. I'll murder the creep, he thought. Then he remembered that she was too smart to pick a turkey.

"But . . . ?" he prodded.

"There are some problems," she admitted.

"Aren't there always?"

She thought about something for awhile, then said, "I just don't know what to do. I want so many things. So does he. Here I'm going to be finishing up college—if they let me graduate, that is—and I want to go to work, to teach. Maybe be on my own for a couple of years. Uncle Emil, I don't know anything but going to school and being a daughter and living in St. Cloud. . . ."

"Want to try your wings, is that it?"

"Yes!" She spoke emphatically.

"And you want him, too?"

"Yes!"

"What about him?"

"He wants to get married. Right now. Or as soon as I graduate."

"This kind of thing *has* happened before," Emil observed drily. "Why don't you let me have a look at the fellow? I'm not a bad judge of character, you know. Or why don't you take him home to your ma and have her cook up a bunch of chicken, or something. That's the way we used to do it in the old days. Sarah's ma stuffed me with so much fried chicken I thought I'd start to cluck."

Dee-Dee laughed, and Emil was glad to hear it.

"I'm not ready to do that yet," she said. "To introduce him around. It's not the right time. For either of us."

"Well, you be the judge of that. I bet I'd have seen him though at Bunyanland, if my eyes'd been a little sharper?"

She looked away guiltily. "Yes. We met there. We were going to have lunch, but I had to intercept him before he came into the Boom-Boom Room."

"You sure this isn't just a 'tree across the road' story?"

"No. It's the truth."

Emil believed her. "Well, only thing I can tell you is that you two'll have to work things out on your own. What bothers me just as much, I guess, is this hearing you've got to face."

She looked downcast again. "Me too. But I'm not going to lie or come up with a fake excuse."

"Want me to take this matter up with Vice-President Dexter, next time I see him? With the murder case and the vision, he and I have only begun to do business. I could mention you sort of off-the-cuff?"

"You shouldn't waste your time on my problem. I made it myself."

"I love you," said the sheriff, "and that means your troubles are mine. Let me know when that hearing meets."

"Thank you."

Emil stood up and shifted his gunbelt. "I better warn you," he said, "that your faculty advisor could be considered a suspect in the homicide. Maybe you better be a little careful."

"Professor *Torbert?*" Dee-Dee couldn't believe it. "He's the best teacher I ever *had*. He's the best one *here*. Why do you think that he . . . ?"

"Can't go into it. Just a word to the wise. Are you all right? Since the killing?"

"I feel a little . . . funny, out on campus at night. A lot of kids do. But we stay together when we're out, or we don't go out."

"Good. Keep it up. Oh, by the way, didn't you tell me that Rusty and Alicia had a date once?"

"Oh, that. Yes. But it didn't last long. She came home early, laughing."

"Why?"

"Uncle Emil, I don't know quite how to put this"—the hint of a blush appeared on her cheeks—"but, as I told you before, Lish could be mean. Rusty's a nice guy, not her type, but she got some

178

jollies playing with boys like that. She told me all about it, with relish. Apparently, she . . . she made herself available to him, and then cut him off."

"Stood him up, you mean?"

"More than that. She let him think that . . . that she'd, you know. She took her clothes off. But then she said no."

My God, Emil thought. Not a whole lot of men, whether they were good guys or not, would treat that sort of ploy with equanimity. No wonder Rusty hadn't admitted to the "date." But, wait. Muffy had indicated that Alicia must have known her killer. What was it that Miss Stanhope had said, while unbuttoning her blouse? ". . . If that's all you want, here it is. . . ."

Until this very moment, Emil had considered Rusty by far the least likely of the three jocks to have been capable of murder. Well, it looked as if he might have to make a reassessment now.

He kissed his niece on the forehead, cheered her with his favorite saying, "*Non illegitimati carborundum*" ("Don't let the bastards wear you down"), and left Halston Hall. A mid-afternoon lull had settled over the campus, and a rising wind slanted the rain into buildings and trees. Even the resplendent Sacred Steeple stood like a big shard of gunmetal against the scudding clouds. Emil cut behind Tobias Hall, where the faculty offices were, and headed toward his parked car. His head was bent against the rain, but out of the corner of his eye he caught a glimpse of movement and looked back. Somebody had edged ferretlike out of a Tobias fire exit. Emil's sixth sense, more than anything else, discerned something surreptitious. He stopped and turned around.

A slight figure in a blue slicker stood just outside the exit, looking around nervously.

Brewster Titchell, Jr.

He recognized the sheriff.

"Hey, Brew!" called Emil in a friendly way. After all, what had happened was history. He had nothing against the kid. "How you doin'?"

Brewster seemed to shiver once, then began to run.

"Hey, don't be scared . . ." Emil began, smiling a bit at the

179

whippersnapper's frantic flight. Titchell was carrying a big bundle of books under his thin arm, but when he rounded the corner on the run and disappeared from sight, something he'd been lugging fell onto wet ground. Shrugging, Emil walked over and picked it up. A notebook, on the cover of which was scrawled, in magic-marker: *Interpretive History 305—Contemporary Ideological Trends.* Kid would probably need it for class. Emil hurried to his car, got in, and took a quick gander. The notebook was about one-quarter filled, this early in the term. Titchell had unusual hand-writing, thin and rounded, quite readable. Charlie Hollman apparently taught this course because the notes followed a pattern. "Plato thought. . . ." followed by long paragraphs. "Machiavelli believed . . ." followed by more information. "Disraeli held . . ." etc. Lastly, to clarify everything, "Professor Hollman maintains . . ." Charlie always got the final word. There was what looked like a typed theme on unlined paper stuck between pages of the notebook, too. More stuff that Emil didn't know too much about. He skimmed a few lines:

> *. . . when we approach the question of individualism, it is clear to all dispassionate observers that societies, both in general and in particular, tend to support, in their later stages somewhat more than at their inception, the rights of the many as opposed to the needs of the few. It is also clear that . . .*

Whew! Emil had had enough. The kid would probably turn out to be a judge just like his sententious old man. What amused Emil was the phrase "it is clear." Didn't anybody in colleges know that *nothing* is clear? It's piled seven miles to heaven and it's forest all the way!

He riffled through the notebook's empty pages and, hidden away toward the back, found expressions of Junior's young heart, in his oddly refined scrawl.

*Alicia Stanhope*
*Alicia Morgana Stanhope*

*Lish Lish Lish*
*Alicia Titchell*
*Alicia Stanhope Titchell*
*Mrs. Brewster Titchell, Jr.*

So. What do you know? The illustrious Miss Stanhope had made yet another conquest, he concluded, tossing the notebook into the back seat.

Emil started his car and drove off campus, passing the pine tree and the golf course, where the crowd had continued to grow in spite of the rain. From the third tee to the ninth hole, people were waiting. Gabriel's Guards ringed the tree, as they had earlier. Whippletree did not see Bunny—she wasn't there—but he did catch a glimpse of Roy Riley, chubby Charlie Hollman, Butch Lodge, and Jaques LaBatt, deep in conversation.

The four men saw Emil's car go by, but only Riley waved. The wind caught pages of his reporter's notepad as he thrust it upward in salute, tiny flapping white tatters against the green needles of the pine.

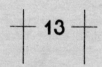

Now's my chance, thought Emil.

He drove back to St. Cloud, fifteen miles over the legal limit in spite of the rain, and went directly to the Hollman house. The two Gabriel's Guards at the front door stiffened like Dobermans when they saw him approach, and moved together, shoulder to shoulder, as he walked toward the steps. One of the guards said something in French.

"Howdy, boys. Bunny in?"

"No," said the bigger of the two.

Emil saw a flutter of curtain at the front window.

"I think you're mistaken," he told the sentinels.

The two looked at each other. "You are not wanted here," said the big one.

Emil put his foot on the bottom step and his hand on his .38. The men leaned forward, as if bracing themselves for contact.

"I'm comin' in, boys," Emil told them. "You better get your butts out of the way."

The little guard began to sputter away in French, but Bunny Hollman opened the door and broke the tension. "It's all right," she told them. "Emil, come in."

"Out of the way, fellows," Emil drawled, stepping past them into the house.

Bunny offered him a chair in the overwrought living room. She was still the woman Emil had always known, but she seemed different: calmer, more confident, almost content. She offered him coffee or a soda.

"No, we better talk fast, before they put you incommunicado again. What the hell's the story on all the protection, anyway?"

"Mr. LaBatt offered his services—he's such a spiritual man, so deep—and Charles felt we needed a bit of help, what with all these people coming here to St. Cloud."

"Bunny, me and my boys could take care of you just as well. Better."

She didn't meet his eyes. "Charles feels that you're . . . that you're not a *believer*, Emil. I'm sorry to say it, but that's what he thinks. It's his feeling that I must be surrounded by believers if my gift is to bear fruition."

"And what would that be?"

"Why, to have a message from Christ through his Blessed Mother."

"And you don't think being guarded by an accused murderer and his fanatical sidekicks will harm your gift?"

"You mean that awful story about Jacques murdering his wife? That's a terrible lie. Mrs. LaBatt was"—she shuddered luxuriously—"an evil woman who sated herself regularly in the pleasures of the flesh"—she shuddered again—"and Jacques is completely innocent. Charlie says—"

"Bunny, do you always think what Charlie wants you to?"

"I took marriage vows of obedience, Emil."

"So the hell did Sarah. But that doesn't mean she gave up her mind in the process."

Bunny looked pained. "Oh, Emil! Please! You! Who were chosen by Our Holy Mother for a message—"

"That's another thing I want to ask. How are you getting your information? About Susan? About those diamond earrings? About Toby Bolthaus and the brakes on that Pontiac?"

"The Virgin is telling me, Emil. Don't you *believe?*"

Emil sat there for a moment. It certainly seemed that Bunny was convinced of her own powers. But he knew, both from his own experience, and from his conversation with Anderson, that conviction can create belief as well as vice-versa.

There *had* to be some explanation, some gimmick, didn't there? "You're sure," he asked, "that Charlie's longtime feud with Coach Avano, and his well-known hostility to the sports program at North Star, isn't somehow behind these visions you're having? And the big crowds that are disrupting campus?"

"Emil," she said, speaking as if she'd been expecting this question and rehearsing her answer, "Emil, nothing in this life is simple. God didn't plan things that way. People must make choices. And in this case they have been given the opportunity to make a choice between God's message and man's frivolous diversions."

"You mean between the Virgin Mary and football, don't you? Have you any idea the kind of trouble you're going to cause? Especially next weekend at the homecoming game?"

"Charlie says—"

"I don't care what Charlie says. Don't *you* see what's happening?"

"I'm not causing trouble, I—"

"Think it over. *You* think it over."

Bunny began to cry. "Don't you believe me, Emil? You?"

"Come on now," he said. Sure, he would like to believe. He would like nothing better than to believe that Susan's death had not been his fault. Perhaps it hadn't been, but that was what he had believed all these years, that was the cruel knowledge with

183

which he had lived and suffered. How could a strange and sudden revelation, under these unconvincing and, frankly, bizarre circumstances be expected so quickly to make him believe, to bring him peace?

"I'm sorry," he said.

Bunny dried her eyes with her fingertips. "I forgive you, Emil. You're not a cruel man. I'll pray for you."

He heard the guards barking briefly outside on the steps. Then the front door opened with a crash. Jacques LaBatt entered, trailed by Charlie Hollman. Both men saw Mrs. Hollman wiping her eyes. LaBatt took a few fast strides toward Emil, his fist drawn back. Whippletree jumped to his feet, surprised at his own agility. LaBatt halted.

"*Get out, Emil!*" Charlie yelled. "Honey, has he been bothering you?" he asked his wife.

"No, no. . . ." she said.

"You and I, Sheriff," oozed LaBatt, with a delicious, slow fire of anticipation in his frightening eyes, "I think (*I theenk*) you and I will one day settle, once and for all."

"Looking forward to it," Whippletree replied, and the coldness in his voice was not feigned.

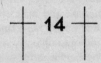

That week, in Washington, D.C., North Star President Rexford Anderson visited the White House, where it was announced that he had accepted the chairmanship of the newly formed Presidential Association for Sports Scholarship (PASS). Interviewed briefly on the South Lawn subsequent to his appointment, Anderson explained, with his usual impressive sonorous conviction, that the association had been established "in order to make certain that college athletes maintained academic standards at levels sufficient to meet the eligibility requirements of the NCAA."

Emil watched the interview on Channel 7, thinking of Gunnar Rutkow's miraculously altered *B*, when an obviously cynical reporter asked Rector Rex, "Isn't PASS merely an attempt to defuse the widely held suspicion that jocks are getting preferential treatment at a lot of major colleges and universities?"

"North Star is certainly a major university," Anderson replied, "and to my knowledge there has never been a single violation of eligibility regulations."

Rector Rex was also asked about the fact that the rooms of three Noble Norsemen had been searched in connection with a recent unsolved homicide on the North Star campus.

"Yes," he said briskly, "you might say that our local law enforcement personnel fumbled the ball on that one." A suave little smile, and the tone of his voice—just the right mixture of sarcasm and condescension—evoked an appreciative laugh, although not from Emil, who groaned in front of his TV. It was difficult to seem credible if you were up against smooth, sophisticated Anderson, especially if you were just an uneducated, down-home country lawman.

That week, in response to President Anderson's reference to the murder, Minneapolis TV came over to the sheriff's office and asked for an interview. First they wanted to film him in his office, leaning back in his swivel chair, with his boots on the desk. This idea was discarded when Emil suggested that the reporter might want to sit on his lap, too. Next the cameraman thought it might look nice if Emil would stand in front of an iron-barred cellblock door, but the lightman pronounced the concrete walls "too bleak" to serve as a backdrop, so this possibility was also dismissed. Finally they just took Emil outside and filmed him in front of the courthouse, so the gold dome would show in the picture, behind the sheriff's head.

Emil figured he'd be on the "State News Wrap-Up," and he was. It was bad enough: his face, sort of long and mournful, had not been designed for the media age. Then things got worse: because of the notoriety of murder at a famous football school, New York picked up on the story, and used the clip of Emil on the national news. Viewers of all persuasions, in every corner of the country, saw the dashing young reporter ask, "Sheriff Whippletree, now that you've failed in your attempt to pin this homicide on three outstanding young football players, what do you plan to do next?" And, after a long, uncomfortable pause, they heard Emil's laconic reply: "Well, not much else to do but keep plugging along, I guess. . . ."

"Maybe you should have worn a blue shirt," suggested Sarah, in the long, embarrassed silence that followed the turning off of the TV.

"A shirt wouldn't have helped me, and we both know it," he groused. "I just look like a big old bumpkin on the tube. Well, dammit, I'm not, and people are gonna know it when I solve this case."

"Of course they are," soothed Sarah.

That week, too, a small herd of feature writers and—it was rumored—two prospective novelists showed up in Stearns County to research the murder or Bunny's visions or both. Stung by his humiliating experience on television, Emil declined to be interviewed, and was later mentioned unflatteringly in seven newspapers, including *The New York Times*, and five magazines, including *Farm Journal*.

But the cruelest blow—not because it was entirely unexpected, but because it added to Emil's local woes—came on Saturday morning. The sheriff, as usual, went out on the porch to pick up his St. Cloud *Tribune*, and, as usual, sat down to read it with his breakfast of oatmeal and honey.

### LODGE ANNOUNCES FOR SHERIFF
by Roy Riley

Raleigh "Butch" Lodge, chief of security at North Star University, announced his candidacy yesterday for Sheriff of Stearns County. "I realize that the election is over a year away," Lodge told a small group of supporters and financial backers at a gathering in Waite Park's

By Charlie Hollman and Jacques LaBatt! fumed Emil, remembering the two of them talking to Butch and Roy Riley under the
pine tree earlier in the week.

He finished his breakfast, wondering what to do about Butch.
He'd been challenged before, of course. Opponents were nothing
new. Fifteen years ago he'd won the job from old Ed Petweiler.
Petweiler had been pretty well established, with most of his many
relatives on the payroll. But Emil'd won with the nepotism issue,
which old Ed had not defused with the avowal that "Petweilers are
the best people in the county and that's why I hired all of them."
Four years later, Emil had whipped Barney Elderkopf handily.
Then Wayne "Bimbo" Bonwit had gone down to defeat before the
Whippletree juggernaut. Last time around, three years ago,
Melrose constable Preston Lakevich had lost in a close race. But
all of those guys had been Stearns County types, like Emil. Butch
was different. He'd made a record for himself out in the Big
World, and if he worked up a good campaign, he might just be
pretty damn tough to beat.

Especially if I can't solve this homicide, Emil reflected, finishing the last of his coffee.

"What are your plans for today?" Sarah asked him.

"Not too damn much," he grumbled. "Probably watch the game
on TV this afternoon."

"Barb and I are going out to campus. She wants to see Dee-Dee.
And we'll probably pray awhile with Bunny."

Emil told her "take care," left the house, and drove to the office. Alyce was off all weekend—Emil was paying her back for

187

working last Saturday—and Jamie Gosch, reading the *Trib*, was alone in the Day Room.

"Where is everybody?"

"Well . . . ah . . . Pete Poll's wife called in to say he's sick again, Axel's out having breakfast, and I don't know where Farley is."

"Well, we damn well better get our act straight for that big homecoming game next week. Any calls?"

"Oh. Right. Wienie Pappendorf. He said you can ring him right at home."

Emil ambled into his office, sat down on the edge of his desk, and dialed the bookie.

"Spread's four points, Norsemen favored. You in?" asked Wienie.

"Yep. A hundred."

"A *hundred* bucks? You?"

"I'm gonna take a chance," Emil drawled. Bunny has got to be right at least *once*, he thought.

"Well, it's your money. Enjoy the game."

His bet placed, Emil hung around the office all morning, feeling sort of mournful and gloomy and ill-used. At a little after noon, he shuffled over to the Courthouse Bar and Grill for a beer and a roast-beef sandwich—wasn't even anybody around to jaw with—then climbed into his car and drove home. Titchell's notebook was still in the back seat. He pulled into his driveway and turned off the engine, feeling lonesome already with the knowledge that Sarah was gone. He debated calling Doc Divot—they could watch the game together—then decided against it. Divot would just rib him all afternoon about Butch Lodge. Sometimes that kind of joshing might make him feel better; today was not one of those times.

Big odds against you, Emil, my friend, he thought, settling down in front of the TV with a tall can of Hamm's. You can either fold or come back fighting.

Trouble was, he wasn't sure which to do.

Notre Dame won the toss and elected to receive. The two teams took their positions on the field. Emil leaned back, sipped beer, and looked forward to a couple of pleasant hours. Athletic events offered a certainty of outcome that real life so often withheld. Either one side would win, or the other, or there would be a tie. Three possibilities, no more and no less. Compared to the constant ambiguity of real life, sports weren't even one-tenth as complicated as nursery school. That was their big attraction.

The front that had crossed Minnesota earlier in the week was now stalled over South Bend. Intermittent spates of rain fell upon Memorial Stadium, home of the Fighting Irish. The helmets of the players glistened wetly, gold for the Irish, red, white, and blue for North Star. The TV announcer babbled about slippery conditions; his sidekick and "color" man recalled a field even more slippery on which he himself had skidded thirty years earlier. "I would have to say that these conditions might tend to favor Notre Dame," the announcer informed Emil. "They are dangerous in the air, whereas Snopes Avano, in spite of Rusty Rollins's talents, continues to pay homage to that grind-it-out running game of yore."

"Good old Snopes," said the color man. "I remember when he and I . . ."

The kickoff was high and deep. Notre Dame managed to get the ball back to its own twelve-yard line. Then, yard by arduous yard, the Irish began working their way upfield. You had to give them credit. Gunnar Rutkow, bulwark of the Norse defense, was everywhere. A series of short runs, however, and a couple of quick passes, brought Notre Dame to the midfield mark. Here Gunnar succeeded in sacking the Irish quarterback, which produced a skittering, tumbling fumble that North Star recovered. Rusty Rollins and the offensive unit took the field and prepared to roll.

"Now we'll see what the Norsemen can show us today," the announcer said.

Fans didn't have to wait long. Rusty, looking cool and even cocky out there on the rain-slick turf, ran straight into the line for two yards, then two more yards, then caught the Irish napping with a long pass. It was not the Fool's Gold play; he just dropped back about ten yards and threw the football straight and true to Duffy in the end zone.

"What a pass," the color man raved, "like a bullet . . ."

But North Star missed the conversion, and it was 6–0. Still, the Norsemen had drawn first blood. Momentum was on their side.

"All you need to do me some good is four points, fellas," Emil reminded them.

The Irish were more successful in their second drive, working the left of the Norse defense, then the right, until, at the beginning of the second quarter, they stood poised to strike on the North Star eight-yard line. Emil got himself another beer, and squatted in front of the TV, watching closely. Just as the Irish quarterback began calling signals, the phone rang.

"Goddamnit," Whippletree muttered. He would have liked to have taken the thing off the hook, but with a job like his, no way.

The nearest phone was out in the kitchen, and he couldn't see the TV from there. He managed a gruff "Hello?"

"Sheriff Whippletree?" Female voice, unfamiliar, sort of smarmy and seductive.

"It is."

"This is Trudilynn Steinhaus calling. Mrs. T. R. Steinhaus. May I talk to you for a moment?"

Butch Lodge's ex-wife! Now what? "Sure, go ahead," Emil said.

"Sheriff, I saw in the *Trib* where my ex-husband is planning to run against you. I just want you to know that I'm on your side, and I think I can help you if you want."

Emil heard wild cheering from the television and knew he'd probably missed an Irish touchdown. "How's that?" he asked.

"I can give you information about Butch."

"No, that's okay." He wasn't about to deal in backstairs dirt. If he was going to lose, he'd lose clean.

"But this is important," Trudilynn persisted. "Butch is not the guy he seems, and people should know it."

"Well, maybe, but I—"

"Please listen. This is hard for me. I would have come to tell you in person, but I didn't think I had the nerve. You see, Butch is a violent man. He beat me . . ."

"Why didn't you do something about it when you were still married to him?"

"I did. I *divorced* him. You see, he was not always . . . *effective* in our marriage. Do you know what I'm trying to say?"

"I think so."

"And when he . . . when he couldn't, he'd get violent, like he blamed me for what he couldn't do."

"That's hardly the thing I want to use in a campaign, Mrs. Steinhaus. Thank you, but—"

"Wait, Sheriff. Don't hang up. There's more. You know, there are rumors floating around about that murder on campus last week."

"Wouldn't doubt it."

"About how the killer was supposed to have used . . . one of those things that men wear."

A rubber. "I get you," Emil said.

"Well, Butch always wore one. Always. There was something about it for him. It was the only way he could."

"Mrs. Steinhaus, are you accusing your former husband of—"

"No. No, not in so many words. But when I heard the rumor, I made a connection. Maybe I'm wrong, b. t isn't it something to consider? Most men would do almost anything not to have to wear one. Because of the sensation, you know?"

In his whole sexual experience, which was exclusively with Sarah, Emil had never worn one, so he didn't really know.

"So I think you ought to keep it in mind," Trudilynn continued. "Why would a *rapist* bother to wear one of those things, unless . . ."

Unless it was the only way he could perform, concluded Emil. Frowning, he went back to the football game. So old Butch's marital problems had extended into the bedroom. It was something to remember.

Midway through the second quarter, the Irish led 7–6. But the Norsemen were on a roll, in spite of the increasing rain. Rusty shot Duffy a short pass, then a long one, both complete. Then, with the Notre Dame defense expecting further assault by air, Rollins shifted gears, and used his running backs to churn out three first downs in seven plays. A North Star touchdown just before the halftime gun was capped when Rollins himself ran for the conversion, and the second quarter ended with the Norsemen ahead 14–7.

Emil went out into the kitchen again, got himself a bowl of unsalted peanuts, and returned to watch the halftime show. Sarah always accused him of wanting to see the high-kicking legs of the cheerleaders and majorettes. He always defended himself by claiming to love the marching songs played by the bands. Sarah was right.

The announcer and his sidekick recapitulated the first half while the Notre Dame band marched up and down the field, playing a medley of patriotic tunes. Emil watched the girls.

"There seems to be some kind of a disturbance down at the far end of the field," said the announcer casually. "Perhaps if the cameras would swing down there . . ."

Emil, and everybody else watching television, saw five young women in the stands holding aloft a banner fashioned of bedsheet and paint. It was not an elegant job, but it certainly got the message across.

### KILLER ON THE FIELD? NSU! MURDER ON CAMPUS? SHAME ON YOU!

Within a minute, several security men and a handful of fans succeeded in ripping the makeshift message from the hands of its bearers. The cameras moved quickly back to the marching band, but not before showing the protesters being led away by Security. Emil thought he saw one of the girls trying to bite a guard's biceps.

"Now what do you suppose that was all about?" the color man inquired.

"Tempest in a teapot," his partner replied. "There was a homicide on the North Star campus up in Minnesota last week. A couple of the Norsemen were apparently suspected for a short time. Some sheriff up there got things all mixed up. The young coeds we just saw are obviously just as confused as that sheriff was."

The announcer and the color man had a good laugh.

"It takes all kinds," the color man pronounced.

"So said a wise man," seconded the announcer.

Emil fumed helplessly, but at least they hadn't mentioned his name.

"President Anderson of North Star phoned me just before the game," the announcer said, "and assured me that nothing is amiss in his domain."

"I should say not," exuded color.

Emil felt defeated. Killer on the field? NSU!

Snopes Avano, chewing his pipe, dogtrotted from the gate out onto the field, leading his warriors back for the second half. In a heartfelt, spontaneous gesture of affection and respect, the crowd rose and cheered the legendary old coach. He stood for a moment on the Norse bench and waved his visored hat. Rain, falling more heavily now, ran down the lenses of his sunglasses and across his forehead. There might have been a few tears there, too, but it was impossible to tell. Play resumed.

Notre Dame kicked off to start the second half. The Norsemen commenced a long, ugly drive—two players were injured and had to be carried away on stretchers—that was ultimately rewarded with a touchdown. Gunnar did the kicking, parting the uprights neatly, and it was 21–7.

But the Irish did not give up. They had a terrific team, and the fabled homefield advantage. They came roaring back, yard by grinding yard, never slacking, never stopping, to eke out a touchdown in the final minutes of the third quarter. Taking a risk, particularly with Gunnar on the prowl against them, the Irish passed for the conversion. It was 21–15.

At home in front of the TV in St. Cloud, Emil was getting excited. His hundred bucks was on the line, but more than that he was thinking of Bunny's prediction.

He sat bolt upright in his chair, and dropped a half filled can of Hamm's, when, three minutes into the final quarter, North Star made a field goal, going ahead 24–15.

"Look at the rain come down now," the announcer said. "And I guess the Norsemen are prepared for it, too."

Emil didn't quite know what the guy was talking about at first; then he saw that North Star's team managers were passing out sleek, hooded raincapes to the players on the bench.

"Hell, I don't blame 'em a bit," he said.

The Irish, showing some desperation now as the minutes ticked by, moved across the midfield mark, running the ball, passing, running again. But, with four minutes remaining, they got careless and fumbled on the Norse thirty-seven. North Star recovered.

A great whoop sounded from the Norse bench as the offensive unit, led by Rusty Rollins, tossed away their blue raincapes and took the field for the final segment of the game. The capes fluttered to the wet turf and slowly collapsed, like dying bats.

Rusty got into position behind the line, head snapping this way, that way, in total and exultant control. Young and strong and perfectly confident, he took the snap and dropped back. Notre Dame, along with Emil, had been expecting a slow, clock-killing sequence of plays, but Snopes had apparently decided to test-run Fool's Gold. Emil saw Lem Duffy, fast as a streak, moving down the sideline. Rollins was in the pocket, seemingly undecided, and every second was an hour. Emil recalled that the main feature of this play was the intricate blocking designed to spring Rusty from an apparent trap. The rush was on by the Irish defenders. Emil leaned forward and peered at the screen. Rusty flicked his arm once, faking a pass, then clutched the ball to his belly, feinted left, right, and then plunged forward. A hole appeared in the surging Irish line where none had been before.

But something went wrong. Timing was off by a millisecond, or human error beset Avano's best-laid plan. The hole closed just as Rollins tried to dash through it. Three powerful bodies met in one place at the same time, with Rusty crushed in the middle.

Whether there was an actual fumble or whether a Notre Dame player pulled the ball from Rollins as he lay on the ground, Emil couldn't tell. But when the players untangled themselves from that heaving pile of armored bodies, the referee signaled a turnover, the South Bend crowd roared in ecstasy, and quarterback Rollins lay on the ground, his outstretched arms beating a tattoo on the turf, his legs jerking in spasms. Emil had once seen a prizefight in the old Minneapolis Coliseum, had witnessed a brutal battle ending in a knockout. The defeated fighter's legs, as he lay on the canvas, had twitched sickeningly, just like Rusty's. Next morning, Emil read about the fighter's death in the newspaper.

Snopes was on the field, on hands and knees beside his fallen star. Players gathered around. Then Snopes was on his feet, signaling the bench, and two stretcher-bearers trotted onto the field, like corpsmen in search of bodies after a firefight. But, before they reached the scene, Rusty sat up.

"Wait! I think he's . . . I think he's all right," the announcer said, with fully as much relief as Emil felt. Tens of thousands of young people were injured playing football every year—the risk of disaster outweighed by promise of glory—and not a few were marred for life. Rusty Rollins, of Sleepy-Eye, Minnesota, would not be one of them. He was sitting, crouching, standing. The spectators gave him a vast cheer, in which gratitude and appreciation were delicately commingled, and he walked slowly toward the Norse bench.

"Under his own power, too," the color man said. "That's always a good sign."

Rusty, thought Emil, if that was your private alley, I'm glad the gunman missed.

Play resumed, with one minute and twelve seconds on the clock. It would take more miracles than Bunny Hollman could imagine to win the game for Notre Dame now, but they did not give up, not even bothering with the huddle, using each second, every play, but getting only as far as the North Star twenty-eight-yard line, where it was fourth down and one to go, with nine seconds remaining.

Well, Bunny my girl, Emil thought, as he saw Notre Dame preparing for a field goal attempt, you came close again. Even if the kick were good, the score would be 24–18. Emil had beat the spread, he was in the money, and he felt damn good.

So it was with incredulous consternation that he saw the kicker charge the snapped football, take it on the fly, and head for the right sideline, picking up blockers as he ran.

The game ended at 24–21, with North Star victorious. But with Emil Whippletree one hundred dollars poorer.

Sarah came home at a little after five.

"How'd Dee look to you?" Emil asked.

"Oh, pretty well, considering. We spent an hour with her, then she had to go to the library. After that we went to pray with Bunny."

"Big crowd?"

"Emil, it was huge. I heard somebody say that over ten thousand people were there today, and I believe it. We never even got close to the pine tree. But there were speakers set up all over the golf course, so everyone could hear."

"Did she have a vision today?" he asked, with some trepidation. There was only a week to go before the big Illinois game, but each incident adding to Bunny's renown meant a larger crowd of worshippers, and he was going to have to deal with them in one way or another.

"Yes, she did. That is, I *think* she did. . . ."

"I thought you said you could hear everything?"

"Well, yes . . ." Sarah seemed a little evasive.

"I'm waitin'," Emil said.

"There was . . . some sort of a disturbance today," Sarah told him. "I didn't see it. I just heard about it. I didn't . . . want to bother you with it."

"Bother me. I might need to know."

Sarah sighed. "Emil, it was different out there today. I felt good the other times. Happy. Peaceful. But today was . . . different. It started when Bunny recited that . . . sort of verse or poetry."

"Bet it was about sex again, wasn't it?"

She nodded. "I don't understand that part of it. . . ."

Emil laughed. "You've sure been fooling me for a long time then."

"Oh, Emil. I mean, I don't understand why that . . . that rather flagrant verse is a part of what she does. It was pretty extreme today. About climax and everything. Some people laughed and

196

shouted. There was a big commotion. I heard later that some of the Gabriel's Guards got into a fight with the hecklers."

"Anybody hurt?"

"I don't know. I'm just telling you what I heard."

Office would have called me if they needed me, Emil figured. But he had a feeling that the fight, which he was sure had occurred, presaged bigger trouble to come.

"Then Bunny announced that the Virgin was in our midst," Sarah went on. "There was no message from Jesus, and a lot of people were disappointed, but Our Holy Mother admonished everyone that Saturday would be crucial to us all."

"Sure, game day," said Emil.

"No, Bunny implied that Jesus' message would come on Saturday."

"Charlie is going all out in his battle against the athletic program, isn't he?"

"Is that all you think it is? How do you explain the messages Bunny has given us before? They have to come from . . . somewhere, don't they?"

"That's true. But I sure as hell don't think they come from heaven."

"It never pays to be impious," Sarah said. "There's always a comeuppance."

"Then somebody better inform Mrs. Hollman," Emil snapped. "Sorry," he added in quick apology. "It's just that I don't care for the most private and tragic part of our lives to have come up again."

Emil stopped in at the office after dinner. Wienie was there, settling up. Axel had made the spread, odds had been five-to-one, and the big deputy chortled as he counted and recounted his haul. Poll was there too, and Farley. Both had lost and both borrowed from Axel to pay the bookie. Emil paid up too, and the deputies were amazed at the size of his wager.

"Wow!" exclaimed Axel. "Did you think you had a private tip, or something?"

"I'm working with a system," Emil growled, "only I haven't got it figured out yet."

"There's always next week," Wienie said cheerfully.

"You boys hear anything about a fight out at North Star?" asked Emil, after the bookie had left.

The deputies exchanged glances. "Well, kinda," said Axel.

"You care to elaborate on that?"

"There's a kid from St. Paul, maybe about twenty-two or so. Jacques LaBatt beat him up when he laughed at Bunny Hollman."

"He didn't like her poetry?"

"I guess not. He's not hurt bad, though, and he isn't gonna press charges."

Dammit, Emil thought. That would have been a good way to get at LaBatt.

"There was another incident, too," offered Poll. "You know Nora Sherman? The one who lost her baby last spring to Sudden Infant Death Syndrome? Well, apparently the baby hadn't been baptized. Bunny had a message from the Blessed Virgin to Nora. Said her baby would be in Limbo forever and would never see God. Said it was Nora's fault for not baptizing the kid. Poor Nora went sort of berserk. They had to haul her away."

Strange, Emil thought. Bunny's messages seemed to be assuming a dismal cast, a reflection of LaBatt's self-righteous rigidity and dark fanaticism. Certainly it was the height of cruelty to have laid such a burden on poor Mrs. Sherman.

"Maybe Bunny just had a bad day," he said. "I'm going home. Call me if anything comes up."

"Sure thing, Sheriff."

Emil had intended to try and get a good night's sleep, but he was restless. The constant interplay of good and evil preyed on his mind. What if Mrs. Hollman was indeed experiencing communion with a powerful but shadowy Beyond? What if people had been gulled by bright messages of peace into a Faith that would now be betrayed as evil raised its horned head? No good could possibly be served by torturing a poor woman who had lost her child.

Sarah finished the historical romance she'd been reading—*Fires of Delight* by Vanessa Royall—and dozed off. But Emil couldn't sleep. He went downstairs, fixed himself a thick braunschweiger sandwich with mustard and onions, poured himself a beer, and tried to find a movie on TV. There weren't any good ones, so after a while he found himself staring at something ponderous on the public station. It turned out to be a videotape of hearings held by the Federal Committee on Urban Harmony, which had met this week in Boston and had been chaired by Dr. Rexford Anderson. Rector Rex, flanked by aides in dark suits, presided from a courtroom-looking bench as, one by one, ordinary citizens rose from the audience and spoke into a standing microphone on the floor. They talked about poverty, prejudice, crime, dirt, and urban decay. Anderson listened and nodded a lot. Now and then he made a note on a pad in front of him, and when each speaker finished with a respectful thank you, Anderson said that great strides were being made, that things were getting better.

Then a dark, little man stepped to the microphone. He may have been Hispanic, or Lebanese, or Indian. Emil could not judge by his accent or appearance. He was not at all respectful of Anderson's presence and authority. He was, in fact, very angry.

"Who you think you are?" he demanded, shaking his finger at Rector Rex, who stiffened suddenly in his big leather chair. "Who you think you are, to come here and tell us things are getting better, things are changing? We live here, in all this disease and muck and drug dealing. You come for a day and then you go. Only thing changed is the name of your committee. Used to be Committee on Urban Strife. Now it's Committee on Urban Harmony. Hah! That's the only change, because you don't know a damn thing about what goes on here. . . ."

The camera moved in for a close-up of Anderson, and Emil was certain that he saw on the president's handsome, distinguished face a momentary flicker of fear and loathing. It was quickly replaced by a hard look of decision. Rector Rex made an abrupt gesture, and the speaker, still yelling, shirtsleeves flapping, was unceremoniously dragged away by a couple of cops.

Emil was astonished. He'd just had a glimpse of a part of Anderson's personality, the existence of which he'd barely suspected. Were the man's basic values reflected by his summary behavior here? Emil felt like cheering for the gutsy little guy who'd told the truth as he saw it, had not kowtowed to the image of reassurance and authority on the high bench before him. Emil also recalled the girls who'd been led away this afternoon, for the offense of having displayed an unpleasant message on a bedsheet. That was how things went in Anderson's league: you minded your manners, you kept your place, *you* paid obeisance to *their* vision of reality.

*Or they hauled you away!*

By God, he thought, chomping on the braunschweiger sandwich, what was wrong with me that I even debated whether to fight or fold? There wasn't any choice at all.

*I'm fighting.*

Buoyed by this decision, his mind began working lickety-split, going over all the facts and impressions he'd stored up. A parade of data passed behind his eyes, and ended with a vision of those blue North Star raincapes.

He'd made a big mistake by asking for warrants to search the rooms of the players. The raincapes would be kept in the locker room beneath Granitelli Stadium. And—he'd bet his job on it— *one* of those raincapes, slightly torn by Alicia Stanhope's fingernails, hung now in the locker of a killer.

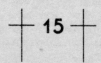

Business was good in St. Cloud. The crowds of prayer pilgrims continued to grow; motel and restaurant owners rejoiced. If Snopes Avano raged against the mobs that would block access to the stadium, if Emil worried about possible violence, others saw naught but pots of gold. Luther Proctor, manager of Bunyanland, reported the largest weekly receipts in the three years he'd been on the job.

"I'd like to get down on my knees and thank Mrs. Hollman,"

Proctor was reported in the *Trib* as saying, "but I'm too busy right now selling food."

"Good for you," muttered Emil, finishing his honey and oatmeal at the kitchen table. "Sarah, I've got to run. What are your plans for today?"

Emil's wife, busy putting dishes into the washer, looked up. "I'm going to xerox my genealogical materials and mail them to the Historical Society. They're having a contest. The person with the most thorough record of family history will win a hundred dollars."

"Is that right? You wouldn't want to invest that with Ethan Pappendorf, would you?"

"It's funny you should mention him, Emil. I looked in the phone book under 'Investment Counsellors' and his name wasn't listed. Are you sure he's legitimate?"

"Oh, yeah, sure," Emil said, buckling on his gunbelt. "He's too busy to take on any more clients. Doesn't even need a listing."

He got into his car and drove to the office. There was a chill, early morning sharpness in the air; cold droplets of dew clung glistening to blades of grass; avenues were shaded by leafy plumes of red and gold.

"What's up, Alyce?" Emil asked as he came in.

His secretary swallowed some coffee and checked a sheet of paper. "Vice-President Dexter's secretary called. She wants to know if you'd care to join Dexter and Mr. Stanhope later this morning. They're meeting to discuss bringing in outside agencies to take over the case."

"Hummmpppph," he replied scornfully. "Call back and tell 'em I'll have the whole thing wrapped up by the end of the week."

She looked after him in wonder as he strode into his office.

He put a big plug of Copenhagen into his mouth and went through the mail. A couple of law-enforcement brochures, some advertisements for weapons, handcuffs, radios, and about a dozen letters. Three asked him what he was going to do to solve the Stanhope murder. Five told him who had committed the murder—naming everybody from town drunk Fred Stroheim to a devil called Ogulomiah—two said they were supporting him against Butch Lodge, one said Butch Lodge was a great man, and the last, unsigned, said Emil was too dumb to figure anything out and he ought to go back where he came from.

He called Alyce in and dictated polite replies to the people who had written, adding to one letter a postscripted request for further information on the local whereabouts of Ogulomiah.

"Who's that?" Alyce wanted to know.

"Don't play innocent with me," he told her. "A whole bunch of people saw you dancing with him at The Bucket on Saturday night."

Doc Divot called to ask if Emil wanted to meet for lunch. The sheriff had to decline; he didn't know what his day would be like. Norb Heffner phoned to ask if Emil had come up with any buyers for his worthless stretch of land along I-94. Emil had to disappoint him. He sent Axel and Poll out to Kimball to investigate a case of suspected arson in a bar. Cowboy John had gotten into a fight with the tavern owner on Saturday night; perhaps the fire was retributive. Farley had the day off, so Emil told Jamie Gosch to mind the store. Then he watched at his office window until he saw Judge Titchell climbing the steps into the courthouse. Emil put on his hat, left the office, crossed the street, and entered the courthouse too.

The place had won architectural prizes in its time, and indeed it was rather imposing, with all the marble and the sweeping staircases. Titchell's chambers, however, suggested the dowdy fussiness of their self-important, crochety occupant. The judge's tastes ran to religious bric-a-brac and languid, sensitive plants that shrank and trembled when anyone came close. There were a lot of books on the mahogany shelves, and reams of files on Titchell's oversized desk. He looked inconsequential behind it, like a high-school kid playing judge on Boys' County Day, when the best and the brightest showed up to see how the real world presumably worked.

"Emil," nodded the judge, peering through the wire-rimmed spectacles that balanced on his great, beaklike prow of a nose, "it's a rare privilege indeed to see you on this side of the street."

"It's a big surprise for me, too." Emil didn't sit down or ask for a chair. "I'm here because I need another warrant. I made a mistake last time. Now I have to search the North Star locker room."

Titchell yanked off his glasses, a gesture of exasperation. "What in hell for?"

"Because that's where I'm going to find the evidence I need to convict a killer."

"That's what you told me last time, when you wanted to go rummaging around inside Valhalla. We all know how that worked out. You made, frankly, an ass of yourself, and everybody knows it. In fact, a lot of people are blaming you—I'm not one of 'em; I'm just telling you—for the close showing our Norsemen had against Notre Dame on Saturday. The boys should have won in a walk, but you—*you*, Emil—upset them."

"A lot of people are saying this?"

"A hell of a lot of them, Emil. Exactly what is it that you're looking for in the gym?"

"Certain articles of clothing."

"Even if I'd be disposed to issue a warrant—which I'm not—you'd have to be more specific, particularly after your fiasco in Valhalla."

I'm not telling him about the raincapes, Emil thought. He's tied into Anderson's VIP network, and he'd go blabbing right away.

"No can do, Emil," the judge was saying. "I'd be derelict in my duties if I cooperated in another one of your laughingstock wild-goose chases. I hold elective office, too, you know. You may want to blow your job, but I'm more responsible than that."

"Well, thank you for your aid and advice," said Whippletree acidly.

Titchell smiled with what he apparently meant to be sympathetic understanding, but which looked an awful lot like glee. "I'm sorry about your situation, Emil," he said. "I know it's tough. Want to know what I'd do if I were in your shoes?"

This should be good, thought Emil. He nodded.

"Nothing," said the judge. "Let the case go. Anderson's been working on it, and everything's about to jell now. Keep messing around, and you'll only be humiliated."

"What do you mean, 'everything's about to jell?'"

"I can't talk about it."

"Rexford Anderson is not Sheriff of Stearns County. I am."

"Well," snapped the judge, "when you're not doing the job, somebody has to."

Emil was furious now, but he didn't want to give Titchell the satisfaction of witnessing a blow-up. In a way, he owed the judge a bit of thanks. Because now he knew that something was up, a new twist, and that the imperial Anderson was behind it. He recalled how impressed he'd been upon first meeting the university president, and how he'd wondered if a lot of formal education truly made a man better in a deep, personal sense. Depends a lot on the man, he realized ruefully.

"Oh, by the way," he told Titchell, just before he left the judge's chambers, "your kid dropped his notebook out on campus and I picked it up. If he wants it back, I guess he knows where to find me."

"I guess he does," replied Titchell, without much interest.

Emil plodded back across the street to the office, trying to figure out what to do now. Was Anderson back in Minnesota, or was he still off in the Big World beyond Stearns County? But even if he decided what to do about Bunny Hollman, Charlie Hollman, Coach, Torbert, and Dee-Dee, what would Rector Rex do about the murder?

He couldn't just come jetting back here to the prairie and sweep away a homicide, could he? Unless—Emil realized with a start— unless President Anderson knew something crucial that Emil did not.

*And had known it all along!*

Emil knew something unusual was up as soon as he saw Alyce's dreamy-eyed smile. She possessed, perhaps in excess, a Stearns County reluctance to be impressed by much of anything. Yet training and heritage had crumbled. Alyce glowed like some daffy sophomore who'd just made the cheerleading team.

"Sheriff! Sheriff!" she hissed ecstatically, jumping out of her chair and pointing frenziedly at his office door, "He's *in* there! He's *in* there!"

"Yep, he sure is in there," corroborated Deputy Gosch, who was studying promotion materials again.

Emil shrugged and walked in to see who *he* was.

Rusty Rollins stood up immediately, respectfully, as soon as he saw the sheriff. Rather shyly, he offered his hand. Emil shook it, told the young man to sit down again, and lowered himself into the creaking swivel chair.

"Guess I'll have to arrest you," he said.

Rollins looked stunned. His face paled slightly, and he stared at Emil in bewilderment.

"Yep," said the sheriff. "You gone and got my secretary all excited"—even now Alyce was peeking around the doorjamb—"and I won't get a lick of work out of her for the rest of the day."

Rollins relaxed, then smiled. He really was a hell of a handsome young guy. He wore his usual perfectly pressed slacks and a V-neck sweater with a soft-collared polo shirt. Emil noticed a neck brace. "Hurt yourself?" he asked.

"Saturday's game. Nothing serious. I'll be fine for Illinois."

"I was watching TV when I saw you get tackled on that play," Emil said. "And I want you to know that I was scared."

"Well, thanks, Sheriff. I wasn't sure what was going on for a minute or two. But it's one of the risks of the game."

There was a moment of uncomfortable silence. Emil sensed, on the part of the star quarterback, a reluctance to introduce whatever business he had come here to discuss. The youthful nervousness, however, was altogether natural and attractive. Rusty glanced at the floor, then at the open doorway to the outer office.

Without comment, Whippletree got up and closed it.

"Shoot," he said, returning to his chair.

Looking simultaneously relieved and flustered, Rusty screwed up his resolve. "Sheriff Whippletree," he began, "I have a confession to make—"

"Just as long as you know I'm no priest," Emil interjected. "I can't give absolution."

"I could probably use some, too," Rusty said. "You see, Sheriff, I wasn't completely accurate . . . that is, I guess I lied to you when you asked if I'd ever dated Alicia Stanhope. . . ."

Now it comes out, thought Emil.

"The fact is," Rusty continued, "that I didn't want anyone to know. I was ashamed of myself."

"Why? For having a date with a good-looking girl?"

"No. For the way she made me . . . for the way I behaved. There were . . . things happened. Do you understand? I just wanted you to know I *had* a date with her, if it's important to your investigation, and also that I'm not the kind of guy who's interested in girls like that. It was just one of those things . . ."

Emil, who'd already learned from Dee-Dee that Rollins and Alicia had shared a disastrous "date," was more interested in the possible ulterior motive for Rusty's confession. The old sheriff judged himself as more than fair-to-middling when it came to down-home sagacity, and right away he reached a conclusion: Rusty was telling him these things, making a clean breast of it, so to speak, because *he* was Dee-Dee's secret boyfriend, and he wanted Emil to think well of him, both now and when, eventually, the troth was pledged. It had taken Rusty a lot of courage—not to mention honesty—to come here this morning. And, as Emil saw the boy struggling, slightly flushed now with embarrassment and resolve, to state his case, he was genuinely touched.

You've got a good man, Dee, he thought. God bless you both.

". . . I have to say this," Rusty was telling the sheriff, "for my own sake if not for yours. There was no *actual contact* between us, ever. . . ."

"Son, it's okay. That's your business. I don't care."

"But I wanted you to know. Jenny, my girl back home, was good. *Is* good. So are . . . all the other girls I know . . ."

*Another* clue, thought Emil. Not only will Dee and Rusty have to wait until graduation to get married, Rusty's probably agonizing over what to tell poor Jenny, back there in Sleepy-Eye. The problems of the young.

". . . but in spite of the fact that I let myself be weakened by

206

lust," Rusty was saying fervently, "it doesn't count against me, does it, because there was no contact. . . ?"

"Hey, look, I told you I wasn't a priest."

Rusty managed a smile. "You're right, Sheriff. But, after what almost happened to me Saturday on the football field in Indiana, you have to admit that I might have a sudden inclination to make sure my slate is clean."

"Lightning never strikes in the same place twice," encouraged Emil.

"It doesn't have to," Rusty replied. "You know, when those two Irish defenders hit me, I was out on my feet. I mean, I was unconscious before I ever hit the ground." He paused. "Sheriff, there'd be no time to make amends. There'd be no way. You have to be ready, I guess."

"In everything, all the time," agreed Emil. Smart guy, and pretty darn mature. He was thinking of Rusty as sort of a son-in-law. He also wanted to go, find Dee-Dee, and give her a big hug and a blessing. But, of course, he wasn't supposed to know.

"Son," he said, standing, "I appreciate your stopping by and telling me this. "I'm sure it'll be of use."

Rollins looked pleased.

"We'll see a lot more of each other in the future . . ."

Rusty looked startled, as if his secret had been found out.

". . . at football games and such-like," added Emil hurriedly, lamely.

"Oh, sure," the quarterback replied, relieved. He got up too. He seemed to hold his neck a trifle stiffly.

"It's only the brace," he said, in response to Emil's worried stare. "I feel great. Really. Our trainer put it on for insurance."

"Want a ride back to campus?" Emil asked.

"No, thanks. I took our red-, white-, and-blue bus."

Aha! thought the sheriff. Rusty and Dee had taken separate buses to Bunyanland on the day he'd spoken to Muffy Huff. Dee-Dee's secrets were falling into place. Emil wished only that his current problems would be as felicitously resolved.

After Rusty left the office, Gosch and Alyce were beside themselves. "What'd he want, Sheriff? What'd he want? And why didn't you introduce us?"

"Oh, for Christ's sake," Emil told them. "The guy's a twenty-one-year-old college kid, innocent as the day is long. You should have talked to him, not stuffed him alone in my office. He's a regular human being, just like me."

There was a long silence, then Alyce said, hesitantly, "But we're scared of you, Emil. We admire you too much. I guess that's how I felt about Rusty Rollins when I saw him walk in."

Doc Divot roared when, at lunch in the Courthouse Bar and Grill, Emil related Alyce's comment. The sheriff thought he was in for some of Divot's typical razzing, but the coroner surprised him.

"You know, Emil," he said, sipping a Cold Spring beer and waiting for his roast-beef sandwich, "Alyce finally hit it, whether she's aware of it or not. I don't think you have any idea of your own powers."

"What? To scare people?" Emil chugged some beer.

"No," said Divot. "It's awe. Everybody around here holds you in tremendous esteem, but they don't want to mention it to you, or maybe even think about it themselves, because they know deep down in their hearts that you don't give a damn for pomp and circumstance. This is what gets 'em. You don't put on any airs. If any of them were able to do the job you do, they'd have somebody to polish their boots and badge, they'd assign themselves a driver for their car—"

"Hell, no they wouldn't," protested Emil.

"Don't you know what people are even *like*?" the coroner wondered. "I sure as hell do. I cut 'em open when they're dead and can't lie any more."

"I don't buy it," said Emil. Alf, the bartender, slid big, hot steaming gravy-covered roast-beef sandwiches at them. "President Anderson is a guy for awe."

Divot knifed and forked a corner of the sandwich. "Emil," he said slowly, chewing, "I'm not saying this because I'm your friend, even though I am, and even though you ain't half worth the aggravation you cause me, but Rexford Anderson can't hold a candle to you on any human scale that I know of."

Emil heard, in Divot's voice, a trace of the gruff tenderness by which male love is revealed. He felt a pure surge of faith in himself. But it would not have been good form—it would have been incredibly gauche—to thank Doc for his support.

"You want to borrow money, or what?" he said instead.

"There are a lot of ways to give a guy the business," Doc went on. "Right now, seems to me, Anderson is giving you the business. Only he's doing it by proxy, sort of. Hell, I read in the Minneapolis paper this morning that he's flying down to San Antonio to study the plight of illegal aliens who come in across the Rio Grande from Mexico. Now, he may have had that scheduled for months in advance, but the fact is that he doesn't *want* to be on campus right now."

"Why not?"

"Things are too hot. He's worried about something, Emil. And he's scared of you."

"He's got to come back sometime."

Divot chomped some sandwich, swallowed. "Emil, awhile back I took my grandkids to this movie, *Star Track*. You know, the one that has this guy with the pointy ears? In it, the good guys were up against some bad guys with a spaceship that could become invisible. But it took them all their power to *stay* invisible. If they wanted to fire rockets at the good guys, they had to become visible again, and then they were a target themselves."

"I don't think I get you," Emil said.

"It's simple. You just wait for Anderson to become visible again. That's your cue. Then you hit him with both barrels."

"I'm not sure my gun is loaded," Emil said.


Doc and the sheriff were finishing lunch when Roy Riley dropped in for a quick one.

"Hey, you guys," he said, "what's up?"

"Not too damn much," allowed Doc. "How about yourself?"

"I don't know yet. But I got a call from Vice-President Dexter, out at the university. He says he's got a big story for me. I wonder what it's about."

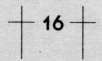

## 16

### UNIVERSITY CALLS FOR ACTION
#### "APPEARANCE OF INCOMPETENCE," DEXTER SAYS

Dr. Fagin Dexter, interviewed yesterday in the president's office at North Star University, called upon Stearns County Sheriff Emil L. Whippletree to admit his inability to handle the Stanhope murder case and turn over the investigation to what Dexter termed "competent outside agencies, whether state or federal. Details will have to be ironed out," Dexter continued, "but the appearance of incompetence on the part of Sheriff Whippletree demands a new direction immediately."

Also present at the interview was Mr. Robert Bruce Stanhope, Edina businessman and father of the victim.

"I'm not withdrawing from anything, now or ever," Whippletree asserted in a telephone interview with this reporter. "I intend to solve the case by Saturday."

"How are you going to do that?" inquired Sarah worriedly, reading the article at the breakfast table Tuesday morning. "You haven't given yourself much time."

"*They* haven't given me much time," he growled. "But I know what's gonna happen if a bunch of outsiders come up here and stomp around. First they'll have to get familiarized with the situation and locale. That'll take awhile. Then they'll have to go over ground I've already covered, talk to all the people, so on and so forth. And all the time they'll be getting the royal treatment from President Anderson. That'll distract 'em. And in the end nothing will be done."

"But from the story it seems that North Star wants action right away."

"That's what it seems like, but if I've learned one thing from Rector Rex, it's that appearances are deceiving."

Anderson's "basic value" is somewhere at the bottom of this, he thought, with a feeling that was less than wholeheartedly charitable.

He didn't go directly to the office that morning, but instead drove to the house on the west side in which Muffy had a rented room. He wanted to talk to her before she left for her job at the Boom-Boom Room. The other occupants of the place were out—the Jelineks, an older couple, both of whom worked—but the fragrant Miss Huff was there, watching a game show on TV. She looked startled to see the sheriff, and stood inside the doorway, pulling an old and inadequate bathrobe more tightly around her substantial endowments, which merely served to enhance them the more.

"Mind if I come in and chat a minute?" he asked.

She was suspicious and unenthusiastic. "About what?"

"Some help that you can give me. Big help."

Muffy let him in and led him to a denlike room. The game-show host on the tube was raving about the virtues of a refrigerator, which one of three frenzied contestants could win if only they knew the letters missing from a word: _R__I_O__.

One of the contestants pressed her buzzer before the others, and got a crack at trying. A frazzly-looking orange-haired woman, she danced up and down in glee.

"You get to choose five letters," the host babbled. "Hint: the words refers to a place of activity."

"Ohhhhhhhh!" mewled the woman, beside herself with intellectual frustration and pressure.

Muffy left the picture on, but turned down the blasting volume. She and Emil sat down on opposite sides of a battered coffee table.

"How've you been?" he asked.

"I'm not sleeping too well. There's a killer out there."

"I know, but you're going to help me get him."

The woman contestant had guessed "I," and she'd been correct because the word now appeared: _RI_I_O_.

"But I told you I was afraid to get involved," Muffy protested in a little voice. "I want to keep my record clean for when I leave Stearns County."

"You give me a hand and your record is gonna be *shining!*" he promised.

She looked interested.

"It might be dangerous, though," he told her honestly.

Her interest diminished.

"I'll be there with you all the time," Emil went on, "or one of my deputies will. You'll be guarded round-the-clock."

"But my job . . ."

"We'll be with you at Bunyanland, too."

There was a long, long pause. The contestant had made another accurate stab, and the word on the television screen was now _RI_I_ON.

"Tell me what you have in mind," Muffy asked fearfully.

Emil tried to be as enthusiastic as he could. "It's simple, really. I plan to tell the radio stations and the *Trib* that a witness to the murder has come forward. We'll mention your name and address, and where you work. Then we'll wait."

Muffy paled, leaning forward in alarm. Her robe fell open a little. Whippletree could not help but see the creamy swell of her breasts, with small blue veins visible just beneath the skin. "Ohmigod," she said. "Are you *crazy?*"

The contestant missed a letter. She had two chances left.

"It's the only way," Emil said, as persuasively as possible. "The way I see it, you're the only person in the county who can help me now. Think of what that means."

"It might mean I'm going to be *dead!*" Muffy cried.

"We'll have somebody with you every minute."

On the screen, time was running out. The woman looked as if she'd bitten through her lower lip. A *place of activity* . . .

"No," Muffy said, her platinum-colored hair flying as she shook her head, "no."

Emil felt discouraged. He tried to think of a way to approach her. Basic value. Deepest belief. Everybody had one, Anderson had said.

"Muffy," he said slowly, "you're an ambitious girl. Your life hasn't been the easiest, but you haven't given up. I admire that—"

"Now don't go trying to soft-soap me . . ."

"I mean it. And I know how dangerous my suggestion is. But you look like the kind of girl who's got the courage to take a risk in order to help others . . ."

On the tube, the contestant seemed on the verge of tears. Come on, Emil thought encouragingly, there are twenty-six letters in the alphabet.

". . . and I bet very few of those North Star students would have the guts to do what I'm asking you."

"Do you think so?" Muffy asked.

"I sure do. You go out there on campus and try to fit in, don't you? Why, hell, I think you *already* fit in. Unless I miss my guess, you're already ahead of plenty of 'em, and you can prove it by helping me."

His praise was, in truth, part flattery. But she had a strong spark of determination in her, and he wanted to fan it into a flame. People, he knew, can always do more than they think they can. But they need encouragement, because the habits of defeat are learned so easily, so early, in all too many lives.

"You've got the stuff to beat 'em all," he said. "You and I are going to break this case wide open. But we have to work together."

The woman on the screen was wailing now, in frustration and defeat. Time was almost up, but she had already *given* up. Muffy, thinking over Emil's proposal, glanced idly toward the TV. "Gridiron," she said. "Okay, Sheriff, I'll give it a try. There's just one thing."

"Yes?"

"If it gets too dangerous—if I get too scared—then I want out, all right?"

"I'm not gonna *let* you get scared," he said. Then he thought of Susan. "I'll be with you all the way, every minute. You just hold my hand, and trust me. Everything's gonna be fine."

*  *  *

Back at the office, Emil first called Luther Proctor, manager of Bunyanland, to explain the plan. Proctor was less than wild about it.

"Deputies around here all the time?" he complained. "It looks bad, scares people away."

"They'll be discreet."

"Ha! I know your deputies. Axel Vogel is about as inconspicuous as a chartreuse elephant."

"I'll have them wear civilian clothes."

"And some nights Muff works until the last customer leaves. Two A.M. sometimes."

"I'm taking care of her. You don't have to worry about it."

"This is on your head, Emil. I don't know . . ."

"Come on, Lute. Be a pal. Remember the time Lucy Steinschwagger shot her husband in the Boom-Boom Room? I made sure Riley didn't get the story. Saved you a lot of embarrassment."

"Hell, it probably would've been good for business. Well, all right, Emil. I'll go along. But just because it's you who's asking."

"'Preciate it, Lute, thanks."

Next, Whippletree called Riley and gave him the story, Muffy's address included. He also called the local radio stations, and, after contemplation, the TV stations in The Cities as well. Mindful of Poll's alcohol problem and Luther Proctor's observations regarding Axel's eye-catching bulk, he ordered Farley and Gosch to change into sports clothes and get out to Bunyanland on the double. "Soda only, if you're thirsty," he stipulated. "But you can have a beer with dinner."

"How long we gonna have to *be* there, Emil?" wailed Gosch.

"Time will tell. Get moving."

They complied. By mid-afternoon, everything was in place. By suppertime, practically everybody in Stearns County had heard of Muffy Huff. She'd once been voted Miss Ice Fishing Queen, and the *Trib* planned to run her picture in next morning's edition. By the time Emil went home for his own quick evening meal—he planned to hang around Bunyanland too that night—Alyce was exhausted from answering all the phone calls.

214

"Everybody's mad," she told Whippletree. "They all say you're putting Muffy's life in danger because you're desperate."

"They're not far from right," Emil said.

Sarah didn't like the plan either. Oh, they'd had their small disagreements over the years—what married couple doesn't?—but never to the extent that one told the other he or she was making a potentially irredeemable mistake.

"Emil, do you know how badly you're going to feel if something happens to that girl?" she pointed out, fiddling disinterestedly at her helping of rice and tenderloin-tip casserole.

"Nothing's going to happen to her," he hoped.

Her silence was disapproving and premonitory.

Tuesday night, and the Bunyanland parking lot was jam-packed, almost as if it were the weekend. It was two and three deep at the bar in the Boom-Boom Room, and most of the tables were filled too.

"Maybe your idea wasn't so bad after all," manager Proctor told the sheriff. "Check out the gang that's come to take a look at Muffy. You made her famous."

Jesus, thought Emil. He certainly hadn't envisioned *this*. What murderer in his right mind would strike at Muffy here, with a hundred witnesses around?

But then, he realized, how many murderers are in their right minds?

Muffy herself was ambivalent about the situation. "You won't *believe* the tips I'm getting, Sheriff. A hundred and thirty dollars since lunch! But"—and this was the other side of the coin—"every time I serve a customer, I can't help but worry if he's the one. Do you think the guy'll make a move pretty soon?"

"Your guess is as good as mine."

The evening dragged on. Farley and Gosch went home at around nine-thirty, and Axel appeared to back up the sheriff. He wore his only sports coat in an attempt to look low-key and conservative. The coat, unfortunately, had a garish plaid pattern.

"Stay at the dark end of the bar," Emil advised.

At ten minutes to eleven, Lute Proctor came hurrying up to Emil, who'd retreated to the pinball game in the corner of the lobby.

"Guy calling on the office phone for Muffy," he hissed.

"Tell her yet?"

Proctor shook his head.

"Is there an extension?"

"It's behind the bar."

"All right. Get her and take her to the office. Tell her to agree to do whatever the guy suggests. I'll listen in on the extension."

He went to the bar phone, waited until he saw Lute and Muffy go into the manager's office, and eased the receiver gently out of its cradle.

"Hello?" Muffy said, her voice about an octave higher than usual.

"Hey there, Muff."

There was a lot of noise in the bar; Emil could barely hear the conversation.

"Who is this?" Muffy asked tentatively.

A crude laugh. "I think you know me. How about a date?"

"I'm working," said the girl.

No, thought Emil. *Agree* to the date. He wished he were in the office.

"What time do you get off?"

There was a pause while, apparently, Muffy and Proctor conferred.

"Well," said the girl, "it's sort of slow here. I could be ready pretty soon. Who is this?"

"Heh-heh. Don't you like surprises? How about I meet you in the amusement area? Say half an hour from now?"

A longer pause this time, then Muffy said yes.

Click of receivers.

Muffy was shaking when she came out of the office.

"Did you recognize the voice?" Emil asked.

"Maybe. I'm not sure. What are we going to do?"

"I'll wait in the shadows outside the amusement park. Axel will

216

be inside. We may see the guy going in before you have to show up at all."

"And if you don't?"

"We'll play it by ear."

The next half hour took about a day. Axel doffed his jacket, stuck a .38 in his pants pocket, and lumbered outside to take up his position. Emil slipped into a parked car near the amusement-park entrance. Paul Bunyan, motionless, gazed dolefully down on the bowed head of Babe. The park was gloomy in half-light; shadows of Paul, Babe, and the ferris wheel fell muted and fantastic on the ground. The half hour was up, then five more minutes. Muffy appeared, wearing a plain white dress. At least she would be visible in the darkness. She paused at the entrance to the amusement area and looked around.

"Haven't seen a thing," whispered Emil, from the car. "Just walk on in. Slowly."

Muffy took a deep breath for courage, lifted her chin, and went through the small wooden gate separating the park from the parking lot. Emil eased out of the car, keeping his eyes on her.

She walked slowly, staring into the shadows, toward Paul and Babe. Emil didn't know exactly where his deputy was concealed, but he hoped that Axel could see Muffy, too. He had considered using walkie-talkies to stay in touch with Axel, but had had to discard the idea because of the awful squawk they made.

Muffy was approaching Paul Bunyan now. She halted next to Babe and looked up at the electronic lumberjack. Then, from behind the hulking blue ox, a figure appeared.

It seemed to grab Muffy, dark arms wrapped around the white dress.

"Hey!" yelled the sheriff, already on the run.

Muffy screamed.

Axel bellowed from somewhere in the darkness.

Emil reached Muffy and her assailant in a matter of seconds, running as fast as he could. She was struggling furiously, and, even as Emil leaped upon the dark-shirted figure, he heard, "Easy

217

now, honey. What the hell is the matter with you? I thought you liked a good time?"

Then Whippletree had the guy pinned to the ground in the shadow of Paul Bunyan. He drilled one fist into a rib cage, and felt the other strike a hard jawbone.

The assailant yelled in pain.

Muffy was still screaming.

Axel thudded up. He and the sheriff yanked the intruder to his feet, and out into dim light.

"What the hell is going on here?" cried an outraged Johnny Pflüger.

Muffy was sent back inside, while the lawmen dragged Cowboy John to their car for a quick interrogation.

"I just wanted a date, is all," claimed the loser. "Jesus, is there a law against that? She *said* it was okay. Hell, I already scrogged her a coupla times. She's a good piece—maybe a little flakey—and I wanted some more. Is there a law against that? We're both contending adults, you know."

"Consenting."

"Whatever."

"You been listening to the radio at all today, John? You hear Muffy's name mentioned?"

"What? Hell no. I been sleeping all day. I got laid off from the paper mill again, and I didn't have nothing else to do."

"Where's Byron, your buddy?"

"Home, probably. I don't take that dumb bastard along when I go out to get scrogged. He ain't no good with women. It's just he ain't got no class."

"What do you think, Sheriff?" asked Axel.

Emil shook his head. Cowboy John was not the man they were looking for. "You just stay away from Miss Huff," he warned.

"Are you kidding?" Pflüger said. "Man, you better believe I will. I don't have to go through this much trouble to get laid. You guys scared the hell out of me."

"I doubt it," Emil said.

218

Nothing happened after that. Bunyanland closed at one forty-five A.M. Emil drove Muffy home. Deputy Poll was already parked outside the house, ready for overnight stakeout duty. Emil saw Muffy inside, sent Poll around to make sure the back door was locked, and quickly checked his deputy's thermos. Nothing but coffee . . .

Poll appeared before Emil got the thermos back into the lunch-box. He looked hurt and crestfallen. He knew what Emil had been up to.

"I swore off, Sheriff. For good this time. Don't you believe me?"

"Sure I do," said Emil apologetically.

Whippletree had always possessed a great deal of natural sympathy for people who had problems, but he sometimes thought he lacked a really true understanding of what they were going through. He liked a good belt himself, got grouchy if he didn't have a chaw now and then, and enjoyed betting on football games even if he lost. But he'd never developed a mania for any of life's common vices.

Sarah, waiting up for him, was relieved to learn of Muffy's safety—Emil refrained from mentioning the incident involving Pflüger—and they both got a fairly good night's sleep. Sarah had put a second blanket at the foot of the bed—it was getting to be that time of year—and just before dawn Emil reached down and pulled it up over both of them.

The next morning he stopped at the office, ascertained that Stearns County had lived, fairly uneventfully, through another night, and drove over to the west side to relieve a sleepy Pete Poll.

Muffy's landlord, Stanislaus Jelinek, stopped to jaw a bit with Emil when he left the house on his way to work. "That's a good girl in there, Sheriff," he said. "She's gettin' to be like a daughter to me and the missus."

"I know. I have a niece about the same age."

"Yeah, but you're not using your niece as bait for a murderer."

The morning passed slowly. Kids went to school and people

went to work. An occasional delivery van passed through the neighborhood, a quiet, neat section of town with small, well-kept lawns and homes. Emil read the *Trib* twice. The president—the real president, not Rexford Anderson—said that a three-hundred-billion-dollar deficit was "small potatoes" and everybody should "stop yammering about it." Butch Lodge had held a campaign fund-raiser at the Elks Hall, netting fifteen hundred dollars to make war against Whippletree. Illinois was favored over the Norsemen in Saturday's game. Bunny Hollman's followers had swelled to twenty-five thousand on the previous afternoon. Gabriel's Guard leader Jacques LaBatt predicted upwards of fifty thousand worshippers by the weekend.

Just before noon, the mailman came ambling up the block. He nodded to Emil and dropped a handful of stuff into the Jelineks' postbox.

Muffy stuck her head out the door, waved to Emil, snatched the mail, and withdrew.

Her scream came, about half-a-minute later, from inside the house. Whippletree crashed inside on the run, .38 in his hand.

Muffy stood, terror-stricken, against the living room wall. She looked as if she'd jumped away from a mouse, or maybe a snake. Wordlessly, she pointed at the floor, on which the mail lay scattered. Baffled, Whippletree stared a moment, then bent down to see what had caused Muffy's panic. One envelope, bearing Muffy's typewritten name and address, had been opened, and two instamatic photos were lying on the floor beside it.

They showed Alicia Stanhope, half naked, a Nerf football jammed into her mouth, dead in the bushes near the Sauk River.

"Who would do this?" cried Muffy, over and over. "Who would *do* this?"

Tests conducted that afternoon showed Muffy Huff's fingerprints on the envelope, and two separate sets of prints that proved to belong to postal employees. Only Muffy's fingerprints were found on the photos. Whoever had sent the deadly message had been extremely careful. The envelope carried a St. Cloud postmark, with the previous day's date, so the murderer had lost little time warning Muffy, after hearing her name on radio or TV.

By Thursday afternoon, with the big Illinois game only forty-eight hours away, Muffy was still safe. She had received no further messages or calls, and had at least pretended to believe Emil when he told her, "Maybe the guy won't make another move. Sending those pictures was a risk. He knows we're closing in."

If only we were, he thought to himself.

Then he turned his attention to crowd control. Butch Lodge, his previous promises notwithstanding, had suddenly called for back-up support from Emil's office, to assure that both football fans and worshippers would have "easy access" to campus on Saturday. Bullshit, thought the sheriff, brooding in his office. Butch was part of a plan to humiliate Emil by demonstrating the sheriff's impotence to do anything about the massive numbers of people on campus. Inflaming the issue further, Jacques LaBatt had announced that his "troops" were stretched "to the limit," and outside help would have to be forthcoming "if disaster is to be averted." Vice-President Dexter, doubtless speaking for the still-absent President Anderson, sought to drive a final nail into Emil's coffin by telling reporter Riley, "If Sheriff Whippletree would only aid us by stating that he cannot handle the situation, which we must admit is rife with the potential for bodily harm, then President Anderson could legitimately petition Governor Bauch for a contingent of the National Guard."

Bullshit, Emil thought again, the National Guard is not going to come into *my* county, but the Gabriel's Guards are gonna leave, and damn soon.

Thinking of the County Charter, he drove out to campus in

order to reconnoiter the situation, which was worse than he had imagined. There were at least forty thousand people spread out all across the golf course, from the tree-lined drive on one side to the woods on the other, beneath which the Guards had their tents. Hundreds of prayer pilgrims had erected tents as well, and the place had the look of an encampment.

Gabriel's Guards had maintained a narrow aisle for traffic between two rows of parked cars and tourist buses lining the drive. A Guard carrying a walkie-talkie stood on duty at the entrance to the drive and flagged down Emil's car.

"State your business," he said, stooping slightly to study Whippletree. "Oh, good day, Sheriff."

"I understand you boys can't handle these crowds any more," said Emil drily.

The Guard was young, tough, clever. "We're doing the best we can." He grinned.

"You know that North Star just wants to put the onus of moving these people on my back, don't you?"

"That is not true. President Anderson has assured Professor Hollman and Mr. LaBatt that his commitment is primarily to Faith. This will be proven on the day of the football game."

Emil laughed. "I've been learning quite a bit about Rector Rex these past couple weeks, and I think *your* big lesson is coming up pretty soon. Where is Jacques, anyway? I want to have a little confab with him."

"He is at the pine tree with Mrs. Hollman. She has just arrived."

"Glad to hear it."

Whippletree drove slowly between the rows of cars. People walked here and there, impeding his passage, and some of them darted carelessly into his path. It took him ten minutes to get near the pine tree.

The Sacred Steeple and Triumphant Jesus dominated campus as always, and today there seemed to be an aura of neutrality emanating from statue and church, as if both were waiting to learn the outcome of all the whirl and chaos below. Whippletree sensed, dimly, an indefinite current of unresolved strife in the air, and, without knowing why, he was suddenly sure that President Anderson had returned to campus. His trips were faithfully recorded by the *Trib*, but, come to think of it, there'd been no mention of him since the "illegal alien" conference in San Antonio.

After driving as close to the pine tree as he could get, Emil slipped between two carelessly parked cars and halted on the crest of the embankment that led down to the Sauk River. Then he got out and walked over to the pine. It was circled, as always, by a platoon of Guards, as well as by—Emil counted—nine separate camera crews from all over the country. There was even a crew from Quebec.

Bunny, flanked by Charlie Hollman and Jacques LaBatt, was kneeling, head bowed, beneath the tree. There was a microphone on a little stand in front of her. Butch Lodge, with several of his security men, was standing outside the circle of Guards. He saw Emil, glanced away, thought the better of it, and then walked over, offering his hand. "Emil?"

"Hey, Butch," said the sheriff. "Good luck in the campaign. Always advantageous to get an early start."

"Emil, it's something I felt I had to do."

"Tell me something, Butch. Did you ever beat up on Trudilynn? When you two were married?"

"How do you . . . ? Is that what she . . . ?" The ex-master sergeant was totally flustered. "Not really," he concluded lamely.

"And I understand you had a penchant for rubbers?"

Lodge looked stricken. "That's my business. You wouldn't . . . you wouldn't *dare* bring that out!"

Emil shook his head. "Course not. But it makes me mighty curious, since the guy who killed Alicia used a condom when he raped her."

Butch, between a rock and a hard place, decided to level. "Emil," he said confidentially, "I got something contagious. I didn't want Trudilynn to catch it, and I didn't want her to know."

"I see."

"It's the goddamn truth."

"I didn't say that I didn't believe you, did I? Now, what I'm here for. I understand you need me to move this mob?"

Butch seemed very nervous. "That's right. I do. By Saturday."

"Okay," said Emil casually.

Butch stared at him. "*Okay*? How are you going to do it?"

"I don't know yet. But I *am* going to do it, because neither you nor Hollman nor LaBatt nor Anderson are gonna run me out of town on this issue. I still have a little time to maneuver and"—he stuck his forefinger into Lodge's wide, hard chest—"you are not gonna feel too much like running against me when I'm through."

Butch thought it over. "You're bluffing," he said uneasily.

Whippletree allowed himself a grin. "I might not always do so hot betting football games, but I never lose in poker. Or didn't you know that? Now, tell me, what's Charlie got planned out here today?"

"How would I know? The Virgin appears when *she* wishes, not when—"

"Sure," snorted Emil. He turned abruptly away from Butch—no harm in showing the guy who was in charge, was there?—and strolled along the circle of cameras and Guards. LaBatt saw him there, and grinned maliciously. Whippletree touched the edge of his hatbrim and smiled back.

The Quebec television reporter, microphone in hand, eyed Emil's badge. "You are the sheriff, of whom I have heard?" he asked formally.

"Yep. But no interviews. What've you heard?"

"That you are not getting along very well with our own Monsieur LaBatt."

"Yep. And you can quote me on that. You here covering him, or what?"

"That is correct. The people in our province have an interest in him."

"He's sort of a hero, I guess."

The reporter, who spoke English with a fairly heavy French accent, laughed. "It is not quite so," he said. "In Quebec, Jacques LaBatt is known as a probable murderer, a possible pederast, a religious fanatic, and—how do you say?—a sheethead."

"We don't pronounce it quite that way, but I get your meaning."

Emil was about to ask the man what he knew of LaBatt's acquittal on charges of murdering his wife, but a sudden flurry of unsettling sensations struck him. It seemed hard to breathe; he felt a constriction in his chest; the world lost shades of color before his eyes. He thought that he might be on the verge of a heart attack—not now, for Christ's sake, I'm still young—but then Bunny cried out into the microphone: "Ah, yoni . . ."

As one, the crowd on the golf course shouted and fell to desperate silence. This was the moment they had awaited; this was what they had come for.

Emil took a series of deep breaths and felt a little better, but that eerie sense of another world, another dimension, came to him again. This time it was more definite than it had been before: no mere doorway to the rolling fields of abyss, but something finite and almost tangible. He knew that he was in the presence of strange power, a force fashioned perhaps of evil, and certainly of untruth.

Bunny's voice was strained, shrill, breathless. The passion for which flesh is meant had seized her once again.

> "Ah, yoni, musk of ancient
>     yearnings on your walls,
> The more you ride, the more you milk.
> Cry out
>     Hot seep of seed unto your longing . . ."

Cameras whirred. Tape recorders turned. "Ahhhhhhh . . ." Bunny gasped.

> "Ah, lingam, stay your prideful
>     Burst, prolong your joy
> Within her pulsing cave.
> Thou shalt, in splendor,
>     Gasp upon sweet breasts,
> Devourer come and come
>     And come again . . ."

"That woman," whispered the Quebec reporter in astonishment, "I would swear she is experiencing *joiir.*"

"Huh?" asked Emil.

"I believe that you here would say 'to come.'"

"Yep," Emil said.

"*I see her!*" Bunny shrieked then. "*She is here with us. Our Holy Mother has come unto us again . . .*"

Then she fell silent for a long while, communing with the tree. People were crying out, fainting, falling. They began to surge forward toward the tree. Gabriel's Guards, along with Butch and his men, sought to hold them back. A crowd of this size, Emil knew, could easily trample plenty of its number.

"*Is Zelda Schrieffels here?*" Bunny asked then. "*The Virgin has a message for Zelda Schrieffels.*"

"I'm here," a thin voice quavered.

Not poor Zelda, thought the sheriff. Why would heaven—why would Bunny—pick on her? She was a pale, wasted, and very confused woman of thirty or so. She'd studied to be a nun, left the convent, taken up social work and the guitar, and been seduced and abandoned at least a dozen times, with three interracial children to show for it. She was one of the few people in Stearns County actually on welfare.

"*The Virgin is telling me,*" Bunny called, "*that your sins are beyond number, beyond absolution. You must go forward from this time and place, banished and exiled. Do penance, Zelda Schrieffels, do penance for all your days, which shall be short . . .*"

Poor Zelda, whose only crime in life had been an innocence too pervasive to grasp even the softest edges of reality, fled wailing across the drive and into the trees along the Sauk. There were those in the crowd, and their number was not small, who shouted angrily as she ran. Emil was glad that there were no stones on the golf course. Mob psychology was at work now. Mob psychology, which Rector Rex had predicted and feared.

"*Wait!*" Bunny cried. "*The Virgin is telling me more! Yes?*" She seemed to be listening to someone high in the branches of the tree. "*Yes? Yes! The Virgin is telling me . . . the Virgin is telling*" *me . . . that Alicia Stanhope was killed by . . . Professor Dale Torbert!"*

The cameras got it all, for later broadcast everywhere, ineradicably linking the murder and the visions in the public mind. Who could doubt that heaven would err in identifying a killer? Nobody in Stearns County.

"God damn it!" Whippletree said aloud. He was furious. Of all the damaging, irresponsible, vicious and loony things Bunny could have gotten it into her head to say, this was the worst. Even if it were true—and it might very well be!—this kind of public spectacle was criminal in itself.

*"Our Holy Mother has no message from her Divine Son today . . ."* Mrs. Hollman was saying sadly, as Emil charged through the ring of Gabriel's Guards. He meant to ask her a few damn hard questions, right now.

The people on the golf course howled in disappointment and the Guards were shouting in alarm as Emil rushed toward Bunny, Charlie, and LaBatt.

*"Bunny!"* he said, reaching her just as she fell forward in a daze upon the grass. He got close enough to hear her mutter something about twenty-four–twelve, close enough to see Charlie's chubby face, his little eyes filled with surprise and hatred. Then he felt hands clutching at his shoulders, felt himself spinning around. He saw LaBatt's hard fist coming toward him, had time to turn his face slightly. But the impact was like a sledgehammer on his left cheekbone, and he was down on the ground. LaBatt was grinning as he advanced. A circle of Guards blocked any chance of escape. I'm gonna get the shit kicked out of me, Emil thought. He grabbed for his gun in desperation. LaBatt kicked it out of his hand and drew back his boot to kick again.

The kick never came. There was a cry of savage outrage, a blur of motion, and Emil saw two Guards slammed simultaneously to the ground. Disbelieving—or perhaps believing finally in miracles after all—the sheriff saw Jacques LaBatt lifted bodily high into the air, saw him flung down brutally upon the earth, so hard that he bounced. Two more Guards, who'd leaped forward to aid their leader, were knocked senseless. Then the blur of motion slowed, stopped, composed itself into the image of young Tony Wiggins, weightlifting champ, the "brain" from Ely.

"Thought you could use a little help here," said the boy, almost apologetically. "The odds didn't look even to me."

LaBatt lay on the ground, out cold. The fallen Guards were moaning. Their mates looked on in impotent rage. Charlie hovered fearfully over his wife. She was starting to come around, exhausted now, her reverie flown.

Emil sat up. He saw Butch Lodge, standing no more than ten feet away. Butch hadn't done a thing to help! Of all the . . . Why, hell, the guy was sweating. He looked as frightened as if he'd just seen a ghost.

"Thanks a hell of a lot," Emil told Butch pointedly. "I see why we did so well in Vietnam."

Butch worked his jaws together but said nothing.

"Mr. Wiggins," said Emil, picking himself up and retrieving his weapon. "Much obliged. I guess I'm all alone out here. It won't happen again. How'd you like to be deputized for a couple of hours until we get this shithead here"—he gestured toward La-Batt—"behind bars?"

"Whatever you say, Sheriff."

The cameras had captured all of the fight, of course, but the crowd was not sure what had happened. Emil tossed a pair of handcuffs to Tony Wiggins, who clamped them professionally around LaBatt's thick wrists. Then the sheriff grabbed the microphone and addressed the mob.

"Settle down now, everybody. It's all over. Bunny's fine. Go back to praying, or whatever you want. Just make sure you keep the road clear so Mrs. Hollman can go home and rest."

His message had its intended effect. The crowd quieted, for the time being, and began to pray: *I believe in God the Father, almighty creator of heaven and earth . . .*

Mrs. Hollman was on her feet now, leaning against her husband.

"You say something about twenty-four–twelve?" Emil asked her.

"I . . . I don't know what I said."

Today's vision, Emil saw, had taken a lot more out of her than usual. Well, didn't they say that evil required more energy than good?

"All right, you boys," Emil said, addressing the Guards, "Jacques has just won a free stint of room and board in the local pokey. Any you fellows want to join him, just make some trouble."

He was answered by sullen stares. They were as conscious of the TV cameras as he was. The Guard leader was still out like a light. Wiggins and Emil dragged him over to the sheriff's car and dumped him unceremoniously into the back seat.

Butch Lodge, who appeared to have shaken the paralysis that had overcome him during LaBatt's attack on Emil, came over to the car with three of his men. "We'll see you get off campus with no trouble," he offered.

"I'll take you up on it," Emil said. "Wait here a minute with Wiggins. I've got something to do."

He slid down the embankment through leaves, vines, and shrubbery. Be a good idea to find poor old Zelda Schrieffels and take her back into town. She'd be pretty shook up about what had happened.

"Zelda? Hey, Zelda, it's Emil Whippletree. Come on, now. Everything's gonna be all right. Nobody believed that crap up there before . . ."

Incorrect. Zelda had.

Her feet were about ten feet off the vine-tangled earth. She had somehow managed to clamber up into the big old birch, behind which Muffy Huff had hidden on the night of the murder. She'd twisted her brassiere around her neck, hooked it over a branch, and swung free. Emil saw that she'd buttoned her blouse after removing the bra. Her tongue was lolling, froth ran from her blue lips, but she was still kicking feebly and in her bulging eyes he thought he read a plea for help.

Still alive.

"*Help!*" he shouted, knowing that the sound of the prayerful mob, the thick leaves of the trees, would muffle his cry. There was no time to run up to the road for help.

How he managed to get up the thick-trunked birch, he never knew. But he did, ripping the bra apart and dropping Zelda to the earth. He hoped the fall wouldn't hurt her, but that was of little importance now. Then he was back down from the tree, kneeling over her, blowing air into her lungs. When she started choking and coughing, he gathered her up in his arms—she couldn't have weighed more than ninety pounds soaking wet—climbed the embankment and stumbled out onto the asphalt drive.

"Emil!" shouted Butch, "What . . . ?"

"Little accident," he explained curtly. "Look, we got to get her to the hospital. Butch, you drive my car. Wiggins, put Jacques in the front seat and sit on him."

Emil stretched Zelda out on the back seat of Stearns County One and, kneeling beside her, resumed mouth-to-mouth resuscitation.

Siren wailing, red-and-blue lights flashing, they shot off toward St. Cloud.

Jacques LaBatt was down on his knees beside his bunk in the Stearns County jail, running rosary beads through his fingers, when Emil unlocked the cell, entered, and relocked it behind him.

"Don't waste your time," Emil said. "The only one who can save your ass now is me, and I'm not particularly inclined to do it."

The Guards leader looked up, then glanced at the locked cell door.

"You speak so bravely, Sheriff," he replied. The arrogance was all in his voice; his eyes showed doubt and, yep, just a little bit of real fear. He got off his knees and sat down on the bunk. "What do you want?" he asked coldly. "I demand a lawyer. I demand my freedom. My men will come here and take care of this, and you will be sorry."

Emil allowed himself a thin smile. "Shut up," he said. "Your

230

case is complicated by the fact that you're a foreigner, or didn't that cross your mind? Fact, if I wanted, I could probably get away with holding you here until you couldn't stand your own stink."

LaBatt's frightening, hate-filled fanatic's eyes shot again to the locked cell door.

"But I have other plans for you."

Nobody becomes a coward more quickly than a bully. LaBatt shifted uneasily on the bunk. "You can't mistreat a prisoner—" he began.

"There's still a bit of dignity in the word 'prisoner.' Whyn't we just call you a fraudulent, self-serving jackal?" Emil spoke very quietly. But his rage was so pure, so magnificent, that LaBatt seemed to shrink away. "This won't matter to you," he said, "because in your whole life you probably haven't thought of anyone else's welfare, but Zelda Schrieffels is going to be all right . . ."

LaBatt had regained consciousness on the drive to the hospital, and been apprised of Zelda's condition.

". . . and what I want to know from you now is this: Who plans those things that Bunny Hollman ascribes to the Virgin Mary?"

LaBatt smirked. "Still an unbeliever, are you, Sheriff?"

"That may be, but I also may be the only sane person left around here. When Bunny started, her messages were basically good. Now they're not. They're mean and evil and degrading. And I want to know why the change occurred."

"I believe Mrs. Hollman's insights come directly from heaven."

"All's I ever had in the way of theological schooling was Catechism from old Father Mauslocher. But he taught me that heaven was good, and I figured I'd elect to believe him."

"Heaven's goodness is only for the Faithful," snapped LaBatt. "Unbelievers must suffer."

Emil shook his head. "Jacques, my boy, you're just another two-bit fanatic in a military suit. The only power and glory that matter to you are your own. Fanatics like you destroy people and bankrupt their own beliefs."

The Gabriel's Guard lifted his chin defiantly. "Neither I nor my men are leaving—"

Whippletree laughed outright. "Axel," he called, "Come in here, please?"

The huge deputy lumbered into the cellblock, wrapped his gigantic hands around the iron bars of the door, and scowled menancingly at LaBatt. "Got a little problem with this here piece of shit, Sheriff?"

"Oh, I don't think so. Nothing I can't handle. But I do have a little job for you. Take Poll or Farley, drive out to campus, and tell the Guards they have until sundown today to get out of Minnesota."

"They will never (nev-air) do that," sneered LaBatt.

"Sure they will. You're gonna write them a nice little letter telling them to do exactly that. Axel, fetch a piece of stationery and a pen."

Axel shrugged and left.

"You are a dreamer, Sheriff." LaBatt grinned. "I shall not write such a missive."

Axel came in again and handed paper and pen between the bars. Emil dropped them on LaBatt's bunk.

"Thanks. That's all, Axel.

"Now, Jacques," said Emil, when the deputy was gone, "do you want to start writing, or do I have to show you what kind of a man you are first?"

The Guard looked wary.

"You'll do as I say," Emil explained, "because you don't want to stay in a cell with a gutless coward."

"What?" asked LaBatt. "Who?"

"Yourself. I'm gonna prove it to you. Now, I'll let you out of here scot-free—"

"Hah! No deal. You cannot contrive to manipulate me!"

"Hold on. I wasn't through. I won't bother taking you to trial on charges of assaulting me if, first, your men all leave peaceably by nightfall and, second, if I receive from each of them a letter, postmarked Quebec, informing me of their presence there and fervently requesting your release."

"Positively not," said Jacques.

232

Emil just grinned. "You know, I may not be all that much in learning, but I've observed a few things. One of which is that when the head fanatic is gone, the followers suddenly disappear. I wonder just how many letters we *will* get from your troops?"

LaBatt said nothing. Suddenly, he was wondering too. "A deal can only be struck by equals, Sheriff," he said finally. "You have the gun, the key."

"Even with those you couldn't get close to being my equal. But, if you insist . . ."

Emil unholstered his .38 and slid it out of the cell, under the iron bars of the door. Next he took the key from his pocket, dropped it on the floor, and kicked it against the concrete wall behind him. Then he faced LaBatt and made a come-on gesture with both hands.

"Man-to-man," he said. "But I warn you, I'm ready this time."

LaBatt half-stood, then sat down on the bunk again.

"You have some trick (*treek*)."

"Nope. One against one. No holds barred."

LaBatt thought it over, then shook his head. "I am a Christian," he said. "I do not provoke."

"Just like I figured," said Emil. "You're a coward. Start writing that letter to your boys." He turned away and stooped to pick up the key on the floor. And, as he'd expected, Jacques LaBatt attacked, leaping from the bunk and rushing Emil from behind.

The old sheriff sidestepped neatly, grabbed the charging LaBatt by shirt collar and asshole, and rammed him as hard as he could into the concrete wall.

LaBatt scribbled the message—in English, because Emil didn't trust him to do it in French—and Whippletree handed it to Axel for delivery.

"By sundown," he emphasized to the deputy.

"Gotcha, Emil. It'll be a pleasure."

"Well, Jacques," said the sheriff, locking the door on LaBatt, "all's I can tell you is that belief in the hands of a fanatic is a lethal weapon to everybody concerned. You know what Rector Rex told

233

me? He said Belief was the reason for Alicia Stanhope's death. And I believe him."

One down, he thought, leaving the cellblock and going back to his office, and three to go. Rector Rex. Bunny Hollman. And the killer.

In that order.

"Hey, Alyce," he said, "check the regulations and see what kind of commendation we can give Tony Wiggins for helping me out."

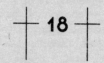

The Torbert flak had already begun in earnest by mid-afternoon. Nameless people were calling to ask why Emil didn't arrest Professor Torbert, since the Blessed Mother herself had identified him as a murderer. Newspapers, television, and radio stations were calling for interviews. And the evening news awaited with its exciting footage of Emil and LaBatt battling beneath the pine tree.

The flak had already begun, but the sheriff had other things on his mind, too. He dialed Corbett Daffleby at the Hannorhed Bank.

"Good afternoon. This is the Hannorhed County Bank, Personal Account Executive Daffleby at your service."

"Yeah, Corb. How you doin'? This's Emil Whippletree over at the jail. I want to check the balance in my special account."

His "special" account, separate from the checking and savings he held jointly with Sarah, was to be used for the upcoming Rose Bowl trip.

There was a slight pause as Daffleby consulted his computer. "Sheriff, you have two thousand and twenty-one dollars and eleven cents, interest compounded daily. Now tomorrow it will be up to—"

"That's fine. Thanks, Corb."

Then the sheriff dialed, in order, the Courthouse Bar and Grill, the Press Bar, the Club Valmar in Lake Eden, and the Quail and

Tail in Pearl Lake. He finally caught up with Wienie at Buster's Lounge in Sauk Rapids.

"Hey, Wienie. Workin' hard? What does it look like for Saturday?"

"Illinois to win. Spread of seven points. Odds are still moving around, but I'd say it'd be about five–one, maybe six–one. North Star's powerful. You want in after your experience last weekend?"

Risky, Emil thought. Bunny had murmured something about twenty-four–twelve. But had she meant that the Norsemen would win, or Illinois? Also, she'd been wrong in every one of her past "predictions," but only by one scoring episode, whether touchdown or field goal. She had not been consistent, either, in naming the winning team. She had to hit it right sooner or later, didn't she? He smiled to himself. Heaven couldn't be wrong *all* the time.

"I'm in, Wienie."

"How much?"

"Two thousand bucks."

There was a gasp at the other end of the line. "C'mon, Emil. You don't want to do this. Only man in town who comes close to betting that kind of money is T. R. Steinhaus, and he usually loses."

"You in business or not?"

Wienie sighed. "Okay, Emil. It's your funeral."

"Got to have one sooner or later, don't I?" said the sheriff, hanging up.

"Divot on the wire," called Alyce from the outer office.

Emil picked up the phone again. "Yep, Doc?"

Divot was not one for small talk when he had something important to relate. "Emil," he rasped, "whyn't you bring in this here Torbert fellow for questioning, at least? Be a good move to cover your ass. The whole town's full of talk, and none of it is good."

"Look, Doc, thanks for the advice. But Torbert seems pretty well covered himself. He's given me his itinerary on the night of the murder, not to mention the whole weekend, and I buy it."

"*I* will if you do. But the grand public clamor has set in. I don't want to see you wind up with your ass in a sling."

"No sweat, Doc."

Jesus, Emil sighed, after he'd ended the conversation. It was easy to see how witch mania got started. Old woman comes out of her house on a fine morning, sees that her cat has croaked overnight. Loved poor puss so much can't believe lazy ball of fuzz died on its own. Somebody had to have killed it, right? Who? Old woman puzzles and puzzles, finally remembers hassle with neighbor over virtues of cat five years earlier. Aha! Supreme logic. Neighbor must have hexed puss during the night.

Still, crazy as it seemed, one could see the human mind at work here. *Somebody* had to be assigned responsibility for the cat's demise, since all red-blooded Americans were taught to believe that life was not chaotic, that God did not play dice with the laws of the universe, that Cause led inexorably to Effect.

Emil sat at his desk, toying with the insight. Bunny Hollman had named Torbert for a *reason*, and however illogical that reason might seem to others, it made perfect sense to her . . . or to Charlie.

This is part of Charlie's fight with Torbert, Emil realized. He wants to root "liberalism" out of sacred North Star soil by any means possible, and discrediting Torbert is certainly one such means. If only Bunny would stand up on her hind legs for once, and stop being her husband's mouthpiece!

He noticed Alyce standing in the doorway, waving her arms to get his attention. "Sheriff, there's some professor on the phone from St. Paul. Says his name is Paul Barnes and he has to talk to you. Says it's extremely important."

Paul Barnes. That was Torbert's buddy, whose wife Torbert had stayed with on the murder weekend. Emil grabbed the phone. "Whippletree here."

"Sheriff, I just heard some rather disturbing news on the radio. About a friend of mine being accused of murder up in your area."

"Right. Dale Torbert. You see, we have this woman who claims to see visions—"

"I know. I heard that too. But my wife, Sandy, told me just a few minutes ago that your office called awhile back? Asking Dale's whereabouts that weekend?"

"Yes?"

"Well, I have to say . . . I'm sorry to have to tell you . . . but she didn't . . . uh . . . exactly . . . uh . . ."

Emil snapped forward in his swivel chair. "You mean Torbert was *not* at your place that weekend?"

"That's . . . about the size of it. Please understand. Sandy didn't know what was going on. She just covered for him automatically. You see, we're old friends . . ."

"I see, all right."

"She didn't *know* about a murder. Any friend would have done the same, don't you think? After all, the call *was* sort of like an anonymous inquiry over the phone."

"Well, I'm darn glad you called now. Thanks." Holy mud, thought Emil. Torbert's whole story is starting to collapse.

"I know he didn't kill anyone," Barnes was saying reassuringly. "He's a wonderful guy, in all ways. But I figured it was my duty to contact you."

"Have you spoken to Torbert?" Emil asked.

"No, but I will. I tried to get him at North Star and at his apartment in St. Cloud, but . . ."

Emil didn't listen to the rest of it. "Vogel! Farley!" he bellowed. The two deputies rushed in on the double, wondering what the big commotion was all about.

"Axel," ordered the sheriff, "get on out to the university right away. Find Torbert and bring him in. *Now*," he added emphatically. Axel chugged out. "Benny, Torbert lives in that condo complex on Ninth Avenue South. Get over there. If he's home, arrest him. If not, talk to the neighbors and ask if they've seen him lately."

The phrase that Doc Divot had used, "*ass in a sling*," ran through Emil's mind, over and over, as he dialed North Star.

"History Department, please," he told the switchboard operator. There were some clicks, then a woman's voice, light and giggly, said, "Good afternoon, History."

"Who am I speaking to?"

Offended pause. "This is Sylvia Bromley, Departmental Secretary. May I help—?"

"Connect me with Professor Torbert."

The extension rang and rang. Miss Bromley came back on the line.

"I'm afraid he doesn't answer. Who's calling, please?"

Emil told her. "Maybe he has a class now?" he suggested.

"No, sir. He's supposed to be holding office hours now. But he's not in his . . ."

Emil felt his stomach drop a couple of feet. Torbert had heard about Bunny's accusation, and whether he was indeed guilty or just plain scared, he'd flown the coop.

And the flak I'm gonna get now will be unbelievable, Emil thought ruefully. *"Did you hear about old Whippletree? The Virgin Mary told him who the killer was. But did he do anything about it? No . . ."*

"Anyone around that I can talk to?" he asked Sylvia Bromley. "Charlie Hollman, even?"

"No, I'm sorry. The only faculty member in his office just now is Professor Beauchamp."

The bright, chirpy little guy Emil had seen in the corridor on the day he'd spoken to Torbert. "Connect me with him, would you?"

Beauchamp's voice was crisp and chipper; he sounded as cheerful as a TV weatherman predicting rain all weekend.

"Yes, I saw Professor Torbert," Beauchamp said. "He almost ran me down on his way out of the building."

"When was this?"

"Several hours ago. Shortly after noon, as I recall."

"Which way was he headed?" Emil asked.

"Why, toward the parking lot, I believe. I'm certain that he'll be back, however."

"Why's that?"

"Because his hearing before the Ethics Committee, which he requested, is scheduled for ten o'clock tomorrow morning. Unless, of course, he has decided to throw in the towel, so to speak."

"Yes, that reminds me," said Emil, "I heard you were the only one of three professors who wasn't exactly certain about the existence of a tape recording, and some transcripts made from it . . . ?"

The silence was short, but cold. Beauchamp's reply was as sassy as ever. "I have no idea what you're referring to," he said.

Axel returned from campus to report, as expected, that Dale Torbert was not to be found there. Benny Farley brought news that was even more disturbing. A Mrs. Penny Thruston, who lived across the hall from Torbert, had seen the professor "come flying in" at about one P.M. She had just gone out to check the mailbox in the lobby of the building. He'd left "on the run" about five minutes later carrying, Penny had reported, "either a big attaché case or a small overnight bag."

"Put out a statewide bulletin on Torbert," said Emil gloomily. "He's got one of these foreign sports cars. Alyce, get his license number from Motor Vehicle in The Cities. There's nothing more we can do about him now. I'm going home for supper."

Sarah, who had not been to campus today, and thus had not heard about Bunny Hollman's efficacy in matters of criminal identification, met Emil at the door. She was ecstatic.

"Honey, I won!" she cried, giving him a big hug. As usual, she caught her blouse on his badge, carefully twisted free. "The Historical Society phoned this afternoon. I won the genealogical prize. Let's go out and celebrate. I'll buy you a steak at Bunyanland."

"Geez, I'm sort of tired . . ."

"Oh, Emil. I *won*. Nothing's defrosted, either . . ."

"We could have canned soup."

He saw her disappointment, changed his mind. "Oh sure, I'm being a drag. We *should* celebrate. Congratulations. You deserve the prize. Matter of fact, I wouldn't mind a steak at all."

"I even made reservations." Sarah smiled, as Emil went to wash up and put on a suitcoat.

Sarah chattered triumphantly on the drive to Bunyanland,

which cheered Emil a bit, and he saw that the Boom-Boom Room was enjoying only moderate patronage this evening.

"Hi! My name is Muffy and I'm your waitress . . . Oh! Hello, Sheriff."

"Sarah, this is Miss Huff. You know, the girl—"

"Yes, of course," exclaimed Mrs. Whippletree, giving Muffy the once-over. "I recognize you from your picture in the *Trib*. You're a brave girl, helping Emil and all."

Muffy blushed. "I don't know how much I'm helping."

"Anything happen out here today?" Emil asked.

Muffy shook her luxurious, artificial head of hair. "Unh-uh. Nothing. No, wait. That man was here for a little bit."

"What man?"

"The one who picked me up that night, when I was hitchhiking back from campus."

Torbert! "What did he want?"

Muffy shrugged. "I don't know. He just looked in the door, saw me, and left right away."

They gave their orders. Sarah had a small filet, but Emil opted for the twenty-four-ounce sirloin.

"Want to get my money's worth out of family history," he said, "seeing as how family history's gonna end with me."

"Oh, don't go bellyaching now and ruin our good time," scolded Sarah.

The dinner was excellent. Lute Proctor himself came over to ask if everything was all right. Sarah commented on Muffy's perfume a few times, not favorably, but charitably allowed that tastes varied. Then she talked about Dee-Dee.

"You know, Emil, Barbara is sure it's a man."

"What's a man? I mean, who's a man?"

"The cause of Dee's behavior lately. The reason she won't tell about that 'lost weekend.'"

"Could be," said Emil neutrally.

"You don't seem too worried about it. The first person in the relationship to have a chance at finishing college, and now all this fuss about sign-ins . . . I just don't know. What if North Star expels her?"

"They won't. You know what I think? They're just putting Dee through the wringer because I haven't rolled over and played dead."

"And I was so looking forward to the big dinner we'd give for Dee-Dee at the Persian Inn on Commencement Day."

"Don't cancel the reservation, hon."

"Emil, do you know something? Did Dee tell you something?"

Women, dammit. "Oh, no," he lied badly. "Anyway, it's her business, isn't it? And wouldn't she pick a good man with a fine future?"

*Heismann Trophy. Rookie of the Year. Most Valuable . . .*

Maybe *free* tickets to the big games . . .

Sarah, as good as her word, gave Emil money to pay for the dinner, and they drove home. The night was warm, stars out, and it looked like an ideal football weekend coming up.

Emil had taken his "civilian" car, a five-year-old Chev, and as he swung into the driveway he pushed the dashboard button to raise the garage door.

The door didn't respond. He braked to a stop only inches away from it.

It had happened before. "These damn modern gizmos," he grumbled.

"Emil!" cried Sarah, pointing toward the house.

Behind the living-room windows, for a brief instant, he saw the shadow of a figure appear and retreat.

"Somebody's in the house," Sarah whispered.

"Did you lock the door?"

"I think so. I'm sure I did. I always do."

"But you were excited that you'd won the prize?"

"Emil, I *always* lock the door. You better call—"

"The sheriff?" Emil said. He opened the car door quietly. "You stay here. Let me check this out."

"Emil. Be careful."

He never wore his weapon when he went out in mufti; he'd stashed it in the trunk. Now he strolled around to the back of the car, keeping his eye on the house, and stuck his key in the lock. The trunk lid popped open, concealing him from the eyes of whomever was inside his home. He pulled the .38 out of its holster, slipped it into his hip pocket, and slammed the trunk shut.

"Emil . . ." cautioned Sarah from the car.

He walked slowly toward the front door, fumbling with the keys, trying to appear completely unaware of intruders. There was a thick, tall hedge of arborvitae running along the porch, however, and when Emil reached it, he ducked down and hustled around the corner of the house, through the breezeway, across the patio, to the back door.

The lock barely clicked. He stood inside the darkened kitchen, gun in hand.

"I thought he was on his way in," someone whispered. Low voice. Probably male.

"I'll look again." This was a woman. "I don't see him now. And Aunt Sarah's still in the car."

*Aunt* Sarah? Emil edged quietly through the kitchen and slid along the dining room wall, peering around the doorjamb into the living room.

Dee-Dee Tiernan was standing behind the draperies, looking out at the darkened lawn and driveway. Light from a streetlamp shone in through the front windows on the close-cropped blond head of a man sitting in Emil's favorite rocking chair.

Dale Torbert.

"Just relax and make yourselves to home," said the sheriff, flicking on the inside lights and putting his weapon away.

Dee-Dee jumped about three feet and let out a startled yell. Torbert, squinting in the sudden light, leaped to his feet.

"Sheriff Whippletree . . ." he began. He looked at least ten years older than he was. Stress showed in his eyes, his jaw, his very posture, taut and slightly bent. "I hear you're looking for me," he said. "I can't believe you'd listen to Mrs. Hollman. You've got to help me."

"Uncle Emil, you've got to help *us!*" pleaded Dee-Dee.

Emil looked from his niece, whose shining beauty not even desperation could fully subdue, to the handsome young man beside her. And he understood. Now things were really complicated. Pro-

242

fessor Dale Torbert, blood type A and current fugitive, was Dee's "secret" boyfriend.

Dee-Dee and Dale Torbert sat on the couch holding hands, facing Emil in his rocker and Sarah in a wing chair. Emil noticed how their fingers were interlocked, how his niece caressed her lover's arm, up and down, up and down.

"We didn't want to announce our engagement until after Commencement," Torbert was saying. "You know how schools can be if faculty date students, especially in the case of a straitlaced place like North Star."

"You mean you're engaged . . . ?" said Sarah.

The two youngsters smiled and nodded in unison.

"And that's why you've been so secretive?"

"We didn't want to be," Torbert said. "It's just that we decided it was best, for the time being. The secret's got to come out now, though, I'm afraid."

"You mean the weekend of the murder, don't you?" asked Emil. Sarah was a little mystified, but he'd figured things out. "Where were the two of you, anyway?"

"We stayed at the Pine Tree Inn up at Big Falls," Dee-Dee said, without hesitation.

"Oh dear," said Sarah.

"It's my alibi, I guess," allowed the professor. "It has to come out now, and it's going to put Dee in a bad light, but she is old enough to do as she wishes."

"Oh *dear*," said Sarah again, thinking of scandal.

"As if you'd never heard of such things," growled Emil affectionately. "You forget about that night at Grand Lake, the fallen tree and all?"

"That was a little different . . ." said Sarah, actually blushing.

"Not for those days," countered Emil. He turned back to Torbert. "Maybe we don't have to rush out and proclaim everything to high heaven just yet," he said. "Tell me a few things, though, so I can figure out how to handle this. First, why did you 'disappear' this afternoon? Why didn't you just call my office when you found

243

out that Bunny had accused you, and that I had a bulletin out for your apprehension?"

"I . . . I had to talk to Dee," Torbert replied. "We had to decide what to do."

"So you came here?"

"Yes. In a roundabout way. You see, our meeting place was usually Bunyanland . . . We didn't want to be seen together on campus."

Emil understood. That was why Muffy had seen Torbert at Bunyanland this afternoon. That was why Dee had been there for lunch when he'd gone to talk to Muffy.

"Then," the girl continued, "we drove out into the country this afternoon. When it got dark, we came back to town. Dale's car is in your garage. I knew where you kept your spare key, behind the loose shingle on the side of the back porch."

"So here you are," said Emil. "There's another thing I need to know, however. On the night of the murder, you told me you'd left campus and driven to St. Paul"—*a lie*, he thought to himself—"but on the way you picked up a hitchhiker. She said you were alone in your car. Where was Dee, if you went off to spend the weekend together?"

"I took the last campus bus into town," she interjected hurriedly. "I had the driver drop me off at Bunyanland."

"So that's why you took Miss Huff to her home instead of Bunyanland?" Whippletree asked Torbert.

"Yes, sir. I didn't want anybody to see me meeting Dee-Dee."

"And now the whole weekend, the Pine Tree Inn and everything, has to come out," mourned Sarah. "*Oh dear!*"

"Not necessarily," said Emil. "Let's wait and see."

He considered the situation. Obviously, Torbert and his niece were very much in love. They'd taken some risks, but love was always a risk anyway. What did matter was the fact that Torbert *could have* killed Alicia Stanhope in the twenty minutes to half an hour he admitted it had taken him to leave the seminar, go to his office, and get to his car. But Emil chose to keep this suspicion to himself.

"I have a request," he said to the professor. "Will you voluntarily allow one of my deputies to search your residence?"

"Why . . . yes," came the reply, somewhat surprised but unreluctant.

"But why?" asked Dee-Dee, looking a little worried.

"In my line, there are things that have to be done. All right. I'll rescind the all-points that's out for you and your car. Professor, there are two things I want you to do. Take Dee back to campus, but first stop at her mother's place and . . . I believe in the old days the phrase was 'state your intentions.'"

"That was the phrase," Sarah said.

"I don't know how Mom will take this," Dee-Dee said skeptically.

"Much better than the way she's taking things now," Emil said. "You know, one of the problems of growing up, for both sides, is forgetting that people can get smarter as well as older. You go on over there. It'll be all right."

They went outside and Emil backed his Chev out of the driveway. Torbert eased the BMW out of the garage and Dee-Dee got into the car with him. Emil walked over to say good-bye. "I understand your hearing is set for tomorrow morning, Professor?" he said.

"That's right."

"Who's chairing it?"

"Dexter, I think."

"Any way I could sit in on it? As an observer, or something?"

"No. Wait. The faculty charter says I can have present witnesses of my choice. But you're hardly involved . . ."

"Maybe I'll be there anyway."

"I wish you'd come to my session in front of the Honor Committee," Dee-Dee said. "That's in the morning, too."

"Just stick to your guns," Emil told her. "What else can I say?"

"Oh my goodness, the younger generation," said Sarah, when Emil came back inside the house.

"Look at the bright side, hon. Now you'll get to plan a wedding

245

as well as a graduation dinner. And if nature takes its course, which it has a strong tendency to do, you'll be able to enter new names on the family tree in years to come."

This observation cheered his wife considerably, as did Barb's call a short time later. "Isn't he a nice boy, though?" she babbled to the Whippletrees.

The sheriff showered, put on pajamas and robe, and watched the national news wrapup on TV. It wasn't as bad as he thought it would be.

"While tension continues on the campus of North Star University in Minnesota," the announcer said as the camera panned Bunny's mob, "local Sheriff Emil Whippletree stepped directly into the fray today and arrested a man that many claim to be an 'outside agitator'"—here the screen showed Whippletree and Tony Wiggins dragging an unconscious Jacques LaBatt to the sheriff's car—"and, moments later, Sheriff Whippletree forestalled a suicide attempt by a local woman who had responded emotionally to the words of self-proclaimed mystic and visionary, Bunny Hollman." There was a shot of Bunny, collapsed upon the ground beneath the pine tree. "Whippletree has said that the crowd crisis at the university will be under control in time for Saturday's clash between North Star and Illinois," the announcer concluded, "and countless football fans undoubtedly hope so as well."

Not bad, thought Emil, turning off the set. They didn't even show me getting knocked on my butt.

The phone rang just as he was settling into sleep. It couldn't be Farley, who'd already called to report finding neither a blue slicker nor rubber gloves in Torbert's apartment. Emil sat up in bed and grabbed the receiver. "Yeah?"

"Am I speaking to Mr. Emil Whippletree?"

An accented voice. Emil couldn't quite place it, but the intonations were vaguely familiar.

"Yep," he said.

"I believe I just saw you on the telly, did I not?"

246

English. "I guess you did. That was me, all right."

"Sir, allow me to introduce myself. I am Osbert Whippletree, from Great Britain. I do quite a lot of traveling in my business—I am in New York at the moment—but, in spite of numerous perusals of telephone directories, I have never found a Whippletree outside England."

"There are Whippletrees in England?" Emil exclaimed.

"Of course there are. There are hundreds of us in Hampshire. I myself am a resident of Salisbury."

Emil told him about his own trip to Godalming, in Surrey, and his failure to find anything other than a lonely tombstone.

Osbert Whippletree laughed. "I am afraid you inquired in the wrong locale," he said. "The family moved to Hampshire centuries ago. Really, we must plan to get together sometime."

Emil allowed as to how that would sure be nice. He and Osbert chatted a little while longer.

"Hundreds of us, did you say?" Emil could not help asking.

"Oh, yes. We're rather ubiquitous in Hampshire, if I do say so."

After thanking Osbert for the call, Emil got out the dictionary and looked up "ubiquitous."

"Hot dog," he said. "I'm not alone."

## 19

After a breakfast of Egg McMuffins on West Division Street—one serving for the sheriff and five for Axel Vogel—Emil and his deputy headed out to North Star in Stearns County One. Whippletree riffled through the *Trib* as they drove along.

"Riley's got a story in here," said the sheriff. "Instead of staying at the St. Cloud Holiday Inn tonight, the Illinois football team is holing up down in The Cities. Seems it's not entirely safe for them to come up here. Or so they claim."

"Unnnnnnnhhh," observed Axel, belching.

Emil read on. "Snopes is calling for the National Guard. Bunny Hollman isn't answering calls. The university has no comment."

Axel belched again. "You'll find a way, Sheriff. You always do."

"Nothing like faith," said Emil.

He couldn't be sure, but when they turned into the drive leading toward campus, he thought that the crowd on the golf course was considerably smaller today. At least the Gabriel's Guards were gone. Emil hoped none of them knew how to write. Jacques LaBatt was stuck back in his cell in the jail, and although Emil hated to admit it, he sort of enjoyed seeing the fanatic twist in the wind.

Butch Lodge and a couple of his security men were standing around the pine tree, where young Father Ryder was saying Mass. Emil told Axel to stop the car. He got out and walked over to Butch, who looked jittery and disconsolate. The crowd of worshippers seemed to match his mood: an air of dour, almost hopeless resignation seemed to hang in the air beneath the mighty arms of the statute of Jesus.

"Mornin', Butch. How goes it?"

Lodge shrugged. "I don't know. I'd like to talk to you sometime."

"Well, not now. I've got a hearing to attend. Say, I don't think there are as many people out here as yesterday. Of course it's early. Is Bunny coming today?"

"I don't know. I haven't heard."

"*The Lord be with you,*" Father Ryder intoned.

"*And with your spirit,*" responded the crowd.

"The people seem pretty demoralized, or something," Emil observed.

"So am I," said Butch.

"That's funny. I feel damn good."

Then Emil got back into the car, and Axel wheeled into the parking lot behind Cuthbert Center. The Torbert hearing was to be held in a conference room on the second floor.

"Might as well come with me," said the sheriff. "Bring the radio with you. If anything comes up back at the office, we'll want to be in touch."

The two lawmen got out of Stearns County One, entered Cuthbert, and found their way to the conference room. Dale Torbert was already there, seated at one side of a long, felt-topped table. He looked a little nervous, but composed, and, as usual, he was well-dressed in a plain navy-blue business suit. He was studying notes written on a yellow legal pad, and nodded his greetings to the sheriff.

"Axel, better wait out here in the corridor," Emil suggested. "Come in if you need me."

"Gotcha, Sheriff."

Emil entered the conference room, and took a look at the other men waiting at the long table. He saw snappy Professor Beauchamp, seated with two colleagues, and four gray, somber-looking men who, he figured, were members of the various faculty committees involved in a hearing of this sort. He also saw chubby Charlie Hollman, seated near the head of the table, where a big, high-backed chair stood vacant. With Hollman was Brewster Titchell, Jr. They saw him simultaneously. Titchell opened his mouth and stared. Charlie's face turned red. He got up and approached the sheriff.

"What are *you* doing here?"

"Trying to learn something. They tell me this is the place."

"You can't come in here."

"I sure can. According to the rules, Dr. Torbert has the right to invite anybody he wants."

Hollman looked over toward Torbert.

"You're such an expert on rules for everybody, Charlie," said the young professor. "Guess I caught you on this one."

Hollman scurried back to the table and began to pore through a blue-bound manual in front of him. He slammed it shut angrily.

"Guess I might as well sit down," said Emil. He took a seat right across from Charlie and Titchell, just adjacent to the big, high-backed chair. "Nice room," he said, looking around. He couldn't figure out why young Brewster seemed so terrified of him.

Emil's back was toward the door, so he was a little surprised when, at about ten seconds after ten o'clock, Charlie Hollman suddenly shot to his feet like a frantic cadet.

Everybody else stood up, too, and Emil turned to see President Anderson striding into the room. Rector Rex had gotten himself quite a nice tan, probably down there in San Antonio, and he looked even more distinguished than usual, white-silver hair set against sun-bronzed skin. He reminded Emil of a chieftain, old, wise and weathered.

Yet—and Emil was surprised by his own reaction—he felt little awe in Anderson's presence any more, quite unlike all the professors present, who snapped to their feet as Charlie Hollman had, with the exception of Torbert, who rose perfunctorily, courteously. Emil wondered for a moment why he felt as he did. Then he knew. Anderson had gotten out of town and stayed out of town during a crisis. Whatever the president's reasons, the old sheriff was disappointed. To Emil, Rector Rex was no longer the man he'd seemed to be only weeks ago.

Emil also remembered what Doc Divot had told him about the spaceship with the cloaking device: when it wanted to attack, it had to become visible. Then you could take a shot at it yourself.

Anderson was elegantly visible now, as he slipped into the big chair at the head of the table.

"Empty chair right here next to me," Emil said, gesturing expansively to Dexter, who had entered with Anderson. "Have a seat."

Dexter skirted Emil briskly, and sat down.

"Good morning, gentlemen," the president said.

"Good morning," came the chorus.

Anderson looked around the table, at Charlie and Titchell, at Torbert, at the four faculty committee professors and the three history-department tenure committee guys. Then he stared curiously at Emil. "What are you doing at this proceeding, Sheriff?"

"Seemed like a good idea to me," Emil said.

"I asked Sheriff Whippletree to attend," said Dale Torbert. "It's my right to have anyone I choose, according to the faculty handbook."

"Make a note, Fagin," Anderson said to Dexter. "We must review the faculty handbook for possible revision."

All the professors nodded sagely. Emil shifted in his chair and took a look at them. The members of the faculty committees were soft-looking, unimpressive generally, except for eyes that showed, if not intelligence, at least a canny alertness. They had the restrained, self-righteous air of bureaucrats, safe themselves, sitting in judgment on someone else. Emil had seen plenty of rubber stamps in his lifetime.

The history-department professors seemed less sure of themselves, and they differed as to physical type. Emil already knew Beauchamp, dapper as ever this morning. Binlow was a big fleshy man, who seemed simultaneously vapid and querulous. Bowers was probably the ugliest man Whippletree had ever seen, grotesquely obese, with a fat lower lip that sagged into his chin.

"This proceeding is now open," Anderson proclaimed casually. "Professor Torbert, you may state your case against the committee's decision not to grant you tenure."

Torbert stood up, poised and cool. He was an impressive-looking young man. Emil caught Rector Rex appraising the plaintiff, he who had gauged and judged so many an adversary in his time. The president's eyes showed, for an instant, an old man's envy of a young man's youth.

Dexter and Charlie Hollman, however, glared at Torbert with a mixture of fear and outrage. Who was this *subordinate*—who had already been given his notice—to challenge a decision of those older, if not wiser, than he?

"President Anderson, Vice-President Dexter, Gentlemen," Torbert began, "I'll be brief. What, after all, is the fate of one man in a distinguished and powerful institution? I speak not only of North Star, but of the larger academic profession of which we are all a part. When I accepted a post here, I believed—and I continue to believe—that freedom of inquiry, the unhindered examination of ideas, constitutes the primary work, indeed, the obligation, of everyone in our world. I thought, upon joining the faculty here, that I would not only be allowed but encouraged to pursue this goal, which I consider as noble as anything on earth. Instead I found, to my chagrin, that many sacred cows may not be milked, nor even examined—"

"This university stands for freedom of intellectual inquiry in every respect," interrupted Rector Rex, with some heat.

Torbert just nodded. ". . . I found," he continued, "that the beliefs, attitudes, ideas, notions and, frankly, intellectual fallacies of my chairman, Dr. Hollman . . ."

Charlie lifted his chin and waited for the blow.

". . . were the standards by which men were measured, particularly those seeking tenure. Not only that. Dr. Hollman, acting in a manner that must be condemned by every person in a nation which claims to be democratic in principle, and in an institution which, through its president, claims fealty to free inquiry, violated the standards of decency, the letter of the law, and the integrity of two students of this university, Brewster Titchell, Jr., who is here with us, and the late Alicia Stanhope.

"He violated their integrity by directing or encouraging them to tape one of my lectures secretly, unbeknownst to me—"

"It's a lie!" roared Charlie, in his best Henry Kissinger voice.

Emil noted that Dexter was copying down everything being said.

"You'll have your chance to speak, Professor Hollman," Anderson said.

"I assure you," Torbert continued, "that had Dr. Hollman come to me at any time, or called me to come to him, and inquired as to what I am teaching, I would have told him frankly and completely. But he chose not to do this. Instead, he resorted to the cheapest, the basest, the most cowardly of *illegal* practices in order to manipulate the work of the tenure committee."

Emil glanced at Bowers, Binlow, and Beauchamp, who were following Torbert's presentation with cold interest.

"In light of the fact that this university is supposed to be a bastion of inquiry and thought, free speech, and publication," Torbert concluded, "and because illegal means were used in the tenure process, I ask—not automatically to be reinstated—but to be reconsidered on a fair and open basis. I also do not hesitate to say that, if not given the satisfaction I seek, I will have no choice but to take the matter of the secret taping to appropriate authority outside this university, for we are men of laws as well as of tenure."

Then Dale Torbert sat down.

Emil studied Anderson. His face was bland and expressionless. The sheriff could not tell what was going on in the president's mind. He glanced across the table at Hollman and Titchell. The professor was smouldering; Junior looked close to panic.

Emil turned to Dexter. "Could I have a piece of paper, please?"

The vice-president, showing irritation, ripped a sheet from his pad and handed it to Emil, who, in the long pause that followed Torbert's unexpectedly brief remarks, wrote, "Axel, bring me Titchell's notebook, it's in the back seat," and motioned his big deputy into the room.

Axel's colossal appearance, and noisy retreat, eased the tension that had been building in the room.

"A little unfinished business," apologized the sheriff, "I don't like loose ends."

"Commendable," observed Anderson. "All right, are there any reactions to Professor Torbert?"

Nobody said anything for a moment, then Charlie Hollman raised his hand. "Mr. President," he said pompously, "I say with all charity that this is not the first time a young man has erred through lack of experience, or sought to save himself by unjust accusations against his superiors. You yourself, Mr. President, have told me that the old ideas and beliefs are legitimate occupants of the academic throne, and that modern, so-called liberal notions must be excised ruthlessly from the halls of learning. . . ."

Emil frowned. Had Rector Rex really said something like that? If so, it was at variance with his reputation as a modern thinker. Had he simply been engaging in politics with Charlie, flattering him? Or did Anderson, down deep, really believe as Charlie Hollman did? The sheriff irreverently pictured the president as a great big onion, from which layer after layer must be peeled away before the essential core could be reached.

"This university is committed to long-standing, time-tested ideals," Anderson averred.

"As to the canard about secret tapes," Charlie went on, "let me now lay that matter to rest, though it embarrass my young colleague. Mr. Titchell," he asked, turning towards Junior, "did you or Miss Stanhope *ever* tape record a lecture of Dr. Torbert's?"

"No, sir," Titchell quavered.

Axel returned then, and as discreetly as possible—which was not very—set the notebook on the table in front of Emil, and retreated.

"Furthermore," Charlie went on, "did any of the members of the tenure committee *hear* such a tape?"

"No," said Bowers.

"Never," said Binlow.

"Not that I can recall," Beauchamp chirped.

"I understand there were *transcripts* made of the tape," Torbert interjected.

"Is that correct?" Anderson asked Charlie.

"Absolutely not," answered the chubby professor.

Emil looked at young Brewster. His eyes were on the notebook. He seemed to be suffering the torments of the lost and damned. He glanced once at Emil with eyes full of fear, then looked away.

What the hell is going on here? Whippletree thought.

"I shall now prove," intoned Charlie, "that our inexperienced friend is a liar in this matter as well. Professor Binlow," he inquired portentously, "are you aware of, or have you ever seen, the mythical transcript to which Professor Torbert refers?"

"Not at all," replied Binow dutifully.

Emil reached for the notebook and opened it. He was wondering why Titchell seemed so agitated, and he was looking for a reason. As soon as he flipped back the cover, Brewster's agitation mounted.

"And you, Professor Bowers," Charlie inquired sarcastically, "what's this about a transcript?"

Emil paged through the notebook and reached the typewritten theme that had been inserted there. He began to scan it.

"I have not seen, nor do I know about, nor have I ever heard of any transcript," Bowers proclaimed.

Emil couldn't help himself. "Wait a minute," he said. His eyes dropped again to the typewritten paper.

> . . . and when we take up the matter of secu-
> larism, we find—yes, a question, Mr.
> Rutkow? (Laughter.) What is secularism, Dr.
> Torbert? (Laughter.) Secularism is . . .

Wait a minute here, Emil thought. This is no student theme! "Subject to verification," Emil growled, "I think I have the do-jiggy right here." He held it up for everybody to see. The faculty committee boys looked as stunned as old maids who have just discovered a carrot or cucumber of unmistakable shape. The history-department professors—"the three bozos," Torbert had referred to them—gaped in fearful astonishment. Charlie Hollman lost his red-brick complexion fast, and Junior Titchell sagged backward in his chair.

"Let me see that," demanded Vice-President Dexter, snatching at the paper.

"Sorry," said Emil. "Dr. Torbert," he asked, as Anderson looked on with an impassivity that took energy to maintain, "is this the lecture you gave in seminar on the night of the murder?"

He handed it across the table to Torbert, who glanced at it with interest, then triumph.

"Yes," he said. "It's a typewritten transcript of everything I said, everything anybody said, that evening."

"Show it to Beauchamp," Emil ordered.

The document was passed on down the table and the dapper prof, now visibly nervous, took a look at it.

"I don't quite know what to say," he observed then, gazing thoughtfully at the ceiling.

"The truth will do," said Emil. "Isn't that right, Dr. Anderson? You know, I bet Sylvia Bromley, the departmental secretary, typed the transcript—"

"This is some sort of stunt," raved Charlie, "a stunt unworthy of this high meeting—"

"The truth will do, Dr. Beauchamp," said Anderson wearily.

And Beauchamp, having been thus directed, let everything out: how there had been a secret tape (how he hadn't approved); how there had been transcripts (how he'd been alarmed); how Charlie had called and told him to destroy his copy (how he hadn't because he thought "something fishy was going on"); and how suddenly the transcript had been missing from his office.

Brewster Titchell, Jr., said he was not feeling well, and asked to be excused.

"Do you have any further remarks, Dr. Hollman?" inquired Anderson with exquisite courtesy.

Charlie Hollman, as defeated as a man could be, said nothing.

"Then I shall take this matter under advisement—" the president began.

"Just a moment," interjected Dale Torbert, "if you please. I don't see why 'advisement' is necessary. I think my case has been proven, if not by me, then by Sheriff Whippletree. I think the facts are clear. I've been maligned. I want an answer now, or I call a lawyer today. Will you overrule the tenure committee's decision or not?"

Good for you, kid, Whippletree thought.

"Comments from any of you gentlemen?" asked Rector Rex, still trying to get off the hook.

There were none.

"Then," said Anderson, "the tenure committee's decision is rejected. I will appoint a new committee to assess this matter."

"Thank you," said Torbert. "That's all I ask."

Charlie hustled out of the room before anybody else rose from their chairs. Anderson looked tired, Emil observed, or angry. Perhaps both, but more too. Instinctively, Emil guessed that, at heart, Rector Rex tended to favor Charlie's conservative ideas, rather than Torbert's more liberal notions. He would not really have cared if the young professor left North Star. But Anderson demonstrated no true passion for Hollman's tenets either. His basic belief lay somewhere else. The layers of the onion are peeling away one by one, Emil thought.

Anderson and Dexter huddled briefly at the far end of the room, discussing something in serious undertones. Emil congratulated Dale Torbert, and walked over to the administrators.

"Sorry, but I've got to talk to you a minute," he said to the president. "Too bad you haven't been around; I could have used your help."

"Go ahead," said Anderson coldly.

"First, I understand there's a disciplinary hearing coming up involving my niece."

"Yes, I'm chairing it," said Dexter.

"Cancel the thing," Emil told him. "Wipe her slate clean. She was engaged in confidential family business that weekend. I'll vouch for her. North Star has always claimed to be a strong supporter of family sanctity, and—"

Anderson threw up his hands. "Cancel it, Fagin," he said quietly. "What else is on your mind, Sheriff?"

"Well, I want you to call Judge Titchell in town and have him issue me a warrant to search the locker room under the stadium."

"Why do you think the judge would listen to me?"

"Let's not kid ourselves. You may have been thousands of miles away, but you've been hindering my investigation. I need that warrant."

The answer was as definite as it was sharp. "No," Anderson snapped. "It's enough that my university has been subject to—" Then he broke off, collecting himself smoothly. "There *are* things I am unable to do," he stated blandly, "just like you, I'm afraid. I note that those big crowds of worshippers are still out there. And I believe you promised they'd be moved by game time tomorrow?"

"I may not be able to do it," Emil said.

Rector Rex brightened. "Then you'll admit you can't, and I can have Governor Bauch send the National Guard in here—"

"No," corrected the sheriff, "I didn't say I couldn't move them. I said I may not be able to move them. But, if I can't, I'll control the situation so both the football fans *and* the prayer pilgrims will have access to their respective entertainments."

Dexter and Anderson were incredulous.

"County Charter," Emil told them. "I have the authority to deputize and arm any number of men I need in an emergency. You'd be surprised at how many guys I can dig up. And you might be surprised at the depth of support I still have here in the county. Besides, people love an adventure."

"You mean to say you'd run this campus with unpredictables from the little towns?"

"Not one of 'em's half as crazy as Jacques LaBatt, and you gave *him* free rein."

"No, Sheriff," decided Anderson, digging in his heels. "If those people are not off the golf course by nine o'clock tomorrow morning, I'm calling the governor. We'll take it out of your hands, County Charter or no. I have plenty of IOUs to call in."

"So do I," said Emil. "So do I."

Rector Rex laughed then, and shook his head. "Move those people, Sheriff, and I'll invite you and any guests you choose to share the presidential box for tomorrow's game."

"That right?" said Emil. "You're on."

Pete Poll, who usually spent Friday nights at the bottom of a quart of Jack Daniel's, requested duty instead.

"One of my problems," he told the sheriff, "was leisure time. I didn't have nothing to do. I got bored. So I started drinking to kill the time. What I need is plenty of work, plenty of responsibility. That's the ticket."

Emil, who'd overheard the other deputies grumbling about the fact that Poll hadn't been assigned stakeout duty at Bunyanland, decided to give it a try. He planned to spend the evening at Bunyanland himself. What could happen?

"Okay, Pete," he said, "let's go."

The Boom-Boom Room was jam-packed with folks launching

their weekends. The sheriff installed Poll at a table near the door and told him to keep an eye on Muffy.

"That won't be hard," said the deputy, ogling the buxom, short-skirted waitress.

Then Emil asked the bartender to keep an eye on Poll and to give him all the root beer he wanted.

"I'll be in Lute Proctor's office if you need me," he told Muffy.

"I'm real nervous about this," sighed the girl. "When will it end?"

Emil didn't know, so he couldn't tell her. He entered Proctor's spacious but cluttered headquarters, sat down behind the desk, picked up the phone and got to work.

First, he called the Highway Department and the State Police. "We're gonna have a colossal mess of cars up here tomorrow," he informed a honcho down in The Cities. "I plan to park 'em along the highway. Yep, I've got the manpower and the thoroughfare won't be blocked."

Having received verbal authorization for this strategy, Emil next began phoning the constables in all the little towns around Stearns County. His message, his request, were identical in each conversation.

"Look here," he said to Rafe Withers in St. Rosa, and Elmer Bromenschenkl in St. Joe, and Herman Spoden in St. Alazara, "I'm gonna need you tomorrow. We'll meet at five A.M. by that big football billboard outside North Star. I'll give instructions then. Come armed. You'll be deputized for the day."

And, in each case, the response was, "Sure thing, Emil, you can count on me."

Finally, the sheriff called all the managers of all the amateur baseball teams in the county. Baseball, during the short, hot summers in the upper Mississippi Valley, ranked right up there with going to church as Sunday recreation. Every town had a team. Emil spoke to the Casey Stengels of the St. Augusta "Gussies" and the Luxemburg "Lux" and the Rockville "Rox" and the St. Alazara "Angels" and the St. Stephen "Saints" and the Brooten "Bulls" and on down the line.

"Five o'clock?" some protested.

"Hell, you'd be up at three for fishing or hunting deer, wouldn't you? Bring the whole team. And come armed." This would be no problem. Sportsmen abounded in the county. Everybody had a weapon of one sort or another.

"We'll be there, Emil," came the responses. "You can count on us."

Whippletree made his final call and put down the phone with a feeling of gratitude and exultation. *This* was why he loved his county, his land, this was what he'd worked for all his life. In spite of what some people had said about him in recent weeks, in spite of what had been in the *Trib* and on TV, he could still count on the people, *his* people out there in the little towns. They knew he was theirs, a hell of a lot more than North Star was theirs, or Judge Titchell was theirs, or Rector Rex was theirs.

"I cannot *believe*," Dexter had said to Emil after the tenure hearing broke up, "I cannot believe how you spoke to the president today."

"What'd I say?"

"It wasn't what you said, it was the way you said it. And now you're promising to deal with the crowds? It seems to me that you recently boasted of solving the murder, too."

"I never boast," Whippletree had responded evenly, "never. I always find a way to do what I say I'm going to."

"I doubt you'll be reelected next year."

"Maybe not. I can live with that. But can *you* live with not being president of North Star?"

Dexter showed a bit of anxiety. "What do you mean?"

"Why do you think Anderson was away for the past few weeks? If somebody's gonna get blamed for the way things were mishandled here, who do you think it'll be?"

Fagin Dexter had beat a quick retreat. He knew.

But the sheriff knew too, now, that he had to deliver on his claims. He put his boots up on Lute Proctor's desk and helped himself to a big pinch of Copenhagen. There was a hesitant rapping at the door, and Muffy came in. She looked frazzled.

"Something wrong?" asked Emil.

The girl shook her head, and pulled a package of cigarettes out of her apron pocket. "No, I just needed a minute of peace and quiet. It's a madhouse out there tonight." She leaned against the closed door, lit up, and took a deep drag. "Friday nights are always the worst," she said. "It's a date night. There's a lot of tension."

"Why is it different from any other night?"

"Well," Muffy replied, slipping out of her high-heeled shoes and massaging one foot with the other, "on a regular night people are just here to unwind. On Friday—Saturday, too, I guess—they come in as couples and the atmosphere is all different. It's a male–female thing. It's sex. Everybody wants it on a night like this. Badly. That's why the tension."

"Men and women," said Emil.

Muffy smiled and puffed her cigarette. *"The soul of man is a knife upon the altar,"* she said, *"of woman it is silken softness for the piercing."*

"What'd you say?" asked Emil, sitting up straight. Bunny Hollman had said exactly those words at her first vision.

"Something wrong?" said Muffy.

"What you just said. Where'd you hear that?"

"I didn't hear it anywhere. I read it. That's from Paolo deVilliers, the poet I told you about. I think he's just the greatest. Those lines are from *Paeans*."

"*Paeans?*"

"Yes. A book of love poems. They explain everything about life. *Paeans to Lingam and Yoni* . . ."

Ginny's words again! "What does that mean?" he asked.

Muffy stubbed out her cigarette in an ashtray on the desk. "It's Hindu, or something. *Lingam* is man and *yoni* is woman. The poems are all about men and women together. It's very erotic, really."

"Sure sounds that way," observed Emil. So Bunny Hollman had taken her verses from an actual poet! They hadn't just miraculously entered her head out of heaven's thin air! That meant everything about her episodes or spells or seances was now suspect, with the possible exception of the physical reactions she enjoyed.

Muffy slipped back into her shoes with a groan, and returned to work. Emil did a little thinking, left Lute's office, and walked to Pete Poll's table in the Boom-Boom Room. The deputy was talking to a couple who'd sat down with him, Tod and Jill Canby. They were big drinkers, and they were ribbing Poll good-naturedly and ruthlessly.

"One can't hurt ya, Pete," Tod was saying as Emil approached. "What the hell, ya turn virtuous on us, for crissake?"

"I'm working," said Poll sheepishly, rotating a glass of root beer in his hands. "I can't drink while I'm working—Oh, Emil!"

"How you doing, Pete? Tod? Jill?"

"Hey, Sheriff," cried Jill. "Let him have a beer, at least."

Emil ignored them. Trouble with being an ex-toper, you sober up to find that all your friends are drunks.

"Pete," said Emil, "I want you to look sharp. I've got to run over to the Hollmans' place for a little while. Keep an eye on things."

"Sure thing, Sheriff. I can handle it."

Whippletree roared away from Bunyanland and piloted Stearns County One to the north side. There were no Gabriel's Guards standing sentinel at Charlie's front door any more, but all around the block, in a column of twos or sometimes threes, marched Bunny's supporters, each one holding a flickering candle in the falling September darkness. They still believed, but in spite of the vigil lights there was a spiritlessness in this demonstration that matched the mood Whippletree had perceived on the golf course earlier today. Somewhere, somehow, a corner had been turned, and everyone involved—Emil included—was headed down a road, or perhaps an alley, the landmarks of which were still unidentifiable.

Roy Riley, carrying a tape recorder and brandishing a small microphone, was standing on the walk and attempting to interview the marchers. He wasn't having much luck. They filed past him without comment.

"Emil," he called, "what brings you here?"

"Oh, I figured I might try and do a little negotiating."

"About getting the worshippers off the golf course tomorrow?"

"Could be."

"Everybody's talking confrontation, Emil. They've heard about your posse. Or is it army?"

"Both."

"Think you'll be in control tomorrow?"

"Hell," said the sheriff, thinking of Paolo deVilliers, "I'm in control now."

He walked up the steps and was just about to rap on the door when he heard voices inside. Charlie and Bunny. Arguing. This was something new, at least to Emil. It takes two people to argue, and never in a million years would he have suspected Bunny of the guts to stand up to her overbearing husband.

He knocked.

The voices ceased abruptly.

Bunny opened the door cautiously. "Emil?" she said, with some surprise. She wore an old housecoat and her hair was in curlers. He noticed lines of tension around her eyes and mouth.

"Got to talk to you. May I come in."

Wordlessly, she edged aside. He entered. Bunny closed the door. Emil stood in the living room, looked around, and saw Charlie Hollman seated at the table in the tiny dining room. Charlie stared at him but said nothing. The table was piled with envelopes and bills of various denominations.

"We've been receiving a lot of donations," Bunny explained, leading Emil into the dining room. "I don't know what we're going to do with all this money. Give it to some charity, probably."

Charlie had not yet spoken. He attempted to put a touch of defiance in his gaze, unsuccessfully. This morning's defeat and humiliation at the committee hearing had taken a lot out of him.

"Charlie," said Emil in greeting.

The professor nodded. "What brings you here, Sheriff?"

"I need to talk to Bunny."

"About what?" Hollman demanded. Bunny just stood there, holding one hand in the other.

"'Fraid that's between me and her."

"Now look here, Sheriff—" began Charlie, rising from his chair.

"Charles, no more!" snapped his wife, in a voice that combined decision and desperation. "I won't have it any more. I can't stand it any more. Nothing has gone the way you said it would. Everybody's angry and disappointed. I didn't mean for it to be like this—"

"Watch your tongue!" cried Charlie, alarmed, tilting his head slightly to remind his wife of Emil's presence.

"If Emil wants to talk to me," said Mrs. Hollman, "that's fine with me." She screwed up her courage and faced him down. "Leave," she said. "Go outside and talk to our friends. Try and tell them why everything's gone wrong, if you know. But just *go!*"

Stunned by her vehemence, and embarrassed that Emil—who'd already beaten him once today—was present to witness it, Charlie got up and left the house.

Bunny motioned Emil to a chair at the dining-room table. She was trembling, but in her eyes the sheriff saw a glint of satisfaction, if not triumph. She had exercised her will.

After all these years.

Bunny sat down, too. Emil reconnoitered all the bills. There were at least five thousand dollars on the table. "Religion continues to pay," he said.

"Emil, it's all ruined," said Bunny passionately, "and it could have been so wonderful."

"What do you mean?"

"I prayed for the message from Christ, the message Our Blessed Mother promised. But it will never come now, not with all the animosity that's built up."

"You really have seen the Virgin Mary?" he asked gently.

"Yes."

"And she's given you the messages about Toby Bolthaus? And Mavis Tuckerman's earrings? And my daughter, Susan?"

"Emil, yes."

"And the football scores?"

Mrs. Hollman was bewildered. "Emil, what are you talking about?"

264

"Forget it. You're certain, though, that what's been happening to you has nothing to do with Charlie's battle against Snopes and the athletic program?"

"Well, Mary has made it clear that the faithful must choose between—"

"All right, Bunny," said the sheriff, allowing a hint of sharpness to enter his tone, "I'm here to talk good old-fashioned Stearns County turkey. So let's level."

Bunny looked hurt, but also wary.

"You do know, I'm sure, that each of your visions has been preceded by a sort of poem?"

She glanced away for a millisecond, then her eyes returned to his. She nodded.

"Those verses just sort of come to you?"

"Yes. I don't know how or why."

Emil looked at her for a long moment. "I know about Paolo deVilliers, Bunny."

Mrs. Hollman did not collapse. One great raindrop of a tear formed at the corner of her right eye. She brushed it away.

"I wouldn't mind taking a look at the book, Bunny, if you happen to have it handy."

She seemed as defeated now as Charlie had been, but in her case it was a sad thing for Emil to witness. He still had no idea what had caused her to mount and sustain a bizarre campaign of faith based, apparently, on deceit.

Bunny left the room for a moment, then shuffled back with a thin volume, its gray paper cover wrinkled, its pages dog-eared, underlined, annotated.

### PAEANS TO LINGAM AND YONI
by Paolo deVilliers

Emil riffled through the thirty-six pages and saw many of the erotic verses that Bunny had recited beneath the pine tree, as if they'd come from heaven. On the back cover of the little book, the sheriff read that deVilliers had been a champion of hedonism, a twelfth-century resident of Venice, burned at the stake in 1185 for witchcraft, immorality, blasphemy, fornication, adultery, and consorting with the Evil One. They'd thrown the book at the poor bastard eight hundred years ago, and here he was again, causing trouble in Stearns County. His work had been suppressed, of course, only to reemerge now and then over the centuries. The volume Emil was holding had been published by Shakespeare and Co., Paris, 1923.

"Why, Bunny?" Emil asked quietly, turning to look Mrs. Hollman in the eyes.

Perhaps it was something she had always wanted to discuss, and he was there at the right time. Or maybe she had not realized, and had never been able to face until now, the diverse strands by which the fabric of her life was bound. But, with the candle-bearing marchers circling outside in her honor, and her tyrannical husband absent for once, Bunny confided in Emil, who had already smelled the stench of her fraud but had not condemned her.

"I never felt like anybody," she began, "not for as long as I can remember. I never felt . . . I never felt *special*. Do you know what that's like, Emil? To be a human being, a person, a little girl, a *woman*, and not to feel special? Not even *once*!

"But it never happened. I thought, when I got married, that it would. Change, I mean. After all, if a man chooses you, he must think you are at least special enough to be his wife. But Charlie is . . . well, Charlie. It became clear from the beginning that he was the sun and I was to be . . . not even a moon, just one of those satellites. Orbiting around him. And with us it wasn't . . . it never was . . . good. As I'd expected and so desperately wanted. He didn't even want children.

"So I built up a secret life. I fantasized. There was tremendous guilt. I was always going to confession, but that just made me feel more guilty. And then I joined the Charismatics.

"It was wonderful. For the first time, really for the first time in my entire life, I thought I had . . . something. A talent, maybe. When we prayed in tongues, I did it better than anyone. When we tried to imagine heaven, and the face of God, I could do it! At least I could describe what I imagined. The people in the group began to look up to me. Emil, it was wonderful!

"And there was something else, too. During the years when I was leading my guilty secret life, I would read . . . things. Things I oughtn't to have been reading. But I needed those things. I needed *something* to make me feel alive, like things never really were between Charlie and me. And in Charismatics, I found that if I thought about certain things, certain words and passages, I could . . . you know?"

Whippletree had already guessed. Bunny used *Paeans* to induce physical excitement, to rouse herself to bliss.

"But, Emil, I want you to know this, and I swear it's true. When we were driving onto campus for the football game two weeks ago, I did see something in that pine tree. I did not simply *imagine* it. I saw, as if it were *behind the sun*, the gentlest, the most beautiful face I have ever beheld."

"Just once?" he asked.

"Just once. That first time."

"And since then?"

"Since then I've been trying to see it . . . to see her . . . again. Do you think I'm crazy?"

"No," replied Emil slowly, "no. You just want to be happy, like everybody else. But you really do go into a trance? You really pass out at the end?"

"Yes. It's so intense. I guess I do it to myself. The more I hope to see that face again, the more upset I become."

"What about the messages?"

Bunny looked sheepish. "Everybody knows that Mr. Bolthaus blames himself for not fixing the brakes on Toby's car. And, shortly before her death, Mavis Tuckerman had a big fight with her sister, who told me she'd hidden the earrings to spite Mavis."

Emil swallowed hard. "And my daughter, Susan?"

"That comes from a long time ago. Shortly after your little girl drowned, Sarah more or less broke down once at a meeting of the Rosary Society. I was there. She said she didn't know what was

267

going to happen to you, that you were destroying yourself with guilt and worry because you thought Susan's death was your fault.

"Emil," she said plaintively, "I didn't want to hurt you. By bringing it all up again. I wanted . . . I truly wanted . . . to make you feel good. I'm so sorry if—"

"It's all right," he said gruffly, deeply stirred by Sarah's long-ago suffering in his behalf. People never really understand, do they, the richness of the hoards of unclaimed love that drift about this earth? Perhaps, in time, evolution will equip human beings with sensitivity sufficient to perceive and possess the shining radiance all around. After all, one must die to see the face of God. Love is at least as great a mystery, isn't it?

"Why did you change?" he asked. "Why did you turn on Zelda Schrieffels?"

Bunny put her face in her hands, her elbows in the piled stacks of bills. "I . . . I don't know. I think it was . . . I was so upset when I didn't see the Virgin again. And LaBatt came. He and Charlie were planning, scheming. The whole . . . the whole *mood* turned ugly. I turned ugly. I didn't feel special any more." She fell silent.

"So here we are," Emil said. "With about a hundred thousand people to deal with tomorrow."

"I really thought," Bunny said, composing herself, "that Rector Rex would be on Charlie's side. That he'd stand up for intellectuality, and start downplaying the football and everything. I was wrong. Emil, I don't want to go out there to that mob tomorrow. I don't think I can stand it again."

"*I've* got to be there," Emil said drily.

"I know. It's my fault. I've caused you all this trouble. But what am I going to do now? Those people believe in me. They expect something from me. What . . . ?"

"You know," said the sheriff, "I think I just had an idea. You willing to spend just a bit of this money to take some of the heat off both of us?"

Bunny looked at him, scarcely daring to hope. "If you have a way," she said, "I'll spend *all* of it."

Then the sheriff was on the phone, calling Norb Heffner at his gas station in Avon.

"Norb," he said, "you know that big parcel of land you own along I-94? I think . . . no, I haven't found a buyer for it, but I think I have some people who might want to rent it temporarily. At least until the snow flies. Yeah, they want to hold some meetings and stuff. Sure, they'll pay. I think they'll be willing to pay"— he winked at Bunny Hollman—"a pretty fair price."

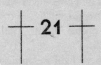

The call came just as he was saying good-bye to Mrs. Hollman, and telling her that he'd see her on the golf course early in the morning.

"Sheriff!" Lute Proctor yelled over the wire. "Sheriff, Pete Poll got drunk with the Canbys, lost track of Muffy, she went out behind the restaurant to dump some garbage, and a guy in a ski mask grabbed her. . . ."

Proctor was waiting at the Bunyanland entrance when Emil turned into the parking lot and braked to a skidding stop.

"Come on around back," he said to the sheriff.

The two men dogtrotted around to the rear entrance of the Boom-Boom Room, which led into the kitchen. Two dishwashers and a cook were standing there. Pete Poll was slumped down on a case of empty beer bottles.

"Emuhl, we got a li'l problem," he blithered, trying and failing to get on his feet.

"Exactly what happened?" Emil asked.

Proctor nodded to one of the dishwashers, a slim kid in his late teens. "Muffy and me was talkin' in the kitchen," he said. "Then she stepped out here to dump some junk in the trash. I heard her sort of yell, like somebody scared her or something, and when I went to look I saw this guy in a ski mask carrying her out into the meadow."

Behind Bunyanland, and all along the highway, fields and grassy meadows, separated here and there by treelines of poplar and box elder, rolled on to the Sauk River and North Star.

"Carrying her?" Emil asked.

"Yeah. Over his shoulder. She was fighting, but it wasn't doing no good."

Emil stared out at the meadow. There was no sound. It was a dark night, too, with cloud cover. "You have some floodlights back here?" he asked Lute Proctor.

"Right," said the manager. "Matt," he ordered his cook, "go inside and hit the switches."

The cook obeyed. Every light in Bunyanland went on, including those in the amusement area. Mighty Paul awakened, too, lifted his axe and resumed his spiel in mid-stride, booming, ". . . *Bunyan, and this is my blue* . . ."

"Kill the damn giant!" shouted Proctor to the cook.

". . . *ox, Baaaaabbe* . . ."

A great semicircle of illumination swept out over the meadow.

"Muffy?" yelled the sheriff.

He thought he heard something, a groan of an answer. But he wasn't sure.

"Somebody's out there," said Lute. "Let's go. You want I should get some of the guys in the bar to help us?"

"Not yet," said Emil. "We don't know what we're dealing with."

"Let's go!" declared Poll, bracing himself against the back wall of the Boom-Boom Room. He staggered out into the meadow. Emil was just about to restrain his deputy when he—and the other men—heard a sharp, ugly crack, like a blow, and saw a dark figure rise from the grass and race away into the distance.

"That must be the guy," said the sheriff. "And nobody could run that fast while carrying another person."

The men entered the meadow on the run, fanning out as they went, calling Muffy's name. Pete Poll stumbled along behind, blubbering "Muff', Muff', I'll make it up t' ya, Muff'."

270

They'd gone roughly a hundred yards when one of the dish-washers yelled in alarm, "Here she is! Over here!"

Emil trotted over to where the dishwasher was kneeling in the grass. He came close, saw Muffy's wide-open eyes staring into the dim light, glazed and expressionless.

*God, no!* he prayed, bending down.

Then she blinked once, twice.

"Ohhhhh," she moaned.

Alive.

A huge bruise was darkening on the left side of her face. Twisted in the fingers of her right hand was a ski mask.

"Are you all right?" Emil asked the girl.

"I . . . think so . . ." she answered, touching her cheekbone gingerly, wincing.

"Let's get you to the hospital."

"No, no, I'm . . . okay, I think." She sat up and Emil put an arm behind her shoulders. "He . . . he didn't mean to hit me . . ."

"What?"

"No, I don't think so. He carried me out here and when he heard you guys come out the back entrance, he made me lie down in the grass and be quiet. He was next to me, holding me down. I couldn't move. When the lights came on he got scared. His elbow hit me in the face when he jumped up and ran away. I grabbed his ski mask, though."

"Get a look at his face?"

"Not . . . really. Maybe a glimpse."

"Be able to recognize him again?" asked Emil.

"Maybe. I don't know. He was already turned away from me when I grabbed the mask. And the light isn't good. But he was big, very strong. He picked me up like I was a sack of potatoes. He had light-colored hair."

"Blond?" asked the sheriff.

"That, or maybe a light reddish color," Muffy said. "I couldn't tell for sure."

"Did he say anything? Other than telling you to keep quiet?"

271

Muffy nodded, touching fingertips to the burgeoning bruise. "Well, he said he wasn't going to hurt me, he just wanted to talk to me about the pictures. The ones that came in the mail. He wanted to know exactly what I'd seen along the river that night. But there wasn't time to tell him anything. You guys came out of the kitchen, and then the lights went on . . ."

"Loo's like a' ope' 'n' shut case, eh?" observed Poll, one arm around a dishwasher for support. "Loo's openenshut, fer sure . . ."

Emil got Muffy on her feet. "Ow, I've got a headache," she said.

"Lute," said the sheriff, "call an ambulance and have 'em take Muffy to the hospital. She might've had a concussion, or something. Then call Axel Vogel. Tell him to post a guard at Muffy's hospital room."

"Will do, Emil."

The sheriff looked across the fields toward the university. It was perhaps two miles away, as the crow flew. An easy distance to cover for a young man in prime physical condition.

"I've got something to do at North Star," he said.

Driving to the university, Emil experienced again that feeling of imminence he'd had at Bunny Hollman's house, a perception that some kind of corner had been turned, that the parabolas of disparate events were now converging. Yet his sixth sense conveyed intimations of danger as well, and it was this apprehension that caused him to drive off the highway and conceal Stearns County One in the shadows behind the big football-shaped billboard at the entrance to North Star. It was after ten now. Emil didn't want anybody to know he was here.

He crossed the highway on foot and set out over the darkened golf course. Vigil candles flickered beneath the distant pine tree, and he saw the shadows of worshippers moving against the light, like darkened figures bent to a mystical rite.

And he sensed too, once again, the eerie current of rare power that had touched him here before. Anderson that morning in his office, had casually spoken of people who possessed, perhaps unbeknownst to them, the gift of inexplicable insight regarding forces that existed just beyond the borders of reality. Guess he might've meant me, thought the sheriff, I sure as hell feel strange out here.

Keeping his distance from the prayer pilgrims—in the darkness he estimated that there were several hundred of them—he reached the rearing walls of Granitelli Stadium. This was where he would find what he needed to know, if he could find anything at all.

The gates to the huge sports complex were all locked. Moreover, they were identical. Emil tried to remember which one he'd entered on the day he'd seen Snopes Avano introduce Fool's Gold to the team. That had been the gate that led to the locker rooms. He walked around the granite wall until he thought he had the correct location, and confronted a padlock the size of his fist. Couldn't use his .38 to blow it apart—too much noise—and he couldn't whack away at it with a rock either, for the same reason. He stood there in the darkness for a few minutes, wondering what to do. The sounds of laughter and chatter reached him from the open windows of a distant dormitory; he saw a security guard strolling toward the gym, and ducked back close against the stadium wall.

Then his eyes fell upon a wire-mesh trash container near the gate. A veteran of many a Saturday afternoon, its strands of metal had been corroded by ketchup and cola. He found a weak spot in the mesh without difficulty and twisted loose several strips of wire.

After ten minutes of pushing, jiggling, and fiddling, he heard the padlock click. He opened the gate, slipped through, and closed it behind him.

Darkness was his only problem now. It took him at least five minutes to find the stairwell that led to the locker rooms, and another five minutes to grope his way downstairs. Here it was safe to try a light, and when his hand finally located a switch on the wall, he found himself standing at the doorway to the locker room itself. Using the wire, it took him only a few seconds to open the door.

He switched on the big banks of fluorescents that ran along the ceiling and headed for the players' lockers.

Rollins and Rutkow had lockers side by side. The sheriff's inspection was thorough and fast. Rusty hadn't bothered to use a padlock at all. His uniform, helmet, shoes, and pads were inside. Also a neatly pressed pair of chinos, a sports shirt, and a sweater. His steam iron rested on a metal shelf at the top of the locker, and his big blue raincape, with name label attached, hung from a hook in the back. Emil took it out for examination. Not a mark.

Gunnar's locker was safeguarded with a dinky little dime-store padlock that a two-year-old could have breached. Inside was a clutter and jumble similar to the huge lineman's dormitory room, with GUNNAR written on every piece of equipment in magicmarker. Gunnar's raincape showed neither scratches nor tears, but way at the bottom of the locker, far in back under a pile of mouldering sweatsocks, the sheriff uncovered a pair of rubber gloves.

Gunnar? he thought, with a sinking feeling. The massive jock had the strength to kill, and he might have thought he'd had a motive. But how had he actually mustered the necessary *will* to snuff out a life?

Saddened, Whippletree made his way down the long row of lockers and came to the one marked DUFFY.

Lem's gear was more or less in order, safeguarded by a medium-sized lock that took about a minute to spring. Lem hadn't gotten around to getting the name labels on all of his stuff yet—the effort was haphazard, at best—but the tag was in place inside the nape of the neck on his raincape.

Which showed a few faint, superficial tears just beneath the right shoulder, and a tiny triangle gone.

Alicia had had blood beneath her *right* fingernails and blue fabric under the fingernails of her *left* hand.

*This is it!* thought Emil.

He felt like throwing up.

Then he folded the raincape into a tight bundle, closed the

locker, turned off the fluorescents, locked the outer door, too, and started up the stairway.

Butch Lodge was standing at the top of the stairs. He held a truncheon, drawn back as if he were a baseball player waiting for a high, hard one, right down the chute. He looked mean, but he was sweating profusely, and Emil saw that the truncheon was shaking in his hands.

"Emil!" he croaked. "You scared me half to . . . what are you doing here? I found the padlock open out on the gate and . . . what's that you're carrying?"

"Just my raincoat. It's a cloudy night." Whippletree climbed the last of the steps and stood before Butch. "Put the club down, why don't you? Say, is something wrong? You sick?"

Butch lowered the truncheon and mopped his forehead. "Emil, you're not supposed to be here. I got to ask what you're up to."

No point in beating around the bush. "Frankly, Butch, it's part of my investigation. I couldn't get Judge Titchell to issue a warrant, so I came in here on my own."

Lodge looked more closely at Emil's neatly rolled bundle. "Say, that's one of those capes the players wear, isn't it? You needed *that?*"

"Yep. And I'd appreciate it if you'd let me move along. I have to get this thing to Doc Divot for examination."

Responsibility and indecision were at war in the security boss's nature. "I don't see how I can ignore this, Emil. Maybe you better come with me."

"Butch, why, for Christ's sake?"

"Breaking and entering? Trespassing? Theft? Really, Emil, you better come with me. I've got my job to think about."

"Your job? This? I thought you were planning on being the new sheriff?"

Lodge ducked his head abashedly. "Well, Emil, I don't know about that any more. Charlie Hollman was gonna be my biggest supporter, but he looks pretty bad because of what you did to his buddy, LaBatt, and I don't think he's all that interested in me now."

275

"You don't need them," Emil told Butch encouragingly. "You've got a good military record to stand on."

Lodge, who was already pretty downcast, suddenly seemed even more discouraged. "It's not all that it appears to be, Emil."

"What do you mean? You have all those decorations. You've got the Purple Heart. You were recommended for the Congressional Medal of Honor."

"A lot of stuff happens in the Army, Emil. Remember the famous invasion of Grenada a couple of years ago? *Everybody* involved in it got a medal, and some of them got two. I wasn't wounded in battle. I got the Purple Heart because a truck ran over my foot, sent me to the hospital for two weeks. And on the Congressional Medal, my commanding officer and I cooperated. He said I was a hero and I said he was one, too. I'm glad it was never awarded to me. I don't think I'd have the guts to wear it."

Emil didn't say anything. There's not a whole lot you can say when a man admits to you that he's a fraud . . . and offers considerable evidence to back it up.

"I always *try* hard," Butch was saying. "I go into a new situation full of piss and vinegar. But something always happens. Every time. I just flub up, I can't keep things under control . . ."

"You know something," Emil said, "I think I have a proposal here that might just change your luck."

"Oh? What's that?"

"Look, this raincape is important, very important, to the murder case. I swear it. You and I keep this between ourselves and, in return, I guarantee that I'll have the crowd off the golf course early tomorrow morning."

Butch shook his head. "How are you gonna do that? It's too late. It's impossible."

"Nope. I've got things pretty well in place. And if you make a big fuss about me being here, I'll have to make a big fuss about my needing to be here."

Butch thought it over. "Whose cape is that?" he asked.

"Can't say."

"You sure you're not pulling a fast one on me?" wondered Butch dismally.

Emil carried the folded raincape back across the golf course, got into his car, and drove to Doc Divot's place in St. Cloud. It was almost midnight, and the coroner came to the door in robe and slippers.

"Well, what the hell now?" he grumbled.

"Run tests on this thing," said Emil, handing over the cape. "Right now."

"Right now? You mean *tonight?*"

"Please. Do it for me. Special favor. There's something in it for you."

"What's that?"

"Inside information. Call Wienie and put every loose cent you have on the game. You'll thank me tomorrow."

"What happened to you, Emil?" Divot laughed. "You have a vision, or something?"

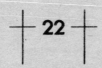

## 22

Four hundred and fifty-seven men, counting Whippletree and his deputies—Pete Poll, too—gathered around the Noble Norsemen's football billboard in hazy, pre-dawn light. The men wore hunting jackets or windbreakers, sweaters or sports coats. A few of them had even come in overalls. Each of them also wore, pinned to pocket or collar or cap, a laminated plastic badge that read, SPECIAL DEPUTY, STEARNS COUNTY, MINNESOTA. Emil and Alyce had been up most of the night preparing the badges, but in spite of the two hours' sleep he'd managed to get, the sheriff felt great as he climbed atop the roof of his car and flicked on an electric bullhorn.

"Like to thank you all for coming," he told the group, which quieted to hear what he had to say, "and there'll be a reward for you later, after the game. I've arranged with Reuben's Beverages in

St. Cloud to have a truckload of beer delivered for your consumption."

His words were answered by a rowdy cheer. "We want it now!" somebody yelled, which brought a burst of good-natured laughter.

"Now this is the deal," Emil resumed. "The prayer pilgrims are going to start arriving very soon. Their cars will not be allowed on campus, or in the campus lots. Those lots are for the football fans, who generally start showing up in late morning. Kickoff's not until two P.M. So we stop the cars driven by Bunny Hollman's people. Park them along the side of the highway—it's all cleared with The Cities—and have the folks walk over to the pine tree. Bunny told me she'd be here around eight. I think—I *hope*—that she's going to give them the word and move them to another location up along I-94. Axel and Jamie Gosch are going to put up signs to that effect. So, with a little luck, by game time the campus ought to be pretty much under control,"

"What if these prayer people give us grief?" asked Walter Bedelmeyer of rural Melrose, who had a .458 Magnum at his belt and a 30.06 deer rifle strapped to his shoulders. "From what I've read in the *Trib*, they're pretty convinced God gave them the golf course."

"That's another thing," answered Emil. "Keep your weapons out of sight. I think we can assure good order by our numbers alone. The big threat to safety was LaBatt and those Gabriel guys. But we don't have to worry about them today."

"Thanks to you, Sheriff," a gruff voice yelled.

Emil smiled to himself. Jacques LaBatt had received a couple of telegrams in his behalf, but he was still safely in jail. He'd retained the services of Tricky Ricky Stein, Pflüger's lawyer, but Whippletree had told Stein to string things along a little bit.

"Now go get 'em, boys!" shouted Whippletree into the bullhorn. "Be courteous, but don't take any guff. You have trouble, send for me or Axel, Ben, or Jamie or"—he caught sight of Pete Poll, standing at the rear bumper of the car, looking sick and ashamed over his disaster of the previous evening—"or send for Pete. Any one of us can back you up."

278

The look of gratitude that Poll sent his way almost embarrassed the old sheriff.

"Good luck," concluded Emil.

The army of special deputies spread out along the highway. Emil and Axel Vogel set up a checkpoint of sawhorses at the turn-off to North Star. Buses and cars began arriving at about dawn. They were halted without incident and ordered to park along the side of the highway. There was some grumbling among the early arrivals but, human nature being what it is, the people who showed up later automatically assumed that parking along the highway was the thing to do.

Besides, they were preoccupied with the possibility of another vision. Today was the day that Bunny had promised them a special message from Jesus Christ.

It was a good day for such a message, too. The dawn was brilliant, splendid, and the soft, golden light of autumn danced in the crystal air. Emil leaned against Stearns County One, watching the sun climb, remembering years gone by. Shocks of corn stood in stubbled fields, straw piles blazed yellow against the sky. Fragrant apples fell oozing upon thick, frost-touched grass. The hay was in the barn, the milk cows fat, and the horses, their work complete, grew lazy in the pastures. Whippletree had always loved the fall.

At least fifteen thousand people had arrived by seven o'clock. Anderson himself, in slacks and sweater, walked over from campus to see how things were progressing. He seemed a little annoyed at the efficiency of the operation.

"I've got an open line to Governor Bauch and the National Guard," he said, reminding Emil of his nine o'clock deadline.

"Might as well close it," the sheriff responded. "I'm in charge here. See you at the game this afternoon."

But seven-thirty came and went, with still no sign of Bunny. Emil was about to give her a call when the radio crackled in his car. It was Alyce, too excited over the day's events to complain about working on a Saturday, or even about her lack of sleep.

"Sheriff, I just heard from Doc Divot," she said. "I thought you'd want to know right away."

"Shoot."

"Well, he ran the tests. That raincape was definitely the one that Alicia Stanhope got her fingernails into."

"Way to go, Doc!" exulted Emil, signing off.

And the good news continued when Bunny Hollman came chugging up to the checkpoint in the little blue Datsun, unaccompanied by Charlie. She parked and got out, looking nervous and frightened.

"How you doin'?" said Emil in greeting, masking his anxiety. She didn't look in any shape to command a hungry crowd's attention.

"I don't know, Emil. I don't know. What's going to happen?"

"I thought we had that figured out. You're going to take them all up along I-94 to Heffner's."

"But I've been praying," she said, "praying for a way. *This* was where I saw Our Holy Mother, and if we leave here . . ."

"You think you might not see her again?"

Bunny nodded bleakly.

"Isn't once enough?" asked the sheriff. "Look, I'll walk you over to the tree. If you can't handle the situation, I'll step in for you."

He walked beside her up the drive toward the pine tree. The crowd became aware of her presence—and of Whippletree with her—and the prayer they'd been reciting stuttered to an apprehensive silence. When Bunny and the sheriff reached the tree, she knelt down. Emil stepped back as Father Ryder set up the portable address microphone.

A vast, waiting silence came over the crowd, which was growing minute by minute as more worshippers arrived. Mrs. Hollman closed her eyes, lowered her head, and began to pray silently.

Emil studied the mood of the crowd, decided that the people seemed peaceable enough for the time being, and looked up into the branches of the pine tree. The puzzle of Faith. Or was it really Hope? Hope that somewhere beyond this bewildering world there existed a Reason by which Faith would be redeemed?

"*She is here! The Virgin is among us!*" cried Bunny into the microphone, refraining this time from invoking the passionate lines of Paolo deVilliers.

The ascending sun was now at a point midway between the Sacred Steeple and great Jesus, and from where Emil stood, it would soon intersect with the fragile upper branches of the pine tree.

*"She is about to speak!"* Bunny Hollman called, as a low hum of wonder rose from the people.

Emil waited for the sensations he had experienced before on these occasions, the feelings of physical discomfort and alarm, but they did not come. Instead he felt a soothing peace descend all about; his heart beat slow and strong within his breast. An inexplicable aura of quiet hope took him into strange embrace, and he gave himself up to it, even though he knew now that Bunny probably wasn't seeing anything in the pine tree at all.

*"Our Lady has a message,"* Mrs. Hollman cried, and the crowd let out a vast suspiration of awe, *"a message . . ."*

Emil felt a sudden wind wash over him, but when he looked up into the pine, not a branch, not a needle stirred. The sun was approaching the treetop now, and in moments it would hang behind the fragrant branches.

*"She is telling us . . . she is telling us . . ."*

"Yes! Yes!" the people called in anticipation of ecstasy.

*". . .that our Faith is to be rewarded, that the great numbers of you who have come here . . ."*

Emil had to give her credit; her conviction was absolute and undeniable.

*". . .day in and day out require a larger plot of land set aside specifically for our worship . . ."*

"Yes!!!"

*". . .an accessible place not far away. We shall leave here and I will lead you there . . ."*

Good going, Bunny, Emil thought. He looked at the crowd, gauging its reaction, and he knew that they would follow her to Heffner's property, that things would be all right.

*". . .Our Holy Mother is smiling now and blessing us,"* Bunny went on. *"She will meet us in a short while at the land Our Lord has set aside for us. . . ."*

Emil looked again at the pine tree. The sun was behind it now, still rising, a pure glittering ball of golden light. Perhaps he glanced too long at the fiery lord of earth and life and living things, but for an instant brief as a breath, long as eternity, he saw—he truly *saw!*—the sweet face of his daughter, Susan, looking down at him.

She was smiling.

And, just as he'd seen her behind the train window in the dream, she was not afraid.

"Well, Butch," said Whippletree later, as the caravan of Bunny's believers pulled away from the sides of the highway, following her little Datsun to the promised land beside I-94, "I delivered the goods. Looks like we're in the clear."

"Thanks, Emil," Lodge replied, with genuine gratitude. "You coming out for the game?"

"Wouldn't miss it. I intend to arrest a murderer today."

"*At* the game?" Butch seemed alarmed.

"Yes. What's the matter?"

"You know who he is?"

"I think so. Why do you say 'he'?"

"Well, I thought . . . I just figured . . ."

Then two big buses turned in and came rolling up the drive toward campus.

"Here come the Fighting Illini," Emil said.

Whippletree managed to steal an hour-and-a-half's worth of sleep while Sarah prepared fried chicken and chilled two bottles of Sauterne for the pre-game feast. While Sarah was upstairs dressing, Emil stole a drumstick and a wing. Then he called North Star to say that there'd be five in his party, receiving assurance that President Anderson was expecting him, and that there would be room for the sheriff and his guests in Anderson's box on the fifty-yard line.

Driving his civilian Chevrolet, Whippletree and Sarah stopped at the Jelinek house and picked up Muffy Huff. She'd been released from the hospital that morning with a clean bill of health.

"Oh, I'm so excited," bubbled the girl, climbing into the back seat, "I've never been to a college football game before."

She wore a flouncy pink sundress that showed a lot of shoulder and cleavage, and her strong fragrance soon obliterated the aroma of fried chicken in Sarah's wicker basket. "I thought you said there'd be some others with us," Muffy said.

"Yep," replied the sheriff, "my niece Dee-Dee and her fiancé."

Traffic moved like a dream on the highway out to North Star, up the long asphalt drive, and into the big parking lots. Butch and his men were in full control, operating efficiently once again. There was a small group of people still praying beneath the pine tree—some of them were busy removing bark or slivers of wood as souvenirs—but the prayer pilgrims were gone. The people on the golf course today were football fans eating picnic lunches and waiting for kickoff.

Dee-Dee and Dale Torbert were waiting, as planned, soaking up the sun and sitting against the bronze hem of Triumphant Jesus robe. They all ate a rather gay, chatty lunch on the grass near Granitelli Stadium, deliberately avoiding serious topics, talking instead of the game.

"I'd give the Norsemen a pretty good chance," Torbert said, "even though Illinois is supposed to win. Poor Snopes."

"Nope," Emil disagreed, helping himself to a second plate of potato salad, to which Sarah had added a touch of the pungent brown mustard that he liked, "it won't even be close. The spread is seven points, but I predict the score will be twenty-four to twelve, favor of the Illini."

"Oh, Emil," Sarah replied, "there you go again. I hope you didn't go and bet a bundle. You almost never win."

"Well, I admit that I did put a tiny bit on fate," he said, thinking of the two thousand dollars. "Makes the game a little more interesting."

"Oh, gee," exuded Muffy, looking around excitedly at the campus, at all the people, "this is just about as much fun as I've ever had!" She seemed somewhat in awe of Dee-Dee, the North Star senior, and Emil noticed that she didn't miss a chance to lean way over in front of Torbert whenever she reached for something from the picnic basket. The professor tried hard, but he could not keep his eyes from a fervent admiration of Muffy's spectacular bosom, and Emil didn't blame him.

The sheriff took the wicker basket back to the car after they'd finished eating, and when he returned to join the others and enter the stadium, he was carrying a small leather tote bag.

"What's in there?" Dee-Dee wanted to know.

"Just my binoculars and some other stuff."

They entered the stadium, part of the vast, spirited human throng here for the game. As always, Emil felt a thrill of pleasure and anticipation, coming out of the long concrete passageway and into the great bowl of the arena. It was something of a kick, too, to give his name to an usher and be escorted down along the sidelines to the presidential box. President Anderson had not yet arrived, nor had his other guests, if any. There were ten seats in the box, and Muffy exclaimed happily over their thick cushions and back rests. She took a seat next to Torbert, managing to look only a little envious when the professor took Dee-Dee's hand in his own. Sarah sat down next to Muffy, but Emil continued to stand. He wanted to sit next to Rector Rex. Although looking forward to the game, he also had hard business to do here this afternoon.

The band played and cheerleaders leaped and cavorted as the stadium filled and the clock moved on toward two. Finally, the public address system crackled into life, and the announcer's voice boomed: "Ladies and gentlemen, please greet the president of North Star University, Rexford Anderson, along with Congressman and Mrs. Sylvester Starkopf."

A great admiring roar rose as Anderson and his guests made their entrance onto the field and walked, waving and smiling, toward the box. The president managed to look casual and commanding at the same time. Starkopf, young and in his first term, was lithe and athletic. He had played football here at NSU. Mrs. Starkopf was a pretty, long-legged brunette. Emil noted that Dexter was with them, although the vice-president's name had not been announced.

"Oh, what will I say to them?" worried Muffy.

"Just say hello and you're glad to be here," suggested Sarah.

The dignitaries reached the box and introductions were made all around. If Anderson was surprised at Emil's choice of guests, he gave no sign, greeting everyone—even Torbert—courteously and heartily.

"Hello and I'm glad to be here." Muffy smiled up at the president, who sniffed the air appreciatively.

Emil maneuvered himself next to Anderson—Mrs. Starkopf sat at his other hand—and everybody took their seats. Emil was seated directly behind Dale Torbert, and he noticed, when the professor loosened his tie and shirt collar, the ragged ends of three scratches on his neck, almost healed.

"Ladies and gentlemen," called the announcer, "make welcome the Fighting Illini of Illinois!"

A lusty, good-natured cheer greeted the opposing team as the players raced out onto the field and ran to benches along the opposite sideline.

"Oh my but they're big!" Muffy said. "Oh my!"

In the hullaballoo following the appearance of Illinois, Whippletree leaned forward and whispered to Torbert. "Must have been nasty scratches on your neck there."

Startled, the professor half turned, touching his neck as he did so. "It was Dee," he whispered back. "You know how it is sometimes."

Passion marks? wondered Emil, as Torbert tightened his necktie.

"I hear you've had a bit of excitement in these parts, Sheriff?" asked Representative Starkopf. "I saw you on TV. How are things going?"

"Pretty well. I'm thinking of running for Congress, what with all the publicity."

Everybody laughed except the congressman.

"Ladies and gentlemen, the Noble Norsemen of North Star!"

The Norsemen, led by Snopes Avano in his billed hat and tinted aviator glasses, were welcomed by a thunderous roar as they raced out onto the field. Everybody in the stadium rose, screaming and cheering, a tide of sound that went on and on and on until the team reached its bench right in front of the presidential box.

"Aren't they just wonderful?" Muffy exclaimed, putting her hands to her ears and shouting. "Oh my, they're so *big!*"

Everyone stood at attention for the national anthem, and when it was over, but before the teams could take the field, Emil slipped quickly out of the box, carrying his tote bag, and approached the Norse bench. The players were milling around, jumping and flexing and affectionately slapping the behinds of their buddies. He saw Lem Duffy, number 27, walked over, and put his hand on the tight end's shoulder pad. Duffy turned around.

"I think you lost this last night," Emil said, reaching inside the tote bag and handing Duffy the ski mask. "You might need it come winter."

Duffy looked at the mask, then at Emil. His face contorted, he swayed, then dropped to one knee, as if he were genuflecting. Fear looks the same on the face of a little kid as it does on a two-hundred-and-twenty-pound bruiser, with hard muscle in every ounce.

"It's not what you think . . ." Duffy began.

Snopes Avano came over. "What's going on here, Emil?"

"Nothing," said the sheriff, as Duffy hid the mask behind him. "Good luck in the game."

Avano looked puzzled, but he had other things on his mind. "Thanks. And thanks for getting rid of Mrs. Hollman and those morons."

"All's right in your world, I guess," the sheriff replied. "Let's have a victory for Homecoming."

When he returned to the box, Anderson glanced at him sharply, but said nothing.

North Star won the toss, and Captain Rollins elected to kick. The ball soared high and deep. Illinois returned it to their twenty-three-yard line. The game was on.

Working hard, Illinois ground out a first down, another, but then Gunnar Rutkow and the defensive unit dug in and settled down to work, stopping the drive and taking possession of the ball at the midfield mark.

Rusty Rollins, on the first Norse offensive play, lofted an easy pass to Lem Duffy, who had streaked into the clear beyond two Illinois defenders.

Unbelievably, Duffy dropped the ball.

"That seldom happens, does it?" observed Congressman Starkopf, as a great collective wail filled the stadium.

"No," said Anderson coldly. He turned to Emil and asked quietly, "What happened out there before?"

Emil didn't answer him directly. "I know now who killed Alicia Stanhope," he said. "And I'm going to make the arrest right after the game."

Rector Rex stared at the sheriff for a long time; the two of them might have been alone in the stadium, so intense was the current that passed from one to the other.

"You think it's Duffy?" the president asked. "What evidence do you have?"

"I've got all too much evidence on Lem Duffy," Emil said sadly.

On the field, Rusty had turned to the powerful running game that had made the Norsemen famous. He sent fullback Tim Steinmetz into the Illinois line for five yards, once again for three, and then took the ball himself, slanted left, feinted, cut out around the end and raced for a twelve-yard gain before being driven out of bounds on the Illini thirty.

Oh Lord, my money! Emil mourned, but then it was still very early in the game. A lot of things could happen. He felt a tingling along his scalp. Excitement. Concentration. Almost an overload of concerns. He had the forthcoming arrest to handle—how to go about it was a problem—he was worried about his big bet, *and* he wanted, once and for all, to get to the bottom, the "basic belief" of Rexford Anderson's personality.

Catching Illinois off guard, Rusty threw again to Lem Duffy, who dropped the ball in the end zone.

"I give the kid credit anyway," Emil said to Anderson. "He's got balls even to be out there today."

"One of my boys!" the president said, with a disconsolate grimace he could not suppress. "Unless you can convince me, there's no way I'm going to allow any arrest."

"He's one of *my* boys, too," Emil said. "Don't forget that."

This time the Illinois defense did its job, stopping the Norsemen two yards shy of a first down. Snopes sent in a kicker, the field goal attempt succeeded, and it was 3–0 with minutes to go in the first quarter.

"Dale," asked the sheriff, leaning forward as the two teams regrouped on the field, "on the day Bunny announced that you were the killer, somebody in your building saw you running out with an attaché case or an overnight bag."

"Yes?"

"Why? And what was in it?"

"Well, it was an overnight bag. I'd packed a few things in case Dee and I decided to go away and talk things over. But, as you know, we eventually decided to come over to your house instead."

"What are you two conspiring about?" Sarah wanted to know.

"Nothing," replied Torbert quickly.

When Emil turned back toward Anderson, intending to resume their conversation, he found the president deeply engaged with the Starkopfs. They talked about the tribal nature of Homecoming for a little, then about the financial burdens borne by impecunious young representatives, of which Starkopf claimed to be one. It seemed to Emil as if Anderson did not wish to return to the subject of homicide, and in a way the sheriff could not blame him.

So Emil took the binoculars from his tote bag and, along with everybody else in the box, gave his attention to the game. Illinois, stung by North Star's field goal, had mounted a major drive downfield; each play was a combination of crackling power and almost mechanical perfection. They were double-teaming Gunnar Rutkow, who had not as yet sacked the Illinois quarterback. Gunnar did not seem to be playing as well as usual today, looking a little slow out there on the turf.

Muffy and Sarah chatted and watched the game. Dee and Torbert studied some plays, but ignored the rest and concentrated on each other. Emil's niece put her head against Torbert's tweed-jacketed shoulder a lot. Rector Rex and the Starkopfs exclaimed excitedly over just about every play. And Fagin Dexter, Emil noticed, stared out at the action disspiritedly, distant and morose.

The first Illini touchdown and conversion sent the North Star cheerleaders into a frenzy of activity intended to rouse the Norsemen. It seemed, at first, to be effective. Rusty Rollins, flawlessly executing plays that Coach Avano sent in from the bench, brought his men deep into Illinois territory midway through the second quarter, but the Norsemen drive collapsed on the sixteen-yard line. Once again, Snopes had to resort to a field goal, and the score was 7–6 in favor of Illinois. Less than a minute before the end of the first half, however, Illinois scored on a forty-yard pass into the end zone, succeeded in kicking for the conversion, and left the field with an eight-point lead when the gun sounded.

If this were the end of the game, Emil thought, I'd be in the money.

As the Norsemen jogged toward the locker rooms, Emil caught a glimpse of Lem Duffy. The magnifying power of the binoculars showed a young man who looked almost ill. Not a nice business, Emil thought.

Anderson hadn't said a word to Emil since the mention of Duffy's name earlier, and he didn't during half-time. In honor of Homecoming, a mid-game ceremony—in addition to the usual show by the marching band—had been organized, during which Anderson presented a Distinguished Alumni Medal to Congressman Starkopf, and then spoke briefly from a microphone in the center of the field.

"What does North Star mean to those of us who have spent parts of our lives here?" he asked, his mellifluous voice resounding in the stadium. "It means what it always has and what it always will: a place where eternal verities withstand the passing fads of modern times, where thought and study, rooted in ancient Truth, put the lie to the frivolous, transitory temptations of secularism. . . ."

Is this what he really believes? Emil wondered. It was not the first occasion at which the president seemed to express yet another "deepest belief." Maybe he just has a lot of beliefs, Emil figured. Maybe that's how it is if you're really smart.

Dale Torbert groaned audibly when Anderson concluded: "The price of victory is always high, but winning is a North Star tradition, which I believe we shall see as the afternoon progresses."

"Pablum for the masses," Torbert said.

If so, the masses loved it. The appreciative cheers that Anderson received nearly equaled, in volume and length, those that had greeted the football team a little earlier in the afternoon.

The president did not return immediately to the box, but hobnobbed and politicked along the sidelines with the hordes of alumni who wanted to shake his hand and tell others, later, that they'd talked to him. Emil felt like a chaw, but there was no place in the box to spit—besides which Sarah would have been mortified—so he got out and walked around a little. He saw Butch Lodge standing in the shadow of the bleachers on the forty-yard line.

"Butch," he said, "I'd like to use a corner of the golf course to give my special deputies a little beer party afterwards. That okay?"

Lodge nodded gloomily. "Is this gonna be before or after you make that arrest?"

"Probably after."

"Emil, who *is* it?"

"Can't say. I want to see how the game turns out."

"A *player?*"

"Can't say."

"Won't, you mean. Do you think you'll have trouble? With the arrest? Will you need a hand?"

"I'd appreciate that. Could be I will need some help." Actually, he wasn't sure. You never know how people will react.

He bought a half-dozen boxes of popcorn from a vendor and carried them back to the box, getting to his seat just as the two teams came back onto the field. Whatever Snopes had told his boys in the locker room, it must have been invigorating. The Norsemen pranced and galloped like an entirely different team.

Only problem was that the Illini were in the lead, an advantage they were not about to relinquish. North Star received the kickoff and Rollins directed a brilliant series of running plays that brought the Norse down to the Illinois thirty-two. Then he dropped back and let fly a beautiful spiral pass that whistled bulletlike through the dazzled air. Lem Duffy was waiting, he could not miss, his huge hands were outstretched, but suddenly an Illinois defender appeared out of nowhere, streaked in front of Lem and intercepted the ball. Pandemonium. He shot down the sidelines, picking up speed all the way, and he was still accelerating when he crossed the goal line.

Kick. Good. 21–6. Illinois.

An air of uncharacteristic gloom settled over the Homecoming crowd in Granitelli Stadium.

"What was that you were just saying about victory?" Emil asked, leaning toward Anderson.

"That's the kind of thing one must tell people." Rector Rex smiled uncomfortably.

"Then you don't believe it?"

"Of course I do. But events don't always go the way one plans."

"Don't I know. Remember that conversation we had in your office concerning belief?"

"I do."

"What do you really believe anyway? Way down deep? First it seems you're a liberal, like Professor Torbert. Then again you sound a lot like Charlie Hollman. But I think it's deeper. The university maybe. Football maybe, because that's what keeps North Star going. Or is it something else?"

Emil wasn't such a country boy that he couldn't recognize a look of condescension at fifty yards, and Anderson was sitting right next to him.

"I asked you once about *your* deepest belief," the president said, "and you didn't know."

"Well, if you're asking again, I'll tell you. I believe those who can take care of themselves must also take care of those who can't."

"Are you referring to anyone in particular?"

"Alicia Stanhope."

"The murder again," said Rector Rex, scarcely bothering to veil his disgust. "Do you have any idea of what it would do to the university if you arrested Lem Duffy?"

Emil let a minute go by. "Doctor," he said, "I think I've figured you out. You care about Duffy, of course, and so do I. But you have all your beliefs in a kind of rank order, like ducks. I think you knew that Charlie and Alicia and Titchell were setting Torbert up for a fall. But nobody counted on the murder. So, suddenly, liberalism versus conservatism didn't matter all that much. You had something else to protect."

"What? The football team?" A trace of sarcasm.

"Partly. I know enough about this place now to know that only one person around here would change a player's academic record to keep him eligible . . ."

Anderson's eyes narrowed, and Emil knew that he had guessed right.

". . . but if a player committed homicide," the sheriff continued, "and if that murder caused a scandal, your very deepest belief, your basic value, would be in jeopardy. Unless you managed to disassociate yourself from it. Which is why you spent all that time out of town. Your only hope was to cover it up, play for time, and wait until everybody forgot."

"You were speaking of my basic belief?" said the president coldly. "What is it?"

"Yourself," Emil said.

Anderson laughed. "Perhaps we ought to give you an honorary degree in psychology, Sheriff."

Emil realized that he and the president were profoundly different. The president used his vast stores of power and fame, at least in part, for his own glorification. Emil had never considered his own little cache of authority as anything but a temporary trust. Indeed, it was quite often a burden.

"Will you look at that?" said Anderson to the Starkopfs, dismissing Emil and turning toward the playing field. "I think we're finally on the move."

The game was now in the waning minutes of the third quarter, with the score still 21–6. Prospects of a North Star victory were grim, though not yet hopeless. Muffy Huff was chewing at her fingernails. The Norsemen were in possession with fourth down and less than a yard to go on the Illinois twenty-eight.

"Quarterback sneak should do it for a first down," said Dale Torbert to no one in particular.

Emil had been aware that the professor had been listening intently to his long, quiet conversation with President Anderson, but that was all right. Torbert had, as he'd once stated, been a pawn in a larger game. He'd earned the right to be an interested observer.

On the field, Rusty was calling signals. The Illinois line was poised for the quarterback sneak, perhaps for a charge by fullback Steinmetz. They were mistaken on both counts.

At first, Emil thought Rollins had called the Fool's Gold play, but the blocking pattern was different. Lem Duffy was in the clear, having eluded *three* Illinois defenders. Nor did Rusty fake or feint as he dropped back into the pocket. Rather, with a ballet dancer's delicate grace and a born athlete's aplomb, he set himself, cocked his arm, and shot the ball straight over the heads of the battling linemen, and right into Lem Duffy's embrace.

The tight end held on.

Touchdown!

The cheers that erupted in the stadium were born more of renewed hope than of faith in victory, because, after the attempted conversion failed, Illinois began the fourth quarter with a 21–12 lead. I've got the spread beat right now, Emil was thinking. But, God, the score's really close to Bunny's prediction!

Stay calm, he advised himself.

"Duffy did pretty well on that one," said Anderson, aware that time was running out. "I must tell you that arresting Lem is madness, and I'll back him all the way. You may, in one sense, have been right about me holding a series of beliefs, each one deeper than the last. But, in this instance, you *will* be satisfied that my conviction rests with Lem Duffy's welfare."

"May I ask," he inquired after a pause, "precisely what evidence you have against the boy?"

"It's pretty cut and dried," replied Emil unhappily. "Alicia had toyed with him, played him for a fool. He's strong, hot-tempered, unsophisticated. He didn't care for her one bit. Also, she insulted Gunnar, and the other players look after Gunnar. So do you," he added, in pointed reference to the grade change. "Then, too, Lem signed in late. He had the time to commit the crime, and that time is unaccounted for. The photographs he mailed to Muffy, in order to frighten her, are just another nail in the coffin of circumstance. The raincape in his locker was the one that Miss Stanhope clawed while she was being killed."

Emil also told Anderson about the ski mask and last night's attempted abduction at Bunyanland.

"I returned the ski mask just before the game," Emil concluded. "It was Lem's, all right."

"Couldn't you at least have waited until after the game," said the president bleakly. "His performance hasn't been any too good today."

Anderson and Emil fell silent for a time, and the crowd in Granitelli Stadium grew more subdued as the fourth quarter progressed. Neither team made much headway. Illinois was intent on protecting its lead. North Star struggled ever more desperately to score again. One more touchdown, just one more, would make the score 21–18 or, with the conversion, 21–19, and even with only a few minutes remaining, that might make all the difference. The Norsemen, like true champions, might then find a way to fashion a victory out of blood and luck alone.

Snopes Avano, almost distraught, paced in front of the bench, one more chance of closing on Rocco Granitelli's record slipping away.

Emil was thinking of the point spread. If North Star scored again, even a field goal, he'd be out two thousand hard-earned dollars.

"Oh, Jesus, I was a damned fool," he moaned, as Snopes sent in his field goal-specialist to make an attempt from the Illinois thirty-two.

Cursing himself for lack of courage, he didn't even look up until the groan told him that his money was still safe. What were the odds today? Four to one? Five to one?

"I'm gonna be rich," he muttered.

"What are you going on about?" asked Sarah, turning and looking at him.

"Oh, nothing."

On the next series of plays, Illinois got close enough to try a field goal, and succeeded! Bunny! Emil exulted. I ought to pay you a finder's fee or something.

Now all he had to do was sit here until the last two minutes ticked away. But the Norsemen hadn't given up yet. Their mettle, forged and tempered by Snopes himself, was solid stuff. They took the kick and came charging back upfield as if the game had just begun.

"It's not over 'til it's over," Congressman Starkopf said.

Dee-Dee and Torbert had their heads together. They'd forgotten all about the game. Muffy was weeping quietly, her first college game a home-team loss. She fit right in. Not a few fans were crying.

Then, from the Norsemen's own forty-three, Rollins called Fool's Gold. Duffy was heading down the sideline, trying to elude a clutch of Illini tormentors. They expected another long pass. But the blocking worked beautifully, and Rusty was free, running like the wind. He was finally brought down on the Illinois one-yard line.

*"First down and goal!"* boomed the announcer over the public address. *"First down and goal!"*

A touchdown, of course, wouldn't win the game. But it would make the score more respectable. A touchdown, however, would make the score 24–18, one point within the seven-point spread that Emil had to beat.

"I see that you're sweating, Sheriff," observed Anderson. "Having second thoughts about arresting Lem Duffy?"

"It's not Duffy I'm arresting," Emil replied, as fullback Steinmetz tried and failed to crack the Illinois line.

*"Second down, goal!"* cried the announcer.

"What?" wondered Anderson. "I thought you said you had all that evidence . . . ?"

"I said I had *too much* evidence. Duffy was set up. He didn't kill anyone."

Rollins tried a pass to Lem. It was batted out of bounds by Illinois.

*"Third down, goal!"*

"No," said Emil. "Somebody hid behind the fact that Lem signed in late that night. And somebody used his instamatic and sent Muffy those pictures. Lem tried to see her last night to find out what was happening. He was in a panic. Clumsy. Careless. The killer isn't like that."

"What about the raincape?" Anderson asked.

On the field, Rusty Rollins tried a quarterback sneak. He failed.

*"Fourth down, goal!"* called the announcer, with waning hope.

"The raincape in Lem's locker wasn't his," Emil told Father Tad. "Somebody switched with him."

"Who?"

"The killer," Emil said. "Rusty Rollins."

Ten seconds remained in the game. The Norsemen got set for one last try. Emil didn't know whether to hold his billfold or his heart. Rusty, he thought, with exquisite sadness, good luck, this is your last chance for glory. The Norsemen were taut, the Illini braced and hovering.

Then the snap.

It was a play that would become part of Norse lore. Emil himself would think of it again and again over the years, even as he tried to forget it. Funny thing was that it took only a few seconds from beginning to end. Yet, in memory, time slowed as it does in dreams, as Rusty took the ball from center, leaped upward, forward, attempting to dive over offense and defense across the goal. He may, at one instant, actually have been in the end zone. But he was in midair, so it was difficult to tell. A couple of Illini linemen hit him, one high and one low. His body, strong as it was, could not overcome the massed force against it, and he dropped, angled and twisted and defenseless, to the grass.

Perhaps he fumbled. In any case, Illini and Norsemen piled on. The whistle blew, ending the play. Refs tried to get the mess untangled, and to determine what had happened.

"Rusty?" said Anderson. "*Rusty?*"

"Has to be," replied Emil, talking to the president but watching the multicolored ball of bodies unsnarling in the end zone, becoming individual players who rose wearily to their feet, wondering if Rollins had been successful.

"Has to be," the sheriff said again. "He had access to the Nerf footballs, and to Lem's cameras. He knew that Lem had signed in late. And he hated Alicia Stanhope more than anybody else."

"That's incomprehensible, Sheriff. Why would he hate her? Rusty isn't capable of hating."

On the field, the refs were still trying to figure out if Rollins had gotten the ball across the goal line.

"Remember, Doctor," asked Emil, "when you told me that belief defines person? Rusty Rollins believed that he was a good boy, pure, incorruptible, better than the rest."

"He is!" said Anderson.

"But Alicia Stanhope ruined him by proving, to Rusty anyway, that he was just like all the others she'd conquered or teased. And Alicia, by the way, looked very much like Rusty's girl back home. Miss Stanhope was unfortunate enough to destroy Rusty's belief in his own purity. Coach Avano once told me that you have to watch out for the boys who never get into trouble, because they're the ones who are going to go off the deep end one day. And Rollins did."

"But, Sheriff," doubted the president, "no 'good boy,' to use your expression, could live with himself after what he'd . . . that is, after a murder and a rape."

"Rusty justified the murder," replied Emil, "probably in a manner quite similar to the reasoning of a man like Jacques LaBatt. He was good, Alicia was evil. So her death didn't matter. As for rape, he denied that, too, at least in his own mind."

"A man can't deny a sexual encounter," Anderson scoffed. "It either happens or it doesn't."

Emil recalled the day that Rusty had come to his office and declared that there had been "no contact" between himself and a woman. Emil had thought, at the time, that the quarterback was referring to Dee-Dee. He knew differently now, and he knew why the phrase had meant so much to Rollins.

"I guess Rusty figured that it didn't count somehow if he used a condom."

Anderson stared right into the sheriff's eyes. "Emil, you're crazy," he said. "That's the wildest speculation I've ever heard." He smiled thinly. "I guess I'll have to withdraw my offer of an honorary degree in psychology. You've got no evidence."

Under the goalposts, a referee was signaling that there had been no score. The crowd groaned.

"But I do have evidence," Emil stated. "Rusty put rubber gloves in Gunnar's locker, probably as a diversion."

"You'll never be able to prove it."

"And he switched raincapes with Lem. Rusty put the one he'd worn on the murder night, the one Alicia had clawed, in Lem's locker."

"How do you know?"

"By the very neatly ironed-on name label. Lem would never have bothered to put a name label on that carefully, if he'd bother to put one on at all. And I found Rusty's steam iron in the locker room. Funny place for it . . ."

Emil and Anderson, locked in conflict, slowly became aware of an odd hush in Granitelli Stadium, an unsettling silence that meant more than defeat. They looked up and saw that, alone among all the players, Rusty Rollins had not risen from the grass.

Snopes Avano was trotting across the field toward his fallen star.

"Oh, Emil," said Sarah, reaching back and touching his knee, "I'm afraid . . ."

The sheriff and Anderson got to their feet. Snopes was kneeling over Rusty now. He stood up suddenly, waving frantically toward the sidelines.

"Oh, my God," Anderson said.

Then the team doctor was on the field, ministering to Rusty. Players stood around, turning, pacing, tense and anxious. Emil had once shot a fox on suspicion that the animal had been killing chickens, back on the farm in the old days. He wished, to this day, that he hadn't. He'd shot from a distance, but before he could reach the carcass, a litter of cubs had appeared. They'd sniffed and nosed their elder's body, approached and retreated and approached again, just as the Norse players were now stalking around the downed body of Rusty Rollins.

Gunnar left the pack then, and raced toward the presidential box. "Rector Rex! Rector Rex!" he bawled as he drew near, tears streaming unchecked down his broad kind face, "please come quick. Rusty's dying, or he's dead already."

Anderson was older than Emil, yet the sheriff had a hard time keeping up with the president as he ran from the stands across the field to the end zone. The people in the stadium were frightened now. Later, Emil would remember their strange, mournful muttering, and would recall too how the shadows of the arms of Triumphant Jesus stretched out upon the playing field.

But, at that moment, he was aware only of the team doctor's hopeless expression, of Rollins lying wide-eyed and motionless on the grass, and of Coach Avano saying, over and over, "We've got to help my boy, we've got to help my boy . . ."

Anderson knelt beside the injured quarterback. Emil did too.

"He can't speak. He can't move," said the doctor. "The spinal cord may be severed. I've called for an ambulance."

"Can you hear me?" shouted Anderson.

"He can't, I don't think," said the doctor.

"Blink your eyes three times if you can hear me," the president persisted.

Rusty Rollins blinked three times.

"My boy's all right!" cried Coach ecstatically.

Rusty's helmet had already been removed. He seemed to waver out of consciousness for a moment.

Emil was right there. He felt the quarterback's eyes on him, afraid, pleading.

"Rusty," he said, "remember that talk we had in my office? When I said I couldn't give absolution? Well, I think I can help. Aren't you sorry for the murder?"

Rusty Rollins blinked three times.

Emil didn't return to the North Star campus until a few days before Thanksgiving, and it was only an impulse that led him to turn off the highway at the big football billboard and stop his car next to the row of white pines at the side of the asphalt drive. He'd been out to Sauk Centre investigating a series of petty thefts there—Cowboy John seemed a logical suspect—and he had a little time to kill before supper.

Strange how different everything looked now, with winter on the way. All leaves were long gone. The darkening sky was cold and iron gray. Jesus and the Sacred Steeple appeared smaller, weathered and temporary and out of place. This was the time of year when the work and artifacts of man were diminished by the immense, naked vastness of the land. Up along 1–94, Bunny Hollman's crowds had dwindled to a few dozen hardy souls in parkas, and there was no one here on the frigid golf course at all.

Emil pulled his hat down low and his collar up high, and slid out of Stearns County One. The white pine in which Bunny had once seen the face of the Virgin Mary was gone now, needles and branches, bark and trunk taken away by forgotten believers, like relics of the One True Cross. They'd dug away at the roots, too; only a depression in the earth remained.

It was all very hard for Emil to understand, but he'd come to accept the fact that not a whole lot of things in life could be understood. Was that the beginning of wisdom, or the end of it? Yet once, behind the branches of the pine, beyond the sun, he'd seen Susan smiling down at him. Once was enough, and he knew, too, as he looked out across the golf course toward the forest, that soon, very soon, he'd find those silver rails again

and follow them
to his daughter
and the heart of peace.


Sarah was all excited at supper that night.

"Emil, good heavens!" she exclaimed, putting the crackling roast chicken on the table, "I had to stop by the Hannorhed bank today and I checked the special account. How on earth did you come to have twelve thousand dollars in there?"

"Oh, that," said the sheriff casually. "Well, the investment I made with Mr. Pappendorf paid off, I guess."

"You *guess!* What was it anyway?"

"Futures, I think it's called. You see . . ."

But she wasn't all that interested in the technical details, which was just as well since he didn't know anything about futures either.

Later that night, settling into sleep, he felt something hard on the pillow, sat up, and switched on the light.

"Something wrong?" asked Sarah drowsily.

"Another pellet of buckshot," he said, picking it up and carrying it to the jar.

"Why do you save those things anyway?" she wanted to know.

"Because they've been a part of me," he said, getting back into bed, "and because they remind me of something."

"What's that?"

"How lucky I am," he said. "How lucky we are." He leaned over and kissed her on the cheek. "Did I tell you that Dale Torbert asked me to be his best man?"

Sarah was quiet for a moment. "Well, I guess you are," she said then, "but don't let it go to your head."

"And I love you, too," he said. "Good night."

Sheriff Emil L. Whippletree
Stearns County Sheriff's Office
St. Cloud, MN 56301

Dear Sheriff Whippletree:

On behalf of President Anderson and North Star University, I wish to thank you for your most valuable aid, effectiveness and discretion during the recent unpleasantness. In recognition of your efforts, therefore, the President has asked me to arrange a reception in your honor, when classes resume after the Christmas Holiday. Please contact me as soon as possible with times and dates convenient to you and your wife.

All of us here at North Star wish you Merry Christmas, Happy New Year, and good fortune in all of your endeavors. As Rector Rex remarked to me just the other day, "Emil Whippletree is a man who knows what he believes." I daresay there is no greater compliment.

Most sincerely,

*J. Dexter*

Fagin Dexter, Ph. D.
Acting Assistant Chairman
Campus Events Committee

Dear Chairman Dexter,

Nice to hear from you. But I don't know about that reception. Sarah and I are heading out to California for the Rose Bowl, and then we're going to a big family reunion with my kinfolk in Salisbury, England. I figure I'll be pretty much partied out by the time I get back home.

Thanks anyway,

*Emil*

# CRITIC'S CHOICE

## For action-packed suspense thrillers.

# CRITIC'S CHOICE
## The greatest mysteries being published today

# CRITIC'S CHOICE

## The finest in HORROR and OCCULT